About the Author

Zara Stoneley lives in deepest Cheshire surrounded by horses, dogs, cats and amazing countryside. When she's not visiting wine bars, artisan markets or admiring the scenery in sexy high heels or green wellies, she can be found in flip flops on the beach in Barcelona, or more likely sampling the tapas!

Her most recent releases, *Stable Mates*, *Country Affairs* and *Country Rivals*, are fun romps through the Cheshire countryside and combine some of her greatest loves – horses, dogs, hot men and strong women (and not forgetting champagne and fast cars)! You can find out more about Zara at www.ZaraStoneley.com or follow her on Twitter @ZaraStoneley.

PRAISE FOR ZARA STONELEY'S BOOKS

'A great treat for readers who love their books jam-packed with
sexy men and horses'
Bestselling author Fiona Walker

'Fans of Fiona Walker will love this book'
That Thing She Reads

'A delightful romp stuffed with fun, frolics and romance'
BestChickLit.com

'Stable Mates is up there with Riders and Rivals'
Comet Babes Books

'Move over Mr Grey, the Tippermere boys are in town! Highly
recommended'
Brook Cottage Books

'A seductive fascinating novel. Mucking out the horses just got
sexy'
Chicks That Read

The Holiday Swap

ZARA STONELEY

A division of HarperCollins*Publishers*
www.harpercollins.co.uk

Harper*Impulse* an imprint of
HarperCollins*Publishers*
1 London Bridge Street
London SE1 9GF

www.harpercollins.co.uk

A Paperback Original 2016

First published in Great Britain in ebook format by Harper*Impulse* 2016

A catalogue record for this book
is available from the British Library

ISBN: 9780008210458

Set in Minion by Palimpsest Book Production Limited, Falkirk, Stirlingshire

Printed and bound in Great Britain by
CPI Group Ltd, (UK) Ltd, Croydon, CR0 4YY

This book is for you – whether your dreams are small, or mighty visions, believe in them.

'The moment you doubt whether you can fly, you cease for ever to be able to do it.'

— J.M. Barrie, Peter Pan

PART 1

Chapter 1 – Daisy. Cheshire

Daisy Fischer wound the baling twine round her finger twice, effectively attaching herself to the gate, before she realised what she was doing, and stopped.

She had to be losing her mind.

Jimmy, her long-term, on-off boyfriend, could not have asked her what she thought he just had. Could he?

She sneaked a sideways glance at him under her fringe, hoping he wouldn't spot her peeking.

Jimmy was swinging the spade he was holding effortlessly from side to side, showing off his best rugged-man-in-the-country look. Over the years she'd known him he had relaxed into his role a bit; there was the first hint of middle-aged spread spilling over the waistband of his jeans (quite noticeable from this angle), but the forearm on display was still muscular. He was grinning, showing off the dimple she loved.

And he was staring at her bum. Which simplified matters. He didn't look like he'd just asked her marry him. He looked, well, like Jimmy always looked.

Daisy straightened up, pushing her dark hair behind her ears. She really had to say something, because it was getting to the point of rude if she didn't. And her back was starting to ache.

He winked. The cheeky wink that had every girl in Tippermere fluttering her eyelashes, even though Jimmy really was more than a little bit too old for most of them. Her mum thought he was too old (and too much of a flirt) for her, but what was eight years between friends?

So what the hell did she say now? If she spoke before thinking this through, one or both of them was going to look pretty silly, and more than a little bit embarrassed. Experience told her it was more likely to be her.

He just could *not* have said it.

'Sorry, what was that? I was just trying to…' The scorch of heat on her cheeks had to give her away, but he didn't let on. But how the hell had he shifted from asking if she fancied a pint to *the question*?

'I think you need to lighten up a bit, Dais.'

Maybe he hadn't meant it. Or hadn't said it. It had been a bit of an embarrassed mumble anyway.

'I only said I needed to sort this out before I could go to the pub.' Which she had, immediately after he'd said '*fancy a pint?*', and before he'd said the other bit.

She fished in her pocket for a second piece of baling twine, just to be on the safe side. Safe side as in securing the gate, but also as in buying some more time.

'But there's always something with you, isn't there? People our age should be out getting pissed, not spending the night tying up gates then watching a sloppy film.'

'I like sloppy films,' this was better, much safer ground. And she liked tying up gates and messing with horses. She gave the gate a gentle tug. It opened a few inches. Bugger. 'You know I've got to fix this. If Barney goes wandering into Hugo's food store again he'll throw a real wobbler. You know what he was like last time.' The last time that Barney, her very naughty (his previous owner had referred to it as 'character') Welsh Cob had escaped from his field he'd managed to break the feed-room door open. Hugo's feed room door. After eating the entire contents of a bag of very nice carrots, he'd tipped a tub of half-soaked sugar beet all over the floor and trampled it in. Well, the bits he hadn't eaten.

He'd then wiped his messy nose across the row of pristine stable rugs.

A strange puce-coloured Hugo, with his normally immaculate blond hair stuck up in a very *There's Something About Mary* way, had arrived at her door, Barney in tow.

Even though she'd spent a good two hours clearing up the mess, Hugo still hadn't forgiven her and was gently simmering; she preferred his frosty look, or his macho sneer, to his anger.

'*Your* food store.' Jimmy frowned. He was even less keen on Hugo than Daisy was. 'Hugo's a pompous git.'

'Well he's renting it, and I need the cash.' Inheriting Mere End cottage had been a dream come true. With its rambling cottage garden, and room for her dog and horse, it was perfect. But perfect came with a price, and she'd soon worked out that her dog-grooming business wasn't quite as lucrative as it needed to be. When Hugo had knocked on her door asking if he could continue the rental agreement he'd had with the previous owner – an old woman her mother had helped out – she'd jumped at the opportunity. Some days, though, she wished she had a tenant who was slightly more on her wavelength.

'I'll go and talk to Angie then, if you're going to be boring.'

Giggling Angie, the barmaid, brought new meaning to the name mini-skirt, micro more like, thought Daisy as she added another strand of baling twine. But she supposed you could carry off that look when you were eighteen. And had a waist, and never-ending slim brown legs that were regularly waxed and suntanned.

Whereas Daisy's waist had gone a bit fuzzy and soft-focus, and her legs were pale and, well let's face it, also a bit fuzzy (but in a different way) inside her jodhpurs.

She tutted at him and folded her arms. 'You should leave Angie alone. Her mum's worried about an older man,' she looked at him pointedly, 'leading her astray.' She could have added, like mine was, but didn't.

'If she's old enough to work behind a bar, then she's old enough to be led astray.'

'Jimmy!'

He laughed, an easy, infectious laugh that brought a grin to her own face.

He was cute. But marriage?

'I remember when you were that age, gorgeous.' Leaning forward, he kissed her. The scratch of dark stubble rubbed against her cheek, and Daisy looked straight into his eyes –wondering when things like that stopped making the inside of your stomach squirm and just turned into 'nice'.

Or a rash.

'You were gorgeous, and you're still as sexy. Come on, scrub up and come for a drink. We need to talk.'

Talk? Oh bugger, he *had* said what she thought he had. Jimmy didn't do 'talking'. The last time he'd wanted to talk to her was when he needed to borrow some cash to repair his ancient tractor.

How the hell was she going to avoid giving him a straight answer when he was staring at her over the froth of his pint?

'Maybe I should get some wire. What do you think?'

'I think,' he prised her hands away from the gate post and reaching into her pocket pulled out the last remaining piece of baling twine, 'I've got a chain and padlock that will do a much better job, and,' he shook his head at the horse, who had ambled over to see if there was any food on offer, 'if he can get out of that he deserves as many carrots as he can nick. Go on, you get inside and shower while I sort out Houdini.'

Barney stamped his foot and shook his whole body vigorously, then lowered his head to peer at Jimmy.

'Yeah, you know when you've met your match, don't you, mate?'

'Think you can outwit a horse now do you, Jimbo?'

Daisy and Jimmy both turned to find Hugo watching them.

It wasn't that he was nasty, or that she hated him, he just always seemed slightly superior. Even his drawl was perfect upper-class insolence. As was the ever-present cigarette dangling from his fingers (she'd told him it was a bad habit and very unfashionable and he'd just laughed and asked her when she'd become such a health-and-fashion expert – he had a point).

Hugo's horses never escaped, he never fell in troughs, and he always looked immaculate. 'Dashing' was how her mother had described him (over the moon that he was going to be Daisy's neighbour – so nice to have a bit of class about, you don't know what you're getting these days), which was why, she supposed, there was a never-ending trail of women in and out of his bed. There always had been, despite the fact he seemed arrogant and aloof to her, and just all too much, but he obviously appealed to some women. Well, quite a lot of women. When they were teenagers he'd been the pin-up at the state school, as well as the private one he attended. Hugo had always had it easy, had the pick of everything.

And he made her feel a bit of a klutz. She'd found 'brusque and couldn't care less' was the most efficient attitude to deal with him. Which didn't come naturally at all.

'I tried to tie the gate up.'

He raised what she could only describe as a sarcastic eyebrow, if there was such a thing. 'So I see. I never knew baling twine could be such an asset. You really do put the rest of us to shame when it comes to recycling, don't you?'

She ignored him. 'But Jimmy is putting a chain on. Did you want help with something?' Polite but firm.

'Not really.' Oh God, that drawl could be annoying. There was a hint of 'not that you could help with' sneer lingering in the background. 'I just had the bill for the food stuff he destroyed, plus the cleaning bill for the rugs. I'll leave it in the house, shall I?'

'Sure. Sorry about that. I'll knock it off the rent.'

'Cash would be handy.'

'I bet it bloody would.' Jimmy shook his head. 'We'll knock it off the rent, like Dais said.'

Daisy tried not to visibly cringe. It was lovely to have Jimmy doing his macho-territory thing, but it wasn't his rent to knock it off. She smiled. 'I'll get showered then, shall I?' And ushered Hugo off down the path. No way was she leaving the pair of them together to lock horns.

Chapter 2 – Daisy. White elephants

'Bloody hell, I needed that.' Jimmy wiped the froth from his mouth with the back of his hand, put his pint glass down on the table and raised an eyebrow at Daisy before scrummaging about in his pockets. 'There you go.'

It was a box. An enormous, blue, scary box. Well, it was tiny, actually. As in ring-size tiny. But inescapable. It was that white elephant in the room. Daisy understood now why they called it that. You couldn't actually *not* look at it.

Her stomach lurched. Not the fluttery feeling of anticipation that she sometimes felt when Jimmy started to slowly unbutton her shirt and his fingertips brushed her skin, it was more like the feeling of fear when Barney took off with her and she was wondering how the hell she was going to stop him before they ploughed through a group of unsuspecting picnickers. That heart-in-the-mouth moment before she knew for sure if he was going to slam the brakes on, spin round, or launch his huge body into the air and go for it.

It hadn't been her imagination, or dodgy hearing because her bobble hat was pulled down over her ears. He had said the words that had made her nearly amputate her fingertips with a liberal wrapping of plastic twine.

We should get hitched.

She took a gulp of lager and glanced round, hoping nobody was looking at them, but knowing that she was probably just about to hit the number one slot for gossip-worthy news.

'How about it then, Daisy, are you up to the job of making an honest man of me?'

His Adam's apple bobbed nervously and there was a sheen of anxious perspiration across his brow. Not a look she associated with the solid, dependable, and slightly cocky man she more often than not shared a bed with. She wanted to throw her arms round him, reassure him, and scream with delight, like they did in the films. But it wasn't happening. All she could force out was a wobbly mad-woman laugh.

'Come on.' His grin was all lopsided. Why, oh why couldn't she grab the box? 'You're making me nervous here, put me out of my misery.' He lifted the lid, encouraging a positive response.

'Oh Jimmy.' She put one finger out, not quite daring to touch the diamond that she should have been desperate to see. 'It's lovely, you're lovely, wonderful.' Oh God, she was sounding like a bad greetings card, and she was going to cry. It suddenly hit her, and her stomach lurched as she looked at the ring, the words that had automatically tumbled out of her mouth summed it up. That was the thing. She thought he was 'lovely', which maybe wasn't quite the same as being madly in love in an 'I want to marry you kind of way'. 'It's just a shock. I didn't expect...'

'To be honest,' the look had turned to bashful Retriever now, 'I know we've always kept it casual.'

Yeah, thought Daisy. At the start, Jimmy had always been the one to say it was daft to get too involved; he didn't like commitment of any kind. Not even the kind that meant he'd agree to accompany her to the wedding of one of her best mates. And, to be honest, she realised now that it suited her; it had worked. She'd soon moved on from that crazy-crush elation because the cheeky Jimmy had noticed her as a teenager (which was rather a long time ago now) to the realisation that maybe they weren't a match made in heaven. They were comfortable. In a few years' time maybe they'd be *too* comfortable. Oh God, surely when you agreed to marry a man, your toes should still be curling up and your skin prickling all over when he kissed you?

But she still liked him, loved him in a best-buddy way. Now she felt two steps behind him, when he was finally saying he was ready to commit it all seemed a bit surreal. A bit too late – if he'd said this a couple of years ago she might well have leapt into his arms and a life of washing his clothes and wandering down to the local every night.

'It was my old man that put me up to this, actually.' He really was looking sheepish, and something inside Daisy rose up in suspicion.

'Your dad?' Since when did his father turn Cupid? Romantic proposals were *so* not the image she had of his dad. Not that this was turning out to be particularly romantic, so far.

'He asked when I was going to get my finger out and give him some grandkids; told me to get on with it while he was still young enough to kick a football.'

'Let's get this straight. It was your dad's idea? Your dad told you to ask me?'

'Well, yeah, but then I got to thinking. I mean, why not? We love each other.'

This was going from bad to worse. She had thought maybe they did. But now he'd made her actually think about it, she was wavering. She loved him in the way she loved Mabel, Barney, her best mate Anna, her parents, her chickens (well at least her favourite chicken)… but did she *love* him? As in big heart, forever together. He was cute, he was kind. He chopped wood like a trouper. He knew just the right way to rub her aching feet. He hardly complained at all when she watched 'Love Actually' for the twenty-third time. He still loved her even when she was wearing a fleece with holes in and didn't have any make-up on.

11

They had matching Christmas jumpers. He loved Mabel.

So why was she messing about? It could be perfect. Was it just some stupid unrealistic romantic notion that she wanted to be swept off her feet – not be asked the question in the middle of a field as she wrapped twine round a gatepost, almost like it was an afterthought.

She'd been watching too many rom-coms, read too many happy-ever-afters. This was real life. In real life you were happy, compatible, had known each other since you were knee-high to a grasshopper, as Grandad used to say.

In fact, this probably was how Grandad and Grandma had made the decision.

They were comfortable. Like two old slippers rubbing together.

Oh Gawd, she didn't want to be an old slipper. Not yet.

The groan started to come out of her mouth and she did her best to change it into a non-committal squeak of what could have been mild interest. Or a pig sound.

Jimmy was not deterred. 'I can just give my place up, daft me wasting money on rent. I'll move in with you, and we might even be able to afford to tell Hugo to piss off.'

She didn't want to tell Hugo to piss off, even though he could be irritating. She wasn't really sure she was ready to let Jimmy move into the little cottage, her little cottage.

They seemed to be skipping from infatuation (on her part), to slippers-and-pipe comfortable, without doing the madly-in-love bit in the middle.

Surely there should be one of those, even for her?

'I can help, you know, mend fences to keep that Houdini horse in,' he gave a reassuring smile, 'I know how hard it is for you to keep on top of that place, and I'm not always there, but I can be. So, what do you say? February wedding before I get busy on the fields?'

February! He was giving her deadlines now. She spluttered up the mouthful of lager. 'There's no need to rush into this is there?' And gave a weak smile.

He could move in. Live there. With her. Instead of just spending the odd night at hers, losing odd socks under the bed, leaving the loo seat up, and emptying the milk carton, he could do it all the time. With all his socks. His socks would be happy – paired off. They could fall asleep in front of the TV together (him and her, not the socks) every night. She could cook his dinner while he mended things. They could do couple-things.

All the time.

Forever. Never set foot outside of Tippermere, never meet anybody new. Live on roast dinners and apple pie for the rest of their lives. Okay she was pushing it a bit there. They could go to the restaurants in Kitterly Heath, or rather she could. Jimmy was quite happy doing the same thing day in day out. He didn't want to explore, he didn't want excitement, oh God, he just didn't have any of the dreams she did.

She perched on the edge of her seat. That was it. She'd got it, he didn't share her dreams, he was happy with what he'd got and deep inside she thought, hoped, that one day she'd find a little bit more.

She really did feel queasy now. No way could she say that, it would be more shocking than the proposal, and it had only just occurred to her. And she'd sound deranged if she said it. He'd set off some weird kind of chain reaction inside her.

But he was nice. And maybe nobody would share her mad dreams, well not a man. Maybe this was all there was. She slumped back.

'Go on then, say it.' The pint glass stopped, halfway up to his mouth as he realised that her open mouth wasn't signalling a delighted yes. 'Daisy? Say something, please, I'm beginning to feel a bit of a dick.' His gaze darted round, furtively checking out for listeners-in.

'It's just,' putting her hands under her thighs and shuffling down so nobody could see her didn't seem to be helping, 'I'm not quite ready to be thinking about grandkids for your dad, and…' It was one thing him feeling a bit of a dick, she was beginning to feel a real cow.

'Oh. Silly me.' The glass went down with a clunk and he snapped the box shut, and then it was engulfed by his large hand. He stared at the table and his whole body seemed to close down, block her out.

She could prise his fingers open. Declare undying love. Give up on everything but him.

'Jimmy, I'm sorry, I didn't mean…' Daisy put her hand over his; the rough, weathered hand she was so fond of. If she was clear in her own head what she meant, this would be easier to explain. 'You've just caught me… you mean a lot to me, you know that.' Lame, that was so lame.

'Sure,' the box disappeared back into the inner packet of his waxed jacket, 'want another beer?'

'I just need a bit of time to get used to the idea. I'm in shock.'

'You shouldn't need a bit of time, Dais.'

'I didn't expect…' If she'd had a warning, then she would have talked herself round.

He gave a weary sigh, then stood up. 'I thought you'd be pleased. It's what women want, isn't it?'

She'd ignore the bit where he'd just lumped her in with half the population. 'It's just, well, sometimes I think I haven't actually lived, you know done things.' There were ways to say this without sounding loopy. 'I, we, shouldn't settle down yet. I'm too young.'

'Young? Lots of people get married younger than us; look at my brother Andy.'

Oh yes, randy Andy, who was intent on giving the Tippermere population a boost single-handed.

'And what do you mean you haven't done things? Like what? You do lots of stuff. It's that Anna, isn't it?'

'What is that supposed to mean, it's Anna?'

'Well you're always chatting to her.' He towered over her, begin-

14

ning to look belligerent. 'She's told you I'm not good enough for you.'

'That's just not fair, Jimmy and you know it. I like Anna, she's my friend, but I can make my own mind up about what's right for me.' Anna did think she could do better. Younger. More exciting. 'And she's never said you're not good enough for me.' Well, she had never actually said it in so many words.

'Well, she's the one that's told you you've not lived.'

'Well, actually it was you that just said I needed to lighten up, have a bit of fun.' But he did actually have a point about Anna. She had told Daisy more than once that she needed to get a life (as in one that didn't centre round a grumpy horse, her naughty dog Mabel, and Jimmy), but it wasn't Anna's voice in her head. In fact it wasn't a voice at all, it was her heart pounding so hard it was echoing in her ears, something deep inside screaming out *Help!*

Jimmy's mouth twisted stubbornly. 'I meant *we* needed to get out more.'

'You mean come to the pub more often.'

'There's nothing wrong with coming here for a pint now and then, or isn't it good enough for you now?'

'I didn't say there was anything wrong. But maybe you're right,' switching it back to him had to help, concentrate on the positive Mum always said, 'I do need to lighten up and get out more. I mean I used to have all these dreams about walking barefoot on some beach in Greece, or riding in the Canadian Rockies, or…'

'Or swimming with dolphins. Yeah, yeah, just like in those daft magazines you read. Daisy, that's all crap, real people like us don't do stuff like that, you just read about it.'

'Anna does.'

He scowled. 'People like us don't go hang-gliding, or jumping off cliffs or whatever it is. We're happy as we are.' He paused, the killer pause. 'I bet your parents never did stuff like that.'

Bull's-eye. She didn't want to be like her parents, even though she loved them. They'd spent their lives tied to a farm; milking cows and cutting crops. Making hay between showers. 'No, but *I* want to.' What had he unleashed? An hour ago, before he'd asked her to marry him, she'd thought she'd been more than happy with Mabel and Barney, with him. With mucking out stables, hacking down the lanes, shampooing and clipping dogs, with being Daisy.

Now she was insisting she wanted to jump off cliffs. Which she didn't want to do at all. Ever. She hated standing on the edge of anything, even a high wall. And the dolphin thing was a no-no. It had taken a very patient teacher and a lot of swimming lessons before she'd been able to splash her way across the width of the local swimming baths still clutching a float, mewling like a drowning kitten.

'Right.' He folded his arms, confidence returning. 'Tell you what then, you spend December doing whatever these things are.'

'December!'

He ignored the interruption. 'I'll wait, then we can announce it at Christmas. Go on, you get on with it, go and do things. Then you can come back home, eh?'

He could have added 'when you've come to your senses', but he didn't. She could see it in his eyes though.

'But I can't do much in December, it's too cold, and I've no time to plan, I—'

'Daisy, be fair.' He looked her in the eye, an earnest frown on his normally happy face. 'You can't just expect me to hang around for ever while you *think* about doing stuff. If it's that important to you, then get on and do it. Unless it's just an excuse, and what you're really trying to do is tell me to sod off?' He cocked his head on one side, and the normal twinkle wasn't in his eyes.

'Of course I'm not, Jimmy, we have a great time, it's just...'

'I'll get that drink.'

They had another beer. He dropped her off home.

'Do you really, really want to get married?'

'I've asked you now, Dais. I can't exactly un-ask, can I?'

Daisy crashed onto the sofa and didn't object when her Irish Wolfhound Mabel climbed onto to her lap. 'Why did he have to ask?'

Mabel didn't answer, just flopped sideways so that her back legs dangled over the edge. Whatever happened, it meant things had changed between them forever. They couldn't just go back to how they'd been.

'Oh Mabel, what am I going to do?' The dog wiggled her eyebrows, then rested her hairy chin on her paws and gave a heavy sigh. 'He's right. He's blown it now. You can't un-ask a question like that, can you?' And you couldn't announce an engagement when your fiancée-to-be hadn't said yes, could you? 'I need to talk to Anna.'

***

Anna kicked her Ugg boots off, pushed Mabel's tail out of the way, and plonked herself down on the sofa – stretching her feet out towards the fire. Still clutching her bottle of wine. 'Come on then, spill.'

Wriggling her way out from underneath the front end of Mabel, Daisy wondered what on earth she was supposed to add. Her text to Anna had said it all, and rather succinctly, she'd thought. *Jimmy proposed, what the hell do I do now?*

'There isn't exactly anything else to spill. I'll get some wine glasses and a corkscrew.'

'So you are sure he actually meant to propose, Daisy? He wasn't just mucking around?'

'He had a ring.'

'Wow, I didn't know he could be that organised. Did it fit? Did it have a huge diamond?'

'I didn't try it on, that would have been weird.' She daren't even touch it.

'A ring is kind of, er, conclusive. Shit.'

'I didn't think he wanted to get married.' Jimmy didn't do surprises, and he didn't do organised. He was just Jimmy.

'But you love him, don't you?'

'I thought I did.' Daisy looked glumly at Anna. This was what people waited their whole lives for, wasn't it? Falling in love, being proposed to. Nest-building. Having children. Growing old together. Oh bugger, she'd just written off her whole life.

'I take it from the look on your face that you've worked out you don't.'

'Well, I am very fond of him.' Yuk, what kind of a word was 'fond'?

'Daisy! You either do love the man or you don't.'

'It's not that simple. I mean I do, really, really like him. We get on.' Which was enough for some people. She loved him, they were compatible, had reasonable sex (even if the headboard didn't bang as much these days), they shared a sense of humour, they got on. She loved him like she loved Mabel and Barney (but obviously it was platonic with them).

She'd always just assumed they'd carry on together. As they were. Without a ring. With separate homes. Have fun. It wasn't that she was expecting some man to sweep her off her feet; sexual frisson seemed to have largely passed her by. Which was fine, but did she really want to deny herself the possibility of ever having it? To give up on the hope of even the smallest fizz?

'What are you thinking about? You've got a weird look on your face.' Anna was peering at her, one eyebrow raised.

No way was she going to say sex, or excitement, or thrills. She'd never hear the last of that. 'Nothing.' She wriggled, pretty unconvincing then, even to her own ears. 'Jimmy is great, but,' she'd moved on to squirming, which was better, 'it's not that I'm not grateful.'

18

'You're not supposed to be grateful, you idiot, you're supposed to be excited.'

But she wasn't. That was the problem.

She covered her face with her hands. 'I ignored him the first time he asked.'

Anna laughed. 'That is so mean.' Then she frowned. 'And it's not like you at all.'

Daisy peeped through her fingers. 'Well he mumbled, and I was busy tying the gate together and I thought maybe I'd misheard.'

'You hoped you had, you mean. So you made him ask again, twice, and then said no! Oh, poor Jimmy.'

'Shush, I didn't mean it, and I didn't say no. Oh, Anna, the second I saw the ring I just felt… oh God, this sounds awful.'

'Spit it out then.' Anna was looking more intrigued by the second. 'This is better than an episode of EastEnders.'

'If you're not going to take me seriously, then I'm not going to talk about it.'

'I am. Honest, cross my heart.'

'I just felt,' if she said it quickly it might not sound as bad as it did in her head, 'is this it? Is this all there is?'

Anna giggled. 'Sounds like a song,' and she started singing.

'This is my life, Anna.'

'Another song.'

'Sod off, it's not funny. What the fuck am I supposed to do now?'

'Well, you're sounding a bit philosophical even for you – *is this all there is?* – roll on death and maggots eating your rotting corpse.'

'I didn't mean that, you know I didn't. It's just…' She gazed out of the window into the blackness, but knew that in the morning the beautiful rolling hills that she *did* love would be there.

She had Mabel, she had her horse. It should be enough; she should be satisfied.

'Spit it out then, Dais.'

'Well, I haven't *been* anywhere.'

'And you haven't shagged anybody else? Is this what it's really about?'

Everybody in the village knew that Daisy had never fallen in love with a playground buddy. She'd never sneaked fags or kisses behind the bike shed, she'd just been Daisy. Then Daisy had left school and turned into Daisy and Jimmy.

'I'm not talking about shagging.'

'So? Can't this dog go on the floor?'

'She's asleep, don't be mean. Look, you went on proper holidays when you were a kid, didn't you?' Daisy said, slightly accusingly, at Anna, feeling like she wasn't being taken seriously. 'All we ever got was a week in a caravan in Tenby, cos Dad had to get back to the cows.' And the chickens, and the hay-making. She sighed. 'Not that there's anything wrong with Tenby. But we were supposed to go to France once, then there was a ferry strike. Dad said what will be will be and never tried again.'

Anna topped up the wine glasses. 'So you've *never* even been to France?' Daisy shook her head. 'Or Spain?'

'Nope.'

'Greece? Italy?'

'Now you're being silly.'

'Isle of Wight?'

'You're making me feel worse now, not better. I thought friends were supposed to help. I did go to Cornwall once.'

'Well it's a start, it used to be a separate country didn't it?'

'Dad was competing with a prize heifer in the Royal show. We were only there for two days.'

'Okay, better than nothing I suppose. Just. Won't Jimmy take you somewhere, you know, if you get married? You could have a blow-out honeymoon.'

'He's like Dad, he likes what he knows.' Daisy sighed. She'd actually always liked that side of him, until it had come to the crunch. She knew where she stood with Jimmy, he was like a comfortable old fleece – the one you always grabbed. 'He did go to Ibiza with Andy and the gang for a stag do, but that was it, and he kept saying how glad he was to be home.'

'He is nice though, Jimmy. You do get on.'

'My whole life is nice, Anna, that's the problem and I hadn't really thought about it properly until he asked.' Had her cornered, more like. 'But I do love him,' maybe more in the old-fleece than mad-passion way, 'and all this.' She waved expansively to take in the cottage and everything outside. The world as she knew it. 'But I just sometimes get this feeling that if I'm not careful I'll miss out on a whole load of stuff.'

'Like?'

'I don't know. Everything. I'm being daft, aren't I? This should be enough. I should just know he's the one for me.'

Anne grinned. 'How should I know? Miss Footloose and Fancy-free, that's me, but,' the smile slipped, 'you know what, girl? Maybe you need to sow some wild oats,' Daisy rolled her eyes, 'well not shag around or anything, but get away from Cheshire. I sometimes envy you, you've got everything while I'm just dashing round wasting my life, so I'm not going to hand out advice. But maybe you just need to get out there, go somewhere.' She shrugged. 'Then you'll appreciate Jimmy and all this, or,' she grinned, 'never come back.'

'I'd never not come back,' Daisy protested, 'it's my home.' She peered at Anna over her glass. 'I could go away though, couldn't I?' Actually go somewhere, rather than just think about doing it.

'You could. And you've got a deadline, so we need to come up with a plan, book flights to exotic locations.'

'Anna!'

'He's given you an ultimatum, Dais, and it's the best thing that could have happened to you. You can't put it off – you either live a bit, or,' she paused, and this time did look up, 'or you give Jimmy an answer now.'

'You know I'm not going to do that.' She stared at Anna. She was right. It was her chance to actually do something.

'If you stay here before you know it Jimmy will have moved in,' she picked up one of Jimmy's socks off the chair next to her and wrinkled her nose, then flung it in the air – it hit Mabel on the head, 'and you'll be married and have a brood of Jim and Jemima's.'

'He said you've got until Christmas,' Anna's voice softened, which was dangerous, so Daisy concentrated, 'I know you're still not sure, and you've got to be. This could be the most important decision you've ever made in your whole life.'

'I'll be fine. I'm perfectly capable of making my own decision.'

Anna sighed. 'I'm not having a dig, it's just you've kind of settled into middle-aged bliss without doing the bit before. You said yourself that you didn't want to end up like your mum, giving everything up and becoming a farmer's wife.'

'I don't.'

'Well at least she had stuff to decide to give up, didn't she?'

'I think she had a pretty high-powered job, though she doesn't say much. She used to fly all over the world.'

'Exactly, and what have you done, Daisy Fischer? You said yourself that you've never been abroad. Let's face it, you hardly ever get more than fifteen miles from Tippermere.'

'Okay, I'm hopeless. Can we leave me alone now and talk about the weather?'

'You're not hopeless; you just need to take this opportunity.'

'I am going to. I just need to think, decide what I really want to do, where I want to go.' No way was she going to let Anna book her a ticket to Bangkok, or wherever she had in mind. But she was going to do this. It was just a case of deciding what 'this' was.

'Now you're talking. The world is your oyster.'

Not that she'd ever even had an oyster. 'But who do I go with? I don't know anybody but you.'

'Well actually, it would be better if you went with yourself, just you, Daisy. Otherwise you won't see anything and you certainly won't meet,' Anna's eyes were positively gleaming with fun, 'anybody. But I've got a better idea.'

'What?' Daisy really didn't like that look in her friend's eye.

'I'll tell you tomorrow, when I've done some checking. Come on, drink up, I've got another bottle of wine in my bag.'

Daisy groaned. Anna knew she was a pushover after two glasses of wine, she'd agree to anything.

Chapter 3 – Flo. Paris and back again

Florence Cortes liked Barcelona best when the fierce heat of the summer sun had mellowed and the crowds had thinned, not that you could ever call the city quiet. But in the autumn it was still warm enough to laze on the beach at weekends, and even the more popular tourist bars had the odd empty seat in the evening.

She was nursing a very nice glass of red wine, in her favourite El Born bar, when Oli bounced in. Late as usual.

'Evening, gorgeous.' Oli kissed her, a broad smile on his full lips. 'Same for me, please.' He signalled to the guy behind the bar for a glass of wine before settling down on the stool next to hers. He snuggled in closer, so that their knees touched.

It was like loving a Golden Retriever; hard to be cross when he looked so adorably happy to see you. No, she corrected herself, it was more like loving a cat. A very demanding cat. He might be asking for cuddles right now, but she seemed to be spending an increasingly large chunk of her life trying to please him; he was like a surgeon – he liked having his patients there in the waiting room ready so that he didn't have to waste any of his own precious time. The fact that she could have written an article for their magazine, or done her nails, instead of sitting in a bar on her own waiting was irrelevant to him.

At times it niggled her, but it was silly to let his little bad habits annoy her – and as everybody was always telling her (including Oli himself), she had the perfect life. A lovely apartment, great job, and Oli. She shook off her irritation; he was the perfect man, even her parents seemed to think so.

'Sorry I'm late.' He hadn't missed the way she'd glanced at her watch. 'But I've been busy.'

'You're always busy,' she tried not to sound cross, he was after all working hard for *them*, both of them, 'what deal have you been sealing today, Oli?'

'One just for you.' He grinned. 'You're going to love this. Hang on, I need a leak but I'll be back in a sec.' He tapped his mobile phone. 'No peeking. I'm expecting the confirmation any second now.' He rolled his eyes theatrically. 'The things I do for you.'

Flo was staring at his mobile, which for once wasn't attached to him, and then it pinged. Just like that.

She wouldn't normally dare touch his precious phone (in fact, as it was seldom out in the wild on its own, chance would have been a fine thing), but it *was* for her, wasn't it? He'd just said so. She hesitated for a nanosecond – to give him time to get back from the toilet, which he didn't – then grabbed it.

Oli had always been pretty spontaneous in the early days of their relationship. In the very early days he'd once knocked on her door with a rose between his teeth and tickets for a gig in his hand, and he'd surprised her with a brand new Vespa scooter when it wasn't even her birthday, but things had got a bit more predictable lately. But that was what happened in relationships, wasn't it?

Or maybe not.

She scanned the email. Then read it again slightly more carefully just to be sure. Then a third time (it was a very short email) and the bubble of excitement burst out just as Oli got back from his visit to the gents.

'What are you doing with my phone?'

25

'Oh My God,' she laughed out loud, ignoring the edge to his voice, 'Oli. Really?'

His eyes narrowed. 'What's that you're looking at, Flo?' He put a hand over hers to steady his phone – which she was waving about in front of his face as she jumped up and down – so he could read what was on the screen.

'Christ, what are you doing?' He paused. 'Oh that.' The nervous twitch and flat tone wasn't quite what she'd expected. Nor was the way his grip tightened on her wrist as he tried to tug the phone from her grasp, while she was busy attempting to re-read the message. Just to make sure it really did say what she thought. 'Oh for heaven's sake, Florence, give me the bloody phone.'

Flo froze. Oh shit. Now he was cross (that cat thing again), she'd spoiled his surprise, and he so liked to do things his way. Or not at all. 'Oh no, I'm sorry, you wanted to tell me your—'

He shrugged, pulled at the phone again in what was getting to be a bit of a tug of war. 'This is you all over, isn't it? Why do you always have to interfere and spoil things?'

'I wasn't interfering, the message just came in, and I thought, you said you were expecting… Oli, I'm sorry, honest.' She never normally got a chance to be remotely nosey, he was far too good at being in control. 'I didn't mean to spoil… it's just such a wonderful surprise and now I've ruined it.' Even for control-freak Oli it was a bit of an over-reaction. Flo stared at him, wondering if any moment now he was going to storm out and cancel the whole thing.

There was a moment when he just stood and stared at her, then his normal quirky grin reappeared. 'It's fine, never mind. I know you always wanted to go to Paris, so I thought what the hell.'

'You remembered.' She shrieked, then relinquished control of the phone, as he'd confirmed exactly what he'd done himself, and grabbed him. 'You remembered, oh Oli, you are amazing. I am *so* lucky'

'Of course I remembered.' His expression was a mixture of satisfaction and slight annoyance that she'd doubted him. 'I always remember important facts like that. You said it was one of the most romantic place on earth.'

'No, well yes, but I meant you remembered our anniversary. Oh Oli, I do love you.' And if she hadn't been quite as excited, and convinced that he really, really did love her, she might have noticed there and then that he hadn't reacted to the word 'anniversary' at all. 'And going on the train; that is so romantic.'

He wriggled free of her grip and straightened his top. 'I thought flying was overrated. This way we're doing it in style, making it part of the trip. Flying first class would have been a bit of a cliché and you can pack your own hamper and bubbly. It'll save us some cash too, no point throwing it away.'

Flo didn't actually mind being clichéd, or being wined and dined in style, but she was being picky and ungrateful. And this was all fabulous, and SO romantic, and this way they'd have some spare money to go out on their actual anniversary. Oh God, maybe he had something special planned. Like a ring. For her third finger. She tried not to grin like a simpleton. One step at a time, she mustn't just expect it – that would spoil the actual surprise.

Oli patted her stool, expecting her to behave and sit down again.

'I'm sorry, I…'

'Forget it.' He pocketed his mobile. 'But you know I don't like people messing with my phone.'

She could have said she wasn't just 'people', but that might have seemed churlish, and at least he seemed to have got over it now.

'Blew the budget really a bit as it was, but we're worth it.' He grinned, his good humour fully restored. 'Paris is bloody expensive you know.'

'But *so* romantic.' Flo sighed. She loved all of France, but Paris really was the most spectacular, romantic spot on earth. And this time she'd be with the man she loved, not her parents, or on a school trip with a bunch of teenage boys who thought culture was seeing who could spit their chewing gum out furthest.

She and Oli had been together five years; it was the anniversary of that first date, he was going to propose. She knew it. And where better?

***

Two days later, with a carefully prepared picnic, and a chilled bottle of bubbly, they caught the train out of Barcelona, heading towards ten days of bliss.

Packing had been pretty straightforward. A sexy going-out dress, for 'the event' because he wouldn't have gone to all this trouble just for a break, sexy underwear (there was a theme going on here, but after all, Paris *was* the city of love – and hopefully passion), high heels (more on the sexy theme), and some boots she knew she could walk in (for those romantic excursions on the Seine and the art galleries, where they would stroll hand in hand).

Flo didn't care that the moment they'd sat down Oli fished out his headphones and disappeared into his own little world as he messed about with his phone (no doubt answering work messages), she was happy flicking through the pages of the guide book, gazing in awe at the photographs and working out just where she wanted to go (though Oli, no doubt, would have planned everything anyway – he was good like that – he liked an itinerary).

The next day, Friday, after croissants and coffee served in their room (no point in squandering money on a café, is there?), he spread out a city map on the bed and pointed out a route around the area that he'd carefully marked in red ink.

'I thought we'd do this today. You don't mind going on ahead though, do you, darling? Bit of a muzzy head, too much champagne yesterday.' Oli grinned apologetically.

'Oh no, do you need anything?'

'I'll be fine, honest,' he glanced at his phone and gave an exaggerated sigh as yet another message came in, 'I don't want to spoil your fun.' He tapped out a reply and Flo shook her head.

'A few days' break from work would do you good. It's no wonder you've got a headache. Can't you just let people leave a message, like you told me to do?'

'One of us has to keep things ticking over, darling, and I want you to enjoy the break. I promise not to do much.' He smiled, then pressed a hand to his temple and grimaced. 'You go and explore, I'll meet you for lunch. Look,' he pointed at the map, where he'd put a star, 'the guy at reception said this place is excellent value.'

Flo was not happy. She'd only got a short way down the street when the first spots of rain fell from the sky, and she realised she'd left her umbrella in the hotel room. It wouldn't have mattered if she'd been at home, but no way did she want to look a bedraggled rat when she met Oli for lunch. He'd obviously asked the hotel for a recommendation, which meant the restaurant could be somewhere special, which meant... Well, she really didn't want to count her chickens, but it was their anniversary, and what if he was leading up to...? Flo grinned and a man walking the other way grinned back, but she didn't care. She was in Paris, the city of romance, and her boyfriend was about to propose, and she needed an umbrella because she wanted to look sleek and sophisticated, not frizzy beach-babe.

She ran up the stairs rather than take the lift; she might as well make an early start on being trim. I mean, Oli had probably already planned the wedding, had a date in mind. In fact, she wouldn't put it past him to have booked a place.

As she opened the door of their room, a gentle waft of air blew through from doors they'd left ajar, bringing with it the hustle and bustle of the Paris streets below, and Flo took a deep breath and smiled. What did they say? Heaven on earth? This place really was blissful. Oh God, maybe he'd brought her here because he wanted to hold the actual wedding ceremony in Paris?

'You're fucking gorgeous you know, darling.'

Her grin broadened as she stepped further into the room. 'So are—' The words died on her lips as she glanced at the empty bed. She frowned. It was Oli's voice, but he wasn't there. She peered in the bathroom, he wasn't there either. Sticking her head out of the doors that led to the balcony, she risked getting her hair wet as a very feminine (and definitely not Oli) giggle reached her ears.

His voice was clearer out here, as were the muffled oo's and ahh's.

Flo leaned out further, desperately trying to see into the next room. Then she froze.

'You bastard.' The words choked in her throat. 'You total utter bastard.' This time they came out full throttle.

Marching back through their room and out of the door, Flo careered into the corridor, just as Oli popped out of the next room like a rabbit out of a bloody magician's hat.

'That's Sarah, and she's—'

'Hang on, Flo, let me explain.'

'She's naked, on a bed, and you,' Flo glared pointedly at his crotch, which was now encased in underwear, 'were fucking naked with her.'

He winced. 'Keep your voice down. Do you have to talk like that, you know I don't—'

'Do I have to talk like that?' For a moment she was speechless, but it didn't last more than a couple of seconds. There were so many words trying to burst out of her it was just a case of getting them in a straight line, and the right order. 'Do you have to fuck another woman like that?'

'I wasn't actually fu—'

'You, Oliver, are the only man I know who could split straws over whether you were actually doing it or not. You were naked. You were flesh on flesh. Like this.' She flapped the palms of her hands together, 'I'm surprised you've not got friction burns.'

'If you'd let me explain, instead of flying off the handle.'

'Explain? Explain? What is Sarah bloody Rogers doing here, in Paris, in the next fucking room? You, you, you fuckwit.'

Oli raised an eyebrow. 'Look, you don't normally swear.'

'You don't normally sleep around, or at least I didn't think you did.'

He didn't say anything, just made a move towards their room, so Flo reversed and planted herself firmly in the doorway. 'Did you ask for adjoining doors so you could just pop between us naked and not waste a precious second of your time?'

'Don't be ridiculous. I didn't bloody know they'd put her in the next room, did I? Be reasonable.'

Flo stared. 'Did you really just say that?'

'It was pure coincidence, if I'd have known...'

That was when she slammed the door and emptied every bottle she could find in the mini-fridge into his underwear drawer, and gave it a good jiggle. Shaken not stirred.

'Flo, Flo, be reasonable.' Oli banged on the door, hissing through the keyhole. 'Calm down, you're over-reacting and making a fool of yourself.'

'*I'm* making a fool of myself? I'm not the one in my pants in a hotel corridor. I should have known you were up to something. That's what all those late sessions working have been about, isn't it? All the *editorial* work you've been doing.' She'd been stupid. Accepted all his excuses at face value, trying to keep the status quo when deep down she'd known it wasn't acceptable.

'Flo, open this door, I'm standing here in my underwear.'

She added the olives and peanuts to the mix in the drawer, and hoped his gritty and oily extremities would cause him and the lovely Sarah a fair bit of discomfort for days to come. 'I'll give you friction!'

'Flo, I didn't even know she'd be in the same hotel.'

'Oh, so that makes everything better. Tons better. How considerate.'

He'd urged her to shop that morning, which had seemed perfectly acceptable. Oli wasn't really one to window shop, the odd breaks that they had enjoyed together had been 'activity' or 'visiting ancient monuments' but this holiday had, he'd said tucking her hair behind her ear, been for her.

How sweet. How considerate. What a load of bollocks.

Flo went back to the knicker drawer, pulled it out and emptied the entire contents into the one that held his t-shirts. The bastard. How could he do it?

He'd even bought her a red rose last night. The one she'd thought might be accompanied by a little jewellery box and a bent knee.

'Flo, be fair, just let me talk to you.'

She opened the door a crack, aware that she now looked like a complete mad woman, her hair all over the place and her face, no doubt, bright pink.

'What?'

'It's been all work and no play lately, I thought a break in your favourite place would be nice.'

'Did you mean you remembered it was *my* favourite place, or hers?' She paused as the realisation hit. 'I'm not even supposed to be here, am I? That train ticket was for her.'

'Flo, it was you that grabbed my phone.'

'So all this is *my* fault? You're blaming *me* for being here.' Flo narrowed her eyes. 'So,' she put one hand on her hip, 'what was it you'd organised for me?'

He looked blank.

'When we were in the bar you said you'd arranged something,' she paused, 'something for me, that I'd love.'

'Well, I arranged for you to talk to a guy who's opening a new trendy fusion bar in Barcelona, so you could do a piece for the magazine. The guy is a genius, he—'

'You bastard.'

Oli had a pained expression on his face. 'It's going to be an in-place, you've no idea how hard it was to get that interview.'

'You've no idea how hard I want to hit you right now.'

He ignored her, put a hand on the door jamb, confident he'd be able to talk his way back inside.

'Look it's not you, it's me.'

'You loser.' She stared open-mouthed. 'That is the crappiest line ever, but you're right. It is you. You really are the biggest dick on earth, aren't you?' Throwing all her weight at the door, Flo managed to slam it shut. There really was nothing else she could do. Then she threw all of her clothes into her case, and half of his out of the window. The half that hadn't been caught up in the pre-dinner drinks-and-snacks saga.

It was quite a spectacular sight. A Parisian street, she decided had probably never seen so many Calvin Klein knickers, Armani shirts and designer jeans hooked in trees. The best bit, she decided, was seeing his pretentious Panama hat land in what he'd termed 'cat-shit alley' after treading in something unsavoury just after they'd arrived.

She stared for a moment, out of breath from all her exertions, then clutched the balcony rail and closed her eyes. She needed a drink, but she'd gone and thrown every last bit of alcohol in with his remaining clothes, and she wasn't quite desperate enough to suck it out. Yet. Even her chocolate fix was in there.

Ringing reception, she very calmly reported a fire in room 406, and then waited until she heard Oli loudly declaring there was no such thing, and a member of staff insisting they had to check, before slipping out of room 405 and running down the stairs. She was out of the hotel, up the street, past the underwear-festooned trees, and round the corner before she stopped to draw breath.

It was when she realised she'd left the umbrella behind that she started to cry.

Chapter 4 – Flo. Heading home

No way was she going to sit on a train, decided Flo. The last thing she wanted to be reminded of was the journey out here, when they had shared a romantic buffet laden with champagne, and all things nice, including some chocolates to die for. When her head had been in the clouds and she'd been wondering what kind of ring he'd chosen, and whether he'd go down on one knee.

Bastard.

Instead she headed for the airport, determined to make use of the company card one last time. Oh God, she gulped down the lump in her throat. Their whole lives were meshed together, two halves of a zip. And now it was stuck, with Sarah Rogers caught in the teeth. And when she finally got past that fluffy obstruction and undid it to the bottom she'd be well and truly stuffed.

No job, no man, no apartment if she didn't work out the job bit. Fuck.

That was what happened when you relied on somebody. When you set up a business with them. When you loved them.

A little whimper escaped, despite the fact she was biting her lip. She had to get a grip. And had to get back to Barcelona as quickly, and unromantically, as she could.

Unfortunately it seemed the rest of the world, well Paris, didn't appreciate how quickly she needed to exit. And how little she wanted to queue up behind loved-up couples.

'Our next flight goes out in four hours, and it is full I'm afraid. Would you like to come back later and see if there are any no-shows?' The woman behind the airline desk flashed a professional you've-got-no-hope smile.

'No-shows sounds fantastic. I'll wait.' First in the queue sounded better.

'We won't know until boarding.'

'Not a problem.' What else did she have to do with her time?

'Some people check in very late.'

Flo gritted her teeth and tried to keep the smile plastered to her face. 'It's fine.' She could plan revenge. Or work out how she'd ever been desperate enough to let herself get into this situation. How had she not seen it coming?

Two strong cups of coffee and a rumbling tummy later she knew she had do something before she exploded or dissolved. It was touch and go either way. She had a sudden yearning for Tippermere, the village she'd grown up in. Normality.

Since her Spanish mother had decided to leave the UK and move back to Spain, and she'd followed, she'd spent her time in various places before finally settling for what had to look like an idyllic lifestyle. She had Oli, her own company (well the shared magazine with Oli), and the trendiest part of Barcelona to live in. But sometimes, she had to admit, it felt lonely.

Sometimes she yearned to put her wellies on and trudge through fields, to curl up in front of the fire with a mug of milk and a pile of cookies. Sometimes she just missed her childhood friends.

She flicked through the Facebook posts of her friends, Anna (who posted lots) and Daisy (who obviously had a far too busy real-life and didn't post often at all). Pictures of them sharing a bottle of wine in the local pub, laughing, having fun. She felt a twinge of jealousy and a soft ache in her stomach that brought her to the verge of tears. She wanted to be there, to rush back – but she had to make a go of it here. It had been her choice. Life in Barcelona *should* be wonderful (everybody said so); she hadn't even wanted to admit to herself until now that sometimes it was hard. That sometimes beneath all the perfect stuff there was a gaping hole, something missing.

Now she felt like toddler-Flo who wanted her comfort-blanket back.

Right now she needed a friend. An easy-going, non-judgemental friend – which Anna had always been given her dating and fashion disasters, which she was more than happy to own up to publicly. Unlike her, who just pretended everything was fabulous.

She sighed as she stared at the picture of a laughing Anna, and then, before she could change her mind, she opened Skype.

'Wow, what a coincidence. I was going to call you.' Anna's familiar face, slightly pixilated, beamed at her from the too-small screen of her phone, and she felt even more like crying. The beam dropped a few kilowatts. 'Are you okay, Flo?'

'Not really.' She wanted a hug. She closed her eyes for a moment, took a deep breath and opened them. Blurted it out before she changed her mind. 'It's all a farce.'

'Sorry?' Anna leaned in closer to the camera, her frown was clearly visible even over the dodgy internet connection.

'My life. Oli. Everything.'

'But you're getting engaged, you're going to… Hang on, you're actually in Paris,' she paused, 'aren't you?'

'I am, I'm at the airport.' Don't cry.

'Oh, and Oli…'

'Is still in the hotel room, with another woman.' She spat that bit out. Anger was better; anger she could cope with. 'Oh God, I've been a complete idiot, Anna.' Getting pathetic again, but she couldn't help it. Anna's look of sympathy made it worse. 'I've been so caught up in the idea of this perfect relationship and my wonderful life.' A sob caught at the back of her throat and she swallowed it down. 'He even got a new scooter.'

'Sorry?' Anna looked confused.

'A more powerful one so he could get around quicker, go further. I couldn't see the point, and he said we didn't have much money, but he said we had to project the right image.' It was all about image with Oli. They were both kidding themselves big time. 'He got it so he could whizz up the coast and shag her, then be back before his beer went flat and I've only just realised.'

'Ah.'

'I've wasted five years of my life on that inconsiderate, pompous, self-centred idiot. He wouldn't even let me have a dog, and I listened to him.'

'Sorry, there's a lot of interference, he wouldn't let you have what?'

'A dog.'

'Oh, you did say dog.'

The dog had been a sticking point, and was now symbolic of all the other things she realised he hadn't wanted her to have. 'And it is just so boring working on the stuff he wants me to do for the magazine.'

'I thought you loved the magazine? Writing was always your dream job.'

She studied her fingernails. How could you have your dream job and mess it up? 'I do, it was, but he just leaves the really tedious stuff for me. He does the interviews, and travels around to get the gossip and I end up sorting the adverts out and doing 'how to pack your suitcase' features. Have you any idea how hard it is to come up with a new angle for packing a suitcase?'

'Er, no. I just tend to throw stuff in.'

'Exactly, and if I have to write one more recipe for tasty tapas for tourists I'm going to scream.'

Anna giggled and Flo looked up. 'You're right, it's a joke. I'm a joke, my whole life…'

'Oh don't be daft, Flo. Me and Daisy love reading your updates, your life is much more exciting than ours. You're just in shock.'

'I miss Tippermere, and you guys.'

'Believe me, you don't miss Tippermere. But I can go with the second part.' Her face suddenly went serious. 'I am sorry, Flo, he's a shit. I can't believe he could do that.'

'I think I can believe it.' Flo couldn't look her friend straight in the eye, instead she concentrated on the keyboard of her mobile phone. 'The warning signs have been there.' She sighed. 'I've just been ignoring them. Keeping up appearances.'

'You couldn't know he was going to do that.'

If she'd stopped her determined efforts to live the perfect live, to convince herself and everybody else that things were great, then maybe she could have. 'Sorry to dump on you.'

'That's what friends are for.'

'I'll be fine when I get home.' And throw the rest of his belongings off the rooftop terrace. 'You said you were going to ring me?'

'It'll wait until you get home. What time's your flight?'

'Hang on, the woman on the airline desk is waving, maybe that means they've got a spare seat.'

'Oh Flo, you are okay?'

'Fine.'

'Call me when you get back to Barcelona. I've got an idea.'

Flo pocketed her phone and made her way back to the airline desk, where a smiling girl was already holding a hand out for her passport.

So, that was it. So much for her smug outward journey with alcohol-laden hamper and gorgeous fiancé-to-be. Now she was make-up free, splodgy-pink faced, wild-haired, on the verge of tears and singledom was yelling her name.

She'd been stupidly happy for two days, she thought, as she

trudged down the aisle and took her seat next to a dreadlocked teenager who had earphones in and acknowledged her arrival with a twitch of her pierced nose. Two bloody delusional days. Plus five years.

The whole row shook, as with a cheery grin a large lady heaved her over-sized bulk into the seat next to her, jostling her elbows and wriggling her hips until she'd squeezed her ample frame into the restricted space.

Flo made a grab for the plastic safety card and hoped neither of her travel companions would try and talk to her.

She stared at the laminated card telling her how to evacuate in case of emergency and the pictures blurred. How could her life have gone so wrong so quickly? Even her pep talk with Anna hadn't made it more bearable; in fact it was just making her feel more homesick – and more of a fool. A tear escaped and plopped onto the card, and she angrily squashed the rest with the back of her hand before they could join it. She was *not* going to cry. If she did she might never stop and would arrive back in Barcelona a soggy, pitiful mess.

'Cheer up, love, it might never happen. Ooh it's a bit parky with this air-conditioning isn't it?' A podgy elbow narrowly missed her good eye – the one that didn't have the overflow problem. 'Good job I kept my cardi on. Here, have one of these.' A tin of boiled sweets was inserted between the evacuation instructions and Flo's nose.

Flo shook her head, not daring to speak, and bit down on her lip.

'Go on, there's plenty,' the tin was shaken violently, 'a good suck stops your ears popping.' She leaned across Flo, nearly squashing her with her generous cardigan-encased bosom, and waved the tin in Miss Dreadlocks' direction. The girl, her eyes shut, continued to nod her head to the beat of the music being blasted into her ears, oblivious to her surroundings and Flo wished she'd thought of that.

'Ahh, you don't like flying. That's what it is, isn't it, duck?' She prised the card from Flo's fingers and pushed it back into the pocket. 'I know these planes aren't everybody's cup of tea, though I must admit I love them, means you're on your way somewhere exciting doesn't it when you get frisked at security.' She grinned, completely unaware that she'd just removed Flo's first line of defence. What was she going to do now? Go into the full-on brace position so that nobody could see her face? 'You don't want to be looking at that thing, dear, it'll make you feel worse. If we go down, then who's going to remember that kind of stuff? They'll all be diving for the doors and to hell with taking your shoes off and not pulling the toggle things. And chances are it'll be boom.' She waved her arms extravagantly and Flo dodged to avoid an elbow.

Flo bit down harder on her lip. How come when you really wanted to chat you ended up sitting next to Mr Monosyllabic, and when human interaction was so far down on your wish list it had fallen off the bottom, you found yourself next to the airborne equivalent of the chatty taxi driver?

'Now, now love, there's nothing to be scared of. I know rattling down the runway can be a bit bouncy at times but once we're in the air it's all plain sailing, isn't it? Well, plain flying.' She chuckled at her own joke and popped a sweet into her mouth.

'I'm not scared.' The words juddered their way out of Flo's mouth before she clamped her teeth back over the wobbly lip. The pain in her chest had grown; in fact her whole body was aching. Maybe she should feign death, or once the plane had taken off she could lock herself in the toilet and say the catch had jammed.

The sweet tin was shoved into an oversize handbag. 'Well, whatever it is, there's no use crying over spilt milk, is there? I'm sure it'll all seem better in the…'

Flo burst into tears. She couldn't help herself, she'd held it together at the airport but just couldn't hold it in a second longer.

'Oh goodness.' The sweets came out again, followed by a man-size tissue. 'Now, now, don't you be getting all upset. Don't tell me…' Flo hadn't been about to.

'Sorry, I, I've had a bit of a shock.' The realisation that your life was a disaster didn't exactly lead to happy-dancing. 'I'll be fine, thank you.'

Flo's travel companion finished wrestling the enormous handbag under the seat and sat up red-faced, 'I'm Carol by the way,' then beamed at Flo.

'Florence, Flo.' Just saying her name seemed normal, and for a moment she forgot about *him*.

'Now would you believe it, Flo, we're about to take off. How about I tell you all about my hols to take your mind off it?'

Flo nodded and after blowing her nose a few times, taking a few deep breaths and letting Carol's words drift over her she started to feel more like her normal self.

By the time Flo had heard all about Carol's fun in Paris they were airborne, and the drinks trolley was jangling its way down the aisle.

'I think we need a little drinky to cheer us up, don't we?' She patted Flo's knee and, ignoring her protests, proceeded to order a mountain of snacks and drinks. 'Here you are, love,' she emptied the contents of a bottle into the plastic cup and added a splash of Coke, 'I got you a couple of bottles of Bacardi. They're only tiny little things, aren't they? Cheers, me dears, drink up!'

Flo drank up and blinked, feeling surprisingly light-headed, which could have been to do with the altitude, or the fact that she really couldn't put the drink away as fast as Carol.

'Oh, now look at this.' Carol had moved onto her magazine, and Flo squinted and tried to concentrate on something other than her disastrous life. 'He's a looker, isn't he?'

Flo nodded dumbly at the photograph of George Clooney. Yes, like Oli. He was a looker alright, and a talker.

'Makes it too easy for them, doesn't it?' Carol turned the page round so she could examine the picture more closely. 'If they haven't got looks then they have to work at it, makes them nicer, that's what my mother always said. And those lookers go to seed, you know. Then what have you got left?'

'George Clooney hasn't gone to seed.'

'Well there has to be the odd exception.'

'Nor has Harrison Ford,' chipped in dreadlocks girl, who had removed her earphones at some point, 'he looked hot in *Star Wars*.'

'They're not real life though, are they, duck? You don't know what work goes into making them look like that. Worse than women they are, all titivated up.'

Flo sighed. Maybe Oli hadn't been real life, and the idea of him losing his looks and going to seed cheered her up a bit.

'Oh look, we're nearly there. I'm quite looking forward to this, like my mam always said, a change of scene works wonders.'

Flo stared out of the window. A change of scene, a complete change of scene, was probably just what she needed right now. She just had to work out what it looked like.

***

As the airplane touched down at Barcelona airport, Flo didn't feel quite so tearful. The two double Bacardi and Cokes, plus the glass of Prosecco had taken her from the 'he's a bastard and I want to cry' stage, to the much healthier 'I'm better off without him (maybe) and I hope him and his hussy burn in hell' stage. After swaying in the aisle of the plane for twenty minutes waiting to disembark, spending ten minutes in a queue for passport control and an impossibly long time (impossibly because her bladder was about to burst) waiting in line for the toilets, her alcoholic haze had lifted and all she wanted to do was go home, get so drunk she couldn't see straight, and cry.

Chapter 5 - Daisy and Anna. Barcelona

Daisy was wrestling with a wet and very randy Dalmatian, and trying to ignore her hangover, when Anna reappeared the day after 'the proposal' – practically bouncing with her news.

'God, Daisy, what are you doing to that dog?'

'It's more a question of what it's trying to do to me. He wants to bonk everything with a pulse. Just hold him round the neck and look stern can you?'

'Like a Dalamatrix?'

'Very funny.' She grabbed the shower head while the dog was actually still, and soon had him soaked to the skin and lathered up. There were days when she really thought her dog-grooming business should cater for nothing bigger than a poodle, and nothing with balls.

'Anyway,' Anna hung on as the dog made a bid for freedom, 'I came to tell you it's all sorted. Your big adventure is on; you're visiting Florence!'

'I am?' She stopped mid-lather, which was handy. If she'd still had the shower head in her hand, then Anna might well have been soaked.

'You are.'

It sounded rather final. 'Don't I get a say in this?'

Anna relaxed her hold on the dog in surprise and it was halfway out of the bath, and she was drenched, by the time Daisy made a grab for its collar. 'Well yeah, of course. I just thought you'd like the idea...'

'Florence, that's in Italy, isn't it? I thought it was expensive there,' she sighed, 'you know I'm broke.' Anna giggled and got a firm hold on the dog again, relief flooding her face. But Daisy hardly noticed. 'I'd been thinking maybe I should go to France first on the ferry. You know, a little village.' With cute cafés where she could settle down with a book. 'And beaches.'

'Daisy?'

The more she'd thought about going away, the more she wanted to do it. But she was afraid of different, too different. Maybe she needed to think this through – it was fine thinking she needed to live a bit, but she'd been thinking of starting off with baby steps.

'I was thinking somewhere on the coast, and Florence isn't, is it?' She'd only just scraped a pass at GCSE Geography.

'Daisy will you let me finish, you dafty? You're going to see Flo the person, not the place. Flo, remember?'

Daisy stopped trying to scrub the spots off the dog and looked at Anna in confusion. 'Flo? But she lives in Barcelona doesn't she? Or has she moved?'

'Yep she does, and no she hasn't. It was you who mentioned Italy, not me.'

Daisy decided it would be a waste of breath correcting her. 'That's Spain.'

'Genius.' Anna grinned, pleased with herself. 'Barcelona's got a beach, and it's better than being stuck out in the sticks. Anyhow, December is hardly sunbathing weather and it'll be freezing in France.'

'Have you actually mentioned this to Flo? I mean, I've hardly spoken to her for ages and I thought she had this hectic high-flying lifestyle.'

Totally unlike her own. Totally unlike any other inhabitant of Tippermere. They might have gone to the same primary school, played kiss chase with the same boys and even hit puberty and agonised over their A levels together. But there all similarities had ended abruptly. Daisy had stayed in the village and Flo had swanned off to Barcelona with her Spanish mother, who had decided that she couldn't cope with the damp English weather any longer.

'The last Facebook status I read of hers she was going on about this Michelin starred restaurant she'd been to, and how fab the magazine she'd set up with her boyfriend was.' And she'd hinted at spring weddings on the beach. Weddings had been the last thing on Daisy's mind (up to a few days ago), and her extent of fine dining with Jimmy was limited to the village pub. Which was very nice, but they didn't tend to have 'foams' or 'amuse-bouches' as far as she could recall – unless you counted pork crackling. 'I know we're still friends, but it just looks so glam, her lifestyle. Are you sure she'd want me gate-crashing?'

'Well, actually, I do speak to her now and again, and I did ask her, and she does want you to go. It's perfect because she said you can stay at her place for as long as you want and—'

'But doesn't her boyfriend mind?' She was pretty sure she'd screwed her face up in a way only animals found attractive, but she was positive Flo had posted pictures of a guy on Facebook: a very attractive, well-groomed, sophisticated kind of guy. So unlike the type you found in Tippermere. 'I'll feel a real gooseberry.'

'That's the "and" bit. She's just split up with him.'

'But I thought they were on the verge of getting married.' Daisy, who had been towelling the dog, stopped.

'So did she, and she caught him with somebody else.'

'You're kidding!' That was nearly as big a shock as Jimmy waving a diamond ring in the air. 'Really?'

'Really, as in shagging her in the next hotel room.'

'Oh no. What a bastard. Oh, poor Flo.'

'So you've got to go. She needs somebody to talk to, take her mind off it.'

'Needs me?' Daisy's stomach gave a flip, which could have been nerves or excitement. She wasn't sure. A trip to Barcelona would be brilliant, and it would be lovely to see Flo again. See how the other half lived.

'Yep. So I told her you can go at the end of next week.'

An involuntary squeal escaped from Daisy's lips. 'Next week? But, I can't…'

'Whatever you were about to say, you can. Jimmy said he'd give you December, so it's perfect. You need to just get on with it, Daisy. You haven't got time to mess about, before you know it Christmas will be here, and then what?'

A family announcement. Wedding dresses. Bridal bouquets. Oh God, that word 'bridal' it just sounded weird when it was applied to you instead of somebody else. She needed to do something, but how on earth could this work? Next week! 'But what about Barney and Mabel? I can't just leave them, and what if the pipes freeze? And…'

'Jimmy can look after the place for a few days, and your menagerie.'

'But I can't ask—'

'Yes, you bloody can ask him, it was his idea you do it, or,' her eyes gleamed, 'if you don't want to ask Jimmy, you can ask Hugo.'

'No!' No way was she going to ask pompous, disapproving Hugo to look after her dog, or wilful horse.

Anna was waiting, grinning, one eyebrow raised questioningly.

'Okay, I'll ask Jimmy, I suppose.' She was feeling guilty even before she'd gone anywhere.

'Good. It's only for a few days, well as many as you like. Daisy, stop feeling guilty.'

'I'm not.'

'You are.'

She was. 'I haven't even got a passport though, so I don't see how I can go that soon.'

'We'll get you one tomorrow. Come on, before you chicken out. Flo needs you right now,' Daisy thought she might be stretching the truth on that one, Flo had always had lots of friends when they were at school, 'and she knows the city and all the in-places to go. Look, it's an ideal opportunity with having some-where to stay, it won't cost you hardly anything. We can sort a flight dirt cheap and you don't need many spends.'

'I'm not chickening out, I'm just being practical. I've got lots of customers booked in and I can't just abandon them.'

'Oh Daisy, I'm not trying to force you if you really don't want, I just thought… I can always tell Flo… well, I suppose I could go instead.'

'Don't you dare tell Flo anything. You don't think I'm going to let you go off and have all that fun without me, do you?' She straightened her shoulders. 'I'm being pathetic, it's only for a long weekend, I'm sure Jimmy will sort stuff here, after all it was his idea, wasn't it? And if he really does love me, he won't mind helping out.' She grinned. 'Oh, God, he'll think I've gone crazy.'

'Well that'll solve your problem then,' Anna grinned, 'he might un-propose.'

***

The next day Anna drove her to Liverpool to get a passport (which cost far more than she'd budgeted for), then they looked at flights, which turned out not to be exactly dirt-cheap after all. And now the butterflies were doing loop-the-loops in her stomach. There was no turning back.

She knew she had a stupid grin on her face as she put the kettle on. God she was pathetic to be so excited about a few days in Spain; anybody would think she was five years old.

Anna hung her sodden coat over the kitchen chair. Water dripped off, then ran in rivulets over the quarry tiles of Daisy's kitchen floor, coming to a stop when they hit Mabel's rug. 'I swear if it doesn't stop raining soon I'll be coming to Spain too.'

Daisy shrugged. Even the rain wasn't bothering her that much today, although it had made the motorway trip slightly scary, especially the way Anna drove. 'The chickens hate it. They're all huddled together in a sodden heap, refusing to lay.' They had stared at her accusingly with their beady little eyes, looking very bedraggled and sorry for themselves when she'd checked up on them before they'd headed off.

'Well at least it won't be raining in Barcelona.'

'No, Flo's probably sitting in the sun.' Daisy had to admit she was a teeny bit envious of Flo right now. She didn't have a problem with a bit of rain, but this was turning the paddock into a paddy field – and it was cold, sleety stuff which trickled down the back of your neck. She found it hard to imagine not having *any* rain though.

'It'll be fab out there.'

Suddenly noticing the wistful note in Anna's voice, Daisy stopped thinking about offering her field up to the rice gods, and put her mug down with a clatter. Hot coffee splattered out onto the back of her hand. 'Bugger.' She wiped it absent-mindedly down her jeans. 'Why don't you come?'

'But it's your trip.' Anna was studying her mug intently.

'Rubbish! It's only a few days and I know Flo would love to see you, she was your bestie really, not mine.'

'I don't want to gate-crash your adventure.' She still wasn't looking up.

'Anna! How could you possibly think that! Come. Book your ticket!'

'Now who's being the bossy one?' She suddenly grinned and met Daisy's eye. 'You wouldn't think I was awful if I admitted

I'd booked a couple of days off work on the off-chance, would you? It's just I was really hoping you'd say that.'

Daisy squealed and wrapped her arms round her friend. Being adventurous was one thing, doing it with Anna made it much better. 'Really? You're terrible, but it's going to be fantastic, the three little bears back together again.'

Anna rolled her eyes, 'I can't believe you still allow your mum to call us that.' She untangled herself. 'It will be fab though, the three of us. Won't it?'

Daisy paused, excitement was great, but what about the practicalities? She picked at a loose thread hanging from the bottom of her jumper and avoided looking at Anna. If she went to Barcelona she'd need clothes; she couldn't go in these scruffs. But she'd be spending money she should be saving up towards a wedding. Although she doubted Jimmy had even thought about the finances, he was one of those 'everything will work out fine' types, whereas she liked to plan. 'It'll be amazing. I do feel a bit guilty though, I am very fond of Jimmy.'

'I know you are. I'm not trying to interfere in your life, whatever he says, but I'm just scared that if you don't take this chance you'll just say yes cos it seems the sensible thing to do.' Her arm hung heavy round Daisy's shoulders. 'Just for once I want you to stop being sensible, be a bit mad and impulsive like me.' She grinned. 'Then you can marry him if you're sure it's what you really want to do, and you won't spend the rest of your life on what-ifs. I'll even be your bridesmaid.'

Daisy rolled her eyes. 'That's enough to put anybody off.' She paused. 'Come on then, let's get your plane ticket booked. When is Flo expecting us?'

'Next Thursday.' At least Anna had the good grace to look a little sheepish.

'I'll need some clothes.' To hell with the expense, this was one of life's essentials.

'We'll shop tomorrow. Christ, is that the time? I'm supposed to be working in the wine bar in Kitterly Heath tonight. See you at 10 a.m.?'

***

A frighteningly short week and a half after he'd proposed, Jimmy dropped Daisy and Anna off at Manchester airport.

It was a sunny December morning. Daisy's favourite time of the year was actually autumn, when the leaves were a glorious multi-coloured mosaic and the golden sun, low at the end of each day, had lost its harsh stare and instead wrapped everywhere in a friendly- uncle hug. She wasn't that keen on winter, the novelty of cold mornings and ice-covered troughs wore thin after a few weeks. So going away was good, wasn't it?

Or not. What on earth was she doing heading to Spain and wall-to-wall sunshine (although a few hours spent with Google one evening had warned of showers) when she could be riding Barney across the fields and spending the evenings with her toes being toasted by the Aga? It was mad, it was crazy, it was so unlike her.

But she was damned well going to do it, even if looking at Jimmy left her feeling like the worst possible girlfriend in the world.

Then she'd come home and know for sure whether she wanted to waltz down the aisle with Jimmy, or not.

'Stop worrying. It's only three days, Daisy.' Jimmy pulled into the 'drop-off' zone. 'I won't park up, not really into goodbyes. So I'll say bye here, okay?'

'Thanks.' Anna was out of the car and was retrieving her rucksack from the boot almost before the car had stopped moving.

Only three days. Three days to discover the world and experience life seemed a bit of a rum deal, tall order, whatever her dad would call it. But three fabulous days! Oh God, what if it really was as good as it sounded? What if she didn't want to come back? What if she ended up wanting more? She squashed the thought down and was sure that Jimmy had decided she was scared, not excited. Which was probably for the best. If you'd just proposed to somebody you weren't going to be pleased if they looked deliriously happy at the prospect of whizzing off to another country without you, were you?

She set her face to serious mode and tried to squash down the giggles that were leaping up and down inside her like a boxful of frogs. 'You will make sure Barney doesn't get out, won't you?'

'I will.'

'I got a new sack of carrots, they're by the back door.'

'Fine.'

'And he doesn't like that New Zealand rug, it rubs his withers.'

'Daisy I am quite capable of looking after a horse for a few days.'

'And don't let Mabel sleep on the bed.'

'Don't worry, I won't let her near it.'

'I would love you to come.' Prove to me that our relationship could work, that there is something in there that adds up to a happy-ever-after. That we actually do want the same things in life.

'I know you would.' He shrugged. 'Go on Daisy, do this, this thing that you need to do, then promise me you'll come home and we can go back to being like we were.'

'I promise I'll be back home soon.' She couldn't promise they'd go back to how they were because that had already changed. They could either move on to married life, or…

Neither of them mentioned what she was supposed to be coming home to – him, the rest of their lives, setting a date; the words sat like the wallflower at the party, wilting but determined to stick it out until the bitter end. Clinging to hope.

'Go on. Bugger off. Anna's waiting.'

She got out of the car, tugged at her suitcase and tried not to grin, because that wouldn't be fair. She was finally doing it. Finally going.

***

As the plane banked to the right and started to make its way along the coast, Daisy was glad that Anna had insisted she sit where she had when they'd checked in for the flight.

'You need Seat F, the window seat.'

'Why?'

'Because that way you will see the whole of Barcelona as we come in to land. It's dead impressive; you can see everything.'

Of course she would. Anna knew, because Anna had, of course, been to Barcelona before. Everybody had been everywhere apart from her.

'Oh wow, look Anna, it's like a grid. All the streets go across or down.'

Anna grinned. 'Apart from that diagonal one.' She giggled. 'It's called Diagonal.'

'Funny.'

'I'm being serious. Honest. And that's the Torre Agbar,' Anna, peering over her shoulder, pointed, 'there, like that gherkin thing in London. And the Sagrada Familia is up there, and that hill is Montjuic. We need to go there.'

'Do we?' She had spent the last couple of days wondering if she wanted to do this at all. But she had to. She had to prove to, well to herself, yes definitely to herself, that she wasn't a dull-as-dishwater failure heading towards a hermit existence before she even hit thirty. And she wanted to. And now, as the plane started to descend towards the runway, it was as though a switch had flipped inside her and she couldn't stop the smile that was tugging at her mouth.

She was finally doing something.

53

'Come here, we don't need that.' Anna grabbed the map from Daisy's unresisting fingers and crumpled it up with a look of glee. 'Don't look so horrified.' Then dropped it into the bin they were passing with a flourish.

Daisy frowned and was about to complain when the Aerobus they had just stepped off pulled away – and she saw it.

The fountain that she'd seen in the guidebook. Two fountains in fact. 'Wow.'

'God, you are so easy to impress.'

'They're massive.' She took a step off the kerb, she just had to see these close up.

'Hang on,' Anna grabbed her arm, 'unless you can tell me how to say "call an ambulance" in Spanish?'

It wasn't just that the fountains were big; everything was. When the traffic lights changed and Anna let her cross the road into the massive square she found herself spinning on the spot trying to take everything in. Fields were one thing, I mean she expected space in the country – but in a city? Kids were squealing as they chased enormous bubbles, and an… 'Is that really an Apple store?' Anna nodded. 'Wow, Jimmy would have a field day, he'd never come out.'

'Stop thinking about Jimmy, look,' Anna took her by the shoulders and turned her round to face the way they'd come, 'an enormous Corte Ingles – you know handbags, clothes, shoes.'

'I've got a handbag.' She whirled back round at the sound of flapping wings to see a black leggy dog scoot across the wide-open space, scattering the pigeons. It reminded her of Mabel; Mabel loved chasing birds. She missed the big lolloping dog already, they'd never been apart since she'd got her as a gangly out-of-proportion eight week old pup.

'Stop thinking about Mabel.'

'I'm not.'

'You are, so.' Anna stuck her tongue out.

'It's amazing.' Changing the subject was always a good idea when Anna got into uber-bossy mode.

'This is just the start, welcome to the big wide world, Daisy Fischer. Fancy a beer?'

'I thought we were going to Flo's? You do know where she lives?'

'Kind of.' Anna grinned. 'Chill, who needs maps? I'll sort it out, it just looks different to last time I came. Or maybe I'm thinking of Madrid.' The grin slipped into a frown.

'Anna!'

Anna laughed.

'Maybe we should ask somebody?'

'Rubbish, that's cheating. Maps are for wimps. Come on, it's this way I think.' And before Daisy could object, Anna had straightened her rucksack on her shoulders and was marching back the way they'd just come.

It was only when they got to another square – this time with a large cathedral at one side – that Anna's confident march slowed down. Which was actually quite a good thing, as Daisy felt she was in a fast-forward film.

'That isn't supposed to be there.'

'Well it doesn't look like anybody's moved it for a few hundred years. What do you mean, isn't supposed to be there? Can we go in?'

Anna frowned. 'I think we're going in the wrong direction. We'll have a beer here while I work it out.'

'So we can't go in?'

'Tomorrow. Beer. Beer and tapas, then my brain will work better."

Daisy raised an eyebrow. 'Are you sure you should have binned the map?'

'I'm just popping to the ladies, then we'll go and find Flo's place.'

'Fine.' Daisy was only half listening – there was a map on the next table, left by a couple who'd been too busy arguing to remember it, and any second now it was going to get whisked away by a waiter.

Anna turned her back and Daisy made a grab for it.

'I can't believe you came without a map!'

Daisy jumped guiltily, in very much the same way that Mabel did when she'd stolen a chicken leg off the table and still had the evidence in her mouth, then looked up. Straight into a pair of grey-blue smiling eyes.

A tall blonde girl, with the kind of tousled beach-babe look that on Daisy would be more 'I need to wash my hair' than 'I need sex', was looking down at her quizzically, one eyebrow raised. Which was exactly the look she gave Mabel when she caught her in the act, as it were.

'Wow, Flo, is it really you?' She scrambled to her feet. 'What are you doing here? I didn't think you were meeting us. Gosh, you look fabulous. That hair colour really suits you.' It did; it looked sophisticated and casual all at once. But it only partly detracted from the dark circles under her eyes, and the slightly haunted look. 'Are you okay? I can't believe—'

'I'm good,' Flo swatted away the concern, so Daisy bit back all the questions. There was plenty of time to talk later, when she was ready. 'All the better for seeing you. I reckoned I should come and meet you half way.'

Daisy raised an eyebrow. There were coincidences and…

'Well actually, Anna just text me from the loo and said you were lost.'

'*We* were lost?' Daisy grinned. 'She's terrible. She threw my map away.'

'I thought it was weird, you're usually the organised one.' She grinned. 'The one with the tidiest pencil case, and you never forgot your homework.'

'She convinced me she knew where she was going. You know Anna.'

Flo laughed. 'I know Anna.'

Daisy pulled a chair out. 'Sit down. Are we having another drink, or heading to yours?'

Flo shrugged and sat down. 'I'm easy, this is your weekend away. I didn't know Anna had been before.'

'Years ago I think, her family went all over. I'm the clueless one. I'm so glad you came to meet us, she hasn't got any idea where we are. I thought we'd end up turning the rest of the day into a bar crawl, and I really need to shower and get out of these smelly clothes. And to be honest, I'm dying to get these shoes off.' And ring Jimmy – just to check Mabel was okay and Barney hadn't escaped.

Flo laughed, it was the same laugh Daisy remembered, but now she had perfect, sophisticated honey-streaked blonde hair to flick back. 'Ahh. I'm so glad you're here though, you're a life-saver. We can plan loads of exciting stuff, you've never been to Barcelona before?'

'I've never left the UK.'

'Never?'

'Nope, never. And I've got three days to discover my wild side.'

Flo's smiled broadened. 'You're kidding, Daisy? I never realised! You should have come before.'

It hung between them, the unspoken force that was Oli. Flo had always been too busy to see old friends, or so it had seemed. Daisy shrugged. 'To be honest, I never thought I was that bothered until now.' She hadn't, not until Jimmy had changed everything.

'A bit of a tall order to uncover your wild side in a long weekend, although you have got Anna and me to help.'

'Anna said I'd find it in Ravel, she said that's the plan for this afternoon.'

'She did, did she?'

'She was winding me up?'

'Well I don't want to be funny, but it wouldn't be my first

choice, some areas of El Raval are still like the worst part of the city. You know, one of those places where you double-lock the doors and put your spare money in your bra.'

'You're kidding? But the bit she showed me in my book looked nice, and,' Daisy's stomach was started to do a shimmy, so much for the big adventure, she was getting the wobbles before she'd started, 'it can't be that bad. Can it?'

'Well,' Flo frowned, 'it isn't terrible, terrible, if you know what I mean?'

So not double-terrible, just one.

'But honestly? It really isn't a place for a travel virgin. I think we'll re-plan Anna's itinerary.'

'Please, or I'm going to be getting the next bus back to the airport, maybe I never was meant to travel outside Cheshire.'

'More like you were never meant to let Anna make the decisions. You'll love it here, I promise.'

'What's this about not letting me do things? I'm fab at decisions, wow it is so good to see you again, we've missed you.' Anna wrapped Flo in a bear hug and then plopped down in her chair. 'So what's up, and where,' she glared at the map that Daisy was clutching to her chest like a firstborn, 'did you get that from?'

'I found it.' She glared back, sending a 'don't mess with my map' message. 'Flo says El Raval is a dump, it's pants.'

'I didn't exactly—'

'Terrible, but not terrible, terrible.' That was probably like Barney getting out of the field, but not invading Hugo's food store. Or was Flo's 'terrible' these days more on the scale of chipped nail varnish, and her double-terrible like breaking a nail? She looked pretty chilled though, so terrible could mean…

'We'll survive it.'

Oh God, she hated Anna's optimism and positive outlook at times. She didn't want to 'survive', she'd signed up for a city break, not the Bear Grylls' survival academy. 'No we won't Anna, we're not going there. You're out-voted.'

'Stop frowning Daisy, you two are such spoilsports. It's an adventure, I want to go to places I've never been.' She turned to Flo. 'So were me and map-girl heading in the right direction?'

Flo, looked bemused. 'Sure, if you were heading to my place, but if you were supposed to be exploring El Raval you're going in completely the wrong direction, it's kind of straight across in that direction, until you hit La Rambla, then keep going on the other side.'

Anna grinned, completely unperturbed.

'You could come back to my place now to dump your bags if you like, then spend the afternoon exploring your dodgy spots on your own. Meet up later for drinks?'

Daisy lifted her face to the sun. It would be fine. Calm. 'I don't do dodgy.'

'We'll have another beer first, then decide.' Anna wriggled her way deeper into the seat and looked at Daisy. 'I'm not moving until you've chilled a bit. However many drinks it takes, and I'm starving, can we eat?'

With her mouth wrapped inelegantly round a very large baguette, Daisy began to feel much more confident. For one brief moment she'd wondered if Anna coming with her had been such a good idea after all, but they'd have fun. The three of them had always had a good time together. 'So what's on the agenda for tonight?'

'Well, if you fancy it I'll take you to this fab little bar? Only, of course, if you want to. I don't want to tell you what to do – it's your weekend.'

'Well if you don't decide, somebody else will.' Daisy grinned in Anna's direction. 'Won't you?'

'Somebody has to. But fine by me.'

'Here, give me the map and I'll show you where you are and where my place is. It'll help you get your bearings.' She looked at the map. Daisy put it on the table reluctantly, as far away from Anna as she could. 'We're right here in this square, here's my place,' she put a cross on the map, 'then tonight, after you've done your exploring, I'll meet you here,' she circled a spot on the map, 'it's called El Xampanyet, it's by the Museu Picasso, which is right here, you can't miss it.' Daisy wondered if she'd be able to decipher all these lines later.

'Just ask anybody, or there are plenty of signs.' Flo added, no doubt reading her dubious look. 'It's a great bar, tapas, cava okay?'

'Fab.' She reclaimed her map. 'But are you sure you're not doing anything else? I mean we can manage if you're busy.'

'Nothing.' There was a flicker of expression that Daisy couldn't quite pin down, but looked a bit like she felt. Wobbly. 'It's fab you're both here, I can't wait to catch up on the gossip.' She smiled, but it was one of those not-quite-happy, not-quite-sad smiles. 'I get dead jealous of you pair together having all that fun.'

'Jealous?' Daisy stared at her hard. 'You have got to be kidding. You've got all this,' she waved an expansive hand, 'it's amazing.'

'Yeah, amazing.' Flo sighed. 'It is, I know, I'm lucky. Shall we make a move, go back to my place so you can freshen up?'

'Sure.' Flo, Daisy decided was definitely below par, she'd always been so bubbly and positive. 'Come on Anna, let's go before we're plastered. Then *I'll* pick a place to explore, I've got a map.' She grinned and waved it, rather unwisely, in the air, just out of Anna's reach.

Chapter 6 – Flo. Another kind of proposal

Flo stared at her reflection in the bathroom mirror and thought, not for the first time, how bloody amazing decent make-up could be. It almost looked natural – like she was a normal, pre-non-proposal-Paris happy person.

She peered a bit closer, until her nose nearly hit the glass. Well, obviously it didn't actually work miracles, her eyes were still puffed up so that she looked like one of those poppy-out-eyed goldfish, but it was a vast improvement – her face had been rescued from the totally yuk broken-heart look. Now she just looked like she'd had a bad night, or been punched. Which she had, well the bad-night bit, the punch was purely mental. It just felt physical. She rested her forehead against the glass.

Bugger Oli. She had to get a grip. He was a completely useless, two-timing wanker who didn't deserve another second of her life.

She needed to block his phone number, shred his photos. Oh God, there were so many happy, laughing-couple photos, and the ones when he was looking into her eyes like some dashing prince about to…

STOP.

Flo scrunched her fingers into fists and counted to ten. Then looked down at her make-up bag.

She could do this. She could be single again and bloody enjoy it.

The make-up had been a gift from a local business that she'd run a spread on. For their magazine. Their joint magazine. Oh stuff him and his stupid magazine. Concentrate on concealer, foundation. She would obliterate him from her life, wipe every trace away, including the bloody dark smudges under her eyes. And they were because of the copious amounts of alcohol. Nothing to do with him and the fact she couldn't stop crying.

She'd thrown all the expensive products into the bathroom drawer and laughingly wondered who the hell needed stuff like that.

Now she knew.

People that went out with cheating creeps.

Most of the time Flo stuck with a quick flick of eye-liner, a coat of mascara and smear of lip-salve, but she'd just discovered there were times that demanded something more drastic. Like right now.

The red-eye look wasn't quite so in-your-face when your blusher and lipstick were several shades darker, and the concealer had almost obliterated the dark smudges under her eyes. She could probably explain everything away as a bad dose of hay-fever. Except it was winter. Hangover, they'd accept a hangover as a good enough reason.

Flo wasn't sure that she really wanted to go out. But no way was she staying in and thinking about Oli.

When she'd got back from Paris she'd felt wiped out, and crashed into an alcohol-and grief-induced coma. And it didn't seem to get easier as the days went on, even knowing that her friends were coming to stay – and take her mind off him. Off the whole fiasco.

Today, despite a bracing walk along the beach, shopping

therapy and a quick chat to Anna and Daisy, she was still fidgeting inside. She needed to do something that didn't involve throwing things he'd bought her at the walls.

And going out with old friends was far better than an evening with Spanish friends. As in 'their' friends. That was the trouble with being a couple, wasn't it? Who had custody of the friends? At some point she'd have to face the inevitable questions from the Oli-appreciation fan-club – which all her mates seemed to belong to – but right now, with the memory of Oli's bare bum partly covered by another woman's hand still fresh in her mind, she'd rather try and think about something else.

She wasn't quite sure what had got into her when she'd practically insisted Daisy and Anna come out to Barcelona, it wasn't like her at all. But maybe that was how she'd get through this – by being less like her normal self. No hanging about waiting for him to turn up to meet her, no dropping everything to answer his calls, no working until midnight to meet his deadlines. Maybe it would help. Maybe it was time to do what she wanted, and not just try and please some self-satisfied idiot.

Flo stared at her image in the mirror. That's what she'd just wasted the last few years of her life on. The reality hit her. Oli had been the centre of her universe, she'd actually morphed from the girl she used to be into the woman he demanded. She hadn't stopped to think about it until now, but he'd gradually got under her skin, and, because she loved him she'd wanted to please him. Like some pathetic lap dog.

Which reminded her. She'd always wanted a dog, and he'd said no. Think about the mess, he'd said, and we'd be 'tied down' – yeah, she should have spotted that one for what it was.

She could get a dog now. And read in bed, listen to heavy rock, watch weepy films. Get totally rat-arsed on cheap wine.

He'd controlled her right up until the end. She'd been the worst kind of fool, trying to keep up a pretence of being the happiest person in the world, of living the perfect life, and she'd been so determined to succeed she'd ignored the warning signs that were hammering like a battering ram against her defences. Well Oli wasn't going to do it for a second longer.

She just hoped that spending a weekend with her childhood friends wasn't going to make her even more homesick than she already was.

***

'Are you absolutely positive this is where Flo meant, and she said seven o'clock?' Daisy stared at the firmly closed shutters, and the crowd of people which had been steadily growing in the five minutes they'd been standing there.

The route Flo had marked on the map had been easy to follow, but she was now beginning to wonder if Anna had sabotaged it. Despite the fact she'd even taken it to the loo with her.

'You're the map-reader.' Anna grinned. 'I wish they'd bloody hurry up and open the place though, I'm starving.'

'Hey, you made it!' Daisy glanced up to see the welcome sight of a smiling Flo.

'Fab, you found it.'

'We did, but we were just beginning to wonder if we'd come to the wrong place.'

'Or you'd stood us up.' Added Anna.

Daisy rolled her eyes and Flo laughed. 'Get ready for the scramble.' She nodded at the shutter behind them, which was slowly moving upwards. The crowd of people fidgeted and edged forward. The shutter stopped three feet up. They relaxed. It lifted a bit more, people edged closer and Daisy began to wonder just what kind of place Flo had brought them to.

***

The moment the shutter was lifted, Flo dived forward. She swung round to check that Anna and Daisy had followed, then put one hand out in a ta-dah gesture and waited for the reaction.

'Wow.' Daisy stared, her brown eyes opening wide, and Flo grinned in satisfaction as she spun round on the spot, taking in the blue ceramic-tiled walls, marble tables and the artefacts that fought for space on the little shelves running along each wall.

Anna giggled, unimpressed. 'She did that in Placa Catalunya, she's going to go home all wound up and need spinning back the other way. Daisy, stop it and sit down. Wow, look at those tapas, can we try all of them?'

Daisy sat. Craning her neck as she shifted on the narrow bench and tried to read the plaques on the wall above. 'This place is incredible, it's lovely, so cute. I want to live here.'

Flo grinned. She'd always loved the way Daisy just came out with what was in her head. 'It's amazing, isn't it? I love it, even though it's always cram-packed with tourists.' She looked apologetically at Anna and Daisy, 'sorry, but you know what I mean. The owner won't let anybody change it though, the local Barcelonese love the house cava and traditional tapas, and as far as he's concerned the visitors can like it or lump it.' She grinned. 'Most of them like it.'

'I do, it's lovely.' Daisy nearly slipped off her seat as she twisted round again.

'You are acting the complete tourist.' Anna shook her head disapprovingly, but was laughing.

'I don't care, I am a tourist and I've never, ever been anywhere like this before.'

'Wait 'til you try the cava. It's compulsory, I won't let you drink anything else.'

A litre of the house speciality, bubbly, and three coupe glasses were soon on the table, along with tapas. Flo pointed. 'Pan con tomate, obligatory round here, and anchovies.'

'Anchovies?' Anna shuddered and pulled a face.

'You can't come to Barcelona and not eat anchovies. Trust me, they're the best with this cava.'

'I trust you.' Daisy forked one up, looking at it suspiciously. 'I think.'

'Good!'

'Although I do remember you trying to get me to eat a mud-and-worm sandwich once.'

'You've got a memory like an elephant, Daisy.' Flo grinned, 'It's so good to see you guys again, I know I keep saying it, but it is. I've got to meet somebody about work tomorrow afternoon, but how about I give you a grand tour in the morning?'

'Are you sure? I mean you don't have stuff you have to do? We can just get on one of those tour buses.'

'Don't be daft Daisy, no way are you doing that. I need the company to be honest,' Flo took a deep breath. There was something refreshing about talking to old friends, no pretence required, 'I've just had the shittiest holiday you can imagine,' she glanced at Anna, 'and you'd be doing me a favour, give me something to think about and stop me drinking every bottle of wine in the apartment.'

Daisy was staring at her. 'Oh I'm so sorry, Flo, you don't deserve it. I've always wanted your life, you just look the most together person, you always did, not the type to experience shit holidays or turn to drink. That's my job.'

'No, it's mine.' Anna poked her own chest proudly. 'I'm the one that has shit relationships, I hold a special certificate in it.'

Daisy and Flo both laughed.

'Well, I always look like I've been dragged through a hedge backwards, and haven't got a clue.'

It was Anna who laughed this time. 'You usually *have* been dragged through a hedge, Daisy.' She grinned at Flo. 'She's even worse than she used to be. She spends most of her time these days covered in dog hair or being dumped by her horse into water troughs.'

66

'That was only once.' Daisy objected.

'Or trampled by him when he's spotted a monster in the hedge.'

'He's easily scared.'

'Scared my arse, he's massive.'

Daisy shifted her gaze from Anna to Flo. 'She doesn't get horses.' She rifled through the picture gallery on her phone and waved the resulting picture of an out-of-focus hairy horse at Flo. 'I miss him.' Flo wasn't sure she got horses either, and ordered another bottle of cava.

Daisy, who had been staring at her horse photographs, put her phone down. 'That's why I decided to escape from Tippermere for a bit really, because of a man, although I did, of course, want to see you.' She added the last bit hastily.

'Oh no, not you too.' Flo glanced at Anna. 'You never said, you just said Daisy needed to have a change of scene, live a little. Nasty split?' She'd sensed that Daisy was acting a bit out of character, and now it made sense.

'No, Jimmy asked me to marry him.'

'Jimmy?' Flo stopped, mid-pour, and put the cava bottle down. That wasn't what she'd been expecting. 'Jimmy as in dimples-and-dirty-boots Jimmy?'

Daisy nodded.

'I didn't know it was that serious.'

'Nor did Daisy.' Anna grinned.

'And he asked you to,' she stumbled over the word, 'marry him?' The lump that had been resting just below her collarbone for the last week popped straight into her throat and made her eyes water. 'I thought,' she swallowed hard, and tried to ignore the burn at the back of her eyes, 'I thought Oli was going to ask, you know, if I wanted to... and... oh, how could I ever have thought he was taking me on a lovely romantic break?' It came out as an undignified wail.

'Oh shit.' Daisy put her hands up to her mouth. 'I'm sorry, that was so thoughtless, I thought you knew, I'm sorry.'

She swallowed hard. 'It's not your problem I thought he was going to propose.' Now she'd started she couldn't stop. She emptied her glass and bubbles shot up her nose and choked her. She spluttered, which was far more undignified than the noise she'd made. Anna shoved a napkin at her. By the time she'd mopped up and sneezed, and snuffled a bit, and was looking back at the two shocked faces, it didn't seem quite as bad. They weren't used to seeing her crumble.

'It was supposed to be a romantic break for him and bloody Sarah.' She sipped from her overflowing glass, and then took a deep, calming breath. She could do this. She could explain and just not care.

'It just never occurred to me...' She speared an anchovy slightly more brutally than it deserved. 'He didn't even have the decency to wait until after the weekend, or the holiday. He could have put her off, but oh no, the bastard decided to kill two birds with one stone. Why take just your girlfriend on holiday, when you can invite the other woman along as well. My dear, darling nearly-fiancé, work partner, whole life, had decided not to let me ruin his plans.'

'Two for the price of one.' Anna shook her head.

'Bog off.' Daisy nodded.

'Sorry?'

'Buy one get one free, BOGOF.' Daisy bit her lip. 'Seems appropriate in the circumstances, that's what you need to tell him to do.'

'I know. I have.' She sighed, looked at Daisy, then wiped her nose on the back of her hand. 'So what's the problem with Jimmy and you?'

'Jimmy's the problem.' Anna cut in.

Daisy swilled her glass round. 'I feel terrible now I know what's happened to you.'

'No, tell. I need to stop thinking about it, him, he doesn't deserve having this much of my time spent on him.'

'Well, that's it,' she shrugged her slim shoulders, 'Jimmy proposed.' She looked as glum as Flo had seen her.

'But?'

'She doesn't love him.' Anna nudged Daisy in the ribs. 'Do you?'

Daisy screwed up her mouth. 'It was completely out of the blue, I never expected it. His dad put him up to it.'

'He's completely boring,' Anna continued, 'and she'll end up spending the rest of her life darning his socks and growing vegetables.'

'I always thought he was nice, quite sexy, really, for his age, and I do remember his dimples.' Flo took another gulp of cava, 'but you can't marry him if you don't love him, can you?' She propped her chin on her hands, and it promptly slipped off, which had to be down to too much cava and not enough tapas. She sat up, trying to look sober. 'I thought I loved Oli, but you know what? He's a complete control freak, as well as a selfish arse.' She gazed at Anna. 'I'd quite like to grow vegetables.'

'Why?' Anna frowned. 'If God had wanted us to grow our own peas he wouldn't have invented Tesco's would he?'

'I think he did want us to grow peas.' Daisy said. 'That's why he gave us soil and stuff. But by your logic he wanted us to darn socks too, or he wouldn't have put holes in them.'

'My mum used to grow stuff when I was little, in England.' Flo was not to be deterred.

'That's all people do in Tippermere,' interjected Anna. 'Grow stuff, ride horses and gossip. I am so glad I moved out and got a proper job.'

'I'm not. I remember the smell of the tomatoes, all green and fresh.' Flo waved the empty bottle of cava and waited for a refill, wondering just how many bottles they'd had. 'And sprouts, she grew those as well, tiny ones for Christmas. Oh God, Christmas. I love Christmas and I'll have to do all the stuff we normally do together on my own, go round the lights, shop,' she put her head in her hands, 'do the romantic Christmas special for our magazine. Shit, and I just know I'll bump into him with her, doing all *our* stuff.'

'You know what you two need to do?' Anna leaned forward, elbows on the small marble table.

'Drink more cava, by the crate.' Flo watched as the waiter topped up their glasses.

'Nope. You,' Anna pointed at Flo, 'need to get away from that selfish twat, and your job, for the rest of the month. That way you won't bump into him. You need to grow stuff, do your own thing. And you,' she swivelled on her stool to look at Daisy, and pointed with her other hand, 'need to stay out here away from Jimmy. If you go back you'll just end up saying yes.'

'You can't grow stuff in December.' Daisy downed the contents of her glass. 'This is so easy to drink; it's just like pop. And I'm not that weak-willed thank you.'

'Flo can finish off growing *your* sprouts,'

'I don't have sprouts.'

'Oh whatever, while you do the whole going-round-the-lights thing here.'

'What?'

'You can both swap.' Anna crossed her hands over and grinned. 'I'm amazing, go on, say it. It's the perfect solution, and it only took three bottles of cava.'

'Four. But I don't speak Spanish. How can I stay here on my own? It's different being here with Flo.'

'Most people don't speak Spanish here.' Flo grinned. 'They speak Catalan. They throw in some French words, like *merci*, but without the French accent.'

'Really?' That made no sense at all.

'Really.' Flo looked at her best friends. 'I like that idea, Anna, you're amazing, I'd even go as far as to say a genius.' This could work. This could really work. She could escape for a couple of weeks. By the time she came back everybody would know and there wouldn't be all that embarrassing explanation stuff that made her cry, and she'd be over him. Completely. 'Oh wow, yes,' she laughed, wondering if she was drunk or delirious, 'Anna, that does sound an amazing idea. Tell me we can do it, please Daisy? I've always wanted to go back and do the works. You know, a cosy cottage and build a snowman, toast marshmallows. Do all the stuff we used to do.'

'Er, well, I'll have to check with Jimmy.'

Anna rolled her eyes. 'Jimmy's given you until Christmas, you nitwit. Just do it.'

'But he needs me there, and somebody needs to look after everything.'

'Don't you get it? Flo looks after your place, everything, and you look after hers. And stuff Jimmy, he's perfectly capable of looking after himself. Right, while we're on the subject of stuffing, can we have some of those stuffed pepper things?'

Chapter 7 – Daisy. The morning after

'Go away.' Daisy rolled over and buried her head under the pillow, trying to escape Mabel's prodding.

'That's not very nice when I've been out for croissants. Come on, get out of bed, you lazy bug.' Anna grabbed the pillow and Daisy scrunched her eyes up against the sunlight that flooded the room.

Something was wrong. It shouldn't be this light; Anna shouldn't be there.

Then she remembered. She was in Barcelona. She had shared a bed with Anna (who didn't snore and snuffle and make little growly noises in her sleep), not Mabel (who did). She had drunk a gallon of cava last night, and it was trying to explode out of her head.

'Hurry up.' Anna, sounding disgustingly bouncy, had retreated and was standing in the doorway. 'Croissants, coffee, come on. We've got to plan what we're doing today.'

'I was planning on sleeping.'

'We've only got two days, come on.' Anna nudged her foot.

Daisy suddenly felt wide awake (but with a thumping head) as last night flooded back (along with a hint of anchovy, which wasn't quite as welcome). 'You might have but,' she smiled, it hurt her head but still felt good, 'I'm staying.'

'Sorry?'

'Swap, house swap, holiday swap. You know, Flo goes to my place and I stay here.'

'But that was a joke, we were drunk.' Anna frowned and looked like she was waiting for Daisy to laugh. She didn't.

'Well I've been thinking about it, and it sounds brilliant.'

'But you can't...'

'That's what I thought at first.' Daisy sat up and pulled the sheet up to her chin. 'I've got things to do back home. It's not that easy to sort, but if I can do it I'm going to.'

'But you'll be on your own. It won't be like all of us being here.'

'I know. But I'm a big girl now, Anna,' she smiled, trying to soften the blow, 'I can make my own decisions.' She giggled like a naughty schoolgirl – not such a big girl then.

'But you can't afford it, and what about the animals? And work? December is a really busy time for you, everybody wants their dog looking pretty for Christmas, that's what you said before we came here.'

'God knows why, they're only going to get muddy. But, that's the beauty of this, isn't it? Flo looks after the animals, and the house. Though I don't think I'll mention that randy Dalmatian to her.'

'Exactly. She can't do your job.'

'True.' Daisy shuffled about, wondering where Anna's positivity had gone. When they'd fallen into bed and the room had started to spin, thinking about this had been a good distraction. 'But Tiggy can, I've asked her before and she's said no problem. She can use my grooming table and scissors, or whatever stuff she wants, and it did used to be her job before she decided to paint again.'

'Oh. But it isn't exactly fair on Flo, lumbering her with Barney and Mabel, is it? And you just get this beautiful place.'

Daisy frowned. 'This was your idea.'

'We were drunk, and I just got carried away. Thinking about it now though, it isn't ideal, and you don't actually have to stay here, do you? I thought you wanted to do other stuff like ride in the Canadian Rockies.'

'You know I can't afford that. Oh Anna, you might have thought of it after a few drinks, but it's a fantastic idea, it makes sense. And she does know about the animals.'

'Yes, but you didn't exactly describe Mabel.'

'I said I had a big dog. Look, stop worrying, I'm sure Jimmy and,' she paused, 'Hugo will help her out if she needs it. What's the matter? I thought this was what you wanted me to do?' Daisy stared at Anna in frustration. She'd expected her to be excited about the whole thing. Supportive.

'I just didn't expect...'

'Exactly. And I didn't expect Jimmy to propose, did I? If I go home now I'll just get stuck back in and forget all about my dreams. And I love it here.' She hugged her knees to her chest. 'I've got to do this, Anna, for Jimmy's sake as well as my own. And like you said, I'm helping Flo out, she needs to put as many miles between her and that dickhead as she can this Christmas. I mean, can you imagine if that happened to you and you had to spend the whole holiday hoping you didn't bump into him and his new shag?'

Anna frowned. 'You're using emotional blackmail now.'

'All's fair. But it's true, consider it a favour to Flo if you really won't admit you want me to do it. Oh, come on, am I wrong?'

Anna sighed. 'No, you aren't wrong. You're right.'

'I'm right!' Daisy squealed and, jumping up, did a jig on the bed, which creaked alarmingly, so she sat down quick. 'I don't think I want to end up like Mum, giving up her dreams and looking after old ladies and cows, but I won't know if I don't try, will I?'

'You won't.' With a grin that was only a tiny bit strained, Anna wrapped her arms round Daisy and squeezed her so hard she squeaked. 'I knew you'd do it and prove Jimmy wrong.'

'Prove Jimmy wrong?' Daisy wriggled.

Anna released her stranglehold and looked sheepish. 'He said a weekend was more than enough for you, and could I bugger off out of your life and lead somebody else astray.' She lifted her chin. 'That's partly what made me suggest it last night, but I honestly thought it was a mad idea. I never thought you'd actually want to do it. Don't look at me like that! Oh, okay, I'm jealous. I admit it, it will be weird, you doing this on your own.'

'I know, and I don't want to sound selfish, but this is about me, Anna. For the first time in as long as I can remember I'm doing something I really, really want to do.'

***

A shower, one glass of orange juice, two croissants and three cups of coffee (they were only tiny) later, Daisy felt slightly less as though an alien had infested her head, and more than a little bit giddy. What had seemed a slightly dubious idea last night in the bar, sounded absolutely brilliant in the sober light of day. Which seemed the wrong way round. It was like a crazy wonderful dream had come true, but she wasn't quite sure how. And even when she said it out loud, in real words, to a person, it still sounded like a good idea.

She glanced at Flo, who was grinning like she agreed, and it was just Anna who didn't look quite so enthusiastic. Which could have been because she wasn't one of the people doing it.

'What do you think, Flo? I mean, I know we were all drunk last night…'

'Honestly? We have to do this swap thing. It'll be amazing. Stop looking at us like that, Anna! What have we got to lose? We can both be home for Christmas Day, but have a fab time before.

I won't have to risk bumping into Oli-the-arsehole,' she looked at Daisy, 'and you won't have Jimmy waving a ring in your face.'

Daisy laughed, relieved that it wasn't just her that thought this could work.

'It would be great, and it would be so nice to go back to the UK.'

'And rain.' Interjected Anna, then shrugged when Daisy glared at her. 'Sorry.'

'It might even snow. A proper wintery Christmas would be cool.' Flo tore a bit off her croissant.

'Very cool.' Daisy couldn't help but smile at the wistful look on Flo's face. 'As in cold cool, and I have got an, er, dog that would need to be walked. Did I mention that?' She looked at Flo apologetically. 'I mean, it's not like being here.'

'No problem. You know I love dogs, in fact a dog is on my bucket list. I told you, didn't I, Anna? Oli hated them, so it will be great to have a dog to look after.'

'And a horse.'

'Oh God, yes, I'd forgotten about the picture you showed me last night. Wow, that's amazing, you have no idea how much I want a horse again. When I was a kid I spent all my time having lessons and grooming ponies for people. Don't you remember?'

'Oh yes! I remember, you went to Billy. That's brill, I'd forgotten that, so you'd have no trouble at all with Barney. He's a big softy really.'

'So that's decided then?' Anna looked from Flo to Daisy, and back again. 'You both want to do it, don't you?'

Daisy and Flo looked at each other. 'Well, if you really don't mind looking after my place, Flo? I can make sure Jimmy drops off plenty of wood for the fire for you.'

'It sounds fab, a proper escape. So where do you live now? Near your parents' farm? Do you live in a proper country cottage?'

'Well it's quite a way from their place and it's on the edge of the village, over the other side.'

76

'Gosh, you're so lucky.'

'Well?' Anna looked at Daisy.

'Definitely.' She'd never been so sure of anything, which was a bit weird. 'It would be lovely to stay for longer. I mean we've hardly seen anything, really, and it's such a beautiful city.'

'That's settled then I guess. So I reckon we should drink a toast to that.'

'Toast?' Daisy stared at Anna and groaned. 'I need more coffee first. Strong coffee. And a better map, and sunscreen, and better walking shoes, and knickers... and how on earth am I going to explain *this* to Jimmy?'

Flo laughed. 'Well I'm not sure how you explain it to Jimmy, but I can help out with the knickers.'

'Good, because packing for a long weekend doesn't quite cut it if I'm staying for nearly three weeks.'

Daisy did villages, not cities. Wide-open spaces, with the odd elbow-nudging encounter in the corner shop if there were more than three people in there (it really wasn't very big). She wasn't even that keen on shopping, being jostled about while she was looking for the perfect top that didn't seem to exist, and as for the whole trying-on-stuff thing in those open-plan changing rooms. Yuk. Thank God for online shopping. But Flo knew exactly where to go, and took a detour half way through when she could see that Daisy was wavering.

'We're going to Café de l'Opera for a pick-me-up.'

'We are?'

'We are. It's olde-worlde, very kind of Parisian chic but actually Catalan Art Nouveau, and I bet it's in your guidebook. Come on, if it was good enough for Picasso and Gaudi it's good enough for you. You will love it.'

Daisy did. The small, unobtrusive doorway led to what she could only describe as a step back in time. 'Oh my God, it's wonderful.' The ceilings were high – painted a subtle green with large old-fashioned fans, and chandeliers along the length – with edges that were carved and decorated. Below, the bottom half of the walls were wood-panelled, the top sections painted in subtle colours, with paintings and decorated mirrors interspersed. It felt decadent, grand and faded all at the same time. 'It's like being at the opera.'

Flo laughed. 'It is, but wait until you see the cakes.' She herded Daisy and Anna over to one of the small, round wooden café tables and sat down.

And one crema catalana and two glasses of cava later Daisy declared she was more than ready to hit the shops again. To see what they could see.

They saw lot of undies, a very nice pair of boots, a very hip shirt, a figure-flattering long-sleeved t-shirt and a soft leather handbag to die for. And her bank balance was literally dying, even if she wasn't. There would be a hell of a lot of dogs to be bathed and clipped in the New Year to make up for this.

Chapter 8 – Daisy. Saying goodbye

'Oh well, here we go, good old Aerobus.' Anna shifted her rucksack on her shoulders.

'This is so weird, you going and me staying. Oh, I'm going to miss you.' Daisy threw her arms round her best friend.

'Don't have too much fun and forget all about me.'

'I'd never forget you, Anna. It's only for a couple of weeks. Hasn't the weekend whizzed by though? I can't believe it would all be over now if you hadn't had your brilliant idea.' The days had passed in a blur of sight-seeing, shopping, drinking and eating. 'We've had a brill time though, haven't we? Thank you so much for making me come and,' she paused, trying not to sound too excited because Anna looked despondent, 'making me stay.'

'I've never made you do anything, Dais, you've done it all yourself. Stop looking at me like that!'

'I'm not—'

'You are. You feel guilty because I'm being grumpy. Just promise me you'll have fun, and skype me loads. Oh gosh, I'm going to have to go, I don't want to miss this bus.'

'Anna, Anna, wait, I've just thought, I never told her about Hugo.'

Anna laughed. 'Doesn't she know him?'

'I don't think so.' Daisy frowned and tried to remember back to their schooldays – it gave her a headache so she stopped. 'I mean he was at the private school, he didn't mix with us village school riff-raff.'

'He might have mixed with Flo though – she always was a bit exotic.' Anna grinned. 'Oh don't worry, she won't care about him.'

'And I never told her how naughty Barney can be. What if she changes her mind when she realises just what she's letting herself in for – and I have to catch the next plane home?'

'Chill, she's a coping kind of girl and if it happens it happens, just come home.' Anna shrugged. 'Are you sure you want to do this though?'

Daisy looked at her best friend, and realised she was trembling. No Jimmy, no Mabel, no Barney. Maybe she couldn't ride in the Rockies right now, swim naked in the sea or sit on a camel (okay, that one was a bit daft, but she had always wanted to do it). But she could walk barefoot on the beach, discover Gaudi, and explore the gothic quarter, and find out if the Sagrada Familia was as amazing as everybody said.

'Yep, I can't believe I'm saying this, but I want to do it. Seriously.' Even her voice was wobbly, but it was good wobbly.

'I can't believe it either.' Anna hugged her. 'Good for you, Daisy. Love you loads,' she blew a kiss, but was already dashing towards the bus, 'I'll message you when I get back, good luck, give Flo my love when she gets back from doing her interview. Byeee!'

Daisy wrapped her arms round herself. She'd been offered the chance to escape from everyday life and discover something new, and she was going to damned well take it. Now all she had to do was break the news to Jimmy.

***

'This *is* a wind-up?'

Daisy had known Jimmy would not take this well. Maybe it would have been better to skype without the video. She hadn't thought he'd stab his steak pie as though he had a massacre in mind though. She pitied the peas, which were currently rolling around unsuspecting.

'No, we, I, just thought—'

'Ha. Bloody Anna. She's put you up to this.'

She'd slipped up on the 'we' front – how come Jimmy never heard the 'can you move your socks/turn the kettle on/hang your coat up' but a simple 'we' was detected with the efficiency of a Labrador spotting a sausage.

'We, as in me and Flo.' *Ha* back at him, she'd thought that up quick. 'She's the girl I'm swapping with, you know, Flo from school, the one I've been staying with.'

Jimmy snorted out a harrumph that could have meant yes, no, or I don't care.

'Anna has gone home.'

'Well why haven't you come back with her? I thought you'd done your wandering.'

'That's what I'm trying to explain, it's only been a couple of days so I decided to stay on.'

'Three.' He stabbed a chip with what she considered unnecessary force and used it to mop up the blood, sorry, gravy. 'You've been away three days.'

Plenty of time to discover herself, obviously. 'I just felt I should take the opportunity—'

'You sound like Anna.'

Shit, how did he know she'd said those exact words? 'It's not for long, I'll be back for Christmas. Tiggy has offered to groom any dogs that are booked in.'

'And what about Barney and Mabel?'

'Well that's the beauty of this,' she really was beginning to sound like Anna, but it was true, 'Flo does that. Lives at my place and…'

'And what about me?'

'I can't ask her to look after you!' He honestly didn't think it was *that* kind of swap, did he?

'I didn't mean that. I meant don't you think it's a bit selfish, heading off without even asking me?'

'I don't have to ask, do I?'

He frowned.

She shouldn't have said that, at least she'd stopped herself just in time and not added *we're not married yet.* 'You did say you didn't want to come. And it was your idea. I mean, you did tell me to do stuff, get out there and live.'

'So now you're saying you're doing this because I said so.'

'No, I'm doing it because I want to, Jimmy. I've loved the last couple of days, but there are so many other places I want to visit while I'm here and this is a brilliant opportunity.'

'Brilliant for you maybe, what about me?'

'But that's the thing, I do want to do things like this and I know you don't, but we're just different.' Maybe too different she thought, her throat tightening up as the frown turned to a scowl.

'A couple of days is more than enough, you're being daft, you need to come home and we can get on with our lives.'

'I'm not going to, I'm sorry Jimmy. Don't you want me to have some fun, do some of the things I want to?'

'I want you here, where you belong.'

'Jimmy, I don't understand you. I'm not talking about moving out here for ever, I'm just staying for a couple more weeks. People do it all the time.'

'Other people might, people like us don't.'

'There's some gorgeous parks here,' she had to try and make him understand, 'and I want to go on the beach, and there are the art galleries and—'

'Daisy, I don't care. I'm not interested, we've got more than enough grass here and we can go to Formby if you want to see the bloody sea. There's more than enough to keep us happy here.'

He didn't get it at all. It was worse than she'd ever realised. Jimmy's world was self-contained and he was content. How could they ever be happy together when she wanted more, when she wanted to taste new food, see new things, meet new people?

'I don't want to go to Formby, I want to be in Spain, see something new.'

'Well you should be at home with me.'

Screaming would make her feel better. It wouldn't solve anything, but it would let some of the frustration building up inside her out.

'I don't know what your mum and dad would say about this.'

'They'd be pleased for me, Jimmy.'

'My dad will think you're crackers.'

A little pfft of a scream did escape then, she couldn't help it.

'Well you better be back by Christmas or you can forget us.' He ended the call abruptly and left Daisy speechless.

She stared at the blank screen. Why had that sounded like a threat?

A sudden surge of unexpected anger shot through her. How could he not understand? If he loved her surely he would want her to be happy, to do things, not try and organise her life and tell her what she should and shouldn't do.

She tossed her mobile phone down on to the sofa. She wasn't going to feel guilty like she had in the past when he hadn't liked things, because this was important to her – and not even Jimmy was going to stop her.

How had she ever, even for a minute, have thought she could marry him?

Chapter 9 – Flo. Barcelona airport departure lounge

Florence (said the email, no 'dear' or 'Flo', she noted), *why aren't you answering my calls and texts? I have sent several WhatsApp messages, and I know you have read all of them, they have blue ticks.*

Yes, he had. One had said 'have I left my blue shirt at yours?' The short answer to that would have been, '*yes, it fits the nice old man who sits with his dog in Passeig del Born perfectly. The dog likes your favourite black t-shirt too*'. But she had decided not to say that.

The second had said,

Sarah hasn't had your final copy for the next edition, is there a problem?

There was a problem. She couldn't believe he thought they could carry on as normal, without even a discussion. How on earth could they run a business together, when he was sleeping with their only employee?

The email continued (it was pretty short, but not so sweet)

You owe me an explanation. O (no love, or kisses, and he couldn't even be arsed to type out O L I)

And then there had been,

Flo. Sarah has helped with editing, but I need you to do the

84

interview next week. Can't expect her to do everything.

To which the short answer (in her head) had to be. '*I didn't expect her to shag you, but she has been.*'

Flo. The photo for the new tapas bar isn't good. You look grumpy, it makes you look old. (Old, old? How could she have ever thought he was nice? How could she have slept with him? Wanted to marry him?). *Reshoot and send ASAP, deadline Monday.*

Grumpy? He should see what she looked like when she wasn't trying to smile. That had been her happy face. But the problem was, it was their magazine, which meant that working on it reminded her of him. Oli. And her. Sarah. It really wasn't helping at all. She sighed and opened the next, non-Oli message.

> Hi Flo,
>
> Just writing to say thank you for doing this holiday swap, I can't believe it's happening! I've had a fab weekend with you. Thank you so much for showing us round and it's amazing that you offered to do this. Jimmy wasn't too impressed, but I know it's what I need to do.

At least somebody thought she was amazing, even if it wasn't oily Oli.

> I love your apartment and it's just what I need – a proper break. I just know you'll love my place – and hope you will adore Mabel, she's a bit on the big side but a real softy. Any problems you know you can message me. Anna lives a bit of a distance away but Jimmy will always help if you need him.
>
> He promised to stack up plenty of logs for you, and sort out the animals this morning. The door will be open and the keys hung up inside. Feel free to message me if you need anything at all.
>
> Have a fantastic time,
> Love Daisy x

She could do this. She would do this. Idyllic, a country cottage, snow, animals, a proper Christmas like they used to have, before she grew up and life went a bit screwy.

In Cheshire she wouldn't have to see Oli again, well at least not until after Christmas. And she could get to have a real English Christmas, like the ones they used to have. Turkey, crackers, snow. A horse, a dog. No Oli. She had to keep saying that bit, no Oli was important. No typing up magazine articles where every single word make her think of Oli. No having photos taken where she looked grumpy and old.

Oli, taking a break.

Sorry but you'll have to finish the winter edition yourself, with Sarah.

No. She wasn't sorry. She deleted that. And adding 'with Sarah' suggested she cared. That had to go too. Wow, this was the most severe edit ever.

Love Flo x. She had to delete the 'love', and the kisses. Try again.

Oli. I have decided to take two weeks' holiday. I will be back next year. Flo. (She deleted 'stuff your deadline' – that looked unprofessional and immature.)

Hi Daisy,

I'm so excited, it will be fantastic to see Tippermere again! I wonder if it will be just how I remember it? They're just calling my gate now.

Will message you when I get there.

Can't wait to meet Barney and Mabel!

Love Flo x

PART 2

Chapter 10 – Flo. Tippermere, Cheshire

'Oh. My. God. It is gorgeous.' Flo stared out of the taxi window and wished she'd got a Barbour jacket and wellingtons on, instead of leather jacket and heels. Why on earth hadn't Daisy and Anna told her? The glass misted up and she realised she'd literally got her nose pressed against it. She wiped it with her sleeve and shot a guilty look at the driver, hoping he hadn't noticed. 'This is the right place?'

The taxi driver, who had talked non-stop all the way from the station, stared at her, his jaw loose, shocked that anybody would dare to think he'd go to the wrong address. The silence dragged on uncomfortably. She could apologise, before he whisked her back to the station.

He cleared his throat, noisily, offended. 'Little Daisy's place you said, didn't you?'

Well she hadn't, actually. She'd said Mere End Cottage, which was what Daisy had told her, then texted to be doubly sure (Daisy's practical side being in full flow once Anna had left Barcelona). '*Mere End Cottage, Tippermere. You can get a taxi from Manchester Airport, but it's a bit pricey. I normally get the train from there and then get a lift from the railway station or walk.*'

Flo had actually been quite excited about the 'Mere' bit, until

Anna had told her that there was no water for miles, well no actual mere but lots of puddles this time of year.

'Well, yes.' Phew. 'Daisy Fischer.' Just in case there was more than one Daisy. I mean, she'd said cottage. Cute, cosy... tiny was what Flo had imagined. This was more English Country Home. She'd had absolutely no idea that grooming dogs was this lucrative.

'Aye, there's only one Daisy. Staying long are you?' He peered up the path. 'Doesn't look like she's in. There's no smoke coming from the chimney and no sign of Jimmy. I'm sure she told my missus she was away for a few days. Not like her mind, she's a real home bird is little Daisy.'

'I'm house-sitting.' It was easier than giving the full explanation. 'While she's away.'

'That's right, is it? Well if you're here a while you might find you need a thicker coat, love, turned a bit parky.'

'Parky?'

'There's snow forecast.'

'Snow? Really? Wow.' The place really was totally amazing. It would be the perfect retreat, the perfect holiday escape. She'd build a blazing fire, make a mug of hot chocolate and surrender to being completely snowbound until Christmas was over, along with her stupid infatuation with Oli. Then she could dig herself out (well the weather would have turned to drizzle by then) and make her way back to Barcelona and real life.

The taxi driver raised an eyebrow, gave her a strange look, then heaved himself out of the cab. 'It won't be so wow if it ices over like it did a couple of years ago,' he was back to his previous chatty self, 'like driving on a flamin' ice rink, and nobody wants to go anywhere anyway in that weather.'

'Which is good?'

'Good? Some of us need to earn a living, love.'

'Ah, yes.' Nothing like a down-to-earth Englishman to pop your bubble.

'Not from round here then?' He peered at her more closely.

'I used to live here, but I live in Spain now.'

'Tax exile, eh?' He chuckled at his own joke. 'That'll be eight pounds, seeing as you're a friend of Daisy's, though maybe I should double it?' He winked, then opened the car boot, and when she didn't immediately react he took her suitcase out, put it by the gate and pointedly opened her own car door. Then coughed loudly.

She dragged her gaze away from the house and looked at him again. It couldn't really be Daisy's place, could it?

He held a hand out.

'Oh, sorry.' Flo fumbled in her purse, checking she wasn't giving him euros, which was quite hard when she was finding it impossible to keep her eyes off the house.

'Good luck, love.'

She'd obviously outstayed her welcome in his cab, not that she'd noticed any other potential customers on the drive over from the practically deserted station, along the narrow, winding lanes, to here. When Daisy had said she lived on the outskirts of the village she hadn't been exaggerating, Flo hadn't recognised a single landmark and wasn't quite sure how far she was from the village shop, and her old home.

'Good luck?' Snapped out of her daydream by the second mention of luck in the matter of half an hour she clambered out of the car and stared at him. The man at the railway station, who had helpfully called the taxi when she'd asked for directions, had said much the same – accompanied by a cheeky grin and a wink.

'You'll be fine, love. Not here that long, are you?'

Flo frowned. It was a pretty strange thing to say to a house-sitter, and if she hadn't felt in a bit of a daze she would have jumped in front of the cab and refused to let him go until she'd got an answer. Except she was in a bit of a confused state. And he was back in the driver's seat and speeding off, leaving a plume of exhaust fumes behind him, before she had chance to say another thing.

At which point in the conversation with Daisy and Anna had she missed the bit where they said she lived in a mansion? She wasn't quite sure what she'd expected, but from the name surely something cute and cosy, with a rambling roses round the door (well maybe not in winter), and a wibbly-wobbly windy cobbled path, smoke coming from the chimney. That kind of thing. Not this.

Daisy had mentioned a dog, and a pony, and how to make the fire (she'd even drawn a diagram), and what to do with the Aga – so she'd got a picture very firmly fixed in her head. Which apparently was wrong. But there would be a cute pony round the back that she could feed carrots to, and a cuddly dog stretched out in front of the fire.

Dragging her case behind her, Flo made her way up the large pothole and puddle infested driveway and was glad she'd thought to buy some wellingtons. Mud wasn't really on the agenda in Barcelona, and, to be honest, she had rather hoped she'd arrived mid snow-drift, but wet was fine. She rested her hand on the rather higgledy-piggledy gate and it creaked alarmingly. But it didn't matter, because what lay beyond was worth any amount of puddle-hopping.

It was massive and it was amazing. Wow was the word that kept jumping into her head and sneaking out of her mouth, so it was a bloody good job they were miles from civilisation and nobody could hear her. She had a quick glance round to see there were no passing sheep, then did a little skip and hop. Before straightening up, pulling her jacket back down and reaching for the door latch.

She'd actually thought it a bit weird when Daisy had said the door would be unlocked, and the key hung up on the nail just inside. But that was before she realised that 'on the edge of Tippermere' could be translated as 'in the middle of nowhere', which was how it felt when she was sitting in the taxi. Even the farm that Daisy had grown up on hadn't been quite this remote.

She counted to ten, holding her breath, because she wanted the full impact of this – because it was just bound to be mind-blowing. Then she flung the door back.

'Who the hell are you?'

The door hit something and bounced back, just as she felt warm breath on the back of her neck and the kind of upper-class lazy drawl in her ear that she'd always thought was only ever heard on the TV.

Flo swung round, slipped on the moss-covered stone step (and would have ended up on her bum if the owner of the voice hadn't grabbed her elbow), and her outsized tote bag hit him right in the midriff.

The 'oomph' exploded from him as he doubled over and let go of her. So he could clutch his stomach. For a second she teetered, then her feet went out from under her and she landed on her suitcase.

'Who the hell are *you*?' Flo recovered the use of her vocal chords before he did, mainly because she'd managed to punch him in the gut and wind him, and she'd just been left looking silly.

He straightened slightly, just enough so that his face was on a level with hers, and she really wished he hadn't. The grey eyes that looked straight back into hers – down a slightly large, very slightly crooked, nose – were creased with humour. At her. He swept back his blond fringe with one long-fingered, elegant hand and she could have sworn his shoulders were shaking.

'I think I'm more entitled to ask that question, seeing as you're trying to break into my house.'

His house? Oh Christ, this wasn't Jimmy was it? She didn't think he actually lived with Daisy, and she didn't remember him as being this dishy. Or posh. Although she couldn't remember him that well at all, just the dimples and dirty boots. The only question now was why hadn't Daisy grabbed him and raced him up the aisle? He was gorgeous. Not that she should be noticing things like that. Or thinking of him as dishy. She was going red, she knew she was, her face was practically burning up. 'I'm not breaking in! I'm staying here. I'm Flo, a,' she paused, 'friend of Daisy's and I'm staying here.' Shouldn't he know this? Wasn't he supposed to be chopping logs for her?

'No, you're not.'

'I am.' She did know who she was, even if this conversation was getting a bit surreal and confusing.

He offered her a hand, which she ignored. One didn't accept help from people who were laughing at you. Even if they were incredibly good-looking – well, that was even more of a reason to avoid contact, because she really should not be having thoughts like that.

At least he wasn't some random mad rapist, which would have been a lot more worrying considering she hadn't seen another soul on the journey from the station. Well, apart from somebody on a horse, and they were miles away.

Oh God, what was she doing here? She could be sitting in a sunny spot in Barcelona, wrapped up in her scarf and jacket sipping a cortado as she did some serious people- watching. Instead she was freezing cold, she had a damp bum and the only person for miles around thought she was an idiot.

'I bloody am staying here. She said she'd told you. Ask her.' She knew Daisy had thought Jimmy might not be too happy about the swap, but this was ridiculous. He was in denial.

He raised an eyebrow. 'I think you'll find you're staying down there.' Grinning in a self-satisfied, smirking way, he pointed to the far end of the building. To what looked more like an architect's after-thought. Or actually a cow shed. Okay, a posh stone-built home for cows as opposed to a shed.

'There?'

'Yep, the last door at the end. Servants' quarters.' His grin widened, and the cutest, deepest of dimples made him look boyish, and rakish, in an upper-class, slightly arrogant way. Oh God, not that she should be finding Daisy's boyfriend cute or boyish. That was wrong, so wrong. 'This is Mere End Farm,' he pointed to the name plaque at the side of the door. Did she detect a hint of sarcasm? Okay maybe 'boyishly attractive' didn't mean he wasn't a jerk. 'Daisy lives in Mere End Cottage.'

Ahh, the cottage name made sense now, and the fact that it didn't look at all like a cottage. 'And you?'

'I live *here*.' Which seemed pretty weird, even for Daisy. He side-stepped her and pulled the door shut again, before she'd even got a chance to see if it was as awesome in as out.

He paused and surveyed her a bit more closely, which made her feel all squirmy inside, and hot and bothered on the outside. His lazy gaze was travelling over every inch of her body, his full lips parted in a way… stop it, she really had to stop it. And actually he should stop it too. He was practically married. To her friend. 'Hmm, you must be the one Jimmy said is in charge of Mabel.'

Ah, so this wasn't Jimmy, which was a bit of a relief, in fact so much of a relief she made a silly giggle sound. So who the hell was he? How come nobody had told her she had a man who looked like *that* living next door? Just skipped their minds? Crumbs, if she'd have been Daisy she'd never leave home.

He was still smiling at her, and she was going beetroot-red, she was burning up despite the nip in the air.

'Good luck.' The mocking salute made her stomach sink, and brought her back some sense of normality. What was it about all this wishing good luck?

'Hey, who—' He wasn't listening, he span round, and the sight of his very trim hips and toned bum encased in tight breeches distracted her.

With a sigh Flo clambered to her feet and dusted herself down. Not that she could get rid of the damp patch on the seat of her jeans, which had probably, no definitely, seeped through to her knickers.

Okay, no name, shut door. So much for love thy neighbour and friendly, welcoming country folk. In fact he might be the sexiest looking man she'd seen in a long time, with the type of voice she'd be happy to fall asleep listening to, but looks were not everything, were they? Definitely not. I mean look at Oli, she'd been attracted to him and look what had happened there.

He was rude, in fact very rude, and he'd been laughing at her. He was probably very unpleasant, which was why Daisy hadn't mentioned him. And it wasn't her fault – if everybody locked their bloody doors then she wouldn't have made the mistake, would she?

The door to Daisy's cottage was more like the door to a hobbit hole than a mansion. Well, it seemed that way after knocking on Farmer Grump's by mistake.

It could have done with a lick of paint though, and the paving slab that served as a step was a bit dodgy, but it just had to be cosy inside. Far better than the big and draughty place adjoining. And she really did need to get out of her damp knickers, and toast her feet in front of the Aga. She reached a hand out to the door latch. And a glass of wine would be…

Flo completely forgot all about wine as the gently swinging door suddenly flung wide open on its own and a wolf launched itself through the gap, knocking her flying for the second time since arriving in the boring, but tranquil (Daisy and Anna's words, not hers) village of Tippermere.

'Christ almi—'

The ginormous shaggy grey animal had its paws on her shoulders (which was why she'd toppled over – because ginormous really was the only word), slobbery whiskers only inches from her nose and it seemed intent on French-kissing her or eating

96

her, she wasn't sure. There was a loud laugh and she gazed up from her position flat on her back, straight at her neighbour's crotch, which was encased as snugly as his arse. Averting her gaze left her looking into two big chocolatey-brown doggie eyes, topped with waggly eyebrows. Which was probably more polite. And it didn't seem to be about to eat her, even if it was peering down short-sightedly so that she risked a mouth of dribble if she didn't keep her lips pressed together. And it had bad breath. Seriously bad.

'I see you've met Mabel.'

'This is Mabel?' She was having trouble breathing as it had moved one big paw from her shoulder to the centre of her chest. Good that it had shifted back a bit, bad that she was about to die. 'It's more like a wolf.'

It was him again. Her neighbour. She never normally fell over, she never normally looked a complete twit. And she'd done it twice, in front of the same man. Within the space of a few seconds.

He leaned forward, slightly over her, so that this time, when she glanced up, it was to see his face.

'I thought you'd gone.'

'I had.' He chuckled, a reverberation that sent a shiver down her backbone. Or that could have just been the result of being pressed against damp cold earth by a mammoth dog. 'Then I thought I'd come back and see what happened when you opened the door.'

'Hilarious. So pleased I'm providing some entertainment, you must be short of it round here.'

'You must be joking. With dangerous Daisy and her menagerie around there's never a dull moment.'

'You're quite rude, aren't you?' Why on earth hadn't Anna or Daisy mentioned this arrogant sex god? Well, from down here, gazing up at his crotch, he looked like he packed a fair punch, to put it politely. Not that she should be looking, if she was being polite. But he was more or less straddling her head (his choice not hers), and Mabel-the-massive was the view if she looked the other way. 'Are you going to help, or just laugh?'

'Last time I offered you ignored me.' He helped anyway, stepping to one side, he grabbed the beast's collar and hauled it off her in a very masterly manner. Then offered a hand again. This time it would have been churlish to ignore it.

'I can't believe *that* is Mabel. Daisy just said big.'

She forgot to let go of the hand as she stared at the hairy monster, which was wagging a tail that could take your feet out from under you if you got in its path. The monster shook its huge body and tried to break free, but her rescuer hung on effortlessly.

'Yep, meet Mabel. Mabel, meet your servant for the next week.' Mabel grinned, and waggled bushy eyebrows that gave her the look of an unkempt old man. And slobbered.

'That's not a dog.' When Daisy had said she had a dog, a big dog, she'd been thinking Spaniel, or at a stretch Retriever. People tended to exaggerate. It should be illegal to call something this big a dog.

'She's an Irish Wolfhound. Daisy forgot to mention that bit, did she? Here,' he wiggled his fingers and she realised she'd been hanging on. Embarrassing. She let go and he reversed Mabel back inside the cottage, 'she's a softie really. You just need to be firm, oh and don't leave the door open, it's surprising how much ground a dog like that can cover in half an hour. I'm Hugo by the way.'

'Flo.'

'I know.'

'You do?'

'You said. Before.'

She frowned. 'Oh, yes, well sorry. Don't let me keep you.'

'You're not. I've not had so much fun in weeks.' He laughed again, a rich, deep laugh that would have actually been pleasant in other circumstances. 'Actually, there's another reason I came back,' he paused, 'Flo.' He seemed to savour her name, rolling it round in his mouth. He raised an eyebrow, the corner of his mouth cocked up in imitation. 'Flo, Florence.'

It was starting to get annoying. 'Don't wear it out.'

'You've not changed much, apart from,' his lazy gaze drifted up from her feet back to her eyes, 'growing a bit.' He was amused. Still.

'Are you going to share the joke, Mr Funny?'

'You don't remember me, do you?'

She knew him?

He folded his arms. 'Little Florence Nightingale.'

Oh God, she knew him. Rude, nasty little know-it-all James, who was too posh for the likes of them. 'You used to scare the horses so I'd fall off.' During a brief infatuation with horses, before she moved onto a longer infatuation with pop stars, then an even longer one with boys, she'd spent her time helping out Billy Brinkley, the village show-jumping hero, with his horses. In return for riding lessons. And James – who would never lower himself to helping anybody – used to swan in, dressed immaculately, ride some of Billy's toughest horses with effortless ease, then swan out again. In between he guffawed loudly (for attention, she was sure), and flicked bits of rubber off the riding-school floor at passing horses (making sure Billy didn't see). She'd hated him. And he'd had his nose (which wasn't crooked in those days) so high in the air she was surprised he even remembered her. She'd just been a target for his sarcasm, not a real person.

He grinned. 'That's a bit unfair.'

'And you're called James.'

'That's my surname, he used to bellow out surnames.' Ahh yes, after Hugo had nicknamed her Nightingale (he'd caught her singing when she tacked his horse up for him), Billy had adopted it. Which Hugo had found hilarious.

She'd not known him that well, which was why she hadn't recognised him straight away, but now the slightly cruel twist to his full lips, the sardonic stare looked familiar. As was the mocking laugh.

'You don't seem to have changed much either. Now if I've provided enough humour for the day I'll go and unpack.'

'I hope you've brought a spare pair of jeans.' Then, with another laugh, he headed back down the path.

Hugo had made moving Mabel look easy. Shoving her far enough in so she could shut the door was like trying to push a car with the handbrake on.

Shattered, Flo dropped her bag on the floor and leant back against the door, spotting a note that was pinned to the wall at the side. It had an arrow pointing up.

Front door key. I've fed Mabel and she's had a run, so she'll be fine. Hmm, fine was a matter of opinion. *Chickens fed and fastened up for the night.* Chickens? Since when had chickens been part of the equation? *Barney was in the field shelter when I last checked, with a pile of hay. Don't panic if he's not, he doesn't go far, talk to Hugo next door. Cheers, Jimmy.*

Ahh, so Daisy's fiancé-in-waiting had come in to prepare the way, as promised. A shame it wasn't easy-going Jimmy instead of aristocratic Hugo living next door.

Not that she was going to take that last bit of advice and ask Hugo for help. Hugo had already categorised her as 'useless but hilarious' (it looked like he'd done that years ago) and she wasn't going to give him the satisfaction of being proved right. If Daisy could cope with her horse, dog and a few chickens, then so could she. But she might need a drink first.

Mabel gave her a nudge then blundered down the narrow hallway and through a doorway, so she followed, straight into the cutest, comfiest room she'd ever seen. Now this *was* what she'd expected. It wasn't exactly the tidiest room she'd ever seen, and some of the furniture was more shabby than chic, but it was gorgeous. Flo gasped, and Mabel wagged her tail as though pleased with the reaction, then her nails tip-tapped over the floorboards as she wandered through an archway and into the kitchen.

She laughed out loud. It was even more adorable.

There was the sweetest little window and she ran over to see what was outside. And then just had to open the back door and get out there.

The back garden made her forget all about her damp bum. When Flo and her mother had lived in Tippermere, they'd been in the centre of the village, on a small modern housing estate, and she'd eyed up the chocolate-box cottages that surrounded the village green and were scattered along the lanes, wishing she had the same. And now, for a short time, she would have.

The garden was far more cottage-like than the front, and exactly what all her flicking through glossy country magazines in the airport had set her expectation levels at. The borders were cram-packed with evergreen shrubs and an assortment of twiggy bits that she was sure meant it would be a mass of colour in the spring. A narrow path made up of stepping stones embedded in the grass wound its way between the plants and, with the reas-suring mass of Mabel at her side, she followed it. Nestled at the end was what had to be the chicken coop and run.

Flo ducked down and tried to peer into the hen house, then sneezed as Mabel copied and her whiskers brushed against Flo's nose. They both jumped as a there was a squawk and a sharp beak and two beady eyes emerged from the hut. The chicken looked at her accusingly, as though it was her fault it had been put to bed early – and then five more bedraggled and very indig-nant looking hens joined it. One of them flapped at Mabel, and she looked up at Flo for reassurance.

'You're kidding me? You cannot be afraid of a hen?'

Mabel waggled her eyebrows, snorted, and then rocked back on her haunches and sat down.

'You big wuss,' Flo giggled, and dared to stroke the wiry head, which actually was soft beneath her fingertips. Mabel tilted her head and leaned in, demanding her ears be rubbed as well. 'Don't push your luck now.'

Beyond the chicken run was a fence, with a gate padlocked rather firmly shut. It seemed a bit extreme, Flo decided, to leave the front door of the house unlocked and then put a heavy chain round a garden gate, but what did she know? She looked down at the keys that were still in her hand, and couldn't see a single one that looked small enough for the padlock.

'What do you think, Mabel?'

Mabel whined, and she glanced up to see a mud-covered horse surveying her from a safe distance. His head low he ambled closer, leaned over the gate to touch noses with Mabel, then snorted at her.

'So I guess you are Barney?' At least he wasn't a giant, which was what she'd half-expected after meeting Mabel. He looked a pretty normal size for a cob, and just like the photo Daisy had shown her. Shaggy and dirty.

And he was still in his field, which was good and meant she didn't have to go running to Hugo.

He nudged her hand. 'Sorry sweetie, no carrots tonight.' His nose was velvet-soft beneath the tip of her fingers, and when she reached up and scratched under his forelock he stretched forward and sighed. 'Oh Barney, that's just how I feel.'

From the moment she'd stepped out of the taxi she'd felt like a weight had been lifted from her, that for a short time she was free to go back to how she used to be. No expectations, no fear of being judged or found short. She grinned. Apart from with Hugo, now there was a man who needed a 'handle with care' sign on him.

Except she felt instinctively that Hugo wouldn't judge her like Oli always had – he'd tease her maybe, laugh at her, maybe even tantalise her. A delicious shiver ran down her arms. 'He's grown up to be quite a hunk, hasn't he, Barney, but don't you go telling him I said that will you?' Barney gave the closest sound to a groan of pleasure that she'd ever heard from a horse. 'Hopefully he's a bit nicer than he used to be. Though I suppose if I've got any sense I'll steer clear of him, won't I? What do you think?'

She leaned against the gate so that the familiar horsey scent took her straight back to her childhood. The good days. Right now she was a million metaphoric miles from Oli. He had no connection to this place; there were no memories of him tied up here. He didn't exist. Even if Hugo wasn't any kinder than he used to be, it didn't matter, she would keep her distance and chill, remember what it was like to make her own decisions, do her own thing.

'This is going to be a perfect Christmas holiday, isn't it guys? And we're not going to even think about Oli, are we?' Barney snorted down his nostrils and Mabel waggled her eyebrows. 'No we're not. You know, since I got here I haven't even felt like crying, or sticking pins in a doll and pretending it's him. So that's excellent, isn't it?' Looking after Daisy's place was going to be easy, and fun. Roll on the marshmallows and wine, and tomorrow she'd get her horse ride – providing it didn't snow.

***

Flo stared at the fireplace. When they did this in the movies it looked simple. Except normally it was all set up and all they had to do was strike a match.

She had thought that Daisy's instructions had been a bit over the top, and had even felt a bit patronised when she'd insisted on explaining how to build a fire – and emailed her the details (just to be on the safe side, in case she forgot). But that was just Daisy, ultra-practical Daisy.

Which she was glad of now. Because getting a barbecue going and lighting a fire didn't seem to be the same at all. And when she looked at the yawning hole beneath the chimney she couldn't for the life of her remember what she'd been told to do. So now all she had to do was get on to the internet so she could read her email.

Daisy had warned her that the Wi-Fi could be slow. But she hadn't been prepared for this. She went in search of a wine glass while the internet bravely tried to download her instructions on what to do with wood and paper.

The wine Jimmy had left on the table was warming, but she was still freezing cold. Maybe the damp bum wasn't helping. A change of clothes was needed – after she'd got the fire going.

'Bingo!' Mabel looked up in surprise. 'Don't look at me like that, I've unlocked the secret to fire-building. Come on. We'll get this place warm in no time, and you can share my marshmallows. Do dogs eat marshmallows?' Mabel put her chin back on her paws, looking unimpressed. 'Maybe not.'

The instructions worked. Who knew a pile of newspaper was so important? Within seconds the newspaper was curling around the kindling, which had been stacked in one small basket, and she prodded the two logs already in the fireplace, and added a third. 'Right. Time to get dry clothes on. You're impressed, aren't you?' Mabel crept forward, closer to the fire, which she took as a sign of approval. She was talking to a dog. Which was one step up from talking to the furniture, or plants.

But at least nobody could hear her. So that was fine. Probably.

Lugging her suitcase up the narrow staircase wasn't the easiest thing to do. The landing was tiny and there were three doors off it.

The first bedroom looked out onto the front of the house, and had a desk and single bed in. She poked her head round the second door. A small but adorable bathroom, with a tiny tub complete with claw feet, and an old-fashioned basin and toilet (she hoped the plumbing wasn't old-fashioned too). She really could do with a long soak, maybe if she filled it with bubbles and brought her glass of wine up she'd be warmed up in no time. But she needed food as well, and marshmallows beckoned. Reluctantly she backed out and examined the final room.

A heavy counterpane covered the small double bed, rose-smattered curtains framed the small window and an old-fashioned water jug and bowl were sitting on the tall, wood chest of drawers. In the far corner, close to the window, was a rocking chair and everywhere she looked there were pretty touches that shouted out 'Daisy'. Photographs of the animals vied for space on the chest of drawers and on the walls, rugs covered the dark old-wood floorboards, and cushions competed for attention on the bed. Gorgeous was the only word.

She hugged herself and grinned. It was perfect. Apart from the chill in the air, but once the fire had got going she was sure it would warm the whole cottage. Which had to be the main benefit of a place this size. She dragged her suitcase in, stripped her damp clothes off, and grabbed her pyjamas. It was too late to go anywhere and she wasn't exactly expecting visitors.

She had to be hearing things, Flo decided, when there was what sounded like a rap on the front door. Mabel gave a loud bark that nearly made her topple over, one leg half in her pyjama bottoms, then there was frantic banging.

'Ouch.' She'd not even noticed the very low beam at the bottom of the stairs on the way up (she'd been bent double trying to manhandle her suitcase), but she certainly noticed it on the way down. Or rather her head did. Rubbing the sore spot, she wrestled with Mabel with her other hand, trying to get to the front door. Which was still being assaulted from the other size. Jeez, you'd think there was a fire.

'You're on fire.'

She stared at Hugo, who was on her doorstep and forcing his way in between her and Mabel as he spoke.

'I'm what?' She glanced down; she didn't even look lukewarm in these pyjamas, let alone on-fire hot. But he wasn't listening, he'd pushed his way into the house and was already in the small front room.

It was then she noticed the distinct smell of smoke.

'Jesus Christ, woman, what have you been doing?' Hugo was waving his arms about (and rather muscled and attractive they were, thought Flo, now they were only covered by the short sleeves of a polo top, rather than a jacket), and wafting smoke her way.

She looked down at the fire, which was still safely encased in the fireplace and heaved a sigh of relief. For a moment there she was worried she'd set her home for the holidays on fire. 'I'd have thought that was pretty obvious.' What was the matter with the man?

He shook his head, then marching over to the window, threw it open. 'You'd normally use dry wood.' He coughed, which she thought was a bit melodramatic and unnecessary.

'I just topped up the pile with some from the back. It was slightly damp, but fine.' She shrugged. Why on earth did men have to make such a fuss?

'You don't use the new stuff from outside, you use the stuff from the shed that's been drying for at least twelve months.'

Oops. 'Oh, well, nobody told me,' she was about to look an idiot again, 'nobody said that was the new pile.'

He stopped to look at her properly then, as the smoke cleared. There was a strange look on his face, but for once he didn't seem to have a comeback. Fab, she'd outfoxed him.

'You,' one elegant eyebrow was raised, 'appear to have a bit of a wardrobe malfunction.' She did like that upper-class very English drawl, even if its owner was a bit pompous.

But, malfunction? His gaze had dropped, so she did likewise. Shit, how the hell (especially in the frozen cottage) had she not noticed that she'd not got round to buttoning up her pyjama top? Jeez. This time though, she wasn't going to give him the satisfaction of winning. She looked up, straight into those clear grey eyes – that were actually surprisingly darker than she remembered.

'*You* hammered on the door as though there was a fire or something so I thought I'd better get down as quick as I could.' Now did she cross her arms over her chest, or brazen it out?

He glared back. 'I thought there was.'

Oh Christ, he was only inches away and she'd gone red hot all over. If her chest had gone its normal red-blotchy I'm-turned-on then she was in trouble. And she daren't look down and check.

Instead she looked at his square chin, at his mouth, cupid-bow lips that were still masculine, but surprisingly attractive, half-open as though he was going to kiss...

Oh God, she had never in her life wanted anybody to grab her so much. And she did mean grab, and kiss. Thoroughly. There were bits of her that were hot, and bits that were goose-bumpy, and bits that were just desperate to feel his hands on them. He was still gazing at her with a look that seemed more lust than anger. But that was probably just her imagination. And her hormones, and the fact that all of a sudden she felt sex-starved – and was sure going to bed with this man would be like nothing she had ever experienced before. Bits of her body were humming before he'd even touched her, not that he was going to touch her. She couldn't ever remember feeling like this when she'd first known Oli, or even after she'd known Oli for years. Being with Oli had been civilised, measured, this felt like it would spin dangerously out of control.

He swallowed and she stared dry-mouthed at his throat, her gaze latched onto his Adam's apple.

'I can't.' She couldn't, she really couldn't. 'I mean you shouldn't.' Oh hell, her brain had abandoned her. 'There isn't. No fire here. Not at all, I'm not even remotely on fire, hot.' She held a hand up and took a step back, staggering over Mabel, who had rather helpfully positioned herself in a back-up position. 'So you can go.' Go, go she wanted to scream, before I make the biggest fool of myself yet. 'Now.'

Without another word he brushed past her and was out of the house, banging the door behind him.

Flo glared at Mabel. 'You,' the dog lifted her head and gave her a doleful look, 'are supposed to stop people coming in and protect my modesty, not trip me up.' Mabel groaned and put her head down, which just about summed up how she felt herself.

***

Hugo James got back into his own house and, leaning back on the front door, reached into his pockets for the cigarettes he'd forgotten he'd given up. Again.

He should have minded his own business, except if she'd set the cottage on fire then his own half would have gone up in flames as well. When he'd found her on his doorstep earlier it had been faintly amusing. But seeing her half-dressed in the cottage, when they were practically inches apart, had been more than a little disturbing and he'd been alarmed to find himself seconds away from kissing her.

Until she'd had a little pink fit, which made her even more appealing, dressed as she was in a very lacy bra (he couldn't even remember what colour), her washboard-flat stomach disappearing into blue-striped pyjama bottoms.

He could have sworn she was about to slap him. Which was why he'd backed off and gone before she'd noticed his hard-on. Hmm. He rifled through the kitchen drawer and found a packet of fags he'd hidden from himself.

It looked like life was going to be slightly more entertaining round here for the next couple of weeks. Much more fun than grappling with Daisy and her hulk of a boyfriend. He lit the cigarette and stared out into the darkness.

He remembered Flo, even though he appeared to have made less of an impression on her. In his teenage brain she'd been an exotic creature as she flitted round Billy's yard, her naturally honeyed skin a contrast to the pale faces that surrounded him, and she'd looked on his antics with the scorn they deserved. Barely sparing him a glance. Which was why every week he'd teased her, then given up and switched his attentions to one of the many girls who were more than happy to play his games.

Now she didn't seem quite as immune, and she was ten times sexier. With her flushed cheeks and full lips she was the hottest girl he'd seen round here for a long time. And she had a fiery streak, which was what had really turned him on. Life round here could get boring, he liked a challenge every now and again.

He stubbed out the cigarette and grinned. 'Christmas, dear Hugo, has come early.' Playing with the grown-up Flo was going to be much more fun than playing with the teenager would have been.

Chapter 11 – Daisy. New Friends

Daisy opened her eyes and lay there for a moment. It was weirdly quiet. No Mabel blundering about waiting for her breakfast. No birds. No Anna or Flo.

She grinned and spread her arms and legs out like a starfish and felt ridiculously happy. And slightly silly. If anybody saw her now they'd think she'd gone mad. Well Jimmy thought she had anyway, and Anna didn't seem too sure when she'd headed off back home.

So now what did she do? The world (well Barcelona) was apparently her oyster, and she planned to make the most of it. Daisy stopped being a starfish and sat up, cradling her knees in her arms and feeling a bit foolish. The past few days had been a holiday, with friends. Now she was on her own, with nothing to do except enjoy herself, which was a bit odd and unnerving. The last time she'd been in this position… no scrub that, she'd never been in this position.

She clambered out of bed and headed for the bathroom. It wasn't that she wasn't used to being on her own (although, to be honest, with Jimmy popping in, Hugo stopping off to put her in her place, and customers bringing dogs, there weren't often days when somebody didn't knock on the door), but she always had tons of ordinary stuff to do. Unavoidable stuff. Like feed chickens, walk dogs, mend fences, ride horses, make fires.

'Right, I need a list.' Talking to herself would have to do, seeing as she didn't have Mabel. 'And before that I need breakfast.'

***

Daisy stared at the man who was looking at her expectantly. And now slightly impatiently. Every last 'Essential Spanish Word and Phrase' she thought she'd learned from her book while they were on the plane completely deserted her.

How on earth did you say 'I'd like a croissant and coffee' in Spanish? She actually had been quite proud of herself as she'd ignored Anna's scoffing (and attempts to steal the book) and had mastered 'How do you do?' 'My name is Daisy' and 'Can you tell me the way to the railway station' and 'I would like to make a reservation for two people'. Well she thought she'd mastered them. And had thought she was doing quite well, until now, when she realised she'd skipped the obvious food-related stuff.

Now, the only words that her brain would dredge up were 'cafe', which she was pretty sure was French, followed up closely by 'Je m'appelle Daisy.' French again. And 'voulez-vous coucher avec moi ce soir?' this time dubious song-inspired French, which was totally inappropriate when you'd just got up.

'Si?' He stared at her, then rattled off something that could have been Greek for all she knew.

'Croissant?' Was that just French, or multi-lingual?

'Croissant, si.'

Phew.

'Que quieres de beber?'

Oh bugger. Surely he couldn't be asking if she wanted a baby? He gave her a slightly disapproving look. 'Drink? You want a drink?' She must have looked even more clueless, and on the verge of panic, than she thought.

'Oh yes, oh coffee, café, por favour, please.'

'Con leche? Cortado? Americano? You want it with milk, no milk?'

'Er black coffee please, no milk, erm how do you say that in Spanish?' It felt so rude not to even know how to say anything except please and thank you.

'Un café Americano.' He smiled and nodded.

'Gracias.'

Feeling better after her first sip of coffee, Daisy looked at the map Flo had left and the list of ideas. She was used to having structure in her days and she knew she needed something to do, have something planned. Or she'd panic.

'Daisy Fischer, you're crazy.' How could she possibly even think she was about to panic when she was sitting outside a gorgeous little café, in the sun, in December? Okay she had a jacket on, and croissant flakes were blowing about a bit and getting stuck in her fringe, but it was still amazing. At home she'd be knee-deep in mud (or snow) and have been up since 6 a.m. chipping ice off the trough for Barney. Instead she had ab-so-lute-ly nothing to do.

She sat back in her seat and gazed around. The square was only round the corner from Flo's apartment, but they hadn't actually stopped and sat here in the last few days. They'd barely had time to appreciate the Gaudi architecture (not that Anna was particularly interested), or even check out the Christmas market before it was time for Anna to head home. Followed, not long after, by Flo.

The large square was quiet at this time in the morning, apart from the occasional dog-walker. In fact, there were more pigeons than people. It was so peaceful she couldn't believe she was in the middle of a city, that just a short walk away was the hustle and bustle of Las Ramblas.

She studied the striking building opposite through the steam coming off her coffee. Then flicked through her guidebook to see what it said.

This, apparently, was the el Born 'Centro de Cultura y Memoria'. It was historic, it was interesting, it had been a market, it was free entry, it was worth a visit, said the book. So she would. After she'd compiled a list. With that at the top (free was good).

The list Flo had written out for her was split into 'touristy things you might think you have to do' and 'real-life stuff that is fun'. Which was typical Flo. Not surprisingly lots of things seemed to cross over both categories – very Flo, she was brilliant at seeing the positives and trying anything. But she had seemed to recognise that Daisy wasn't quite as adventurous.

My God, how had she ever thought she'd be stuck for something to do? Just looking at Flo's jottings made her feel tired.

Go window shopping on Passeig de Gracia and Rambla de Catalunya (touristy) had an arrow *to Fab beer and olives at La Bodegueta (fun)*

She certainly wasn't going to go home any thinner.

Walk up Montjuic (touristy) had a pointer to *Coffee and snack at café, view of the whole city then get the cable car down to Port Vell (more fun)*

Picasso Museum (this was in both categories with a note, *depends how seriously you take yourself and your art*)

Tapas and wine tours (fun) – *Javier has some ace places on his list, and he's cute.* (Cute? Where did cute men come into this?)

Meet-ups (fun) – *there's a local one just round the corner. I've told Javier to expect you.*

Hmm, sounded a bit dubious, and this Javier got around. This sounded like match-making at the most underhand level, which wasn't like Flo at all. Flo was open and generous.

Jog along the beach (everybody does it, and I know you're a fitness freak).

She wasn't, always being on the go was different than fitness freak.

Vespa tour (can't be much different to riding a horse, can it?)

It probably could, thought Daisy. And no way would she ride a horse on these roads, there were scooters going in all directions (wrong ones quite often), which went right against her sensibilities about doing things correctly.

She would, thought Daisy, as she scanned down the rest of list, have to do some prioritising. It was like being a kid in a pick-and-mix shop, she wanted to grab a handful of everything but she knew if she did she'd probably feel ill afterwards and not appreciate the best bits.

Closing her eyes and tipping her head back, she let the soothing warmth of the sun stroke her face. It was so relaxing, she could just sit here all day drinking coffee and dreaming where she could go and who she could visit.

Or she could check in with Jimmy and then go exploring. Even after his little temper tantrum when he'd found out she was staying, she owed him at least a phone call. He'd have calmed down now, so they could have a quick, friendly catch-up. The time to discuss their future was when she got home. Face to face.

'Hi, you've reached Jimmy but he can't be arsed to answer his phone right now. If you're selling something, bog off, if you need me for a job leave a message and if you're after my body leave a number.' Daisy grimaced; his answerphone message was the most original thing about him, but he hadn't changed it for years. It was like their relationship. Comfortable, stuck in a rut, and, quite frankly, not as funny as it used to be. Jimmy was just Jimmy – totally predictable and happy as he was. He didn't want anything to change in his life, and he wanted her to stay the same as well.

She sighed. They really weren't ready for marriage. Either of them. And especially not to each other.

Leaving a quick message to tell him she was fine, and ask if he could check Flo was okay, she rang off and pocketed her phone.

Dropping some change into the dish to pay the bill, she stood up. Today would be a wandering around getting her bearings day, and she'd look at the list in more detail.

And chill.

***

She'd stick with water. Water was good. Water meant you didn't get drunk, say stupid things, make a fool of yourself or have a hangover. She reached out to push the bar door, then it opened. Which meant she nearly fell in – except she was stopped short.

'Hi there.' The deep, startlingly blue eyes stared straight into hers and she was transfixed by the fine lines that fanned out from them (it was definitely the wrinkles, not the oh-so-gentle-but-slightly-sad eyes, that had caught her attention), and the dark eyebrows above, and the tan. Wow, that was some tan. He was slightly taller than her, but had taken a step back when she'd more or less toppled into the place. Which was good. It avoided that embarrassing being pressed against a complete stranger's body situation. Fine on the London Underground (or so she'd found the one time she'd been there), not so fine in a Barcelona bar.

Close enough to shake hands, not so close to swap fragrances; gently inviting, not overcrowding. Which was nice, and not intimidating at all.

She dithered. Maybe this wasn't a good idea. What on earth was she doing here? But she'd told Flo she'd come, and she always did what she'd promised.

She probably should say something.

'Er.' Excellent start.

'Here for the meet-up?' The broad, genuine smile caught her off-guard and she found herself smiling back.

She nodded.

'You've not been before, I take it? Come in, nobody bites.' The

115

smile faltered a bit when she reversed a step, and he lifted an eyebrow. 'Are you okay?'

'Fine.' Feeling pretty stupid, but fine. 'Sorry, I'm Daisy.'

'You're Daisy?' He laughed, a generous warm, reverberating kind of sound. 'I'm Javier.'

'*You're* Javier?' Phew, she had been thinking she'd spend all evening surreptitiously peering at people, trying to find the mystery man. And she'd have been looking for some Spanish-talking, arm-waving, madly gesticulating, totally outgoing, noisy Spaniard. Okay, she was being a bit stereotypical here, but that was just how she'd pictured him. After what Flo had said. Not a gentle, very English-speaking (but slightly Spanish-looking), reserved type of guy.

'I am.' He nodded. 'Flo told me all about you.'

'She did?'

'She messaged me an hour ago and told me that if you didn't turn up I had to go and winkle you out of her apartment.'

'I don't know how I ever got to have such bossy friends.' Ahh. She must have sounded particularly pathetic when she'd messaged Flo earlier and mentioned she had one hundred and twenty-seven books on her Kindle so wouldn't get bored at all.

'*I'll send you a link to the meet-up group that was on my list, it's for people who want to, well, meet up. It's brill, one of the places is just round the corner, literally. You just sign up online and then turn up and have a few tapas and drinks. And Javier will probably be there, you'll like him, everybody does.*'

'*Javier?*'

'*He's a mate of mine, he runs these tapas and wine tour things so he goes to the meet-ups and hands leaflets out, you know, networks. I did a piece for the mag about the meet-ups and that's how I met him. There, I've emailed you a link. Actually there's a meet tonight. Go! I'll send Javier a message and tell him to look out for you.*'

She'd checked the link and was relieved to find that it was in no way related to speed-dating, or aimed at sad, lonely singletons in the city. It was just a chance to meet people, chat, find out about good places to go to and rubbish places to avoid.

'Come in.' Javier motioned her in, and started to thread his way through the crowd of people, checking she was following. 'Flo's sweet, and very kind.'

'She is, I was kidding about her being bossy. She's lovely.'

'She said you're staying at hers for a couple of weeks?'

'I am.'

'I'll have to persuade you to come on one of my tours then.' He winked, then turned as he reached the bar. 'Drink?'

'Red wine please.' Fail. So much for sticking to water.

'I'll introduce you to a few people.' Mr Wonderful-smile was fed up of her already. 'You can leave your coat and stuff over there, if you want.'

She clutched the Kindle tighter and felt a bit daft. It was her security blanket, she'd not been convinced when Flo had told her that meeting people in Barcelona was easy – meeting new people in Tippermere was as likely as being invited to a royal garden party. If she had her Kindle she could sit in the corner with a drink for an hour if nobody talked to her and she'd be fine. She could make inroads into her to-be-read pile.

'So what kind of tours do you do?'

'Tapas and wine.' He took her jacket and hung it on one of the hooks under the bar, then leaned in to make himself heard. One warm hand rested on her shoulder and she relaxed. He was nice, he was like an antidote to stress. 'No pressure, but they're fun if you fancy that kind of thing, I just take you round to some of the best bars – you know, the ones that are a bit off the beaten track.' He paused and raised his eyebrows, 'unlike this one.'

Daisy laughed. The place was crowded, with the buzz of people getting to know each other. It seemed years since she'd been in this situation, and, despite having to shout to make herself heard it was giving her a novel rush of adrenalin. A happy vibe.

Javier glanced towards the door and a smile of pure adoration settled on his features. Daisy followed his line of sight, smack into a very pretty, petite figure, who was waving wildly, a massive grin on her generous mouth. 'Hang on a sec, I'll be right back. Will you be okay for a bit? I'll introduce you to—'

'It's okay.' For a second she felt reluctant to let him go, she wanted to hang on to him, which was stupid, she'd only just met him. But it had felt safe having a friendly figure at her side, somebody who actually wanted to chat to her.

She swore that Jimmy hardly heard a word she said these days, and he definitely didn't listen when she was talking about what she'd been up to, or what she'd like to do. He just wasn't that interested, she supposed, he tuned out unless she was talking about something that interested him – like food, beer, or how much he should charge to cut a hedge. Which was more about him than her.

Daisy stifled the sigh. It was so refreshing to be having a proper two-way conversation with a man who hadn't got one eye on the TV. Which was why, she supposed, she'd relaxed in Javier's company and found herself chatting away quite happily to a stranger. 'You go. I'll be fine.'

'If you need me, just shout.'

'I will.'

'I'll catch up with you later.'

'Sure.' She put on her best sparkly smile and took a gulp of the wine. It was time to mingle.

***

To say she'd had a good time was an understatement, thought Daisy, as she shut and bolted the door behind her and wobbled her way over to the ceiling-height doors so she could stare out at the star-speckled sky. The same sky she had at home, same stars, same moon, which kind of made everything seem more familiar, closer. Or that could have been the wine talking. She hadn't exactly made friends, but she felt almost like a little kid who'd been to a party. Exhilarated and a bit giddy (or again that could be wine) that she'd done it, got out there, talked to people.

There was a slight chill in the air, and she hugged her arms round her body as she stood on the balcony and leaned over the wrought-iron surround, shifting her gaze to watch the people below. A murmur of noise travelled up on the still night air, a gentle buzz pierced by the odd shrill laugh. The cultural centre was lit up, casting a ghostly blue-white shimmer of light over the square, and beyond it there was a smattering of windows lit up in the buildings that surrounded it like sentries.

She took a deep breath, then gazed back up at the inky-blackness. It could be lonely in a city. How often had she heard that? But tonight it didn't feel that way. Tonight it felt like a beginning. Like she was doing the right thing.

The apartment already felt like home, with its white, arched, high ceilings that were divided by traditional Catalan beams – so different to the heavy oak ones at home. The kitchen was small, functional, part of the open-plan living area, but more than adequate for living in a city like this where she guessed eating out was the norm. And it was light, bright. Welcoming.

But she really needed her bed. Really. This standing up business was so over-rated. She pulled the doors shut and flicking the light off, made her way into the white-painted, modern bedroom that was so different to her cosy cottage one.

***

Daisy launched herself forward as the buzzer went. It might only be a three-legged race but she was in it to win it. She glanced over at Jimmy, who was laughing and holding her back. He wanted her to stay where she was with him, but she couldn't, they had to race. They had to get to the end, get past everybody else. She tugged, tripped up over the hem of her wedding dress. There was a second buzzer, they were in shorts, they could do it this time, she grabbed his arm trying to get him to move, it was another chance. Anna streaked past them, she was on her own. It wasn't fair, that wasn't in the rules. She turned to Jimmy to yell at him, but it wasn't Jimmy, it was Javier. The buzzer went again. It wasn't right, they couldn't keep re-starting the race.

The buzz went on and on; noisy, annoying. She flung an arm out to stop it and her hand hit something hard. It hurt. Daisy sat bolt upright, shocked out of her weird dream. There was another buzz.

'Hell, what time is it?' She glanced at the clock on the bedside table. Ten o'clock. Bugger, how did that happen? And why was somebody ringing her doorbell? She didn't know anybody.

The sheet was tangled round her feet, well that was what happened when you had a race in your dreams, so it took a moment or two to get out – but the buzzing hadn't stopped.

She stared at the intercom. Hmm. So how did she answer this? 'Er, hola?'

The rich, deep laugh startled her. 'Your Spanish is coming on. It's Javier, I've got something for you.' He chuckled and the heat rushed through her body like an express train, no stopping, building up steam as it went. He'd been in her dream. How absolutely, excruciatingly embarrassing. She hardly knew the man – and it wouldn't have been so bad if she never had to see him again. But he was here, on her doorstep.

No more red wine, definitely no more red wine. It had given her hallucinations.

'Can I come up?'

'Er, well yes.' Dressing gown, she needed a dressing gown. But it would take him at least five minutes to get up all the steps, so she didn't have to panic. It was fine. She could dress.

She didn't have time to dress. He must have bolted up the stairs faster than her red-hot flush. He wasn't even panting when she opened the door. A crack. 'Hang on, don't go away.' She could at least have the decency to dress for the man.

He didn't go away. He was still there when she'd pulled on her jeans, sloppy sweater, and dragged her fingers through her hair.

'Hi! Sorry about that, I was just…'

'No problem.' He laughed. 'I'm not surprised you needed a lie-in.'

'Really?' Oh God, how drunk had she been?

'You were one of the last to leave.'

Ahh. So maybe not too drunk.

He grinned. 'You're tougher than me. I'm a lightweight – I'd have a stinking hangover if I'd drunk that much.'

Okay, very drunk.

'Glad you enjoyed it though.'

'Thank you. Did you?'

'Sure, more business than pleasure for me though.'

Apart from your wife, or girlfriend, or whatever you call the woman you gave a bear hug to. 'Oh yes, did you get much interest?'

'A few people took leaflets, but you never know.' He shrugged. 'Keeps me busy enough though. You forgot this.' He held something out.

'Oh my God, I didn't? I did! Oh crumbs, I remember. Oh thank you so much.' She clutched his arm. Oh no, this was in danger of overlapping with the surreal three-legged race dream, she diverted her grip and made a grab for the Kindle instead. Hoping he'd just think she was still seeing double. 'Oh no, I can't believe I left it. You've saved my life.'

He laughed. 'Well I wouldn't quite—'

'No, honestly. I can't survive without my books.' She daren't go back to any more meet-ups if she'd got that drunk, who knows what she'd done. What she'd said. So what else was she supposed to do in the evenings now apart from watch Spanish TV that she didn't understand?

'Would you like a coffee?'

He took a step backwards. 'I better get off actually, I've got to see—'

Her. Why would he want a coffee with some mad English woman when he had a gorgeous girlfriend waiting at home? 'Oh sure, fine, sorry. Thanks though, for this.' She waved the Kindle, nearly hitting the poor man. 'Maybe see you around some time.'

'Sure.' He grinned. Bright white teeth shining out from the megawatt smile. Then rubbed one hand over his lightly stubbled chin. 'You did actually book on three of my tapas tours.'

'I didn't!'

'You did. Don't worry, I'll only hold you to one.'

'Oh good, I…'

'See you around then, you've got my number.'

'I have?'

'You saved it under Tapas Man I think.'

'Ah. Sorry.' She must have been really drunk – really, really drunk. She was surprised she'd remembered her coat and bag, or where she lived.

'I walked back with you.'

So she hadn't remembered where she lived.

'I am so sorry, I don't usually—' Oh hell, what on earth would his girlfriend have thought of her? And everybody else? That was meet-ups struck off the list for good then.

'It wasn't a problem, I was coming this way. Just to be on the safe side, it's confusing down these little side streets in the dark when all the shutters are down.'

Very nice of him to give her an excuse, but it was no wonder he was in a rush to go.

'See you later then.'

She shut the door behind him and leaned on it, then slithered down into a sitting position, and stared at her Kindle. One night on her own and she'd gone crazy. Tonight was definitely a night in. With a good book.

The buzzer went off and she jumped, which wasn't surprising as it was within touching distance. Who the hell was it now? Surely she couldn't have left a trail of stuff last night to be returned by random strangers, or maybe she had, she should check she did actually have her coat. And her bag.

'Hola.' She was getting good at this.

'Me again.' The sound of people walking along the street drifted up through the intercom. There was a pause. The silence lengthened. For a moment she thought he'd gone. 'You said you liked books, I was just wondering, well there's a massive second-hand-book market in Sant Antoni today, I thought maybe you'd like—'

'Oh yes, yes please! I mean yes that would be lovely,' she paused, 'with you?'

'Of course with me. It's my job, showing people round the city I love.' He chuckled. 'I'll come back in a couple of hours.'

'But if it's work.'

'No charge. Honestly, I've nothing planned today. It's a quiet time.'

'Well if you're sure your girlfriend won't...' But he'd already gone. He didn't mind because it was his job. She sighed. Or because Flo had told him to do it.

***

'This looks quite a bit like the Cultural Centre in El Born.'

Javier grinned. 'I'll have to enlist you as a tour guide.'

Daisy frowned. It was an automatic reaction, and Anna was always telling her off and saying she'd get wrinkles. 'I like reading up on stuff, knowing my facts.'

'I wasn't criticising.'

'Sorry.'

'Don't apologise.' He laughed and his blue eyes shone, why had she thought they looked sad?

'Sorry, oops, I did it again. It's a bad habit the apologising, same as the research stuff.' She shrugged. 'I don't do spontaneous, I do in-depth analysis.'

'Okay, so here's a dose of my research. Ready for this?'

She nodded wondering what was coming next.

'Barcelona has lots of historic markets, which serve the different districts. The most famous is La Boqueria – that's the big one on the Rambla that everybody visits – which was first mentioned back in 1217, but it was 1840 when construction started on the version that's there now. Then there's your market in El Born, Ribera, which was a food market at one time. That one was designed not long after in 1873 by a guy called Antoni Rovira i Trias and constructed in iron. It was used as a market until 1971, and then in '77 they decided to renovate it. It's all a pretty long story, but in 2002, when they were excavating, they discovered ruins of the medieval city, and so in 2013 it was re-opened as a cultural centre.' He grinned, slightly sheepishly, 'sorry I'm no good at remembering much more than that, but if you go in there's loads of information boards.' She opened her mouth to comment and he held up a hand. 'Hang on, there's more, I'm getting to the point. The mercat here in Sant Antoni was also designed by the same architect, which is why it looks kind of familiar, it was built between 1872 and 1882 and is one of the oldest in the city.'

'Ah.'

'This one's bigger, on a cross shape, whereas the El Born one is more of a rectangle with extra bits. The architect is pretty well known, there's even a statue of him up in Gracia and he was responsible for lots of other stuff, other markets and well, you can read a proper guidebook to save me boring you.'

'You're not boring me at all. It's much better hearing it first hand.' Daisy smiled. Just listening to his voice was lovely. It was wonderfully soft and syrupy warm, the rise and fall wrapping her in a hug of words that had her hanging on to every syllable. And he sounded as though he really cared, as though it all meant something, even though he was so self-effacing about it. 'But I'm sure you've got stuff to do and want to get on.' Jimmy would have never spent the time explaining something to her – he'd have passed her a book. Not that he'd have been interested in anything like this – his main fascination was with tractor engines, and explaining why she needed to lend him the money to buy spare parts.

'I wouldn't have asked you here if I had other stuff to do. Come on, let me show you the book market – I can't wait to hear what you think.' He winked and his gorgeous dimples deepened. 'I reckon you'll love it.'

A little shiver ran down Daisy's backbone as his gaze met hers. He looked so sincere, as though he did really, truly care. As though her opinion mattered to him. He was sweet, he was adorable, and he was amazingly attractive. And she reckoned she'd love anything and everything if he was there to show her.

She tried to ignore the fluttering in her stomach. He had a girlfriend and he was just being nice, and she really had to make sure he didn't feature in any more of her dreams.

'I reckon you could be right.' Now that didn't sound too desperately keen, did it?

'It's amazing.' Daisy squeezed her way through the people so that she could look at the collections of postcards, the comic stalls, the tables crowded with books. 'It's a shame most of them are in Spanish.'

Javier grinned. 'Catalan, which makes it even harder. I can get by speaking it, but my reading and writing is a bit dodgy.' He put a hand on her shoulder. 'Had enough yet?'

Daisy glanced up at him and couldn't help smiling. 'Well, I could spend another hour or two, but I'm parched. Fancy a beer?' He was the perfect companion, easy going, funny, and she could see why Flo liked him so much. When she thought about it, she could chat to him as easily as she did to Jimmy. Well, in fact, more easily, as he was so engaging, drawing comments out of her, teasing her, murmuring little asides that were almost intimate as they searched through the books, their fingers brushing as the crowd pushed them closer. They were in it together, sharing the experience, not just two people living it out in their own way. And she wanted to draw out every second, to make it last as long as she could.

So it was a bit like being back home, but better – comfortable, but not as in we've-been-together-forever-and-don't-need-to-listen-any-more comfortable. And without the sex and the complications. She hated complications. Why couldn't life just be simple? Oh hell, how was she going to explain all this to Jimmy and get him to see sense, without hurting him?

Chapter 12 – Flo. Scooters are easier

After a disturbed night, when Flo was sure she'd heard a ghost knocking around in the attic, she woke up feeling legless. Literally. Not in a 'I had too much to drink last night', more as in a 'somebody amputated my legs in the night'.

She wriggled frantically and there was a groan. Which wasn't her. She froze, then dared open an eye. One was staring straight back at her indignantly. A big, brown, Mabel eye.

She gave up on the trying to sit up and collapsed back on the bed, looking up at the ceiling.

'How the hell did you get on the bed, Mabel? You're supposed to be downstairs.' It came flooding back to her. She'd actually got up to go in search of the ghost, armed with a hairbrush (she could have backcombed any assailant to death), and only found the sleepy dog. When Mabel had followed her upstairs she knew she shouldn't have let her, but who was going to mess with an animal that size? The reassuring bulk had meant she'd fallen straight back to sleep, well after the dog had stopped snoring.

A bit more wriggling and she got custody of her dead legs back, which meant she was jammed in the foetal position in half the bed, and Mabel had the rest. She might as well just admit defeat and get up.

She flung open the curtains. The thick, grey layer of cloud that had welcomed her to Tippermere yesterday had gone, and the place was awash with a golden winter sunshine that gently lifted and transformed the countryside.

The chickens were already out and about in their run, pecking busily at the ground, jostling each other in competition for the tastiest worm. They were funny, like a group of busybody old women on market day – gossiping, but with an eye on the others to make sure they didn't miss the tastiest bargain. Flo smiled and forgot about the pins and needles in her feet.

'Come on lazy bones.'

Mabel flopped onto her side, taking up even more of the bed. Taking over Daisy's house and animals was certainly a brilliant distraction. Since she'd got here, Flo realised that she'd only thought about Oli about three times. Which was brilliant progress, considering the normal frequency was about equivalent to the alleged rate that men thought about sex.

With a sigh she started to look through the drawers for her thickest jumper. Even though the sun was shining, she had a feeling that the temperature probably wasn't much higher than yesterday.

Daisy's instructions on how to look after her pets were like a recipe for making a Michelin starred tasting menu when you'd never cooked before. Very long, with sections that seemed to be in a different language, and a bit jumbled, as she kept thinking of things she'd forgotten. So there were little scribbled asides in the margins, and lots of asterisks and arrows pointing down to extra bits added in at the bottom.

'We have to give Barney extra hay before breakfast, and feed the chucks.' Mabel waggled her eyebrows, unimpressed, and looked pointedly at the washing-up sized bowl. 'You are next on the list, oh go on I suppose you could jump to the top.' She skimmed over the 'Mabel' bit, wondering if the whole day would collapse into chaos if she didn't follow it to the letter. 'But only because it's easy and out of a bag.' She would worry about handling the raw meat that was under the 'Mabel loves for her dinner' category later. It was worse than feeding a family of five, bang went her idea of vegetating on the sofa eating crisps and drinking wine. If this list was anything to go by, she'd be glad to get home at Christmas.

With Mabel fed, Flo wandered out into the garden.

'Not feeding them in your pyjamas then?'

Flo glanced up to find Hugo watching her from the other side of the fence, a broad grin lighting up his open-featured face.

She blushed scarlet (it was at least scarlet on the heat-ometer, and there was she thinking she needed thicker clothes).

'Those pointy chicken beaks look lethal.' She eyed up his polo-neck sweater and waxed jacket, which made him look like a model for country wear. 'And I didn't think there was any fire risk, unless you're about to tell me otherwise?' It wasn't just the clothes either, he had that confident air of a well-off Englishman (well what she thought one should be like), and the floppy fringe that was a bit Hugh Grant and a bit *Brideshead Revisited*.

Her mother had thought she might miss England when they'd first moved out to Spain, and so taken a huge collection of TV series and movies with her. *Brideshead Revisited* had been one of her favourite programmes, cuddled on the sofa with her mother just before bedtime. And had made a lasting impression.

The cocky, arrogant boy was obviously more 'to the manor born' than she'd realised. She'd just thought he was a stuck-up twat back then.

He had the good grace to chuckle. 'Well, I was rather hoping you'd keep away from matches.'

God that drawl was sexy. She'd always thought that type of accent would come across as affected, but it suited Hugo. Even his name suited him.

She had to stop this; men were off the agenda. Look what had happened with Oli – she'd thought he was arrogant and assertive in a sexy and amusing way and, before she'd known it, he was controlling her life.

'I may be lighting one later, but I'll send Mabel round if I need help.'

'That's telling me.' He didn't seem offended; more amused. Sod him, she could so do this, and he'd just overreacted last night. What was a bit of smoke? 'I'll catch you later then.'

Not if she saw him first.

***

She was going to make the most of this man-free, wonderful holiday thought Flo as she pulled on an extra sweater and grabbed the key for the shed that Daisy referred to as her 'tack room'. The sun was shining now, but the long-term forecast said snow, so if she was going to get her long-awaited horse ride out down the country lanes, then now was as good a time as any.

Barney stood as patiently as a riding-school hack, shooting her the odd quizzical look as she shifted the saddle about on his back. It wasn't that she'd never put a saddle on before (though it was a long time ago, but surely you never forgot?), it was more that he was so broad, and his withers were so low, it was hard to be sure if it was actually in the right place. And every time she tried to do the girth up he gave such a big sigh she couldn't get the leather strap through the buckle. Which convinced her she'd got something wrong. But this had to be his saddle, and his girth, as they were the only ones she could find.

There was at least a two-inch gap between her and victory when Mabel heard a noise and barked. Barney stuck his head up to see what the fuss was about, and he miraculously slimmed down.

'Ha!' Flo pulled the leather strap through the metal buckle

quickly and did up the girth triumphantly. 'You naughty thing, blowing your stomach out like that.' Barney looked at her indignantly and pulled at his hay net.

Using the fence to mount off might not have been her brightest idea, thought Flo, as it creaked alarmingly, leaving her scrambling up and onto Barney before the whole thing collapsed. But at least nobody had seen her, she hoped. She glanced around from her new vantage point on the back of the cob, even standing up as high as she could in the stirrups to peer over the fence, and luckily there was no sight of Hugo.

Not that she was bothered about what Hugo thought.

Hugo was a man, and a very opinionated, arrogant, posh man at that. Who thought she was a comedy act. He'd be crap in the relationship stakes; she'd never know what he was thinking, not that she wanted another relationship.

The lane from the cottage was as traffic-free this morning as it had been when she'd arrived. In the spring there would, no doubt, be farm traffic and tractors, but a winter morning just had to be the most perfect time to go out. Barney ambled along happily on a long rein as she settled into the saddle, wondering if her hips would ever recover from being stretched this wide apart. Crumbs, she might not ever be able to walk again properly if she was out for too long.

Barney came to a stop and tugged on the reins, and Flo stopped thinking about the state of her inner thighs. There was a weird buzz, and she glanced to the right to see a large pylon and then up to see heavy electricity cables overhead, crossing the road from side to side. She guessed that the cold, damp air was probably partly responsible for them making that much noise, not that she was any kind of expert. She had as much knowledge about electricity cables as she did about men.

The horse snorted, so Flo nudged with her heels. 'Oh come on, I know you've been this way lots of times before. Daisy said so.' Barney wasn't impressed, he took a step backwards. Flo kicked gently. Daisy had made it quite clear that her horse was a typical cob, easy-going when it suited him, but lazy and obstinate. 'You really need to show him you mean it or he'll be awful' she'd said, then added 'but if you're too bossy he'll take offence and try and show you who's in charge.' Very helpful.

Barney turned as though to head back the way they'd come, so she pushed him on and they ended up doing a circle and facing the same way. He wasn't impressed. He stamped a foot and snorted again.

'Look, I don't like them either, but it's only a couple of strides and we'll be under.' Maybe she should turn him round and take a run at it, as it were?

Letting Barney turn round was a mistake though, he'd already taken advantage and trotted a few hundred metres up the road, with his nose in the air, before she managed to stop and turn him back again. This time she was determined. She'd been pushed around enough over the last few years, and she really wasn't going to let a woolly gelding do it.

'You boys are just all the same, give you half a chance and you take advantage.' Taking a deep breath she kicked on and set off at a spanking trot. It was easy. This was going to work. It was SO going to work. Three yards short of the cables she realised it wasn't.

It was amazing how agile a horse that bulky could be.

Barney wasn't daft. He didn't just put the brakes on this time; he slid to a halt, spun round and ducked his head all in one impressive motion and Flo found herself in a very damp ditch. With wet knickers for the second time in two days.

Barney peered down at her, and she could have sworn he winked, then off he trotted – straight up the road under the flaming electricity cables!

Flo closed her eyes and swore. Then she heard the welcome clip-clop of horseshoes on tarmac. Brilliant. He'd come back, obviously realising he was heading in the wrong direction and away from his precious hay net.

But it wasn't Barney.

It was a very elegant and well-groomed thoroughbred. With a very upright, elegant rider, who had slowed so he could look down his nose at her.

He grinned. It was Hugo.

Was he the only person that lived within five miles of her? Talk about a ghost town, or village.

She scrambled out of the ditch (which luckily wasn't too deep), staggered to her feet, and gave him a glare that dared him to say a word.

The grin broadened and he laughed, his horse standing motionless, as a well-trained animal should.

'Problem?'

'Can you bloody well stop taking the piss for once, and help?'

He looked her up and down, his eyes crinkling at the corners. 'Makes a change from smoking the place out, I suppose.' He rested a hand on the pommel of the saddle. 'What would you like me to do? Swing you onto my horse and take you home fair maiden?' He raised an eyebrow, and looked decidedly cheeky from where she was standing. Roguish her gran would call it.

But no, she definitely did not want to be pressed groin to groin with him on a horse.

'Very kind, but I think I'll pass. Maybe you could go and catch Barney?'

'Not quite as appealing as catching you.'

Flo stared; she was going pink again. A very bad habit. 'I need to get out of these.' She pointed down at her jodhpurs and the look he gave her made the blushing state worse.

'I could help.'

'You can help, Hugo,' she paused, 'by catching Barney. Please?'

'Some girls are no fun at all.' He sighed.

***

He was as good as his word. By the time she'd got back to her cottage, stripped off her sopping clothes and soaked in a warm bath for half an hour, the feeling had returned to her bum. And Barney, it appeared, when she glanced out of the window, had been returned to his field.

Mabel had flopped on the floor in front of the Aga, and for a moment she felt like joining her. Coping with a broken heart at Christmas surely should be enough for anybody, but sharing it with six scraggy old chickens, a solitary neighbour who thought she was a comedy act, a wilful horse, and a dog the size of a donkey? You had to be kidding.

'Thanks for catching Barney.'

'No problem, I'm a dab hand at it. He has a habit of wandering.'

After doing a bit of wandering herself she'd tracked Hugo down to a small outdoor school adjacent to Mere End Farm, where he was riding a large bay horse in fluid, effortless circles. He pulled up a few feet from where she was standing.

'And dumping people?'

'Well Daisy is used to his ways, it's his habit of getting out of the field which is normally the problem. Hence the padlock and chain.'

'Ahh, so you're saying I'm just a terrible rider?'

'I didn't say that.'

'It was in your eyes.'

He laughed and swung out of the saddle, landing far too close for comfort. 'I can give you a few lessons if you like, to brush up?' The smile reached his eyes, devilish as well as amused.

Flo took a deep, calming breath and tried not to let him fluster her. 'Kind offer, but I don't know if my bum or my pride is up to it.'

'Nothing wrong with admitting you need help. Even I have

lessons.' He paused. 'And you weren't too bad when you were at Billy's, from what I remember.' Faint praise. 'But my memory isn't that good.'

'You just had to spoil it, didn't you?' Flo pursed her lips and shook her head. 'And for a moment there you were almost being nice.'

'Treat 'em mean, keep 'em—'

She held her hand up. 'Now you sound like a dinosaur. What have you been reading the 1950's guide to being a scoundrel and rotter?'

He laughed. 'Sorry, old habits.' He didn't look at all sorry.

'I won't be here long, I mean if the weather turns like it said on the forecast I might not even get chance to go out riding again.' So much for the romantic notion of ambling down the lanes on a gentle hack – scrub that one off the list.

'Well the offer is there.' He paused. 'I can always escort you if you like, happy to help you back in the saddle any time.' His gaze had drifted down to her bum, which she had a strong urge to wiggle, just to see his reaction. But if she knew anything about Hugo at all, then she knew that was just playing with fire.

Oh why did everything he said sound like some kind of innuendo? Or was that just her? She was pretty sure it wasn't though, the grin was never far from his eyes, even if it wasn't playing around his full lips.

'I'll bear it in mind, thanks.' She could just imagine a lesson with Hugo – now that really would give him something to laugh about. Anyway, moving on. 'I came because I had another kind of offer.'

He raised an eyebrow.

'Dinner.' Did she detect a hint of disappointment? 'I can cook, honest! To say thank you for rescuing me. Catching Barney. And the smoke thing, I suppose.'

'I hardly…'

'Just be British, keep it simple and say thank you.'

'Thank you.' He grinned. 'Thank you doesn't always come that easy to us Brits.'

'I'll see you at seven then? At mine.'

'We could do it here, I have slightly more room than you do.'

I bet you do. More room downstairs, more room upstairs... where, no doubt, he had a four-poster bed and no head-banging beams.

'My place.' Safer. 'Nothing fancy, but you can bring wine if you like.'

'You're early.' Flo spun round in mild panic as Hugo appeared at the back door, clad in jeans, white shirt and the type of jumper that would have made some men look like a grandad. Since when did a pullover look sexy? She gulped. 'It's not quite...'

He raised an eyebrow. 'Everything okay?'

'Sure.' She was squeaking. This was looking like a bad idea.

'I can pour the wine.'

She caught sight of the clock: he was bang on time. Typical. Here she was trying to impress for once, and prove that her life wasn't one disaster after another and she'd failed again. She was normally a very together person. She planned, worked to strict timetables, she had spreadsheets. But whenever Hugo was about it didn't seem to work out.

'Smells good.' He popped the cork and started hunting in the cupboards for glasses.

'I was just going to—' Flo waved towards the stairs.

'Sure, you get changed, although you look fine to me.'

Hugo being nice was harder to cope with than Hugo making fun of her.

'I'll wait in the lounge,' he winked, 'make sure you're not about to set the house on fire.'

Ahh that was better. 'Sod off, Hugo.'

Mistake number one (well for this evening, at least): leaving clothes on the bed. Her very nice, but only vaguely sexy (you had to play safe with Hugo around), tailored trousers now had the unmistakeable mark of a very big dog on them. She picked them up with a sigh. Crumpled was not the word. Okay, so it was jeans then, and a cashmere jumper, which she'd wisely put away.

How on earth did a dog that size manage to sneak around without her knowing?

Hugo was standing in front of the fire, glass of red wine in his hand, looking very lord of the manor-ish, when she went down.

'Dinner is served, my lord.'

He grinned and took his place at the table, then transformed into the most charming dinner guest she'd ever known.

It wasn't just his impeccable manners, the way he appeared to actually *listen* to her, or his compliments to the chef – he was actually relaxed and easy company. He made her laugh with his story about the day Barney broke into his food store, made her giggle at his slightly naughty comments about Jimmy, and seemed intent on wiping every sarcastic, mocking, and arrogant comment he'd ever made straight out of her head.

He even cleared the dishes off the table and then led her un-protesting to the sofa.

'It's quite warm in here, you've done an excellent job with the fire.' Was he laughing at her or with her now? 'Think I need to strip off.'

Shit. She was in trouble here. Mistake number two: efficiently building a fire.

The pullover went straight over his head, and the shirt under-neath rose up, displaying a rather toned set of abs. And a long scar down his rib cage.

'That looks nasty.' Gawd it was hot in here, she'd be fanning herself soon. Could you get hot flushes at her age? She stared at the scar, which wasn't good for her, as it meant she was taking in the rest of his surprisingly tanned torso.

He pulled the shirt down unselfconsciously and threw his jumper over the back of the chair. Then he ran long, slender fingers through his mop of hair, leaned back and looked at her through heavy-lidded eyes. 'Offering to do your Florence Nightingale bit and kiss it better?'

A 'red for danger' signal flashed in front of Flo's eyes. You couldn't make it up. He was coming on to her. Seriously. The strip was part of the act. And even though the glimpse of his body had made her question her ability to become a nun (that really had been a stupid idea) did he honestly think a couple of hours of good behaviour and half a bottle of smooth red wine was going to oil the route into her knickers?

'Hugo stop being a wanker. It will take more than a bit of sweet-talking over a trifle to get me in bed.'

'Sorry.' Why did 'sorry' in that posh, languid drawl sound anything but? He raised an eyebrow. 'Your language has got worse.'

'So has your behaviour. No, sorry, scrub that. You always were like this.'

'Call it attention-seeking.' He looked slightly, but not very, apologetic. There was a long silence, disturbed only by Mabel's snuffles as she chased an imaginary intruder. 'I was rather hoping—'

'What? That you could just add me to your list of conquests? I remember what you were like.' Yeah, she'd watched the girls clamour for his attention, and vowed that however attractive he was she wasn't going to join them. He was too selfish, too temperamental, too damned arrogant. She'd always felt like tipping a bucket of water over his head. She had to admit he was sexy, and when he turned the charm on full-force, wow, she'd almost forgotten who she was dealing with.

He didn't smile as she expected, just carried on looking. Which left an uncomfortable hole she had to fill.

'I thought you called me Nightingale because of the singing, not my nursing ability.'

His eyes narrowed and he studied her for a moment. 'Both. It seemed to fit. You always looked after the little people.'

'I was just nice to everybody, that's all.' Unlike you, she could have added.

He shrugged, as though he knew. Held his hands up in surrender. 'Sorry. Uncalled for. I got the scar when a horse I was on went down with me, caught me with a hoof when it was thrashing about trying to get up.'

'Oh, it looks bad.'

'Worse for the horse.' He didn't elaborate, just poured the remainder of the wine into their glasses. 'That was when I bashed my nose as well, not that it was ever one of my best features.' He twisted the stem of his glass in long, elegant fingers and Flo shifted in her seat. Why did he have to make everything look like some, some, well sexual gesture?

'It goes down rather a long way if you ever feel the need to check it out. The scar.'

She rolled her eyes and hoped he hadn't noticed the way her gaze was drawn back to his waistband.

'Don't you ever stop, Hugo?'

'Not when I really want something.' The corner of his mouth twitched. 'Patience never was my strong point.'

'Well go after an easier prey, I'm sure there are plenty of girls willing to humour you and,' she willed herself not to look down, 'check out the full extent of your scar.' Would opening a window, or fanning herself look too obvious?

'I'm sure there are.' One of his arms had somehow sneaked its way along the back of the sofa, and his hand was uncomfortably close to her shoulder, his fingers beating a gentle tattoo that seemed to be reverberating straight through her.

'I seem to remember you working your way through them on the yard.' If she perched any more on the edge of the seat she'd be falling off.

'And you were the sensible one who resisted.' He smiled, a

139

wolfish smile that sent a shiver of goose bumps down her arms.

'And I still am, Hugo. I told you, I'm not falling for your charms.' She wouldn't, she really wouldn't. 'So you might as well pack it in.'

'Really?' He shifted, putting a distance between them. 'That was a lovely meal, thank you.'

Flo looked at him, slightly startled at the change of tone, and the way he'd dropped his arm back down and left a disappointing space. Not that she should be disappointed. She should be pleased. Relieved. 'You're welcome.' Well at least that put paid to her uncontrollable urge to kiss him, then rip the rest of his clothes off. They'd gone back to polite. Well her being polite and him being slightly pompous and overbearing.

'So what is your surname then, if it isn't Nightingale?'

'Cortes.'

'Ahh.' The corner of his lip curled, but he still didn't smile. 'Cortes, polite.'

'A linguist too.'

'I try. I'm not sure if that suits you or not, dear Florence.' He stood up. 'Earlier, when you interrupted, I was going to say I was rather hoping you'd forgive me laughing at you earlier.' His smile was tight. 'Maybe not.'

'There's nothing to forgive, Hugo.'

'Splendid.'

Oh heavens, why did he have to go all posh on her again? He really was the most frustrating man she'd ever met.

He kissed her cheek with firm, dry lips that weren't a surprise at all. But the warm hand that somehow found its way under her hair to the nape of her neck caught her completely by surprise. She froze as his thumb stroked along her jawline, knowing she should push him away, but not really wanting to. Any second now he'd kiss her and she wouldn't be able to say no.

He leaned in, his breath warming her cheek. 'You do realise,' he paused, his voice low, little above a whisper, 'that packing things in has never been an option I've considered?' Then he did the one thing she hadn't expected at all. Stopped. Abruptly moving back, and, with a nod of his head and a slightly sardonic twist to his beautiful mouth, he was at the door. His eyes were hooded as his gaze drifted over her body. 'Goodnight, Flo. Sleep well.'

Gawd. That voice should come with a health warning.

Flo groaned and shook her head as he shut the door behind him. Then put her hand up to touch the spot he'd kissed. Bugger.

She sighed. 'Mistake number three, Mabel: almost forgetting I'm allergic to men. It's a good job he's a totally insensitive pillock as well as incredibly hot, or I might have got into deep water there.'

Mabel shook her whole body vigorously and headed for the stairs. 'No way, you, madam, are sleeping downstairs tonight and I'm sleeping on my own.' The safest way. 'Florence bloody Nightingale. What is wrong with the man?'

Chapter 13 – Daisy. Blue-sky space

She was going to die. She would collapse here on the boardwalk and die. Daisy wavered, her jelly legs swaying underneath her as a bead of perspiration ran down her brow, straight into her eye, stinging like crazy.

She tried to let the beat of the music that was pounding into her ears distract her from the pounding of her heart that wanted to burst out of her chest. But it wasn't happening.

So much for deciding that A: she needed exercise, and B: she wanted a closer look at the beach. Jogging was obviously not the answer. And bloody Flo had put it in the 'fun' category on her list. How on earth was everybody around her bobbling along without breaking sweat, still staying the same colour (instead of fire-engine red) and with both legs going in the same direction?

She took in a deep, rasping breath, which actually hurt, and was pretty sure that any passer-by would be able to hear her wheezing: she just had to sound like a faulty kettle. Oh God, she was going to have to stop, she needed to breath and she couldn't.

A seriously overweight woman with a bulldog on a lead streaked past her like a whippet.

She just couldn't go another step. Her legs didn't want to work any longer. Her shins hurt, her sides ached, she couldn't…

Daisy tripped. The paving stone couldn't have been more than a couple of millimetres higher than its neighbour, but her legs were leaden and her eyes were watering. Not that she was really looking where she was going. She sprawled forward, knowing she was just about to look the biggest, most undignified arse on the beach, when a strong hand caught her elbow. She staggered, it went with her, and then another hand caught her round the waist. Which wasn't quite enough to stop her momentum altogether, but meant she landed on her knees not her face. Not that she thought she cared that much at the moment.

The hands that held her were strong, the warmth seeping through her running gear and straight into her bloodstream, so that for a second she felt lightheaded in a way that she was pretty sure she could put down to jogging and oxygen deprivation. Then it hit her senses: a gorgeous waft of something that was all male, but confusingly familiar. Cedar, musky, fresh, gorgeous. Oh my God, she'd died and gone to heaven.

'I thought it was you.' There was a soft chuckle and she looked around from her position on her hands and knees, mortified. The knees next to her were nut-brown and led up to… the smiling face of Javier.

Bugger.

She rolled over on to her back and he sat back on his haunches and looked at her.

She had to say something, and not just lie here feeling hot, bothered, and embarrassingly flustered. Something normal. 'I think I need mouth-to-mouth resuscitation.' Not that. If she was actually alive, and from the way her heart was pounding she was fairly sure she was, then that was *so* wrong.

The corner of his mouth twitched. 'Right now?'

'Oh God, no, I mean, I wasn't suggesting.' She flapped a hand. 'That wasn't a come-on.' She closed her eyes. 'Please let me die or a big hole open up and swallow me.'

'You're funny.'

143

'I'm not funny. I'm dying.'

'Come on,' he held a hand out, 'get up.'

'My legs don't work. They've gone all wibbly-wobbly.' And holding that hand could make them worse.

Get a grip, Daisy. He's nice, funny. Friendly. She closed her eyes for a second, then opened them again with a mammoth effort and took his hand.

He hauled her to her feet, and they were almost nose to nose, any second now she'd be kissing him. She staggered back to a much safer arm's length.

'Are you okay?' He looked worried, which wasn't surprising given the way she felt. Heavens only knew what she looked like. Gruesome, no doubt. Whereas he was in running gear, but looked like he'd just been out for a stroll.

Her heart had been pounding like she'd just run a marathon before he'd touched her, and now it was off the scale. Deep breaths, that's what she needed. Air and a sense of normality. And distance. Plenty of distance, so that she wasn't tempted to lean his way.

'I think so.' She bent over double to rest her hands on her knees. It might help with the breathing, and the staying-on-her feet bit. 'So how far have you run?' He looked like he'd just set off.

'I've only just started, about seven or eight kilometres, I think.'

'Oh.' That wasn't her kind of 'just-started'.

'You?'

'Probably about, oh, a good kilometre, I'd say.'

He grinned, a grin that reached right to those amazing blue eyes. 'Ah. So you're not a seasoned jogger then.'

'Don't laugh.' He was trying not to laugh, she could tell, but his eyes were twinkling and the corner of his mouth twitching. 'I'm a beginner, I naively thought I was fairly fit, with riding Barney and mucking out and all that kind of thing, and this would be nice. It was a bit of an impulse.'

'Says the girl who doesn't do things on impulse.'

'When did I say that?' She frowned. I mean she wasn't, but she couldn't remember…

'When you were slightly tipsy after the meet-up.' He grinned. 'You said coming to Barcelona had been a bit of an impulse move and totally out of character.'

Ahh, okay, so she just hoped she hadn't completely unburdened her soul on the poor man. No wonder he hadn't wanted to stay for coffee. 'Er, did I say anything else?'

'Not that much.'

'Yeah well, my freedom,' he raised an eyebrow, which she ignored, 'has obviously gone to my head. I don't normally act this rashly.' She groaned as she tried to straighten up. 'I know why now, I'm not doing it again.'

He laughed. 'Acting on impulse can be good for the soul.'

'Can be, but my soul isn't appreciating this particular impulse. It prefers the too-much-wine-or-chocolate kind of impulse.'

'You've got to build up your stamina.'

'I know that now. Can I sit down?'

'No, now you can breathe, you need to walk.' The smile was still in that syrupy-rich voice, but so was a hint of concern. He probably thought she was about to pass out on him, and getting her dead weight up those steps to the apartment would be quite a task, even for somebody as fit as him.

She groaned. 'I don't think I can breathe and I definitely can't move.'

The chuckle was back. 'If you can talk you can breathe, and we'll go slowly.'

'You're cruel.' With a sigh she fell into step beside him, trying to keep a big enough distance so he couldn't smell her or see how drenched with sweat she was, which had to be so unattractive. 'Small world, bumping into you again.'

'Well I do live close to you in El Born, which is a fairly small district if not quite the world.'

'Not as small as Tippermere.'

'Is that your home town?'

'Village. I'm a bit of a country bumpkin.' If she talked then she could ignore the way it felt so natural to fall into step with him. 'I'm used to open spaces, which is the other reason I thought a jog out here,' she waved a hand to encompass the beach, sea, sky, 'might be good. I was beginning to feel a bit like a bird in a cage up there in the apartment. I mean,' she cast him a glance, 'it is lovely, and there's an amazing view, and…'

'Don't worry, I get it. It's nice to escape and get some blue-sky space.'

'I like that, blue-sky space,' she grinned up at him, knowing he really did get 'it', 'it just feels a bit cooped up in the centre of the city, even on the roof terrace. But it's gorgeous down here, when I'm not running, that is. I suppose I'm better off on a horse.'

He laughed. 'You're a bit more of a doer than thinker, aren't you? I guess when you're at home you're kept busy and pretty much hands-on?'

'Very hands-on, mending fences, sorting the garden and the hens, stuff like that. And what are you? A brain box?' She grinned, wondering what he'd say. 'Let's see, you're bi-lingual, know the history of Barcelona, and you're an expert on wine and tapas.'

'I'll have you know decent wine and tapas are very important!'

'I totally agree, but that's probably why you have to run miles.'

'Cheeky. I do like to keep fit though.'

'I can see that.' She said it without thinking, then wished she hadn't, but apart from a brief quirk at the corner of his mouth he didn't seem to have noticed.

'I used to run outward-bound courses.' That figured. Now he wasn't covered up he had quite an impressive physique, not that she was looking. 'But it meant travelling a lot, and it suits me more to be settled here now. I must be getting old.'

'Yeah, there's a time for exploring, I suppose, then when you're not footloose and fancy-free it's only fair to settle in one spot. I got it the wrong way round,' she carried on, when he looked like he was going to say something. No way did she want to start trying to analyse why she'd only now decided to be adventurous, when really she should have got all this out of her system years ago. 'So, the tour business is yours?'

'Yep, I work in partnership with some of the other businesses though, of course. It's fun, I get to meet people. To be honest, I never was much of a talker, but this comes pretty easily – people are interested and they're nice. I've got a script to work to, all planned out just how you like things to be.' He winked.

'Very British.' She nodded approval. 'I take it you are English?'

'My mum was, but she had a love affair with all things Spanish.' There was a slight twist to his lips, and his voice had a sardonic edge, 'One I appear to have inherited. My father was Spanish as far as I know, but I haven't got a clue who he was or how they met, she was always a bit circumspect. That's one secret that died with her.'

'Died?' Daisy put her hand over her mouth and wondered why the wrong stuff fell out of it so often. 'Oh I'm sorry.'

'Don't be.' He shrugged. 'It was a while ago now. An accident. I've spent most of my life here really, with odd trips back to the UK to do the family duty thing, so that's how I picked up the lingo and the history of the place. I like it.'

'I've never really gone anywhere before.' She slowed as they approached a bench, but Javier grinned and took her hand.

'Keep going, you'll seize up otherwise.'

She instinctively curled her fingers round the large capable hand. Then uncurled them rapidly when she realised what she'd done. It was awkward. At what point did you pull away? So it didn't look rude and ungrateful, but you weren't left hanging on. Like you really wanted to hold hands. With a man you hardly knew. Who had a girlfriend.

This was wrong, feeling this right with him. Which showed she'd led a far too sheltered life.

He solved the problem for her by letting go and putting a

hand in the middle of her back, which made her stomach squirm in quite an indecent way that was hard to ignore. 'Look.' He pointed with his other hand.

'What?'

'Miles of empty beach. We can do some sit-ups if you want to stop.'

'Sod off.' It had broken the moment of awkwardness and she relaxed again.

'You can stop when we get to that café up there, I'll buy you a restorative shot of caffeine.'

'Why thank you, kind sir. It is amazing isn't it? Miles and miles of beach, it's gorgeous, so clean, no people.' For a moment she paused to take it in, forgetting that the man she was sharing it with was a virtual stranger.

She had never in a million years thought that Barcelona would be like this, never thought that a two hour flight would transport her into what felt like a totally different world. But one she had relaxed into, that had seeped under her skin, had made her feel like she belonged.

'It's not quite this nice in the height of summer, when they're packed in like sardines.'

'But it is now, in winter. And the sea looks so inviting, just look at the colour of it, can we walk down there?' It was gorgeous. The clear blue of the sky, with the odd white fluffy cloud, giving way to the deep, deep blue-green sea that was still – apart from where white surf sea horses broke the line, cantering in as it neared the wide expanse of golden sand.

It was one of the things on her list, dancing barefoot on a Greek beach – and right now Barcelona was as good as Greece. 'Can we, please? Come on.'

He put out a steadying hand. 'There's no rush. I think your legs could do with a break, but I agree it's an awesome beach. There are some quiet spots a few miles up the coast, I could take you one day if you want? You can roll your jeans up and paddle.'

148

'That would be nice, thanks. Or if you're busy just tell me how to get there.'

'I'm not busy, whatever gave you that idea?' He smiled, the wrinkles fanning out around his eyes and she looked down, suddenly conscious of the fact she was staring. 'It's my quiet time, and besides somebody has to keep an eye on the sweet travel virgin.'

'Less of the sweet, buster. Are you sure we can't stop yet?'

'Soon, tell me about your place then, Tippermere. What do you do in the winter?'

'Well we don't do mad things like jog along a beach.'

'Because you're miles away from the coast?'

'Well there is that, but it's bloody cold in the winter. I'm pretty busy most of the time too, I run a dog-grooming business.'

'You should do it here, catch some rays at the same time. There are lots of dogs in Barcelona.'

'I know! I was really surprised, I mean there are some really big ones, not just diddy ones. Though they're nothing like the size of Mabel.'

'Mabel?'

'My dog, she's an Irish Wolfhound.'

'You miss her, don't you?'

Daisy glanced up instinctively at the gentle note in his voice, and his blue eyes were watching her intently. She shrugged, feeling a bit silly. If she was honest, a lot of her time had been so taken up with new sights and sounds, and the gorgeous man at her side, that she'd hardly missed anything about home at all. But then there were odd times like this when she could just picture her mad dog having fun here.

'She would absolutely love this beach, it's such a fab place. Sorry, that must sound a bit lame talking about a dog when there's all this.'

He laughed. 'You're not lame at all, you're lovely.' He stopped short, as though he'd not meant to say that. 'There's nothing wrong with missing somebody, or something.' The smile was sweet, perfect. 'It's good.'

Yeah, that's what he'd meant to say.

'She keeps me busy, she's good company.' She did miss the big dollop of a dog, more, she realised, than she missed Jimmy. How wrong was that? She'd hardly thought about the man who'd proposed to her. But, there again, it was all the proof she needed that to have said yes and stayed a home would have been the biggest mistake of her life.

'So are you.' The words were spoken so softly that for a moment she thought she'd misheard, then his finger brushed against her cheek and she knew she hadn't. 'Good company.'

Her heart went off at a gallop again, then his hand dropped to his side as though it had never happened. 'It must be strange if you're used to having a dog around all the time, suddenly being on your own. Is that why you came out jogging, to keep busy?'

He looked so caring, as though he really did want to know, that she suddenly felt awkward. 'Well, yes and no. I mean I'm always so busy at home and I felt at a bit of a loose end. That sounds stupid in a place like this, doesn't it?'

He shrugged. 'Not really.'

'I mean, I know there's loads of places to go and see, and Flo left me a massive list, but I needed to do something more—'

'Physical?'

Physical. That was it, that's why she'd had that weird dream. It was her brain telling her she needed to be more active. With Javier. She gulped. Scrub that image. She'd gone all hot again, hotter than she already was, even though she hadn't thought that was possible. Just the way he was so close, and the way he said 'physical'. There was only one way her muddled-up mind wanted to take it. And there she was thinking her libido had gone into permanent hibernation. This was SO inappropriate.

He was watching her, waiting. Nice, inviting, not at all suggesting anything sexual in any way, shape, or form. If she could she'd bang her head on something. Then he really would think she was a head-case. 'Er, yes, I suppose. I ride every day, muck out, take Mabel in the fields, and haul dogs in and out of the bath.'

'What a glamorous life you lead.' He grinned.

'Told you, country hick me.'

'You look sad.'

'Oh I'm not, honest. I was just thinking about how different it is here, and I was being soppy. She's only a dog.' Well that's what Jimmy always told her.

'Oh no,' Javier suddenly stopped dead as his mobile phone beeped. 'Is that the time? Hell, I've got to go and meet Gabi. Look I'm sorry, I didn't realise we'd been—'

'Moving so slowly? My fault. You go, I'm fine now my legs are working again.'

'Take it easy.'

'I will – after I've got up the eighty-five steps to the apartment.'

His hands were on her arms, the warmth drifting through her body like a drug and it took all her willpower not to lean in towards him and kiss that gorgeous mouth. 'I am sorry, Daisy. Look, I'll catch you later. I'll call.'

'Sure, don't worry if you're busy.'

'Drink plenty of water. You sure you'll be okay? You look a bit wobbly still.'

She'd be okay if he didn't keep looking at her in that earnest way. It was the touch of his skin against hers that was making her feel like she was about to dissolve. She swallowed and put on her best smile. 'I'll be fine, I'll drink.' And never, ever go jogging again. 'Go, Gabi will be waiting.' He had a girl. She had a boy. A boy called Jimmy that she had to talk to as soon as she could.

'Hey,' he grinned, 'she's not *only* a dog, she's your dog.' Then with a wink he turned and was jogging back up the beach.

***

151

'Are you busy?'

'Let me think about that.' Well, she'd got up. Had breakfast. Stood on the balcony in the sun and watched people. Which left only one thing on the 'compulsory for today' list – check how Flo was doing. 'No, not exactly rushed off my feet. I was just writing another list actually.'

He laughed. 'Forget the list, I'm downstairs waiting for you.'

She shook her head. She'd begun to think Flo must have instructed Javier to make daily checks on her, in much the same way she made daily checks on Barney's fence. 'You can come up if you like.'

'It's okay, best if you come down. I'll be here.'

He was. Right outside the door, his back to the wall. He pushed away and turned slowly round when she opened the door.

'Meet Poppy.'

Poppy was a dachshund. A wriggling bundle of chocolate-and-tan gorgeousness with the biggest, darkest eyes she'd ever seen. And she looked quite indignant at being presented in Javier's large, capable hands.

'Oh my God, she's adorable. Totally gorgeous.' The heat of silly tears prickled at the back of her eyes and she didn't know if she should laugh or cry. Or just look daft. Then Poppy licked her hand and sealed the deal. She was in love.

Javier laughed and passed the little dachshund over. 'I thought you'd like her.'

She stroked the silky soft ears, felt the wonderful warmth of her doggy body, and the little dog buried its nose under her arm. 'Where on earth did you get...? Is she yours?'

'No, not mine, I'm not around enough. She belongs to my sister, but I asked if I could borrow her for a few hours. You looked so sad when you were talking about Mabel yesterday, I know it's not the same as having your own dog, but it was the best I could do.' He shrugged his broad shoulders and grinned. Gosh how much gorgeousness could she cope with in one day?

152

'Oh thank you.' She acted on impulse, reaching out and hugging him, then quickly retreated when he flinched and she realised what she'd done. 'Sorry.' It was a family joke that she didn't 'do' hugging or kissing, and now she was throwing herself all over a man she hardly knew. First she'd stumbled over him yesterday, literally asked him to give her the kiss of life, and now she was draping herself all over him just because he'd handed her a dog. 'You're welcome.' He didn't seem too flustered, but she hung onto Poppy a bit tighter just in case he decided it was safer to make a quick exit and tried to take her with him. But he probably hadn't noticed, after all he was half Spanish and they did the whole big hugs and double kisses. It was just her that took the whole British reserve thing to extremes. 'Not quite an Irish Wolfhound.'

She laughed. 'She's adorable, and size doesn't matter.' He laughed at that. 'It's daft really, I've not been gone long and she probably hasn't missed me at all, she's only bothered about sitting in front of the fire, and food.'

'It's not daft,' the steady blue gaze didn't waiver, 'it's nice to care that much.'

Nice or, as Jimmy said, a little bit mad.

'I get it, I like dogs myself. I'd have one if I didn't work such crazy hours in the summer season. Come on, let's walk.'

She put Poppy down reluctantly. 'No lead?'

'She's a typical Barcelona dog, she thinks she's a person. No lead, visits bars, eats in restaurants.'

'You're kidding?'

'Well she doesn't get a plate, but people here are pretty relaxed about dogs.'

'I saw a pig yesterday when I was walking back.'

'That doesn't surprise me one bit.'

'It was on a lead though.'

There was, it seemed, a dog-walking time in Barcelona, which she hadn't really noticed before. And it was a little community all on its own. Even if she didn't know the other dogs and owners along the route, Poppy did, and all Javier and Daisy could do was smile as she said her morning hello's to some, and snubbed others.

'She's a real little madam.'

'Determined, like you.'

'What's that supposed to mean?'

'Well some of this scares you to death, doesn't it? But you're determined to do it.'

'I'm enjoying myself, it's just different. I'm not exactly scared, just, well it is all so different. Does it show that much?'

'No, not at all. I just like to watch you watching them, as it were.'

She frowned. 'Watching me watching them?'

'Well you people-watch, don't you? And you care, you react. Sometimes you're shocked, surprised, it's like seeing the city through new eyes. I guess most people just don't react much.'

'Oh but they must. It's beautiful, amazing.' She stopped abruptly. 'What on earth is that?' She whispered and nudged him in the ribs so that he turned to look into a bar window at the food.

Javier laughed. 'That's pulpo, octopus.'

'Eww, should I try it?'

'You're funny.'

'You have just got to take me on one of your tapas tours soon. I haven't tried half of those things on sticks.'

'Pintxos. Don't worry, I'll take you. You can have a private tour if you want. We'll do stuff, I promise.' He patted her hand, then shouted over to Poppy, who was barking at a very large Labrador.

'That would be lovely, if you're not too busy.'

'Stop mentioning me being busy, I'll tell you if I am.' He scooped Poppy up and she licked his chin. 'I suppose we better get back, hadn't we poppet?'

The poppet wriggled.

'This was so kind of you, thank you, I appreciate it. Really. Some people would just think I'm daft.'

He put one finger under her chin. 'I don't think that at all.'

She didn't know what had got into her, but she went up on her tiptoes and leant forward the few inches she needed and kissed his generous mouth. Well, she went to kiss his cheek, but he moved slightly. Honest. It was just a quick touch against his full, slightly dry, lips. Lips that parted slightly. It was an instant, the slightest brush, but it was nothing like the fleeting kisses she shared with Jimmy.

The scent of him teased at her senses, sending her stomach tumbling and she closed her eyes. She wanted to kiss him properly, linger long enough to feel the pressure of his mouth against hers, to savour the unfamiliar taste.

Her chin brushed against the stubble of his and she started guiltily, brought back to her senses. What was she playing at? What on earth had made her do that?

What did she do now? Kiss the other cheek to make up? Kiss the dog?

'Daisy?'

'Sorry.' She patted Poppy on the head, being careful to miss all contact with his hand, and definitely miss all eye contact.

'Daisy?'

Okay, she'd have to look up. Embarrassment corner. 'It wasn't… I didn't mean… I know you're married and…'

'I'm not married,' he paused, 'or anything.' his voice was soft, firm.

'You're not? But…' She'd seen him with the amazingly pretty girl, called Gabi, a girl that he'd been so pleased to see that first night she'd met him.

'It ended a while ago. We've stayed friends, but,' he shifted awkwardly, 'it's just I'm not in the perfect place for a relationship right now,' he shrugged, 'if you can understand that? My life's a bit all over the place. I've got responsibilities, people that rely—'

'I can understand, nor am I. I didn't mean anything by...'

'Fine, my misunderstanding, it's just...'

'I know, I don't normally kiss... it was a sudden... an impulse.'

'You seem to be getting a lot of those lately.'

She was. Dangerous out-of-character impulses. 'Yeah, and they're not working out that well, are they?' She ran a finger down Poppy's long nose, and let her lick it. 'Please say thank you to your sister.'

'I will. Daisy, I like you,' he was waiting for her to look at him again, 'really like you, but you need to know where I'm coming from, and you'll be off home soon. I don't want to hurt anybody, I...'

'Javier stop. I didn't mean anything, honest. I'll see you around okay? Bye Poppy.'

'Daisy?' He put a hand out to stop her opening the door, 'what did you mean yesterday when you said the freedom had gone to your head? At the beach.'

'Oh nothing. Just a figure of speech.'

She shut the door and belted up the stairs, regretting it after two flights when she ran out of breath and had to literally crawl up the rest. She really had to get a handle on this pacing herself business. When she got to the top she collapsed on the sofa.

Oh God, a man was nice to her, and she had an irresistible urge to kiss him, and maybe jump him. Which was so not her, she couldn't remember ever doing that. Not even to Jimmy. She was having a mid-life crisis, the sun had gone to her head. Maybe she needed to go home before she did something really daft. Or frightened the very nice Javier off. Maybe she already had.

So which was the real Daisy? What did she really want? Was she the mad, impulsive girl who decided to stay in Barcelona, kiss strangers, and jog along the beach? Or did she need Mabel, Barney, and maybe even Jimmy to keep her feet on the ground and stop her making a complete and utter fool of herself?

She rubbed her palms over her eyes. She'd kissed Javier because she was happy, because she was on a high. Because he'd been kind. Because she really shouldn't be getting married to Jimmy.

She picked up her mobile. *'Javier, thanks for bringing Poppy, I love her. Can we do tapas soon? Please?'* she could have added, I promise not to kiss you ever again, but thought that was better forgotten. Ignored. *'I need to tell you about my list'* the new list she'd been writing when he'd arrived, *'and my dizzy head.'*

Chapter 14 – Flo. Home sweet home?

Flo did not sleep well. Her dreams were filled with vivid images of her licking Hugo's scar, which then turned into a snake and gave her a deadly bite. It didn't take Freud to work out that one. Maybe Tippermere wasn't that good an idea after all. Had she jumped from the Oli frying pan into the much more lethal Hugo fire?

'Should I go home? What do you think Mabel?' This had all seemed a brilliant idea, and she did love being back in Cheshire. But she wasn't sure it loved her. She couldn't exactly spend two weeks hiding from her next-door neighbour, even if he was insufferable. But there was nobody else to talk to. And Barney had decided she was a pushover, so idyllic hacks in the country weren't high on the agenda. To sort him she'd need Hugo's help, and no way was she going down that route.

Daisy had left car keys though, so she could always go into the village, find out if it had changed. Stock up on food. Wander round Kitterly Heath. She sighed. But she couldn't exactly spend the next two weeks doing that, just to avoid having to face Hugo again.

The toast popped out of the toaster and she lathered the butter on, not hearing the skype call ringing out on her laptop until Mabel nudged her.

'Oh, thanks Mabel.' She was halfway across the kitchen, one piece of toast and a mug of coffee in her hands, when she saw, out of the corner of her eye, the dog surreptitiously stealing the other piece.

When was she ever going to get used to the idea of a dog whose head was at worktop height?

'Oh hi Daisy.'

'Hiya, everything okay?'

'Mabel just stole my toast.'

'She's good at that.'

'I met your, er, neighbour.' She sat down at the laptop and started to eat the one slice of toast she did have.

'My neighbour?' There was a pause, followed by Daisy's eye widening and her hand going over her mouth. 'Oh my God, you've not met his Lordship, I am so sorry I should have warned you, I never... Well, I wasn't sure if you already knew him or not.'

'Lordship? He's a Lord? Oh shit.' She knew he was posh but hadn't realised he was a Lord, and she'd called him an arsehole, and he'd seen her slip on her bum. Twice. And in a ditch. And she'd dreamt she was licking his abs. Eurghh. Her mum would never forgive her.

'No, no he's not an actual Lord.' Daisy giggled. 'We just call him that, if you've met him you'll know why. Are you alright?'

'He's not?' Flo wondered if it would be better to turn the camera on her laptop off, rather than let Daisy see her meltdown.

'He's so bloody pompous. Look, I am sorry, I should have warned you. He's not been horrible has he?'

'Not horrible, no.' Flo spoke slowly, trying to work out the best way of saying this.

'Did you already know him?'

'Well I did meet him yonks ago when I used to have riding lessons with Billy Brinkley, but I didn't recognise him at first.'

'Oh. But he has been alright? He always looks down his nose at me.'

'Fine, we er had dinner last night.'

'Dinner!' Daisy's squeak travelled at high volume all the way from Spain and Mabel lifted her head and cocked her ears. 'Oh Mabel, Mabel, aww she looks happy, it's so good to see her, I miss her. Has she been good? Apart from taking your toast?'

'Fairly.' It was probably best not to mention she'd let her sleep on the bed, and fed her popcorn, and fallen over her a few times. Dogs didn't bruise, did they?

'Fairly?' Daisy frowned.

'Oh she's been perfect, haven't you, Mabel?' Unlike Barney. Please don't ask about Barney.

'And how's Barney? He hasn't got out at all, has he?'

'No, still safe and sound.'

'If you hack him out, be careful when you go under the electricity cables, he's not keen on the buzz, but he will go if you're firm.'

Thanks for that one, Daisy. 'Okay.'

'Oh God, Flo, how come you ended up having dinner with Hugo?' Which was worse, talking about Barney, or Hugo? 'You've got to watch him, he's a real, real—'

'Cad?'

'Something like that. He's a total womaniser, though. God knows what the attraction is.'

Flo had a vague idea what the attraction was, but decided not to voice it. Or think about his abs. She shook her head, hoping it would get rid of the image that seemed to be set on her brain. 'I think he's quite funny actually.'

'Funny? As in funny ha-ha?' Daisy sounded confused.

'He's amusing – he can just be so pompous.'

'Very, so what's funny about that?'

'Maybe he's misunderstood?' Flo grinned at herself. 'Maybe he has this deep, sensitive side that he never lets out.' She could pretend, or just accept he was a bit shallow and wanted a shag.

'Yeah, had a traumatic childhood.' Daisy laughed. 'Jimmy hates him, but he is good in a crisis, he's really kind of assertive and decisive, he just gets on with it, but you can kind of get trampled by him if you're not careful.'

Hmm, she could understand that. 'I think I witnessed the Hugo charm offensive last night.'

'And?' Daisy had leaned forward in anticipation.

'I called him a wanker; it seemed to destroy the romantic atmosphere somehow.'

Daisy giggled. 'You didn't! Oh Flo, I wish I'd been there, I would have loved to see his face.'

Flo decided it was time to change the subject. 'So how's Barcelona? Everything okay?'

'Oh fine, fine. I do miss everybody, and I have been a bit, I don't know, it's so different here, but I met this guy. Don't look at me like that, Flo! It was your friend Javier. Honestly, what do you think I am? He'd dead friendly, isn't he? And he brought the cutest of dogs over for us to walk because he guessed that I miss Mabel – wasn't that lovely? Oh hang on, I think that's my phone. Look, I'd better go, I just wanted to check everything was okay?'

'Everything's okay, including the chickens you didn't tell me about.'

Daisy grinned. 'I knew you wouldn't mind them, have you had many eggs?'

'Eggs?'

'Yes eggs, you know, chickens lay them? Just put your hand in the box underneath?'

'Won't they, you know,' she really didn't like those beaks, 'peck me?' Stick her hand in? Was Daisy mad?

'Don't be daft. I'd better go, catch you soon. Bye.'

'Well, Daisy's having fun, isn't she?' Mabel cocked her ears at the mention of her mistress's name. 'But she hasn't got Cheshire's answer to Don Juan next door, has she? Oh bugger,' there amongst the Skype messages was one from Oli, his smarmy face grinning out at her.

'*Where are you? I need to pick my stuff up from your place.*'

'He really is a jerk, isn't he?' Mabel scratched behind her ear with one massive back foot and then ran her chin along the worktop in search of crumbs.

'*I told you, I'm away. Call me in the New Year. Florence.*' She had just pressed send when Mabel gave such a loud bark she jumped.

'Mabel!' The dog barked again, then again, then put her nose in the air and howled. 'What on earth is the matter, you daft animal?' Mabel stared at the door, her hackles rising, and for a moment Flo didn't know if she should be scared and do a runner. Or go and open it.

The dog cocked her head to one side, as though listening, then barked again – and wagged her tail. So maybe not a mad axe murderer.

She opened the door a crack. There was nobody there. She opened it a bit wider, to take a better look and was just about to close it again when Mabel barged past her, heading straight down the path towards Hugo's place. She didn't stop at Hugo's front door – she kept going. 'Oh hell.' Slipping on the wellingtons that were behind the door, and pulling it closed behind her, Flo started running after the dog, whose lolloping stride was covering the ground remarkably quickly. No wonder Hugo had warned her not to let the animal out.

'Please don't go round there.' Mabel did, straight round the corner towards Hugo's stables. 'Bugger.' Flo slithered on the mossy stones but kept going. 'Mabel!'

Then she heard the bellow.

Hugo.

Which meant he was there. She could creep back inside and wait for him to bring the dog back. Deny all knowledge. No, that was wrong. Wimpish.

What had ever made her think she wanted a dog in her life? For once (just once) Oli might have been right.

Then she realised it wasn't just a bellow. He was shouting her name.

'Thank Christ you heard me. I need help with this horse. Lock Mabel in the stable out of the way.' He didn't even look at her, his gaze was fixed on a horse, a very large horse that was lying flat out on its side, its neck lathered foamy white, its nostril flared, showing a blood-red lining.

For a moment Flo stared, then, grabbing Mabel, she shoved her into the next stable before she had chance to realise what was happening and object.

'He's cast.'

'Cast?'

'Stuck. I think he's got colic and rolled. Go and get two lunge lines out of my tack room over there,' he waved an arm in the vague direction of one of the stables, 'hung up on a hook at the back.' She looked at him. 'Go. Hurry up.'

She hurried. His tack room, like everything else about him, was immaculate and ordered, which explained why he went apeshit with Daisy the day Barney got in.

The lunge lines were exactly where he said, hung up neatly, so she grabbed two and ran back. Mabel had her front paws over the stable door. 'Please be a good girl.' She slipped down soundlessly and sat in the middle of the stable, her large tail slowly wagging a neat semi-circle into the shavings.

'Cheers.' Hugo put a hand out to take them from her. 'Rub his ears in slow circles while I loop these over his legs.'

Okay. Seemed a bit weird, but sometimes it was wise to do as you were asked.

'It will keep him calm, he's normally pretty chilled but I don't want him striking out if my head's in the way.' Hugo's voice was steady, measured, not reflecting at all the danger – and Flo got why Daisy said he was good in a crisis. 'Just keep some pressure on his neck with one hand to keep him steady, fine, there's a boy.' Adrenalin wasn't in his vocabulary, he was as calm as somebody taking a stroll in the park as he murmured to the horse, working away to fasten the lines round his fetlocks.

'Right, probably better if you just stand in the doorway, hold this.' He passed her the end of one lunge line, then wiped his arm across his eyes. There was a thin sheen of perspiration across his brow, despite the cold and the fact he was in his shirtsleeves. This was bothering him more than he let on. He stood back. 'Take up the slack a bit, there, good.' Still he didn't look at her, just had eyes for the horse. 'We're going to ease him over, together, okay?'

It was over in an instant. The moment the horse started to move he took over the roll himself, hooves flailing, as Hugo ducked out of the way and stood in the doorway with her. For a moment the large horse lay on his side, as though exhausted, then he was up on his feet. Wobbling and unsteady.

'Just stand at his head will you? Talk to him.' He was back at work, moving the lunge lines out of the way, then clipping a lead rope onto the horse's head collar. 'I'll walk him round in the school. Colic. Come on, boy. I thought he'd be okay in the stable; he usually is when this happens, but the silly old fool was rolling about too much. Weren't you?' The handsome head, darkened with sweat, rubbed up and down Hugo's arm, then he followed, his head hung low as though he was exhausted. 'I phoned the vet but he was out on a call, I think we'd better keep this old boy gently moving until he gets here. Eh?' The horse faltered, looked round at its flank, then recovered and patiently followed Hugo into the school.

Flo watched, feeling useless, but reluctant to leave as Hugo and the gelding walked falteringly round. 'Go in, it's cold.'

'I'm fine. Isn't there anything I can do?'

He ran his hand over his face, blinking his eyes open wider, shattered, and she wondered how long he'd been in the stable trying to get the horse on its feet by himself before she'd arrived. 'Well, there are a few horses out still that need bringing in.'

'I'll get them.'

'A couple are a bit,' he hesitated, 'lively.'

'I can try.'

He shook his head wearily. 'They probably won't let you near them, they get fresh when it goes cold like this and they can't be turned out for long.' He looked at her, then back at the horse and hesitated, weighing something up. 'I suppose you could walk him round while I do it. I won't be long and…'

'It'll be fine, honest, I'll do it.' She was already walking alongside him, keeping in step.

'I want to keep him on his feet unless he really wants to go down, but we do it at his pace.'

'I know, I'll carry on just like you've been doing.'

'Shout me if anything happens, if there's any change at all.'

'Promise, go on.'

It was a relief to actually be doing something useful. Flo murmured softly to the horse as she'd seen Hugo doing, encouraging him to plod on beside her. 'Good boy, it won't be long now. I know it's boring and cold, but you know it's for your own good, don't you?' The horse nudged her arm in response, and she scratched under his forelock with her free hand, then stroked her hand down the long nose. It gave a low nicker, spotting Hugo coming back before she did, and Flo found herself blinking back tears. She would never have imagined that beneath that arrogant exterior there was such a caring man, but there was evidently a strong bond between him and the horse. The animal trusted him, loved him; a feeling that was obviously mutual.

'Thanks.' His hand rested on her arm, warm, strong, his gaze fixed on hers as he tugged the lead rope gently from her hands and for once there was no mockery, nothing but concern. 'Thanks, really. I'll take him back now. You warm your hands up.'

She swallowed to clear the silly lump from her throat. 'We can take it in turns if you like?'

'Sure?'

'I'll walk with you, if you don't mind, of course?'

She fell into step with him again, not wanting to leave his side, wanting to feel the warmth of his hand again, wondering why all of a sudden she felt wobbly and her stomach felt strangely hollow.

He nodded, his attention back on the horse and Flo risked a sideways glance. His brow was etched with a frown she'd never seen on his chiselled features before as he concentrated on his horse, his voice low and steadying as he coaxed it on – as they stumbled doggedly on, round and round the arena. This caring, determined Hugo was nothing like the mocking man who'd been trying to get her into bed, the man she'd decided was an insensitive idiot.

Flo started as she realised she'd got closer and closer, and was practically leaning on him.

'You're tired – go and sit down for a bit.'

'I'm fine.' She linked her hand through his arm. 'I'm not going anywhere.'

Two hours later, when they were all exhausted, the vet finally turned up.

***

'Come and have a drink with me. I need one.' It wasn't a question, or even an invitation, but Flo didn't mind. He needed company. He was shattered and, with a start, she realised this wasn't physical. He was emotionally drained. Hugo cared. And as he sank down into an armchair and smiled it was the most genuine and open expression she'd ever seen on his face.

'Thanks for helping.'

'You're welcome.' She felt pretty shattered herself, but strangely happy. For the first time in years she'd actually been useful. Somebody had actually thanked her for doing something. 'Will he be okay?'

'I think so. He's getting on a bit though, and he's had a few bouts. Vet doesn't quite know what's causing it. Christ, I'm shattered.' His fingers were brushing through his hair, a habit she'd already got used to, and she had a sudden urge to hug him, to wrap her arms round him, feel his strong body against hers, taste his lips, those strong fingers tangling in her own hair...

Oh God. She opened her eyes, which she hadn't realised she'd closed. She had to stop this; it was totally inappropriate and was going to get her in all kinds of trouble. She could just hug him... no, she couldn't.

Instead she scrambled to her feet. 'I'd better let Mabel out.'

'Okay. Flo?'

'Yep?'

He didn't continue until she was looking straight into those grey eyes, which didn't have any hint of mockery in them at all. 'How about we reset the counter, clear the slate, forget I was such a prick last night and start again?'

'Sure.' She wasn't quite sure what 'start again' meant, but what the hell? It was only a fortnight out of her life. 'That sounds good. I'll catch you later.' She took a step towards the door.

'Florence?'

'Hugo?'

His brow was furrowed as he studied her over the rim of his glass. 'What were you doing last night? You were in the front bedroom with the light on for ages.'

'Have you been spying on me?'

'Maybe.' A hint of the normal Hugo returned, a gleam in his eye.

'I was writing.'

'Writing?'

'Mm, you know, words, sentences. I do it for a living.'

'Do you?'

'I run a magazine with my boyf—' she pulled herself up short, what did she call him that was polite? 'My ex. Well I did, but I'm taking a bit of a sabbatical while I decide what to do next.' With the rest of my life.

'But you were writing last night. Not much of a sabbatical.'

'Just scribbling, ideas. Other, different stuff, you know.' Stuff that was too embarrassing to talk about.

He didn't look like he did know.

'I better go and check on Mabel. Bye Hugo.'

She'd been scribbling. That was the only word for it. After lying in bed for half an hour she'd had a sudden urge to write. It was strange, when she'd left college she'd wanted to be an author, she loved letting her imagination run free, creating characters who could roam free and cause havoc in her head. And then real life had taken over. She'd got a job, met Oli, set up the magazine. Then spent her days proof-reading his columns and writing her own. She did enjoy it, most of the time, but it was only now – in a cottage in the middle of nowhere – that she'd felt compelled to create. Oli had always said it was a waste of time, and she hadn't had a second to spare anyway. But here, now, she had.

And she'd just had a whole new line of inspiration. A hero who was a pompous cad who cared. 'How terribly Jilly Cooper,' she said to Mabel, who waved her tail frantically, glad to have escaped the confines of the stable. 'Come on, we're going to share beans on toast then I'm writing a bestseller.'

Chapter 15- Daisy. Seeing clearly

'I thought I'd find you here.'

Daisy looked up and grinned, totally relieved that she hadn't put Javier off for life. She'd had a horrible feeling that he'd be running for the hills, or at least his scooter. He was obviously taking his duties, as instructed by Flo, seriously. Didn't anybody think she could do this on her own? Although she had to admit, she'd realised last night that she would miss Javier if she didn't see him again. She'd got used to his comforting presence. He felt safe, reliable. Nice. More than nice.

'Am I so predictable?' She'd only been here a few days, but the small corner café in the square had become her go-to place for breakfast. The staff were friendly, the seats were in a sunny spot and the croissants just had to be the best. And it was quiet. She could sit undisturbed and start her day off with a bit of people-watching, and day-dreaming.

'Nope, you look very at home and relaxed though.'

She was – very relaxed. She was finally starting to unwind, to take life a bit slower and not feel like she should be doing something. Speaking of which… 'Don't you ever work?'

'It's a slow time.' He sat down on the chair opposite her and ordered a coffee. 'Another?' She shook her head, she didn't need a caffeine boost, she was already hyper enough these days. 'There's always a bit of a lull at this time of year. People come to go round the shops, see the lights and the Christmas markets. The tapas and wine are just necessary fuelling in between. Spring and autumn are my busiest times.'

'I haven't really done the shops, light, or markets yet properly.'

'Tut, tut, although you're not that type of tourist, are you?'

'I'm not sure what I am.' Many a true word spoken in jest. Isn't that what they said? Which brought her neatly onto... 'I said I'd tell you about my list.'

'Later.'

She really did want to try and explain about being here, about Jimmy. But Javier had backed off.

'I want to take you somewhere. Drink up.' He reached across and took a flake of croissant from her hair. 'And eat up. Then go and get your scarf and jacket.'

***

'Your chariot awaits.'

She'd gone up to the apartment to get her scarf, as instructed, and now had got back down to find Javier waiting. 'You have to be kidding!' With a scooter. A bright red Vespa scooter. 'Oh my God, isn't it cute?' She giggled and put her hands over her mouth. She'd discounted Flo's idea of hiring a scooter because no way did she trust herself to motor unscathed round the city, but she trusted Javier to take her.

'No joke.' He waggled the helmet she hadn't noticed in his hand.

'Where are we going?'

'It's a surprise.'

'I don't like surprises, I like to know.' She always knew exactly what was happening and when. But hadn't she come here to break the mould, get out of her normal routines?

'Well you're going to have to wait this time.' He winked. 'Trust me.'

She did, even without the cheeky wink and the look he was giving her, which was making her forget all her good intentions to think about him as just a good friend who could never be anything more. He was a good friend though, everything about him was good. He seemed to be in tune with her, how she felt, what she wanted. Which was a totally new experience, Jimmy had never known, or, if she was honest, seemed to care.

But Javier had known instinctively that she missed her dog and he'd actually gone to all the effort of trying to make her feel better, which he hadn't had to do at all. He'd made an already good day even better by turning up with little Poppy, and he'd not made her feel bad about kissing him. Not made her feel an idiot.

She just felt like he'd be there for her when she needed him, which she'd never ever felt with Jimmy. With anybody. It would have been scary if anybody else had seemed to read her mind so effortlessly, but with Javier it just felt right. Natural. She trusted him.

He was waiting patiently, watching her, no pressure. Knowing she wouldn't be able to resist.

'Here, let me wrap that scarf round more authentically, then you'll look the part.' His hand brushed against her cheek and sent a judder of cold goose bumps down her arms. 'There.' He didn't seem to notice, or the way she was sure she was gazing at him like an adoring puppy. He put her helmet on, not meeting her gaze, so she studied his mouth – lips pursed as he did the strap up.

It was getting impossible to imagine being here in Barcelona without Javier; he was as much a part of it as the beach, as all the wonderful places he'd taken her. In fact she was beginning to

171

feel like he was some kind of drug – a drug she knew was dangerously addictive, but there was no way she wanted to stop and say
no.

'There you go.' He moved back. She breathed again.

'Let me get on first, then climb on. You can hold these bars,
or put your arms round me – whichever you feel most comfortable with.'

Bars. She'd hold the bars.

'Oh my God, how do I get on?'

'Like a horse.'

'When I get on the horse it's a saddle for one.' Not that she
minded sharing with him, the black leather jacket, tights jeans
and boots suited him. Man in black. 'And there's not a big back
box stuck in the way normally, I just throw my leg over.'

'Well throw your leg over me.' He chuckled, the fan of wrinkles
round his eyes more pronounced than ever, along with the
dimples. She thumped him.

'Do I have to get off and let you get on first, like I do for my
Gran?'

'You are so cheeky. I'm not like your gran, I am an agile young
thing.'

'Ah yes, I noticed that when we went jogging.'

'*We* didn't, I was there minding my own business and you just
happened to join me.' And rescue me. He was shaking his head,
rubbing a hand over his chin that had its normal dark shadow.

'I can lean it a bit – you can either put your foot on the peg
or just go for it.'

She went for it, then wriggled about on the seat.

'Just go with the scooter round the bends, don't fight it or
over-lean.'

'Just like riding a horse.'

'Exactly, you'll be a natural now you've managed to get on.'
The warm chuckle reverberated through them both and she
wondered if she should move back a bit. 'Here we go.' Too late.

He revved the engine and they were off, an involuntary squeak forcing its way out of Daisy. To hell with holding the bike, she was hanging on to him. Or his jacket. It was perfectly respectable, they were both fully clothed. Even if right now it felt as intimate as anything she'd ever experienced.

'Oh my God.' She squealed, and clung on tighter, as he sped up and started to weave his way through the traffic, but she knew that she had the same kind of grin plastered across her face as she did when she was galloping Barney across the fields. Literally plastered. It hadn't seemed windy until they started to pick up speed and she could see why he'd told her to put a scarf on.

At the traffic lights they trickled their way to the front, joined three others that were in pole position, and the moment the lights were on green, engines were revved and they all zoomed ahead, easily outpacing the cars. Daisy leaned forward, gripping tighter. Then, as the smell of his hair teased at her nostrils she sat back. She had to, or she'd be forgetting all her good intentions and trying to kiss him again.

Javier headed through the city, the traffic thinning slightly as the road began to climb. Their speed dropped as the scooter struggled up the increased incline and Daisy hung on, laughing. 'Are we going to make it?'

'I think you've been eating too many tapas.'

'Cheeky.' Even as she spoke, the road evened out and he pulled up. Daisy clambered off and pulled the helmet off her head, fluffing her hair out. She turned round as she did so, then stopped short. All her attention had been on the road ahead, but now she realised how high they'd climbed. 'Wow, look at that view.'

'You ain't seen nothing yet.'

'Where on earth are we?'

'We're where you get the best ever view of Barcelona. Keep going.' He took her hand as she looked doubtfully at the steps, steps that became an uneven path that he picked his way over like a mountain goat. 'Nearly there.'

173

And then they were. It was fantastic, a high point from where there was a 360-degree view of Barcelona. All of it.

'Oh my God, what is this place?' She didn't need Javier's urgings now as she let go of his hand and scrambled on. 'We're on top of the world.'

He laughed and climbed over a wall and railings on to a flat platform, with what she was sure was a sheer drop on the other side. 'It's a Barcelonian's secret, hardly any tourists come up here. I wanted to show you what it's like on a bright day so that you could get the full scale of the city, but it's fabulous at night. I'll bring you one evening. Climb over.' He held out a hand.

'Oh no, no way am I going over there. Railings are there for a reason. I don't do standing on the edge of high things.'

'Come on, trust me, crawl and I'll give you another history lesson.'

'I might be history if I do.' She muttered under her breath, but he heard and grinned.

'You don't have to.' His voice was lazy, but those amazing blue eyes were fixed on her. 'Not if you really don't want to, not if you're happy to miss the most amazing view of the city.'

She took his hand, still undecided, and the quake in her stomach could have been down to anticipation, fear, or those seductive circles he was making on her hand with his thumb. 'I want you to see this city the way I do.' Those blue eyes were a killer, irresistible and yet, when she looked into them, she knew she'd found somebody who believed in her. Who wanted to share something special with her. And how could she even think about saying no?

She wanted to see Barcelona through his eyes too, feel the same passion he had for the place. Share as much of his life with him as he wanted to offer. Which, okay, might not be that much, seeing as he was just being friendly and she was the one with the kissing-impulses. But she could cope with that. Couldn't she?

'But do it for you Daisy, not for me, not anybody else.'

It was as though they were the only two people there. Everything else had faded away and all she was aware of was him, of her own growing need to do this, to prove to herself she could. To experience something nobody else had ever offered her. He wasn't just showing her a view, he was giving her a glimpse of himself.

She couldn't help the nervous laugh, which she knew meant she was going to do this. She had to. Javier would look after her, and she was here as the new, brave Daisy – the one who dared to do things.

'Oh to hell with it, I do, but I might get all clingy.'

'I can cope with that.' He grinned.

'You might have to look the other way though, me clambering over this fence isn't going to be a pretty sight.'

'Promise I won't look.' He strode over to the edge confidently, sat down, his legs dangling over the edge.

'Okay, I'm coming.'

It was a bit like giving a nervous horse the confidence to jump a big hedge she thought, as she clutched the fence and did her best to clamber over. He'd told her she could do it, led the way, and then given her her own time and space to make the leap. And it was worth it. She could tell as she inched forwards towards him, even before she got to the edge.

He had a hand out, had her safe as she shuffled the last few inches. If she leant back and tried not to think about what was, or wasn't, under her feet, she knew it was worth it.

He grinned at her, shared the feeling of triumph, and she clung to his arm, feeling on top of the world in a way that wasn't just down to their height above sea level.

The view was stupendous. It was a clear day, and the whole city was laid out below them, but as much as that, she was aware of the man next to her. The man who seemed to be bewitching her even more than this beautiful city was. 'I think I need distracting. Talk to me.' Not that she'd be able to hear a word.

'We're at Turo de la Rovira, which used to be an anti-aircraft command post.' He waved back, behind them, but she daren't move a muscle. 'These gun platforms and bunkers were built in the Civil War, the bunkers were then used by squatters for a while but the place was tidied up before the 1992 Olympic Games.' He gave a wry smile. 'Lots of Barcelona was tidied up for the Games.'

'So the Olympics had a real impact?' She knew she sounded a bit wooden, but she was interested, despite herself. Maybe it was because she'd glued herself to his reassuringly firm body.

'Oh yes, it was more than just the stadium built on Montjuic, there was a massive investment. The Barcelona you're seeing is way different to before the Games.'

There was a slight note of censure in his voice she hadn't heard before. 'All good?'

'In the main.' He shrugged. 'Some parts of the city were pretty dire, and the whole pickpocketing and prostitute thing needed sorting, so all that was addressed.'

'But?'

'I guess some of the character of the place was lost as well, swept away because it was easiest, tidiest.'

'Somebody got carried away?' She sobered for a moment as she stared out over the city. Since she'd made the decision to come here, she'd felt like she might be getting carried away, swept along, caught up in the excitement, wondering where she was heading. She didn't want to lose any of the good things about her life, she didn't want to lose the real Daisy, but she didn't want to be stuck in a rut, never evolving.

'It's not always good to change just for the sake of it, is it?' He pulled his gaze back from the view and looked at her. 'It's knowing when to stop that's the important part. A few small changes can make such a difference, but you don't need to go too far.'

A tingle ran over her arms. 'I don't. I mean, they don't.'

'Nor do you, Daisy, some things are perfect just the way they are.'

For a moment she thought he was going to kiss her, hoped he was going to kiss her, as they sat perched on the edge of the world, where the opportunities to change seemed limitless. They stared at each other and Daisy wished she could read his mind.

'What would you change if you could?' She had to say something, anything, before she gave in to the urge and spoiled the moment.

His gaze never wavered. 'Right now I'd keep things exactly as they are.'

She wasn't sure what they were talking about now. The city, or being here together. A perfect moment, when she could lean in, touch him, kiss him, and probably ruin things for ever.

She swallowed. 'You love it here, don't you?'

'I do.' There was the slightest lift to the corner of his mouth. 'Faults and all. Barcelona had to change, and it has done, it still is – things evolve, don't they?'

'They do.'

'Sometimes it takes patience, and we never know quite what the future will look like.'

She hadn't a clue what her future looked like; wondered if he had any idea about his. Wondered what it would be like if the passion he had for all this, this place, was transferred to a person. To her. A shiver ran through her and she dragged her gaze away from his and stared out at the city, not wanting him to read her thoughts. A sudden pang of loss had hit her as they'd looked into each other's eyes, a regret that these desires he was stirring inside her were never going to be anything more – and she knew it would be written all over her face for him to see.

The more he showed her of himself, the more she knew she was falling for a man who she'd never even shared a proper kiss with.

He squeezed her hand. 'I like the old character best, and maybe I'm a bit of a country bumpkin myself.' Then he chuckled, leaned in closer, and the sound vibrated through her body. 'Though obviously not as much as you are.'

'Obviously. Tell me more about what they changed.' If she kept him here talking she could stretch this time out, make the moment last.

He shifted so that his arm was round her shoulder, his voice soft in her ear. 'The airport and railway system were redeveloped, the whole waterfront, beaches, marina – you name it,' he pointed as he spoke at the various landmarks that they could see from their vantage point, 'if it looks faintly modern then it was probably built or redeveloped back then. Bored yet?'

'Carry on.' The brief moment of sadness she'd felt was gradually slipping away as the facts brought a feeling of normality back. She should be happy, not sad, she was in a wonderful place with an amazing man.

'That's why we've got the mix we have here, Gaudi sitting next to something ultra-modern. Look,' he pointed towards the Sagrada Familia, 'when that was started in the 1880's it was a big plot of land, around 3 acres I think, hard to imagine open fields round it now, isn't it?'

'It's a shame really that you can only see it properly from up here.' Her body relaxed a bit, then tightened as her brain registered the smell of him, the fact they were so close. She tried to inch away to a respectable distance, but her body was refusing to co-operate.

'Well they are thinking about demolishing some of the buildings. Gaudi's vision was that there was space in front of the Glory Façade, which would be nice.'

'Space is always good. Though not necessarily under my feet.' Daisy looked at her legs dangling over the edge and felt herself leaning back in towards him, purely so she could listen to him, of course, and grab him if the earth suddenly moved. 'It must be incredible to have that kind of mind, you know, get that kind of vision.'

'A dream on a massive scale, eh?'

'Massive. My dreams are much smaller. I've got this list of things I really want to do, well I had Flo's list of places, and I had my kind of dream list of silly things—'

'Nothing is silly if it's what you want to do. One person's dream is building a cathedral, the next person's is conquering a fear, writing a poem, climbing a mountain, they're all equally valid.'

'Well this is silly stuff I'll never get round to, like riding in the Canadian Rockies.'

'Why won't you ever do it?' He smiled, a slow, dangerous smile. Well dangerous because it brought out his dimples, showed just a hint of white, even teeth and made her want to kiss him.

She shook her head. That thought really did need walloping on the head. He'd very politely pointed that out when she was on an adrenalin and perspiration-soaked high after her abortive jog. 'I'm never going to be able to save up that kind of money, it's just a dream.'

'Dreams are just realities that haven't happened yet.' He shrugged. 'You can make more or less anything happen if you want to.'

Easy for him to say. 'Well, anyway.' Get back onto safe ground, Daisy. 'I decided yesterday that I needed a new list, not like a sight-seeing one, but the things that really mean something to me, things I want. Like walking on the beach barefoot, and being a bit more daring.' Things that, deep down, meant something.

'You don't need a list, Daisy. Throw it away.' He was grinning, his eyes dancing. 'I dare you.' Okay, so he'd got a handle on her. 'Let go, surrender.' He was laughing now.

'To you? Never.' If she said it enough times she might believe it.

'Look,' he leant in a bit closer, so his shoulder nudged against hers and she couldn't avoid his mesmerising gaze. 'You don't need lists, it's all in your heart.' Oh God, he'd touched her chest, she'd forgotten how to breathe, 'what you really want to do. Need to do. Listen to it, trust it.'

She was holding her breath, everything tensed up.

'Just for a couple of weeks anyway. Let things happen.'

'But that's what I've done my whole life and I feel like I haven't done anything.'

'Of course you have, don't knock what you've got, Daisy.'

'So you're saying I should just be satisfied.' Like Jimmy. With Jimmy.

'That's not what I said, build on it, don't knock it. You've got a horse, dog, a great home, haven't you?'

'Yeah, but that just came to me, the cottage. I know I'm really lucky to have it,' she glanced up at him, 'really lucky, because it's wonderful, I couldn't hope for a better home, but I suppose having it stopped me making a decision to do anything different.'

'But you chose it.'

'It chose me. Well, it was this old woman in the village that Mum knew. She didn't have any relatives and she'd lived at Mere End Farm all her life, it was passed down to her. I think she was born there actually. I suppose most people used to be like that, they stayed in the same place, grew up, found work. Farming people did anyway. Not like now.'

'Lots of people in Barcelona have been here all their lives.'

'Mum used to pop in and drag us along. She'd take pies and casseroles, stuff like that, and Mrs Webster would let us pick the apples and other stuff from the garden. We lived on a farm, but I still liked going there. We used to say it was a ghost house, me and Em – my sister – would play hide and seek. The place was filled with antiques and old books and all the floorboards creaked.' She smiled to herself. They used to try and scare each other, and they used to try and find out if Mrs Webster was a witch. 'When she died she left Em some money, and me the house. It was Mum she was thanking though, not me,' she shrugged, 'I was just an annoying kid, but Mum looked out for her, chased away salesmen and stuff like that. She's kind.'

'That's where you get it from; the generous and kind nature.'

Daisy felt herself blush, so blustered on. 'If I hadn't got Mere End Cottage though, maybe I would have done more with my life. Been forced to do something.'

'Forced isn't good though, is it? You've chosen to do what you want to, Daisy, and that's good. Your life's fine, from what I can see – you just want a few exciting highlights.'

Highlights like having a gorgeous man like him in her life. Highlights like kissing him. What would he say if she told him that he was number one on her unwritten list of dreams? That she'd be quite happy to let go and surrender if he gave the slightest inkling that he could be part of her life. She shook her head to chase the thought away.

He'd hit the nail on the head though. She did love lots of things about her life, but she wanted to add experiences like this in. Raise her blood pressure – although maybe the way Javier was doing it for her wasn't exactly what she'd expected. Have some fun. Live a bit. 'I just wish I'd been brave enough to do things like this,' she waved an arm to encompass everything around them, 'before. I used to look at Mum when I was a teenager, you know, through those judgemental, know-it-all eyes, and pity her. All she did was look after the family – she never did anything for herself. My parents don't even go on proper holidays because of the farm, they can't get away, Dad doesn't care, but Mum sometimes talks about places as though she regrets not going, doing things. I don't want to get to her age and feel like that.'

'So she's always been on the farm?'

'Oh no, she used to have this high-flying job before she got married. She'd be in Paris one week, Madrid the next, at conferences and stuff and she lost it all.'

He put a hand on her knee. 'She chose to give it up, Daisy, like you're choosing to do something now.'

'I've only done it now though, because I'm cornered. My boyfriend proposed, it took that to make me realise... I'm not ready to get married. I don't think we're even suited.' There, it was out. She'd said it.

The words had never really formulated in her head before, and now they had it felt like a huge relief. They weren't suited. They wanted different things. Javier, a man she'd only just met, understood her far better than Jimmy ever had. Jimmy would never have cared enough to *not* kiss her, which was all a bit perverse because she really, really would have been happy for Javier to forget all about why this wasn't a good idea. Jimmy had just never 'got' her, they'd just been together, in parallel, their lives bumping every now and again.

'Ahh.' Javier's hand retreated, leaving a cold gap. 'What does he think?'

'He just wants an easy life.' She stared across at the Sagrada Familia – one person's vision. A big dream. 'I've tried to explain, but he won't listen.'

'Won't? Doesn't want to?'

She sighed. 'That's what I meant when I said the freedom had gone to my head, you know, getting away from the expectations, normal life, Jimmy.'

There was a pause. One of those long, pregnant pauses, the type that happened when you had verbal diarrhoea and told somebody you hardly knew all about your dreams, disappointments – and marriage plans. Or not.

'Normal is whatever you want it to be. A year ago my normal was white-water rafting and mountain-climbing, now it's tapas-and-wine tours. Slightly different danger levels.' He grinned, a lopsided grin showing a chipped tooth she hadn't noticed before.

'Oh gosh, I'm keeping you from work, I'm sorry. I mean, it's really good of you to spend all this time with me, but Flo shouldn't have asked.' She scrambled to her feet, then hastily took several steps back from the edge.

'Flo? This is nothing to do with Flo.' He was looking at her quizzically. 'What gave you that idea?'

182

'You did, you said at the meet-up…'

'That was just the meet-up, she didn't tell me to follow you round. Is that what you thought?'

'Well…'

'Nobody told me to keep an eye on you, Daisy. I'm sure you're more than capable of looking after yourself. I'm here because,' he shrugged, 'well, I want to be, I guess.'

'You guess?' She laughed.

'You're good company, and' his turn to pause, 'I haven't got anything better to do.'

'Touché. Ha-ha, thanks for that.'

'You're welcome. Ready to go?'

'Yep, then you can have the afternoon to do…'

'I wasn't planning on going back yet, I'm going to give you one of my tours.'

'Oh. Are you sure?'

'Stop asking. I wouldn't offer, and you can count it as work if it helps your conscience. I want to check out some new bars.'

Daisy stared at him and couldn't help the smile that started as a flutter somewhere in her chest then spread through her whole body. He was wonderful company, he'd been kind and generous, but all along she'd had this niggle at the back of her mind that even though he'd said he liked being with her, he was there out of a sense of duty.

'You're sure?' She had to be certain.

He shook his head and grinned. 'Do you honestly think I'd risk ruining my scooter engine taking you up that hill for any other reason than I really wanted to?'

Really wanted to. Daisy hugged the words to her, repeated them in her head, and was pretty sure she had a very stupid grin on her face.

***

183

'You can't believe how starving I am, are you sure they'll still be serving?' Daisy dived down the steps into the tiny corner bar and then stopped abruptly.

'Still serving?' Javier laughed. 'Lunch time starts at 2 p.m. in Spain – we're early.' He was right up behind her and side-stepped, putting an arm round her as he went so that they didn't collide. 'Sorry, is there something wrong?'

'It's lovely. Look!' She pointed up at the ceiling, 'that's amazing. It's made of bricks, isn't it?' It really was the cutest bar she'd ever been in, and she thought the El Xampanyet bar Flo had taken them to had been incredible. But this place was so welcoming, without the crowds of the cava bar, and was like stepping into the past. It was laid-back, a bit like the pubs at home.

'The volta catalana: it's the traditional ceiling here, wooden beams and bricks done in arches. It's been here a while, this place – one of my favourites.' Javier steered her towards a table.

'It's incredible, and what are those wooden cupboards?'

'Fridges.' He grinned. 'Old ones.'

'Look at all the wine, and those barrels.'

'It used to be a wine bodega years ago. Sit down, I'll get us a beer, unless you want cava?'

'Beer's fine. Oh wow! I want all that food.' Daisy stared at the tapas that were displayed behind the small bar and her stomach growled in sympathy.

'I'll get us an assortment, if that's okay? Some of the specialities?'

'Whatever you say, Mr wine-and-tapas, you're the expert.'

On her own she wouldn't have dared order half the food Javier picked out, as she hadn't got a clue what they were. Even the jamon, which she'd thought was ridiculously over-priced, was delicious.

'I can see why this is so popular.'

'You can spend a fortune on jamon, and it's one of those things you can't miss when you come to Spain. This is the best acorn-fed black pig.'

'So is this place on your list?' She smiled, 'you said you were doing research.'

'Well no, this is an old haunt,' he was sitting back in his chair, hair ruffled and looking totally at home, 'but I wanted to bring you here. I thought you'd like it.'

'I do.' And I like you, far too much, Daisy thought with a sigh.

***

'Jimmy, I think we need to call it off.' Well she didn't think, she knew, but she was trying to do this as gently as she could.

There was a clatter in the background. 'Hang on, let me bang this fence post in, bloody thing. What did you say?'

'I don't think we should get married.'

'Rubbish, damned thing,' was he talking to her or the post? 'You've just got cold feet. And anyhow, I've got the ring now.'

'I know, I'm sorry, but I can't—'

'You'll be fine when you get back home and back to normal. Bloody hell, I think I've hit a bleeding stone again.' He cursed a couple more times and Daisy cringed. 'This field is terrible.'

'Jimmy, can't you stop and talk to me?' It was the same as it always was, whether she was standing next to him, or miles away, he wasn't listening. He wasn't even missing her, not really.

'Some of us have got work to do, Daisy. We're not all living it up in Spain and it's getting dark. We can talk when you get back. You don't know what I've done with that new claw hammer I bought, do you?'

'No, sorry.'

'Right. It's not in your shed?'

'No, didn't you say you'd lost it?'

He never had been very good on the phone. Or talking.

Chapter 16 – Flo. Poetry and wine

Flo flung the bedroom curtains open and stretched. Then stopped, mid-way, her arms half in the air like a footballer supporter who thought there was going to be a goal then realised they looked a fool, and didn't know how to back down without being noticed.

She dropped her hands and rested them on the windowsill. Oh, my God, they had snow. Proper, white cover-everything snow.

Snow! Flo pressed her forehead to the cold pane of glass and grinned.

It hung like heavy icing from the shrubs and trees in the back garden, had gathered in a fluffy swathe in the edge of the chicken-coop roof and decorated the tops of the fence rails as though it had been carefully piped out.

On the other side of the fence there were a several large hoof-print shaped holes, scars across the perfect landscape. Barney was plodding his way hopefully from shelter to gate and back again, in search of food. He spotted her and stopped – gazing up at the window, his whiskers and eyebrows comically frosted.

The window had misted over and she wiped it with her sleeve, then flung it open and pushed her head through the small opening. There was an air of quiet expectancy, as though the countryside was waiting for something to happen, to break the spell. Flo took a deep breath and the cold air bit at her nostrils and throat, and the breath she breathed out hung for a moment before drifting away. She giggled. This was amazing. Magical. Exactly what she had really, really missed about Christmas back in Cheshire.

Barney whinnied, and downstairs Mabel barked in response. 'Okay, okay, let me get my clothes on and I'll be out to feed you.'

***

Mabel was standing with her nose pressed against the door handle, sniffing hard and whimpering in anticipation, as though the cold air that was finding a way in through the crack had told her that something exciting, something new, was out there. Her tail banged against the wall as Flo slipped her feet into the wellingtons and grabbed the key for the shed that served as a food store.

'Shall we go on an egg hunt, Mabel?' The dog whined and sat down, pawing at the door. 'You like snow?' Laughing, Flo opened the back door, Mabel shoving her nose into the gap as soon as there was one and forcing her way out first. 'You've no manners, you naughty girl.' She glanced up to see Hugo standing on the other side of the fence, which was wonderful and terrible all at once. She covered up the sudden, and totally unwelcome, rush of affection by saying the first thing that came into her head. 'Like somebody else I know.'

'That's rather unfair.'

'Totally justified – one doesn't lunge at ladies. Did your parents never teach you that?' Okay, he might have a point; it might not actually be totally fair. After all, he had shown just how wonderful he was with his horse yesterday. She'd seen a warm, very human, side to him that she'd never suspected existed and it had left her feeling totally confused. And he had apologised for being an idiot and trying to get her into bed. But it really didn't help her at all.

It had been a lot easier to fight him off when he'd been acting the womaniser he really was (even Daisy said he was, and she had to know him quite well), now he was just a very lethal combination. A very attractive, very smooth-talking, man with a heart. Who'd do an Oli on her if she let him get within a mile of her own, still slightly battered, one.

She'd gone to bed very late, after finding that pouring the fictional version of Hugo down on the page came remarkably easy, and then he'd somehow managed to creep into her dreams. Again. It really wasn't good, but as long as she could keep him between the fictional pages and sheets she'd be fine. The last thing she needed messing with her emotions right now was the real-life Hugo.

For a moment he looked cross, then he laughed. 'Some ladies like it, I had rather hoped you'd be one of them.'

'Well dream on, Hugo. I'm not Daisy you know.'

'Oh, I am well aware of that.' His lazy drawl was disgustingly dirty as his eyes roamed over her from head to toe, sending an equally disgusting image of him naked straight into her head. 'Daisy is sweet, kind, spends her life in wellingtons, and is totally devoted to her animals, and,' his gaze seemed to pause around chin level, then shifted up so he met her head-on, the pause was excruciating, 'I have absolutely no desire at all to sleep with her.'

'If the pipes weren't frozen I'd tip a bucket of cold water over you.' Then she'd run in for a cold shower herself.

He grinned. Wolfishly.

She shook her head, fighting the urge to nod or smile, which would encourage him and take them where she really wasn't prepared to go. 'No hope for you, is there? Poor Daisy.'

'What do you mean poor Daisy?'

'Well I get to escape you soon, she has to come back and live here next door to you.'

'What kind of books do you write? I'd rather imagine there's a girl who kicks ass in there, gets rid of your inner anger.'

'Stop being a pompous prick, Hugo, you haven't seen a half of my inner anger yet. But, for your information, right now I'm imagining the type of woman who would rather a man got off his arse and helped open the chicken coop instead of grilling her from the other side of the fence.'

'No ass-kicking?'

'In your dreams.' She laughed as Mabel, who had bounced up the path ahead pounced on some invisible prey in the snow and then snuffled her nose through it like a mini snowplough, until her whiskers and eyebrows were covered in a fluffy layer.

Following in the dog's rather large footsteps she slithered her way across the lawn, a tub of chicken feed in one hand, and a crowbar (the first thing she'd spotted in the shed) in the other – to break the ice on Barney's water bucket. Her phone rang.

'I could jump over the fence and rescue that from your pocket?'

She swung the crowbar that was dangling from her fingers from side to side, and narrowed her eyes at him.

'Maybe not.' But his gaze was still roaming over her body in a way that was very unsettling. It was making her feel all fidgety.

She opted to put the chicken feed down and answered the phone. 'Oh, that's a bit of a bugger.'

'Bad news?'

'My supermarket delivery might be a bit late; the van is waiting to be pulled out of the ditch it slid into.'

'Maybe the fruits of the countryside will provide.'

He was mad, slightly poetic, but crazy. Then she noticed he was staring pointedly over her left shoulder, so she swivelled round.

'Oh my God, what the hell?' There was something hanging from a hook at the side of the back door, and if she hadn't been so busy looking at snow, and Mabel, and Hugo, she might have noticed earlier.

'You've got a very limited vocabulary for a writer.' He was back to laughing at her again, which was something she'd hoped he'd stopped doing. 'A brace of pheasants. The shoot always leave us some – seems the food crisis is solved.'

'You are kidding? They've got feathers!'

'If Daisy was here she'd have them skinned and oven-ready by lunch time.'

'Well, I think we've already established I am *not* Daisy.'

'We certainly have.' The light was still shining in his grey eyes, but he didn't look quite so predatory now. 'I tell you what, I'll get off my arse as requested, clean them, and cook them for tea tonight.'

Mabel bounced back, her tail wagging. She'd snorted her way into making a nice oval, which was just dying for a snowman to be built in the middle of it. And she had the animals to feed. And she really would rather play with the snow than worry about food for tea.

'Deal, you can have them. Providing you help me get the eggs from under these bloody hens.'

He raised an eyebrow.

'Well you haven't got anything better to do, have you?' She could keep this up, she really could. Then he'd back off and she'd be safe from herself as well as him. Except he was making it pretty much impossible, the way he was hanging round, being helpful. Looking at her in a way that was making her all wriggly inside.

He sighed, rolled his eyes, and shook his head so that his blond hair flopped over his forehead and made him look rather boyishly attractive. Or rakish, yeah, rakish. Bad news. Bad for her.

'Bring back sweet little Daisy. Oh, and Flo?' That innocent look on his face meant trouble, she just knew it did. 'I didn't mean I wanted them, I meant I'd cook them for dinner for the two of us. I'll see you at 8 p.m.'

Oh God, now he was being nice again, cooking dinner for her? There was a lot, she decided, that could be said in favour of chastity belts and chaperones, as without either she was going to find resisting Hugo incredibly hard. Because deep inside she knew she didn't want to.

Well, she could pair the wellies with a dress, just to keep his mind on Daisy and off her body. It wasn't that he wasn't attractive, but if anything happened with Hugo she'd blame it on a massive big rebound from Oli. Another cad.

Okay, she'd be the one doing the leaving this time, but it still probably wouldn't do her much good, would it?

Mabel gave a single thump of her tail when she saw Flo, and stretched her legs out further, as though to say 'shift me if you can'.

'I'm only going next door, but you'd better stay here.' Another thump on the floor, and a groan. 'If you come with me, Hugo's terriers will be all over you and you won't get any peace.' Ha, what was it they said about dogs being like their masters? 'Be good.' She glanced round the kitchen, checking she hadn't let anything out, and then left, pulling the door shut behind her.

Hugo, it appeared, had cleared the pathway between her front door and his. Which was very gentlemanly, but knowing him it was because he expected her to have sexy high heels on.

'Oh you're here, good. I'll crack the bubbly open.'

'Why, what are we celebrating?'

'We need an occasion?' He raised an eyebrow, which she took to mean he liked to open champagne any day of the week.

'Well, it doesn't have to be anything big, how about because it snowed?'

'How about because it snowed us in together, and you're not Daisy?'

'You're terrible. Anyway we're not snowed in.'

'Nice thought though. Here you go.' He handed her a glass and lifted his, 'cheers.'

'Cheers. You wear a pinny well.' She grinned. It wasn't a chef's apron like you'd expect from Hugo, it was flowery, with a frill

191

around the edge. The faintest rose blush hit his face and he looked like a boy, caught out. 'I found it in the airing cupboard, I think my mother left it when she was here one time. I don't often cook to be honest.'

'This *is* going to be edible then?' He still managed to look masculine in floral. The broad shoulders and slim hips did that, she supposed. She had to stop staring – she really did have to stop staring.

'I know how to do a good pheasant casserole – even I can do that. Five minutes and I'll be with you, come in the kitchen or have a nosy around. It is rather a mess in the kitchen though,' he waved a dismissive hand, looking slightly perplexed, 'not quite sure how a meal for two can use up quite so many pans and knives.'

'No problem, I'll stay out of your way.' A safe distance. 'I'd rather nosy.'

'I thought you would.'

'Call it research.' Flo had always liked to watch people, and she liked to look at what they wore, what they owned, what they kept, and what they discarded. 'You've got a lot of books.' She raised her voice so he could hear her from the kitchen, where there was a rattling of pans and the sound of water. 'Did your mother leave these too?'

'What?' He was in the doorway, tea towel flung over his shoulder in a way that really shouldn't be sexy.

'George Bernard Shaw?' She held up the book and grinned. '*Man and Superman*?'

'*"The reasonable man adapts himself to the world: the unreasonable one persists in trying to adapt the world to himself. Therefore all progress depends on the unreasonable man.'* I like to think I'm the unreasonable man.' His eyes narrowed wolfishly.

'I can believe that.' She put the book back in its place, and ran a finger over the spines of the others. They were a total mix: old, modern, novels, non-fiction, poetry.

'My mother started reading to me before I was born and still persists in adding to my library. She says school was but the start of education.'

'And this? Is this helping your emotional education?' She held up the DVD. 'I wouldn't have put you down as a Richard Curtis fan, *Love Actually* eh?'

'You'd be surprised how much more affable girls are after watching that.' The drawl was back, full on arrogant Hugo mode.

'You're so obvious.'

'Well actually,' he shrugged sheepishly, 'that is one Daisy gave me for Christmas. She said I needed help.'

'I can imagine.' What had Daisy said about the constant stream of women doing the walk of shame past her window?

'I'm not a heathen you know. I did have the best schooling—'

'Money could buy?'

'That was available. My father had rather high expectations.' She could have sworn he looked suddenly uncomfortable. He flicked the tea towel down and back as though to dismiss a thought he wasn't happy about having. 'The dinner's ready, let's sit down.'

The dinner was amazingly nice, or she was just so starving that anything would have been good. No, that was wrong, it was more than just a simple casserole.

'This is fab.'

He raised his glass of wine to her, the sardonic smile she'd decided was his way of taking a compliment. Confident and arrogant he might be, but he didn't seem to know how to say thank you gracefully. 'If you live here it would be criminal not to be able to cook game.'

'So, what's in it? This is really scrummy, really, it is just so tasty, and the meat.' He'd jointed the birds, but the slightly gamey meat just fell of the bone the moment she touched it with her knife.

'Good rustic fayre they call it.' He raised an eyebrow.

'Apples, there's apple, so is there cider in it?' She closed her mouth let the flavour of the rich gravy play with her senses.

'Cider, a splash of Calvados, crème fraîche, onions, the normal stuff. You look happy.'

'Almost orgasmic.' She laughed, probably not the right way to keep him at arm's length, but it was good. She suddenly realised he was watching every move she made. Oh God, the last thing she was going to let him accuse her of was eating erotically. She had a carrot on her fork and decided it was a bad idea.

He chuckled. 'Happy and sexy, so at least I know home cooking is the way to your heart and not rom-coms.'

'I like rom-coms,' she swallowed and tried not to moan with appreciation. Now that would be misconstrued. '*When Harry met Sally* is one of my favourites.' Bad choice, but he'd probably never seen it.

'You can act it out for me later.'

Or maybe he had. 'I thought you were too busy to watch films? You know, playing with your horses.'

'I've watched a few.'

Ahh, yes, with his many conquests. The way into a girl's knickers...

'This is actually really tasty. I can't believe it's those poor birds that were hanging by my back porch.'

'It isn't actually. I had a brace a few days ago, so I used them, they'd had time to hang. I've put yours in the shed. I'll show you how to prepare them if you like and we can have a return match.'

'Pheasant showdown?'

'I must inform you, I play to win, always.' Why did that sound like a challenge that wasn't completely related to cooking?

'I don't have to sit for hours pulling feathers off?'

'I'll show you the cheats' way, no time for plucking, there are far more interesting things we could be doing.'

'You don't stop, do you?' She shook her head. Time to change the subject or she'd be the pudding. Unless that was all he'd got in mind anyway.

'I enjoy the chase.' He suddenly grinned, a proper grin that lit up his whole face. 'You haven't changed a bit, Florence Nightingale. Come on, I'll clear up later, let's sit and drink this wine somewhere more comfortable.'

They sat down in front of the roaring fire, and she nursed her glass of wine, staring into the flames for a while. 'You're wrong.'

'I am?'

'I have changed quite a lot.'

'Well, you're more sophisticated, more beautiful.' He was watching her intently, his gaze almost like a caress, and a shiver ran down her spine.

She tried not to squirm. 'I mean on the inside.'

He waited.

'I didn't quite realise how much until I got back here. I got bogged down in acting the part, having the perfect life, if you know what I mean.'

'Oh yes, I do, believe me.' His tone had a rueful edge, but he didn't add anything.

'I was the girl who had it all, and I wouldn't admit to myself that I didn't.' She turned the stem of the wine glass round in her fingers. 'I just did things,' she paused, 'this will sound dotty, but you know that saying about stopping to smell the roses? I haven't just stopped and thought for ages.'

'So that's why you've started to write?'

'Yep. All of a sudden I had ideas, I used to always dream about this book I wanted to write, but then we got too busy. And, like Oli said, it was daft wasting time on stuff like that when we could be making a living out of the magazine. I'd probably never get published anyway.'

'Oli?'

'He was my boyfriend.' How the hell had she ever thought he

195

could be more than that? 'It wasn't just his fault; it was mine. I just abandoned my own personal ambitions, concentrated on his. Anyhow, he was probably right in a way.'

'I doubt that. You never regret the things you tried and failed at, just the things you don't try.' The drawl had dropped to an intimate level. 'So what if you don't get published?' Hugo shrugged his broad shoulders. 'Do it, if that's what you want to do. You're a kick-ass kind of girl, Florence Nightingale, not a yes girl.'

'I'll kick your ass if you carry on calling me that. You put me off singing for life.' Flo knew she was hitting out, making a joke of it, because all of a sudden this conversation seemed far too personal, he was getting to her in a way Oli never had. She could never remember sitting and talking like this to the man she'd thought she'd wanted to marry.

Now she thought about it, Oli had never actually been interested in her dreams. Never encouraged her. It had all been about him. A future he'd planned out.

Hugo laughed. 'Well to be honest you were a bit of a wonky nightingale.'

She stood up abruptly to get away from the closeness that seemed to have crept up on them. Why the hell she'd started confiding in him, telling him stuff that should stay in her head, she wasn't sure. It must be the Calvados talking.

The bookshelves were far enough away for her to get a grip again. She pulled out a slim volume. 'Poetry, is that to woo the girls as well?'

'I'm willing to try anything. Will it work on you?'

Oh hell, he'd followed her.

She ignored the comment, slightly too aware of the heat of his body behind hers as she stood by the bookshelf.

'Robert Frost?'

'Ah yes, The Road Not Taken *Two roads diverged in a wood, and I –, I took the one less traveled by, And that has made all the difference.*"

'Quite a reader, aren't you?' She was surprised, but hoped he couldn't hear it in her voice because she wasn't having a go at him, and she hated it when people made generalisations.

'My mother and I had a game. If I was getting argumentative and wanted something I'd have to give her a quote to justify it. She was very well-read, but it got me actually picking the books up I suppose. I don't like to lose.'

'So what did you use that quote for?'

'To justify riding horses for a living rather than being a lawyer.'

'Ah. So you don't intend regretting things you never did.'

He was right at her shoulder now. His head close to hers as she studied the books. One arm had somehow slipped around her, the heat of his hand on her waist, his other hand reaching out to turn the pages. Effectively trapping her, moving in, and she wasn't sure if she wanted to resist this time. She realised she was holding her breath. Waiting to see what he did next. His nose was so close to her neck she could feel every breath he exhaled. If he kissed her now, right on the sensitive spot near her ear, she'd either have to kick him or keel over.

'So, er,' she wriggled away a bit, feeling faintly stupid as she shuffled her way up the bookcase, 'how are you going to justify cornering me?'

'Shall I compare thee to a summer's day?'

'That's just so unimaginative, Hugo, you'll have to do better than Shakespeare.'

'You *are* demanding.' He gave a short laugh. 'I said you hadn't changed. Just like the girl that used to ride Billy's horses.' He slid a hand under her hair, the warmth of his palm against her skin, and she flinched, practically jumping her way along now.

'You're being lazy,' her vocal chords were doing quivery, weird things, 'and that's cheating. It's not a reason.'

'I'm realistic and just want to get you into bed.'

His thumb pressed gently against her neck, then he lifted her hair, leant in and kissed her.

Turning to look at him was just a natural reaction. As was lifting her face to meet that grey gaze. And parting her lips, and not daring to breathe as his mouth came down on hers.

It was the gentlest touch at first, a caress as his mouth teased her lips. She could taste the sweetness of cider, the fruit of the wine. Then all she could taste was him as the pressure intensified and he ran his tongue over the edge of her teeth. His fingers played at the nape of her neck and her insides started to curl up, heat spreading down between her legs. She edged forward, her hip against his as he turned her so that she could feel the length of his body. The unmistakable erection.

She could do this. She wanted to do this. They were two consenting adults having a bit of fun.

No she couldn't. She was an idiot. He'd wooed her with his bloody cooking and a few choice lines from a poem.

It didn't matter. It did. She was going to choose what she did next and when. If she didn't do this now, it would be too late.

'No.' She pulled back. Put a hand between them on his chest, softened her voice, even though her pulse was doing a staccato beat and making her light-headed. Calm. 'No, Hugo.' Okay, maybe not soft, maybe shaky. 'I think it's time I went back to my, er, Daisy's place.'

He dropped his hold immediately, the expression on his face pretty unreadable, apart from the twist to his mouth.

'Whatever you want. I'm not in the habit of forcing my attentions on anybody, I've never had to. I suppose,' he looked at his watch, 'it's late and you'll be ready for your own bed now if you don't want mine.'

Chapter 17 – Daisy. Handbags and hippy cats

Daisy stared at the shoes in the little boutique window. She'd never really been one for window-shopping, but the shops around the El Born area of Barcelona drew her in.

One clothes shops was full of nick-nacks – old sewing machines, shaving kits and gramophone players scattered in between neat piles of sweaters and carefully folded socks. Another had a stuffed fox in the window – she daren't go in to see what else the taxidermist had been up to. The jewellery shop had a small hatch at the back, through which you could see the artist's carefully crafted silver rings and she'd even discovered a guitar workshop down one of the back streets, with instruments at various stages of manufacture scattered around and the smell of sawdust hanging in the air.

And then there were the handbag and shoe shops. Felt and suede bags hung up in a range of colours that put nature to shame, with samples so that you could pick the patchwork of your choice. And leather. She loved the smell of leather, and just walking round the shops made her feel at home.

She took another look at the shoes.

They were totally impractical of course. Unless you lived in

Barcelona, but she couldn't help look and was more than a little tempted to try them on. Or she could have coffee and cake at a nearby café. Or she could do both.

The impatient beep of her phone, announcing an incoming text, saved her from a crisis.

'*How are you doing?*'

She couldn't help the little lurch of happiness inside that brought a grin to her face. She hadn't seen Javier since he'd taken her out on his scooter, and she'd missed him. '*Fine thanks, rescue me from these handbags and shoes.*'

'*???*'

'*They're seducing me*'

'*Fancy a trip to see a hippy cat commune?*'

It was her turn to wonder what the hell he was on about. '*Hippy cats?*'

'*Meet me at the metro station in an hour.*'

***

The sun was shining by the time they got off the train at the small station of Montgat Nord. Right next to the sea. Daisy grinned. It was perfect.

'Do I get to go in the sea this time?'

'Sure.' He laughed, his blue eyes as gorgeous as any ocean, and Daisy had a sudden urge to throw her arms around him and squeal. Spending time with Javier was like having all your birthdays at once; good birthdays when you got the presents you really wanted instead of the things other people thought you should want. 'Come on, there's an underpass here so we can get to the other side of the railway line. I promised you a beach the other day, so here it is.'

'Race you.' She ran, galloping down the stairs to put a distance between her and her silly ideas, and he chased after her.

'You're crazy.' He was laughing, his blue eyes sparkling.

'Look at it, it's amazing.' And so are you, she wanted to add, but didn't. She waved her arm, then span around.

They'd emerged from the tunnel under the railway line, straight onto the sand. Pulling her shoes and socks off, she curled her toes into the soft, warm sand.

The beach by the station was deserted; a golden blanket that stretched as far as she could see.

'Barcelona.' She turned back to see Javier pointing back the way the train had come. 'The coast curls round so you can see the city from here.'

'I'm not interested in the city, I want the sea.' She giggled.

'You're like a big kid.'

'That's how I feel.' She did, mad, crazy, free. 'Come on, let's walk along the edge so I can paddle.'

The sea was icy cold and Daisy stood for a while letting her feet get used to it. The water lapped around her ankles and she looked out to sea, suddenly sobering.

Standing in a place like this, seeing the amazing colours she never saw at home, gazing at a landscape that stretched on for ever was what she'd dreamed of. And Javier had given it to her – as though he understood. How could it have taken her so long to do this, to book a plane ticket, explore the world? She'd been so close to missing out on it all, never setting foot outside her safe little world. She swallowed down the silly lump in her throat and concentrated on the water.

It really was the most incredible shade of emerald green against the white-gold of the sand, and then, as the sand dropped away sharply, it turned to a deep, deep, blue, mottled with light and dark and broken by the lines of surf that advanced towards them. 'You can see why people call them white horses, can't you?'

The sunlight flickered off the surface of the water, a million tiny shimmering lights that danced as the surface constantly shifted. 'The sky is so blue here, we just don't get this at home.

Well maybe in the summer on the odd day – it's just so clear.' She twisted round to smile at him. 'Thanks for bringing me, I'd have never found this place without you. It's fantastic.' And she wouldn't. She wouldn't have come here without him, and it wouldn't have been the same on her own anyway.

She took another step and slithered down the bank, and would have ended up on her bottom if Javier hadn't caught her elbow. She turned, laughing, her feet sinking deeper into the damp sand, her hand on his chest to steady herself – and looked up.

Talk about serious. He was giving her the strangest, searching look. A look that sent a giddy feeling of anticipation swirling in her stomach. She felt her fingers curl against the warm, solid wall of his chest, but all she was really aware of was the look in his eyes. She was holding her breath, she didn't know why. She wanted to say something, but she was afraid that whatever she said would be wrong.

'It is fantastic.' The syrupy warm voice blocked out the sound of the sea, the birds. Everything. He was still looking straight at her and her stomach was slipping away faster than the sand beneath her feet.

He reached up, brushed a strand of hair back from her face. Still not smiling.

She opened her mouth to say something, anything.

Then the corner of his mouth tipped up, and he glanced away. Took half a step back so that the contact between them was lost. He casually put his hand back in his pocket. Cleared his throat. 'The sand drops away quite quickly, it's difficult to walk along the shoreline unless you don't mind getting wet.'

Daisy searched his face, but she could have imagined he'd ever been looking at her in the way he had. 'I don't mind.' She swallowed, the words sounding strange and distant even to her own ears.

He grinned. 'No you don't, do you?' And the moment had gone, the relaxed Javier back. 'Come on.'

He hauled her back up the small bank as though nothing had ever happened and Daisy fell into step with him. Okay, so there had been a moment there. She had definitely not imagined that. When she'd last seen him and he'd insisted he did really want to be with her it had left her feeling stupidly happy, optimistic in a way she couldn't remember ever feeling. Even if he didn't want to *be* with her in *that* way, he was still spending time with her because he wanted to, not out of some sense of duty. But now her stomach was doing little flips in a way that was leaving her feeling all jittery and she knew that when she went back to Tippermere, the sights and sounds might fade in her memory, but the time she'd spent with this man would have left a mark on her for ever.

They walked in companionable silence. Near enough to touch hands. But they didn't. The only thing missing was a dog.

'You should have brought Poppy.'

'She doesn't approve of the cats.'

'What cats?'

'Come on, it's not far but we need to go back up on the path.' He held out a hand as they reached the steps and she took it. After all, if Flo or Anna had done the same she wouldn't have hesitated, would she?

They walked alongside the railway track, until it snaked its way into a tunnel, and the path meandered its way round the large rocky outcrop. On the right of them was the huge mound, through which the trains continued their journey, and on the left the beach – which ended abruptly in a pile of roughly hewn rocks.

'There's a cat over there.' Daisy screwed up her eyes at the unmistakable outline of a cat sitting on the top of the rocks, and as her eyes adjusted she picked out a second, and a third.

'It's like a cat commune.'

'Hippy cats. Oh my God, look at them sunbathing!'

He laughed at her reaction. 'There's more over there.' His eyes gleamed, the wrinkles fanning out, his full mouth smiling broadly as he gestured towards the mound. 'I haven't a clue how they all came to live here, I guess there were one or two strays and they just multiplied.'

'Well I suppose there's plenty of shelter.' Between the rocks, Daisy was sure she spotted a tail, then another cat disappeared down a crack.

'And people feed them. They've got all they need,' he gave her a sidelong look, 'and freedom.'

She laughed. 'I hope you're not suggesting I come and live down here to get the full hands-on experience.'

'You'd probably get fleas.'

They sat down on one of the rocks and Daisy watched the cats potter around, some stretched out on the rocks soaking up the winter sunshine, others stalking pigeons with a casual carelessness that had to mean they weren't hungry.

'Not a bad life though, apart from the fleas.'

'A bit like mine used to be. Living on rocks. Shall we make a move?'

She gave him a sideways look, unwilling to let him just skip over the comment. He seemed to be so good at finding out about her, and she seemed to know so little about him. 'You're a bit of a free spirit at heart, aren't you?'

'A nomad.' He grinned, then it faded. 'But we all have to grow up at some point.'

'Do we?'

His smile was slightly twisted, he was staring beyond the rocks, at something only he could see. 'You get older, there's family, responsibilities. You know how it goes.'

'And give up white-water rafting and danger?'

'There's other people who rely on you as you get older, aren't there? When Mum died it was a bit of a wake-up call, but it didn't really stop me, I didn't give up. But then my sister's husband died and it hit home; she needed me to still be around. Risking my neck was wrong.'

'God, I'm so sorry, Javier. My dad used to say I was born with an old head, I seem to be doing my selfish bit now.'

'I guess I was very selfish when I was young, like most of us are. But you aren't being selfish, Daisy. You're not letting anybody down.' He sighed, then seemed to dismiss whatever thought had been on his mind and she had a feeling it was better not to press him. 'Come on, it's too beautiful a day to get all serious.'

They made a move, wandered along the coast up towards the next railway station. Apart for the occasional jogger, and one or two people walking dogs, they didn't see anybody.

'It's lovely and quiet isn't it? Hard to believe we're so close to a city.'

'Barcelona is like that. Come up the coast a few miles and it's nearly all locals, or even if you just head up to Montjuic or around Tibidabo you can find some peace and quiet.'

'And space – all this open space, blue sky, and just the sound of birds and the waves rolling in.'

'Soul food. Which,' he glanced at his watch, 'speaking of food, I'm surprised you've not demanded any yet.'

'I was too busy paddling.'

'We can have tapas at Badalona, or head back? I'm afraid I've got work this afternoon,' he gave a broad smile, then winked, 'paying customers, so I'll have to love you and leave you, but I can take you up in the hills to get a night-time view of the city from above if you like? Later?'

***

Daisy still hadn't quite mastered the getting-on-and-off-the-scooter thing, especially in heels, but it was easier second time around. And she knew how to wrap her scarf round properly.

'I'm impressed.' Javier started up the engine. 'I did think about going up to the Battery again, but it's a bit cold up there. This place will be better and the view is nearly as good.'

'And this place is?'

'The Tibidabo mountain, we're not going to the top but to a café in the square just below. Hang on tight.'

She did. Well to his pockets, because wrapping her arms round seemed a bit forward, and dangerous at a hormonal level, and most people riding pillion on a scooter seemed very cool and casual about it. She'd even seen one reading a map. But it was nice with the heat of his body in front of hers, and her head tucked in so that she didn't get quite so windblown.

'I'm used to helmet head with my riding hat,' she pulled the helmet off and handed it over so he could stow it in the back-box, 'but with this all my hair gets tangled too. Look it's gone all into ringlets.'

He wound one round his finger, then shook his head and gave a rueful smile that she couldn't work out. Maybe he didn't like curls. 'Coffee time.'

The café didn't look much from the outside, but once they stepped in, Daisy could see the attraction. It was fairly quiet, so they managed to grab a table by the front window.

'Wow, that is some amazing view.'

He sat down next to her and ordered the drinks. 'We're not quite as high up as last time, but it isn't bad, is it?'

'You can even see the planes going into the airport.' It was like a giant jigsaw puzzle, the criss-cross of streets leading out to the sea in one direction, and across the city to the hills in the other. All lit up. 'It is so pretty.'

Out of the corner of her eye she could see he was studying her intently in a slightly unnerving way, then he put his coffee cup down. 'It is pretty. Amazing. Like you.' And he kissed her. She was pretty sure he hadn't been aiming for her cheek and missed, this one seemed on target. Like he meant it. The taste of coffee teased her nostrils, mixed with the musky scent she'd become accustomed to. He didn't touch her. Didn't reach out. He just leaned in and let his lips make contact with hers. And something inside her melted, all gooey, swirling round. She closed her eyes, felt her lips tremble beneath his. Wanted more, and just as she felt herself falling closer he drew back, wound one of her ringlets round his finger and studied it for a moment before looking up.

'I wanted to do that on the beach.' An unfamiliar note of uncertainty had crept into his voice. 'I wish you were here a bit longer.'

'Me too.' That came out a bit squeaky, like she was being strangled rather than, well, caressed. He stroked down her cheek gently with his thumb. Then picked his cup up again and watched her over the brim. Serious for once. She cleared her throat and tried again. 'I wish I could stay for longer. The time's whizzing by far too quickly.'

'Do you think you'll come back? If you could make it next year... I could show you what springtime is like in Barcelona.'

'I don't know. I er, well it's difficult with all my commitments, the animals and my work, and I'm pretty broke really, and...' no Jimmy wasn't a problem, she wasn't about to add that. She knew. She'd known, she supposed, from the very moment he proposed, that it wasn't right. She didn't want to hurt him, but she wasn't going to send a Dear John. Needed to explain to him that it was over, that his dad wasn't going to get grandkids any day soon. 'I would like to though.' She really would. Leaving Barcelona, leaving Javier would be like leaving a part of her behind. She'd never thought that any place could feel more special than her home did. She had thought this trip would be a break that would be entertaining, fun, a collection of memories that would fade like snapshots over time. Now she wasn't sure. Whatever happened next, whether she came back or not, this journey had changed her forever. Javier had changed her. 'One day.'

'So that's a no, not really, then.' His grin was slightly strained as he stood up. 'I will miss you.'

Daisy looked up, startled at his words, the tone of his voice.

'I wish I could, but I can't follow you back, Daisy, that's why I've been trying to stop this—' he gestured between them, 'happening. I can't do it, I'm not free to do what I want these days. If we'd met a couple of years ago it would have been different, but,' he shrugged, 'I can't just abandon my sister and I don't even know how long she'll need me here for. I shouldn't have kissed you, I'm sorry.'

'Javier I—' She paused, not sure what she was going to say. 'I'll miss you too, but I've not gone yet.' It sounded lame, she wasn't saying any of the things she wanted to say. Like how much she'd really miss this place, and him. Oh yes, definitely him. 'I'm not sorry you did it.' It came out all small and soft, but she was pretty sure he'd heard.

He gave a wry smile. 'Drink up. We'd better get back.' His tone was flat and she didn't know how to respond. 'We'll drive through the centre so that you can see the Christmas lights in style. It's an experience you really shouldn't miss.' The unspoken 'in case you never come back' hung between them.

It was a sight she was glad she hadn't missed, even though it felt bitter-sweet now. They streaked along the main roads and zig-zagged along the minor ones, in and out of the traffic. Each area had a different style of lights strung across the streets – some colourful, some twinkly silver-blue, some flamboyant, some subdued.

The cool air made her eyes water, the wind tugged at her hair, and she leant into his warm, lean body not sure how she felt about that gentle lingering kiss. How she felt about this reserved, warm-hearted man who managed to stir her up even when he was keeping his distance. Why the way he'd stopped so abruptly and decided to head back had brought a pain to her chest.

He didn't say another word all the way down, until he pulled the scooter up right outside her door. He didn't turn the engine off.

'Thanks, it was lovely.' She handed the helmet over and he took it, his fingers just brushing hers ever so slightly, but still sending a flutter of butterflies to the pit of her stomach.

'You're welcome. I'm afraid I've got stuff on tomorrow.'

'That's fine, don't worry, there are loads of things…'

'You could get a train up to Sitges if you're feeling adventurous. There's a beach, lots of cafés and quaint streets in the old part.'

'Sure.'

'The trains go from the main station across the road. Or catch the bus up to Montjuic; it's great up there, lovely gardens.'

'I'll find something to do.' It wouldn't be the same without him though.

'You'll be okay?' He was looking at her as though he didn't want to go, and she really wanted to reach out, kiss him again.

'I'll be fine.'

'You're sure?' He hesitated, still astride the scooter.

'Positive.'

He leant across and kissed her cheek. 'Goodnight then, Daisy.'

'Night, and thanks again.' She watched him speed off, then pushed the old iron door shut behind her and started to walk slowly up the stairs, her hand up to her face, covering the spot where his lips had been.

She couldn't get involved, she still wasn't uninvolved, and she couldn't promise to come back soon, however much she'd like to. She had a home she loved, things she had to do. And he had his own responsibilities, duties, and she knew all about having those. It had been her sense of duty to the life she had that had stopped her exploring, tasting life.

Falling for Javier had been easy because of the man he was, his passion, the way he cared. And he cared for his sister, and needed to be here for her. Which meant he couldn't be anywhere else. It all made sense, perfect logical sense, but Daisy wasn't sure she was quite as keen on logic as she had been.

She sighed. She really was daft. Falling in love with a city was one thing, but falling for a man who kept telling her he couldn't get involved was something she hadn't bargained on at all.

Chapter 18 – Flo. Living the other dream

Flo didn't quite know what to make of the invitation he'd thrown her way.

'You said you wanted to come back and experience the whole Tippermere thing again, so you can't leave without going to the annual charity bash at Tipping House.'

'Well I've never been before.' She hadn't. 'I didn't mix with the posh people like you do.'

'They're not posh – for heaven's sake, Billy Brinkley will probably be there.'

'That's posh where I come from.' Olympic-medal-winning riders, the local huntsmen, footballers' wives (and of course the footballers) from Kitterly Heath. 'They're not really my kind—'

'Nonsense. You'll love it – it's a right piss-up.'

'I won't know what to say to anybody.' She'd be star-struck – they'd all look at her like she was an interloper.

'Now who'd have thought little Miss Nightingale would get cold feet?'

'I warned you about calling me that!'

'You'll be off home soon, so why not try it?' He paused. 'You'd be doing me a favour actually. I keep getting text messages from women, with heavy hints.'

'And you expect me to feel sorry for you? You bring it on yourself.'

'I know,' he shrugged, 'but I don't want to take any of them along, I want to take you.'

For a moment his grey eyes looked completely serious, then the twitch of his mouth was back. 'You're more fun, more of a challenge.'

She'd ignore that one. But, he was right. She'd have to leave all this behind again soon – and at one time she would have killed for an invite to *the* social event of Tippermere's calendar. 'I would like to see inside Tipping House, I suppose.'

'Good, because I RSVP'd last night after you gave me the cold shoulder. You don't think I've given up that easily, do you?' The grin was pure wolf. 'I'll run you into Kitterly to get a frock.'

***

The snow crunched under their feet, already succumbing to the cold night air, as Flo and Hugo walked down the path. It would be like an ice rink by the time they got back, which wasn't a good thought.

He caught her elbow as one heel slipped. 'Is this part of your evil plan then?'

'Of course.' The grin was broad as he inclined his head towards hers so that she got a whiff of expensive aftershave. It had to be expensive because it was kind of not there, but it was. A delicious aroma that made you want to breathe it in, but then you needed more. Rather than the cheap type that caught in the back of your throat and made you gag. 'I had to get you out of those wellingtons somehow.'

She pulled her jacket closer and hoped she wasn't overdressed. She'd fallen in love with the strappy sandals and not thought about the practicalities of the heels in a snowdrift, but the dress had been very much on the 'would look fab on somebody else' list – until the owner of the boutique had found out where she was going and insisted she try it on. It did look good. Very good.

'I hope I'm not overdressed.'

'Darling, you cannot be overdressed at this function.' He put his best upper-class drawl on. 'It's impossible with some of the totty that turns up.'

'Totty isn't a very nice word.'

'Have you any idea the lengths some of the girls go to so they get an invite? Nobody is going to take a dog.'

'Poor Mabel.'

He looked at her through lazy, hooded eyes. 'You're funny.'

'I have never ever spent this much money on a dress and pair of shoes.' She hadn't, despite being wined and dined in some very exclusive Barcelona nightspots and restaurants. 'I feel like it's not me, somebody else.'

'Well pretend you're a famous novelist, I'll introduce you as one.'

'Don't you dare. If you tell anybody I'm writing a book I will tell them all about your melodramatics over a bit of smoke.'

'I'll do it next year then.' He gave her a sideways look. 'I'm sure lots of them will remember you anyway. I did.'

'I told you, they don't know me.'

'Billy does, and I bet you've met his daughter, Lottie. Here we go.'

He opened the car door and Flo wondered just how the hell she was supposed to get into the four-by-four in this dress without causing a split that wasn't supposed to be there.

'I'll give you a boost from behind.'

'You touch my behind, Hugo James, and your days of shagging your way through Cheshire will be well and truly over.'

'I do not shag my way through Cheshire. Whatever gave you that idea?'

'You did. Go and get in the driver's side.' Flo took a deep breath and decided there was no other way. She launched herself into the large four-by-four with her eyes closed, hoping against hope there was no sound of ripping, and wondering whether she really had lost her marbles when she got dangerously close to landing head first in his groin.

It was breathtaking. The moment they walked from the imposing stone steps into the entrance hall Flo felt like she'd been hit in the gut. The hall was massive, wood-panelled and decked out with the most amazing Christmas decorations, just like the glossies had told her a stately home should be – but she hadn't dared hope this would live up to, and surpass, her expectations.

The sweet smell of vanilla mingled with the earthy tone of pine cones and warm note of cinnamon so that all her senses were being teased at once. The large staircase was as wide as the cottage living room, and she nearly cricked her neck when she looked up at the high ceiling to examine the chandelier to beat all chandeliers.

'Can I take your coat?' She hardly noticed who had asked her as she slipped off her jacket, her gaze taking in her surroundings.

'You look amazing.' The whisper in her ear brought her back to her senses, and a rash of goose bumps down her arms. She shrugged her shoulders up in self-defence. 'Although the hay in your hair rather detracts.'

'Hay? Get it out!'

'Kidding.'

She frowned at him.

'You said not to touch,' he held both hands up in mock surrender, 'well I have to get your attention somehow.'

'Childish.'

'I can be very grown up if only you'd let me. Here, have some champagne and I'll introduce you to a few people.' He rested his hand in the small of her back, the naked small of her back. Oh hell, this dress really was a mistake. From the front it looked rather demure, well the neckline did, although the way it clung to her body like a wetsuit, it wasn't exactly wallflower wear. But the trouble really started at the back, where it plunged down nearly to her bottom. Leaving any onlookers in no doubt at all about whether her tan was an all-over one or not.

'Well, well, if it isn't the Nightingale, who'd have thought you'd be here?' There was a loud and unmistakable guffaw that took Flo straight back to being a teenager, and she turned round to see the slightly more portly but recognisable figure of Billy Brinkley. 'Never thought I'd see you two on friendly terms.' He laughed. 'Where did you find her, Hugo?'

'Breaking into my house.' Hugo put on his best upper-class drawl, which sounded even posher against Billy's gruff tone.

'That isn't fair, I wasn't…' She glared at Hugo, completely forgetting to be in awe of her surroundings and he grinned wolfishly back, suggesting he knew exactly what he was doing. He winked.

'You want to watch him, love. Hasn't changed a bit from the days when he used to be on my yard distracting the grooms. You did well to ignore him.'

'Hugo, Hugo!'

He nodded as the excited squeal echoed across the room, as though that proved his point. 'Bit old for your tastes that one, isn't she?'

'Oh shit, it's bloody Lucinda.' Hugo rolled his eyes and Billy chuckled as a middle-aged blonde, waving fingers that were weighed down with what just had to be real diamonds, made a beeline for them.

'This is your bloody fault, Brinkley, it was you who told her I'd give her daughter riding lessons, wasn't it?'

'Well I couldn't be arsed trying to work out how to explain she'd got as much chance of riding internationally as she had of being a page-three girl.'

'They don't do that these days, do they?' Flo frowned.

'Maybe not, love, but with her flat chest the odds would have been the same if they did. Come on, let's leave the charmer to wriggle his way out of that one. Lottie will be thrilled to see you.'

'It's a set-up.' Hugo seemed to be looking for an escape route, but Billy had wrapped an arm round her waist and was already steering her away. Flo glanced back at Hugo. He put on a 'help me' face that made her grin and shrug her shoulders in a 'what can I do?' gesture.

Lottie did seem pleased to see her. 'You're not really going out with Hugo, are you?'

Flo laughed. 'No, who said that?'

'Well, he just kind of suggested...'

'I'm staying next door to him, at Daisy's.'

'Ahh. I did wonder, I mean you weren't one of his groupies, were you?' She didn't stop for an answer. 'He is cute though, isn't he?'

'Cute?' Flo glanced across the room at where Hugo was nursing a glass of what looked like whisky. He was nodding in agreement with the man next to him, but seemed to sense the second she was looking his way, and smiled back. Cute wasn't a word she'd ever associated with him.

Lottie nodded vigorously. 'Well yes, cute. He's got this kind of, 'I want somebody to look after me' side. It makes you want to cuddle him.'

'You're potty, darling.' Rory, who Flo vaguely remembered, wrapped his arm round Lottie's waist. 'He isn't one of your bloody spaniels.' He kissed her affectionately. 'So don't you ever dare try to cuddle him!'

Lottie giggled and kissed him on the cheek. 'I've got you to do that to. But he is rather dashing as well, isn't he?'

Rory rolled his eyes. 'I'm off to find a proper drink and talk about something sensible.'

Flo took a sip of the bubbly and hoped she'd spot some food

soon or she'd be too drunk to fend off Mr Dashing. 'I think he brought me for protection, he said one or two other girls were expecting invites?'

'Well he does flirt rather, lead them on.' Lottie grabbed a canapé from a passing tray, and a bottle of champagne. She looked at Flo apologetically as she topped up her glass. 'Last year he brought two girls, which raised a few eyebrows. Sorry, I didn't mean, he's just…'

'Oh I know what he's like.' Flo smiled back and dared to peek over her glass at the man they were talking about. She'd begun to wonder if she did actually know what he was like, if anybody did. He was busy circulating on the other side of the room, but her eyes instantly picked his athletic figure out. And he did, as Lottie had said, look rather dashing. Definitely more dashing than cute.

'He does seem to have eyes only for you tonight, though.' Lottie had her head on one side and was watching him carefully, her eyes twinkling with laughter.

'Sorry?'

She grinned. 'He's watching your every move.'

'He's not.' Flo looked again, shockingly aware of exactly where he was in the room. 'Well if he is, it's only because he's checking I'm okay. I was worried I wouldn't know anybody.'

The other girl chuckled, a lighter version of Billy's hearty laugh, then linked her arm through Flo's. 'Oh really? Come and meet Xander – now he really is gorgeous. If you don't remember him I'll be shocked.'

Flo didn't recognise Xander, but she could see why Lottie had him down as memorable. 'Look after Flo and tell her about the first time you got on a horse while I go to the loo – won't be a minute.'

He leaned in, so that she could hear his soft voice above the excited chatter and music, and he reminded her a bit of her friend Javier in Barcelona. Slightly brooding and serious, but sincere and gentle.

'Enjoying yourself?' The soft drawl on her other side brought a smile to her face, and she turned to find herself face to face with a rather serious Hugo.

'I am. It's fabulous – thank you so much for bringing me.' She leaned forward impulsively and kissed him on the cheek. 'Do you know Xander?'

Hugo nodded. 'I do. So do you, by the look of things.'

'You can't have her back yet, Hugo.' Lottie had reappeared and very skilfully took Hugo by the elbow. She grinned. 'Not jealous, are you?' Then before he had a chance to reply she stepped between him and Flo. 'Tab wants to talk to you, and she said you absolutely promised you'd dance with her.'

'But I promised Flo…'

'She's having lots of fun without you – go on, shoo, go away.'

Flo found that it was strange to discover just how many people she did know in the village. She supposed she'd assumed that most of them had moved on, like she had, or wouldn't recognise her, or be too posh. But she'd been wrong. She was whisked from group to group, with introductions made and laughter as they realised who she was and quizzed her about Spain.

She would quite liked to have talked to Hugo, but Lottie seemed intent on ensuring she'd spoken to everybody at the party, and it probably was for the best. She'd not had chance to see Hugo dressed up before, and he really was indecently good looking. Which just had to be bad for her good intentions of not getting involved with anybody.

At every turn somebody seemed to be topping up her glass of bubbly, and she wasn't sure if it was that or the laughter that was making her feel a bit light-headed. The one thing she was sure of though, was that every time she glanced up, it was to see the reassuring figure of Hugo. Watching her. His gaze hooded, a slight lift to the corner of his mouth.

After chatting to a rather dishy polo player and his wife about the best restaurants in Barcelona, she was shocked to catch sight of the clock and see just how late it was. The evening had whizzed by, she was high on champagne and very little food, and her feet ached from being in high heels for so long. Murmuring an excuse, she dived off to find the washroom and check out if she really was as flushed and giddy as she felt.

'Dance?'

It was Hugo, catching her as she wandered back into the main hall, wondering if she dared take her shoes off. 'I'm not sure I can in these shoes.'

'You can lean against me.' He quirked an eyebrow.

She did actually want to dance; she loved dancing and it would be somehow liberating after all the talking to strangers, and explaining where she was staying and why.

She thought she'd got used to the feel of his hand on her back, against her skin, but it was different when she was turned to face him, when the hand wasn't guiding but was drawing her close, even though his touch was ever so light. Tantalisingly light.

His laughing eyes dared her to object, but she didn't actually want to. 'Thanks for bringing me.'

Hugo danced like he'd been doing it all his life, which he probably had, she decided. Another social skill that his mother had made sure he had mastered, and something to concentrate on instead of worrying about the effect such close proximity was having on her body.

'You're welcome – thank you for coming. Although I had rather hoped to get a dance in earlier, Miss Popular.'

'Mr Possessive.'

'And what if I am?' He took her hand in his spare one, held it between them, his hips moving dangerously close, as his other hand slipped lower down towards her bum. Was it in her dress or outside? She wriggled, then froze when her stomach brushed against what had to be his erection.

'Can't you keep your body under control?'

219

He grinned, dipped his face lower so that his nose was almost touching hers. 'Impossible when you're clinging to me.'

'I'm not clinging.' Oh blast, she was sounding like she wanted to.

'I'd like you to be, later?'

'Hugo,' his thumb definitely was in her dress. 'I admit I fancy you.'

'I know.' The upper-class drawl played with her mind; he leant in even closer so their foreheads touched. 'Your nipples are digging into my chest.' The grin was so naughty, so bad she should slap him.

His lips brushed hers as his hand pressed her closer and his body encouraged her to dance to the music. Dance to his rhythm.

Flo's lips tingled from that feather-light touch, that brush of his dry mouth against hers and she wanted more. She wanted to taste him again like she had after he'd cooked for her. Wanted to feel his tongue exploring her mouth. She was already damp between her thighs, rocking her body closer to his, even though she knew it was a bad idea.

'You are beautiful, you know.' This time his lips settled on her own parted ones, his tongue traced along the tips of her teeth, and when she sighed he took it as acceptance.

His tongue played with hers, demanded a response and she gave it. Letting him in, resting against his firm body and tipping her head back as he explored every bit of her mouth, the fingers of one hand tangled deep in her hair as the other slipped deeper into the v of her dress, one long finger reaching out to stroke the dip at the bottom of her back, *right* at the bottom of her back so that she wanted to part her legs, invite him in.

Swaying now, incapable of moving her feet because all she wanted to do was taste him, she cupped the side of his face with her hand, closed her eyes, and let the smell and taste block everything out.

He dragged his mouth away and her eyes shot open. She looked at him, feeling drugged. 'Christ, Flo. I can't do this.' He pulled further away, leaving a gap of cold air between them, but his hand was on her waist, his other holding hers. 'Have you any idea what watching you from the other side of the room all evening has done to me? I've never ever fucked anybody on a dance floor, but it is going to happen now if we carry on. Come on, we're leaving.'

Hugo was out of the car and round to her side before she even had the seatbelt off. He grabbed her. 'Sorry, can't wait for you to totter across in those bloody heels.'

'Are we going to—'

'Mine's nearer.' He was panting as he stumbled towards his front door. 'Bloody hell, you're heavier than you look.' He pushed through, kicking the door shut behind them, then staggered on into the lounge, falling to his knees so that she rolled onto the rug. 'I'm having you here.' He was leaning over her, his hair flopping as he kissed her lips and she laughed. 'Then I'm having you on the kitchen table.' He put his hands on the shoulders of the dress then roughly pulled it down and kissed her throat, kissed a trail down her chest, took her nipple between his teeth.

That was bad, so bad. The throbbing need between her legs made Flo gasp. 'I need your clothes off.' She reached up, didn't even think about undoing buttons, just ripped the two sides apart as hard as she could. His skin was surprisingly soft, the smattering of hair across his chest teased her fingertips as she traced over his body.

'Shit, you need to stop that.' He tried to crush her body with his, but the second he stopped kissing she carried on, tiptoed her fingers down, following the trail of hair that was leading down to his waistband.

Flo undid the button of his trousers, tugged at the zip, and then lost track of what was happening.

Hugo could stand it no longer. Years of desire was trying to burst out; he pushed his trousers down to his hips, then lifted the thin chiffon of her dress and groaned at the lacy scrap that covered her.

He paused, looked up to see what was in her eyes and when he saw dark-eyed lust that mirrored his own he eased her legs apart and sank between them.

'Jesus Christ, Flo, I need you.'

'So, that was interesting.' Flo turned her head so that she could look into Hugo's eyes, and grinned. 'What was that you said? You've been waiting nearly twenty years?'

He groaned and wiped a hand over his face. 'Hell, I didn't actually say that, did I? It was worth the wait though.' He rolled onto his side, and started to circle one boob with a finger, spiralling closer and closer until her nipple hardened, and then he moved onto the other one, his face serious as he studied the effect. 'I'm going to have to do it again, I'm afraid.'

'Oh you think you are, do you?' His face stiffened and Flo laughed, then swung her body over his, straddling him. 'I think it's time we did it my way, don't you?'

'I'll do it any way you want, darling.'

'I'm not normally that bossy.' Flo collapsed onto her back and stretched her arms up, before flopping one over Hugo's waist.

'You can be as bossy as you like.' He reached over, groping for a pack of cigarettes that wasn't there. He sat up and scoured the room, spotting them, and then returning to her and rearranging them so that he was propped up against the sofa and she was lying across him. He lit the cigarette, drew deeply, then wafted the smoke away.

'I was never very bossy about anything, actually, until I split with Oli and realised,' she glanced up to see the reaction to her ex's name, but he just shrugged and looked down at her, his eyes hooded.

'Go on, I'm interested to hear about this Oli chap – sounds a bit of a wanker.'

'He is. But I didn't realise at the time. You don't always, do you?'

He didn't comment, his steady gaze not wavering as he took another drag.

'Until I caught him in bed with somebody else. I thought my whole life had ground to a halt, then I started to wonder how I'd ever put him on such a high pedestal.' She shifted around and he put a cushion under her head. 'I'd just let him push me round, stop me writing, just doing the stuff he wanted. Coming here has let me get a grip again, do what I want instead of what somebody else wants all the time.'

'Like write?'

'Like write.'

'Fair enough.' He stubbed the cigarette out, even though it wasn't finished. 'I can understand that.'

'You can, can't you, Hugo?' There was something in his eyes. 'Tell me about your father and his great expectations.' The twitch of his lips told her she'd been right.

'I hope you're not expecting an outpouring of grief or hate that will explain all my faults away.'

She smiled. 'Nothing so simple. I'm just curious, and you seem good at wheedling stuff out of me. You said he wanted you to be a lawyer?'

'I did?'

'When we were talking about quotes the other day.'

'There's a lot to be said for a post-coital fag instead of a chat.' He sighed, then lit a second cigarette and stared into the flames of the fire. 'Not a lot to tell, he did indeed want me to do something useful with my expensive education, and be respected in my field. Law is in the family; another barrister would have suited nicely.'

'But not for Hugo the rebel.'

'I didn't rebel.' His tone was mild. 'I just hate all the stuffiness, all the pomp, and I loved horses. It's one thing that has always come naturally to me, and,' he smiled, 'I'm lazy, so why not follow the easy route.'

It didn't look like it had been an easy road to her. 'Doing what you want rather than what's expected is the hardest thing you can do.'

'We fell out rather spectacularly when I not only started riding for a living, but I shagged his boss's wife. He threw me out, told me never to darken the doorstep and all that kind of thing.'

'Ah.'

'I wasn't that old, and she did rather grab me by the balls, as it were, and make me an offer I couldn't refuse.'

'You told him that?'

'Did I hell! Pompous old fool, I wasn't going to admit to being coerced rather than sweeping her off her feet was I? It was probably the only bit he was proud of, I think he was jealous.'

'Hugo!' She laughed. He flicked the ash off the end of his cigarette.

'I do rather miss my mother. But that, my darling, is why I'm here in this dump. My money supply was cut off, and all my time and everything I earn goes on the horses.'

'It isn't a dump. Daisy's nice, kind, you should be nicer to her and more grateful.'

His hand, she noticed, was trembling.

'I can't be, I don't have any redeeming features – or so I'm told.'

She rolled over and wrapped her arms round him. 'Oh I think you do.'

'I think I should show you my best feature one more time and then have a whisky.' He stood up and pulled her to her feet. 'You are staying, I take it?'

'No.' The look in his eyes made her feel guilty. 'I need to let Mabel out, and…'

'You have to do things your way.' The look had gone, and he'd got his normal, slightly mocking, look.

'People will talk.'

'There's nobody for miles.'

'I will talk. In my head, to myself, and I won't be impressed. I don't want to turn this into something wrong, Hugo, when it actually feels right. I'll see what I think in the morning.'

'After you've talked to yourself?'

'Yes, I'll let you know what I tell myself.' She reached over to grab her discarded dress. 'Night, Hugo.'

Chapter 19 – Daisy. Finding Mr Right

The sun was shining, but there was a cool enough edge to the air to make Daisy grab her jacket and scarf when she returned to the apartment after her morning coffee and croissant.

She'd tried ringing Jimmy again, and got his customary message, which wasn't quite as funny on the two hundred and seventy-eighth hearing. And it cost her a fifty pence connection charge; her next mobile phone bill was going to be of scary proportions. She didn't mind the fifty pence, it was more the fact that she'd paid it to listen to his message and talk to his answerphone. But it seemed wrong to not keep in touch. She'd sent more than one email as well, but knew he wouldn't even bother reading them. He considered all emails spam, and treated them the same way he did paper junk mail – by ignoring them.

She'd had one email from Anna –

Hiya Dais,

How's it going? I'd give anything to swap places, you lucky thing.

The buggers here have got their own back for letting me have those measly few days off, I really hate my boss you'll

226

never believe what a cow she's been and she just keeps saying it's for my own good, ha, you should see the snide look on her face.

Not had a chance to check up on Flo, but she texted and said everything was okay, and she'd met Hugo, and said why didn't we tell her what your place was like? She also said she doesn't like chickens much, but she loves Mabel.

From what I've heard, Jimmy has more or less moved into The Bulls Head now you're not there to cook his dinner. Not being funny, but if you decide not to say I do, then I think Angie will give him a shoulder to cry on. I have never, ever seen a skirt like the one she had on the other day – it made a cummerbund look big. I'll send you a pic.

Better go and prepare stuff for tomorrow, and go to the bar. Reception here is crap or I would have phoned.
Anna xx

It was no wonder Jimmy wasn't answering her calls if he was in the pub all the time. The phone reception wasn't the best in there, and he normally had his phone on silent, and in his pocket, so it didn't interfere with his drinking.

She glanced round the apartment to check she'd shut all the windows, then turned the thermostat down a bit. Double-locking the doors behind her (though any burglar keen enough to get all the way up here had to be deranged or determined) she set off down the stairs.

Daisy opened the outside door then pulled the zip of her leather jacket up a bit higher. There really was a nip in the air today – although it was more like a British autumn than winter temperature – which was why she'd had a sudden urge to go for a long walk rather than catch a train.

She'd abandoned the idea of jogging after looking at a couple of apps that were supposed to introduce you very slowly. So slowly that she'd still be at the stage that involved two minutes' running and the same walking by the time she'd got home, which hardly seemed worth it. Plus, she'd actually found her days were crammed full of things to do. She'd hardly made any inroads at all into the contents of her Kindle – by the time she got in she was usually too tired, or too tipsy, to enjoy it. Which was a bit weird, she'd expected finding time to read to be easier here than it was at home.

Crossing the road, she followed the route she'd jogged down, which meant she got to see a bit of everything. She wandered through the old streets, packed with bars and shops and then re-joined the main street that would take her down towards the port.

On the corner there was an old circus, decorated caravans in a circle around the big old tent and a brightly painted ticket office with kids crowded round giggling and jumping around.

A circus visited the nearest town to Tippermere when she'd been little, and her mum would always take her and Em, and tease her dad until he reluctantly took his overalls off and spruced himself up. They'd been like these families here: expectant, excited, waiting for somebody to add a little bit of magic to their lives. People were people the world over, she supposed. You didn't need to catch a plane to see happy faces, to be happy.

She wandered along in front of the posh restaurants that faced the marina and on a sudden impulse fished her phone out of her pocket as she stared out at the luxury yachts that competed for space and attention.

'Well, this is a nice surprise, Daisy. I was just saying to your dad I wondered how you were getting on. Are you having a nice time?'

'Hi, Mum. Yes, it's great thanks.'

'We've had snow here.'

'It's lovely and sunny here, not exactly sunbathing weather, but I did have a paddle in the sea.'

'That's lovely, dear. I always did think it was a shame we couldn't get away from the farm more when you were little. Me and your dad are thinking of going on a little cruise next year, you've made me get my wanderlust back. I do miss going abroad.'

'But who'll look after the farm?'

'Well your dad has a lad full time now, and he'll get somebody else from the agency, just to help out.'

'That'll be great, Mum, you'd love it here.'

'Oh I did dear, though I bet it's changed since me and your dad went.'

'You've been to Barcelona? I never knew.'

'Oh it was before you were born – we weren't always boring.' She could hear the smile in her mother's voice.

'I didn't think you were. Mum?'

'Yes, Daisy?'

'Did you ever, well,' she couldn't say 'regret' could she? 'Did you ever miss all your trips away, you know all the excitement you had before…'

'Before I decided to help your dad on the farm?' Her mother's voice was always soft, gentle, but now it dropped even more. 'Oh never, darling. This is what I decided I wanted. But I think I know what you're asking, you'll know when you've found what you want, Daisy, and in the meantime you should enjoy yourself a little. I did.'

'But you loved your job?'

'Oh I did for a while. It suited me when I was younger, but people change.'

'I think I've changed the other way. I think I want to see other places.'

'You should do, dear, or how will you ever know where you really want to be? Although, to be honest, it is the people that make the place.'

'I do love Tippermere.'

'I know you do, Daisy, and that is why dear old Mrs Webster said she wanted you to have Mere End. She said you loved the village enough to respect it, and she wanted to give you freedom to explore.'

'Freedom?' She sat down on a bench. 'But it's made me stay there.'

'If you have a base where you feel secure, Daisy, then it gives you the confidence to travel further. She was a clever old lady, she said she recognised a little of herself in you; she knew that once you'd settled and got yourself comfortable, then you'd start looking for a little bit of excitement. She thought it would give you the time you needed to think about it. Do things your own way, in your own time.'

'Oh.'

'You will be back for Christmas, will you love?'

'Yes, Mum.'

'That's nice, it'll be lovely to see you.'

'Mum?' She had to ask, had to know what she was facing when she got home. 'Did you know Jimmy proposed?'

There was a long silence. Which could have been a yes, or could have been shock.

'I'm going to say no to him when I come back. I have tried to talk to him but he's always busy, but I do want to tell him, explain properly, you know, be fair.'

'Well you know we never like to interfere in your life, Daisy, but I have to say I'm pleased.' She paused and Daisy waited for the 'too old' 'too boring' 'no money' spiel. 'You'll find the right person when you're ready, and you'll know, just like I did, and then it won't matter where you are or what you've done.'

'I know, Mum.'

'He's not the one, is he, Daisy?'

She sighed. 'I don't suppose I ever thought he was.'

'I better be off, love, as long as you're okay. I've got some mince pies ready to come out of the oven.' There was a rattling sound of baking tins in the background. 'You haven't met anybody out there have you, Daisy?'

Daisy didn't answer immediately, and when she did she knew she didn't sound entirely convincing. 'No, Mum.' But maybe she had.

She hadn't come here to find anybody, she'd come to find the bit of herself she thought she might have lost. But then she'd met a man who seemed to instinctively understand her, to care about her, a man who wanted to share things with her.

Except he was a man who had a home – and responsibilities she still didn't properly understand – in Barcelona. And she had a home back in the UK. Or maybe the answer would have been different. Maybe, just maybe, she would have said yes.

Her mother was wrong about one thing though. It did matter where she was, where he was. The lives they had.

Or maybe she was just making up excuses, like she had in the past when she had stopped herself exploring the world and doing what she wanted to earlier.

Javier had kissed her and he'd made her feel dizzy, confused, and exhilarated all at once in a way she would never have thought possible.

Then he'd asked her if she'd come back to Barcelona, and she'd just brushed it off, said it was difficult. Not even tried to find out more about his sister and his complications. Not dared to think that they might have a chance to get to know each other better. She groaned inwardly. It was no wonder he'd driven her home in near silence. How could she have done that? Been so thoughtless.

But he *had* asked her if she would come back to him.

'Are you still there, Daisy?'

'Yes, Mum.'

'And you are okay?'

'I'm good.' She was good, but maybe she could be better if she could be brave enough to follow her heart, to really go for it. 'I'll give you a call when I get home. Bye, Mum'

'Bye, love. You enjoy yourself.'

Daisy slipped her phone back in her pocket. She'd expected to feel homesick, wanting to rush back. But she hadn't. She just felt happy. As soon as she got home she was going to write out a proper list of places she really wanted to go, and she was going to find out how much they cost and plan exactly when she was going. And she was going to work out when she could come back to Barcelona and see Javier – if she hadn't already blown her chance. But for now she was going to walk as far along the beach as she could.

Daisy slowed her pace as she neared the cafés that sat at the back of Port Olympic. They were set back a bit from the water and had glass fronts, which she was sure would cut down the effect of the breeze, meaning they'd be quite warm. She really fancied coffee and churros, or even some of the spicy patatas bravas – just something to warm her up and stop her stomach growling. She seemed to be eating more and more since she'd been here – whether it was the fact that the tapas and pintxos were so inviting and tasty, or just the brisk walk, she was definitely in eat mode. It was probably a good job she'd be heading home soon, before the waistband of her jeans exploded, there was a lot to be said for a good percentage of elastane.

She eyed up the menus as she walked, not that she was going to be tempted into anything more than a snack, then narrowed her eyes as she spotted a familiar dark head of hair above broad shoulders. No it couldn't be.

Some instinct stopped her from running over, from waving and shouting his name. Either that, or the fact that he'd said he was busy today and she'd just assumed he was working, not...

She backed up a few steps, then ducked into the restaurant she'd just passed so that she could take a closer look. From this angle there was absolutely no doubt at all.

It was Javier. And he was bouncing a giggling toddler on his knee.

On the seat opposite was the girl that Daisy had seen him with when she'd gone to the meet-up, on her first evening alone. The petite, pretty girl he'd shared a look of pure adoration with.

He'd told her that it had ended; they'd stayed friends. That he wasn't in the right place for a relationship – and she'd just assumed that was because of his sister. Because of family responsibilities. So what was this? This put a whole different slant on the meaning of 'family'.

The girl was watching the man and boy, laughing, putting out a hand to rest on Javier's knee in a way that spoke of a closeness Daisy was suddenly jealous of. Then she leant forward and kissed him on the cheek.

No wonder he'd said life was complicated.

Daisy's hand went up automatically to her own cheek, the cheek he'd kissed when he'd left her the day before. When he'd told her he was busy – with work – today. When he'd suggested she catch a train out of town.

Way out of town, out of his way.

Daisy frowned. She shouldn't be upset. It was one kiss, a few friendly days. Days when he'd warned her off, when he'd said he should never have kissed her.

But the pain in her chest was real, as was the choking feeling in her throat, followed by the sudden sharp taste of bile as her hand dropped to cover her mouth.

Why would he lie to her?

She'd trusted him so much, instinctively, wanted to. Thought that they had something far closer than anything she'd had with anybody before – and suddenly it looked like it had all been built on nothing. If he'd lied about this, what else had he lied about? Did he even have a sister who relied on him?

She couldn't drag her gaze away from the little boy, who was now bouncing and rubbing his nose against Javier's. Then Javier swung him up in the air above his head and he squealed with excitement. They all looked so happy. A perfect family. Which was what she could have with Jimmy. But she didn't want it.

A short time in Barcelona had given her what she'd always dreamed it would, it wasn't that she wanted to spend the rest of her life here. But she couldn't go back to how things were before – with no promise of a better future.

The girl turned, and for a moment Daisy was sure she'd seen her. She had to get out of here. How bad would it be if he saw her watching them like some kind of stalker? She stumbled back, nearly tripping over a table leg, then righted herself and ducked down so she was doubled over.

'Is there a problem?' The waiter was peering at her, a look of concern on his face.

'Fine, er stomach ache.' She clutched a hand to her stomach and carried on going in her old-lady stance. Javier. A girlfriend. A child. The pain wasn't in her stomach, it was in her chest.

They'd stayed friends, he'd said. They were obviously more than friends again now. Which was good. Nice. Families needed to be together. Why hadn't he told her? What was so difficult about admitting to having a family? About being honest.

Instead he'd kissed her and asked her if she'd come back in the spring. And see him. And she'd convinced herself she had to do it.

Daisy took a big, deep breath and waved the waiter away with a smile. It was a shock, that was all, but no way was she stopping for coffee here – or walking over and saying hello. What could she accuse him of? Being nice to her, a simple kiss. Looking at her in a way that made her all squishy inside.

Oh God, how could he have kissed her like that? That kiss had been so gentle, so sweet, like no other kiss she'd never had. Like a promise. Except it hadn't been. Not for him.

She walked on, feeling stupid, her hand over her mouth to stop the wave of disappointment flooding out of her. He'd looked at her like he cared. He'd promised to show her more of the city. He'd said he wanted to show her springtime in Barcelona. She'd thought he wanted her to come back, and she'd been planning on doing just that. But it had all been words. Meaningless. And it shocked her how much it hurt. Physically hurt.

Choking back the tears that were catching in her throat, pricking at her eyelids, she rushed on, past all the happy faces, all the wonderful sights that all of a sudden were just unimportant blurs.

For one brief moment then, when she'd been talking to her mother on the phone, she'd got carried away, started to plan a future that was nothing more than pure fantasy.

By the time Daisy got back to the apartment, out of breath and sweaty hot, she'd made her decision. Tomorrow she'd book a tour of La Sagrada Familia, then she'd walk up the hill to the Parc de Montjuic and check out the waterfalls, and the Museum of Catalan Art. She would pack the last few days she'd got with as much sight-seeing as was humanly possible. At best she'd be blown over by the whole experience – at worst she'd be too worn out to even think about what Javier might be up to. And then she'd go back to Tippermere, and real life.

***

Daisy trudged up the last of the steps to the apartment and leant against the door for a breather. She really was worn out, even with several stops for coffee and cakes. She fished in her pocket for her keys, taking her mobile phone out to make it easier.

With a jolt she saw that she'd missed half a dozen calls. From Hugo (Hugo! What on earth had made Hugo call?), Flo (oh, God, she hoped Mabel and Barney were okay) and a message from Anna saying '*don't you answer your phone these days? Flo needs to tell you something.*'

And another message from Javier. '*Where have you been –*

missed you! Fancy a glass of wine later? She stared at the message, feeling a pang of guilt. She should at least be polite – all she had to do was say no. Except then he'd ask why not.

Although telling him was the right thing to do. If she didn't feel like it would hurt her more than him.

She glanced back at Anna's. Then switched again. Then decided she could cope better with Anna. *'What's up?'*

There was an instant reply. *'There's been a fire.'*

Which made it a hell of a lot easier to decide what to say to Javier – she was typing it before she'd even decided what she was going to do. *'Sorry. Going home. Thanks for looking after me – you're relieved of duty!'* She added a kiss automatically, then deleted it, then added it again, then deleted it. Oh to hell with it, she'd never see him again, so what did it matter? At least one of them should show some honesty. With a sigh, she added it again and hit send.

Chapter 20 – Flo. Past mistakes

Being woken up by a kiss was one thing, a slightly worrying thing, mind you, given the rules she'd laid out last night. But this was sloppy. And whiskery. It would take a vat full of testosterone to result in that type of overnight growth.

Flo opened one eye and a dark-brown one met her gaze from an uncomfortably short distance away. She shuffled her way to the middle of the bed. 'You have got seriously bad breath, Mabel, no way would I sleep with you.' Crumbs, she ached – every muscle was objecting. Even her feet hurt.

'What are you doing up here anyway, dog?' She turned her face away and Mabel padded round to the other side of the bed, giving her a big doleful look, and then plonking a massive paw on the pillow. The little alarm clock on the bedside cabinet caught her eye. 'Oh God, is it really that time? Sorry Mabel.' Lying flat on her back, she pulled the covers up to her chin and wondered if she could ring Hugo and ask him to feed the dog.

No. No, no, no, no. She could not ask Hugo anything. She'd slept with him. Well done everything *but* sleep with him. An image of his naked chest, and that arrow of hairs heading straight down to… No.

She'd kissed his scar – she'd practically ripped his clothes off.

No, there was no 'practically' about it; she had actually done it. She *had* ripped his shirt and screwed his jacket into a ball, and thrown his socks on the fire (and what were the odds they were silk socks?) and let him pin her to the bed...

She grabbed a cushion and put it over her head. It didn't help. Just made Mabel bark.

Flo peeped out from under the fabric. 'Shush, please, Mabel, my head hurts.'

The dog barked again, so she thumped the cushion down over her hips.

Mabel cocked her head, staring out of the window. There was the bang of a car door. Good, he was going out, she was safe from embarrassment. It was lucky she'd slept in until lunch-time.

The rap on the front door made her jump.

So he was coming back not going out.

'Oh hell, Mabel, what am I going to do? Hide?'

But Mabel wasn't listening, she was hurtling down the narrow staircase, her whiplash tail banging out a drumbeat on each wall alternately. And barking again.

It would be cowardly to hide. He'd know she was in, and then it would be worse when she did decide to talk to him. She had to be grown-up about this. Stick her head out of the front bedroom window.

'Hi, Hu—'

It wasn't Hugo's head she could see.

'Thank God I've got the right place.' He stamped his feet on the doorstep, shaking the snow off. 'I didn't realise you were out in the middle of nowhere, it must be so bloody boring. I presume that's why you haven't bothered to get up yet?' Mabel barked louder, and scrabbled at the door. 'Well are you going to let me in? I'm freezing my balls off out here.'

Oli.

'What on earth are you doing here?'

'I emailed.' He frowned. 'That girl you've got staying in your place told me you were in the UK.'

'Daisy gave you this address?' Daisy wouldn't do that, surely?

'Not exactly.'

'What does "not exactly" mean?'

'I rang your mother and asked her the name of the village.'

'You rang my...?' The cheek of it. 'You never, ever spoke to my mother when we were together, and you speak to her now. Now!'

'Calm down, Flo. Why do you have to make such a drama of everything? Come down. I've come all this way to talk to you, so the least you can do is—'

'The least I can do?' All this way? He was making it sound like a trip to the moon, not a bloody two-hour flight.

'Flo, I did email, twice. Didn't you read them?'

'Nope.' She hadn't. She hadn't had time, and she really didn't care.

'You always read your emails.'

'I used to, when I didn't have anything better to do.'

He frowned, then bent down to reach into the bag at his feet. 'I've bought bubbly, and your favourite catanyes. An early Christmas present?' As Oli disapproved of chocolate, all chocolate – including the chocolate-covered almonds that were a Spanish favourite – then he was doing some serious crawling.

She was being mean. She should at least open the door and let him meet Mabel. But her head hurt and her feet ached like buggery. She'd rather go back to bed. She curled her toes over, which hurt more. And wondered why she felt like she'd run a marathon, hmm, maybe better not dwell on that one.

'Are you listening to me, Florence?'

Oh dear, we'd progressed to Florence now.

She decided to lock Mabel in the kitchen and use her as a secret weapon if she needed one. Oli, after all, didn't like dogs – he'd told her enough times that they shed hairs, left muddy footprints, passed wind at the worst times (was there ever a good time?) and licked their balls – whether his objection to the last point was down to jealousy or something else she wasn't sure.

She reversed the huge dog down the narrow passageway, something she'd got quite expert at. 'Sorry poppet, I promise it won't be for long' and took a deep breath. Wondering if being in her pyjamas with 'I've just been shagged' hair was a good or bad idea. But getting dressed would suggest she cared. And he'd expect it, because Oli always liked her to be tidy.

'Bloody hell, it's dark in here.' Oli was in, huffing and puffing and taking his jacket off the second she opened the door. 'I bet you can't wait to get back home.'

'I like it here, actually. Why are you here, Oli, I don't get it?'

'Well, seeing as you're not reading your emails. Look, Flo, I've made a mistake, so I thought we could have a couple of days in London, do a bit of sight-seeing, then home.'

'You've made a mistake?'

'You have no idea how untidy Sarah is, and she just argues about every bloody thing.' He gave her his lapdog look. 'You've no idea how tiring it is.'

You've no idea how much I wish you'd go away.

'I can't come back, Oli.'

'Why not? We can have a bit of a break, no need to rush back to work. Although we could do with sorting out the next edition.'

'No.'

'Sorry?' His look was total confusion. 'I'll make it up to you, have a proper anniversary trip. I made a fool of myself, Flo, I realise that, but we all make mistakes.' He smiled. 'Even me.'

'I haven't got time. In fact, I was going to email you to hand my notice in.'

'But you aren't doing anything! You're in the back of beyond, Florence, this isn't like you at all.'

'That's the point. It is like me, Oli. This is what I want to do right now, I'm not saying forever, but it is for now. And I'm writing a book.'

'A travel guide?'

'A novel.'

'Oh come on, Flo, you know what publishing is like,' he shook his head as though he was remonstrating with a four-year-old, then gave what he thought was a knowing smile but looked more like an idiot, 'you won't be buying designer shoes from selling six digital copies you know, and even somebody like you might never get a deal.'

'What do you mean, somebody like me?'

'Well, you've got your journalistic background, and all the years you've worked for me on the mag—'

She spluttered. She couldn't help it. 'Worked for you? I thought we were doing it together.'

'Whatever. Look, Florence, even though you do write good, very good,' he smiled as he threw a reward her way, 'copy for the magazine, it really isn't the same as being able to craft a novel you know. We all need to know our boundaries, know how we can best make a living.'

Flo stared at him. She didn't honestly know whether to laugh or cry. Hugo believed in her, Hugo encouraged her. He didn't think all she was capable of was churning out column inches for a magazine. He didn't think it was all about making a living, that she was daft to waste her time, that it was all about some swish publishing contract. He understood.

'I don't care where my boundaries are, Oli.' She could be destitute, writing in a garret. Maybe not – that would be a bit over the top. 'I want to kick ass.' He was giving her a slightly horrified look. 'I just want to write it, and I don't need designer shoes while I'm here.'

'But you have rent to pay on your apartment.'

'That's my problem. I'll sort it, don't worry. I will do some freelance writing or something.'

'You're being silly and impractical. Dreams have a place, Florence, and that is in your head when you're asleep. We've got a good life together, Flo, I need you to be there with me, at my side. You're so good at organising everything.'

'We *did* have a good life. You screwed it up, Oli.' 'Screw' being the important word in the sentence.

'I know you have an issue with forgiving people, Flo, but let it go. A man's allowed one mistake, isn't he?'

He was doing his Labrador, disarming look, but it wasn't working now and it had just reminded her. 'Not the type you made. And I've realised I just don't want to live your life, Oli. I want to be here, I want to write, I want a dog,' she looked down, 'and to stay in my pyjamas all day if I want.'

'You're just having a bad reaction, when you get home and everything is back to normal...'

'I don't want to see you. Honestly. I don't want the old normal, I want a new one.'

'I will sack Sarah.'

For a moment she couldn't speak. 'You mean you haven't already?'

'Well no, with you disappearing I can't do everything on my own, but when you come back...'

'Oli, you aren't listening. When I come back to Barcelona it isn't to work with you, go out with you, shag you, wait about for you. I've moved on, so thank you for that, you made me realise that I wasn't being true to myself.'

'Well this isn't being true to yourself, the Flo I know...'

'Exactly. You don't know me. That me isn't the real me. Now I'm very sorry, but I've got things to do and you are going to have to go.' She made ushering gestures towards the door.

'But I've hired the car for two days, I thought we'd stay here tonight.'

'No.'

'I paid in advance.'

242

'You shouldn't have come.'

His eyes narrowed, and he froze like a Pointer. 'What's that strange noise?'

'That is Mabel, a big dog and she's fed up. Would you like to meet her before you go?'

'It sounds like somebody is in there. Have you got somebody else already?' He was frowning again, looking most uncomfortable, a fish (or reptile) out of water.

'No, Oli, it's just Mabel. She's very big.' Well, if he wanted to meet her, why not?

He went to open the door. 'I wouldn't do that if I—' Oli always knew best.

Mabel was so deliriously happy to have been released that she bounded straight through Oli, knocking him spinning, his arms flailing like a windmill.

'But you are seeing somebody?' He panted out, once he'd stabilised and worked out which direction to point in.

'Why would you assume that?' She crossed her fingers behind her back, she hadn't exactly told a lie, but just to be on the safe side.

'Well, you'd come home otherwise, to me.' He advanced cautiously into the kitchen, as though the dog had been a booby trap and there might be more.

Flo sighed. 'There's nobody hiding in my kitchen, Oli.'

'I really don't understand.' He turned to her, the expression on his face pure petulant child. He'd lost his toy, raided the toy box, and hadn't found anything better – only to discover the one he had liked had gone by the time he decided to play with it again.

'No, I don't suppose you do. It was good, Oli, then it was bad, and now it's over.' She shrugged her shoulders.

'I'll check into a hotel in town and you can ring me when you change your mind.'

'I won't.'

Flo watched him march out of the cottage and get into his hire car.

She really wanted to throw a snowball at him. But that would be childish.

Instead she went back into the kitchen and realised that she was shaking, even her legs were trembling. She wrapped her arms round Mabel's neck. 'I thought you were supposed to protect me, you know, see him off the premises.' Mabel licked her nose (and chin and mouth as her tongue was unacceptably large), Flo wiped the slobber off with her forearm. 'Oh Mabe, what am I going to do?' There was only one thing for it, a hangover-busting fry-up.

The supermarket delivery van had finally made its way through the slippery, snowy lanes, which had been partially cleared by a very helpful farmer and his tractor. It was actually a shame he had. She would rather have faced starvation (or a strange diet of pheasant, berries, and Barney's carrots) than have Oli on her doorstep.

She now had a pantry with enough food to last her for the rest of her stay, and she opened the fridge and stared at the contents. Fried egg, bacon, mushrooms, tomatoes, and toast seemed an excellent idea.

Turning the grill on, and splashing oil into a frying pan, the total feeling of panic started to subside. Her hollow stomach was still churning as though she was at sea, but hopefully food would put a stop to that – clog it up. 'We'll have sausage as well.' Mabel wagged her tail and looked up expectantly. Why not go the whole hog? Oli would be appalled. 'Now don't you dare steal anything, I'll be back in a sec.'

Inspiration had struck, which was strange, but she just had to write this bit down while it was still in her head.

When she had started writing her novel she'd had brilliant ideas while she was drifting off to sleep in bed and known they were exactly the twists she needed. She thought she should write them down, then she didn't want to get out from under the warm covers – the cottage would be freezing now the fire had died down. If she repeated it enough times she'd remember. Or she could put a note on her mobile phone, except it was dead, and she was tired, and… Then she'd wake up in the morning knowing she'd had a brilliant idea, and it would be gone. Completely. The only bit she could recall was that it was good. Genius. The quote to outdo all quotes.

So she'd learned that she had to write the thought down while it was there. Instantly. She padded into the cosy living room and picked up her laptop. It had been that look of total disbelief on Oli's face when he'd thought she had another man hiding in the kitchen, when he couldn't believe that she couldn't just not want him. She needed to capture that look, the mistrust, the way it had made her feel before she lost it.

'Writing a best-seller?'

'Hang on.' Flo finished the sentence she was writing and hit 'save' with a flourish, before looking up.

Hugo was towering in the low doorway, looking very country-manor in his breeches and long boots. He also looked quite pleased with himself, in the way Mabel did when she thought she'd been naughty and had escaped detection. No regrets there then. 'Who was that I saw skidding out of the driveway? Somebody asking for directions? He nearly knocked the gatepost out.'

Hugo had obviously decided that a night of crumpled bed sheets meant he needn't knock on the door.

'The door was open. I did shout, but you were too engrossed to hear.'

Ahh, he mind-read as well. She put the laptop down on the table. 'It was Oli.' She wasn't going to let the anger come back. She could be calm.

Hugo it appeared couldn't be. The grin dropped from his face and he swished his whip irritably. 'Who?

'Oli, my ex.' Forever ex. Never to be reconsidered.

He tapped his boot with the whip, hard, and stared at her.

245

More of a smack than a swish and she flinched. 'So you've asked him to come here and stay as well.' He was *not* happy.

'Well no, he…'

'Does Daisy know?' Aloof and cold. The atmosphere had dropped several degrees. 'It is her place.'

'Not as far as I know.' She stood up. 'Look, I didn't invite him, he just turned up.'

'But you told him you were here?'

This was getting a bit ridiculous. 'He asked my mother, who told him we used to live in this village.'

'Keep it in the family. Oh well, at least I know my place in all this.' He spun round, nudged Mabel out of his way, and headed for the front door.

'Hugo.'

He half-turned. 'I came to tell you I'd booked a table in Kitterly Heath for lunch, you can take your boyfriend.'

'He's not my boyfriend.'

'Well it looks like you've got a good evening planned when he gets back.' That drawl had an edge to it she'd never heard before.

For a moment she was confused, then glanced down in the direction of his gaze to see Oli had left his gifts. Bubbly. Chocolates. Bugger.

'This isn't how it looks, Hugo. He's go—' She was about to say gone, but Hugo already had. Storming out and slamming the door behind him.

Of all the insufferable, pompous… she pushed her feet into her wellingtons and grabbed a duffel coat from the hook behind the door, muttering to herself. 'Why should I care, why should I even explain?' Pulling the door shut to keep the heat in she started off after Hugo, who was already rounding the corner of the building, no doubt to go and give his horses hell.

She ground to a halt. Why was she chasing him? Maybe she only liked bastards. Except Hugo wasn't like that. She started walking again. She'd seen the sweet, caring way he looked after his horse when it had colic, he'd cooked her a meal. He read poetry.

Oh crumbs. She stopped again. She didn't want to fall for Hugo, she didn't want to think he was that nice because she'd be going home soon, and she did love Barcelona.

He'd encouraged her to write, to do what she wanted, he was good for her. She set off again, half-running this time, her feet slipping on the cobbled path.

The sex had been amazing, nothing like with Oli, who always hung his clothes up first. It had been impulsive, unscripted. Passionate.

But that's because he was Tippermere's answer to Don Juan. She slid to a halt, nearly falling over.

He loved them and left them, so why was she trying to explain?

Because she was doing it for her, not him. And for him.

He wasn't on a horse, he was leaning over a fence and when he turned to look at her his features were stony. Pure granite. Quite attractive, chiselled granite. Bugger.

He'd made her heart feel like it was about to melt when he'd been looking after his sick horse, and now, when he was acting all angry and superior it was hitting her straight in the pit of her stomach.

He looked so bloody masterful and sexy, and annoying. She wanted to shake him and tell him to listen for once, and she wanted to grab him and kiss him like he'd kissed her after the party.

Now what did she say? 'He's gone.'

'It's none of my business.' He wasn't even meeting her gaze now.

'Well no, it isn't, but I wanted to tell—'

'You do what you want, Flo.'

'I will, Hugo.' She spat his name out; he really was being insufferable. 'It's no wonder you fell out with your bloody father. Do you never listen to a word anybody says?'

247

Suddenly he was meeting her head on, glaring, his eyes steely grey. 'Well actually, I found a one-way conversation where I was expected to do all the listening never helped one bit.' His tone was clipped, controlled.

'Oh, Hugo.' She didn't know whether to hug him or shout at him. 'I'm not your father.'

He turned away, looked out over the field again, blocking her out.

'Hugo, I'm trying to make this two-way. I want to explain.' She lifted a hand to put on his arm, then didn't know if it would make things better or worse, if he'd just shrug her off. She let it fall, brushing against his arm.

'And it's all my fault, falling out with my father, falling out with you, yes that works fine for me.' He laughed, a short, bitter sound that clawed straight at her heart. He kicked the toe of his boot into the hard earth then slowly turned his head to study her. 'I was kicked out, Flo, I wasn't the one that took the easy way. It's you that's just taking the soft option, going back to him instead of following your own dreams.' His jaw was clenched. 'I fought for what I believed in, and I really thought you of all people…'

'I'm, I'm,' Flo could have hit him, and now the words wouldn't even come out. '*I'm* taking the easy option? Look buster, I'm the one who is actually facing up to things. You're the one who's just hiding here next door to Daisy because you can't face your own bloody issues.'

'Flo you don't know what the hell you're talking about.'

'Maybe not, but I know you miss your mum, and you call this place a dump.'

'Leave my mother out of this.' There was a tight control to his voice, but underneath she could hear a tremor. 'I've never hidden from anything. You sound just like him, not giving a shit about how I feel or what I want, just trampling all over my feelings and doing things your way.' The coldness had gone and the anger was bubbling out of Hugo now, and she'd never wanted him more.

'I do care what you want.' The words came out low; she didn't want to shout at him, she just wanted to make things right. He was frowning, hurt and disappointment in his face, and she wished she hadn't lashed out. Except maybe that haunted look was because her words were true. 'I want you to be happy. You're right, I don't know anything about you and your dad, but I know it's not right, Hugo.' It really wasn't right. The real Hugo was loving and warm. The real Hugo trusted and was generous. She couldn't make *everything* right, only he could do that, but she could make this bit right. She could make him listen. 'Hugo.' She took a step closer, and this time put a hand on his arm. 'I know what it might have looked like, but I never asked Oli here, honestly.' His gaze had softened, he was letting her explain. 'I didn't even tell him where I was.' She took a steadying breath. 'He came to try and persuade me to go back, but I can't. I don't want to. This isn't just about my dreams now.' This was the bit where she should tell him she could never go back to somebody like Oli, not now she'd found out what it was like being with him. But first she needed to kiss him.

'Christ, Flo.' The exclamation nearly blasted her eardrums and she jumped back startled.

'Okay. I didn't mean that, well yes, I did actually.' Oh God, how did he manage to get her all confused like this?

'Look!' He had a hand on her shoulder, was spinning her round. 'The fucking house is on fire.'

She looked. Last time he might have been a bit melodramatic, over-reacted over a bit of smoke. But this time there were flames. In her, Daisy's, kitchen.

'Shit, oh Christ, Mabel, I've left Mabel locked in there. Oh God, I've got to go and get her.'

'Here.' He tossed her his phone. 'Ring the fire brigade, I'll run round the front and get her out.'

Chapter 21- Daisy. Heading home

Nobody was answering their phones. Anna had changed her message to a cheery rendition of 'All I want for Christmas, is You', which wasn't at all helpful. Flo's phone just rang out (very worrying), and Hugo had his normal abrupt message concerning his working hours and the cost of a riding lesson.

Daisy stared out of the window and suddenly felt freezing cold. She wrapped her arms round herself. Something was seriously wrong. She had to get home – if she still had a home.

She dragged her small suitcase from the top of the wardrobe and started to shove stuff in as fast as she could. Wondering what the hell she was going to do with all the new clothes she'd bought. Well if they wouldn't go in, they were staying here. Forcing the lid down she tugged at the zip, cursing as she snagged her nail.

Wasting time now trying to book a plane ticket would be stupid; she just needed to get to the airport and then take the first seat she could.

With a last glance round, and a check that the oven was off and the windows shut, she slammed the door behind her and headed down the steps.

The aerobus was quiet, which hopefully meant the airport would be too. She sat down in a window seat and gazed out as they pulled out of Placa Catalunya. Stupid tears prickling at her eyes.

She'd loved her break, fallen for a city that was more than she could have hoped for, and, well, she'd fallen for a man who had 'complicated' in his life, which wasn't such a great move. But now she was going back to reality. To a house that was on fire (well she sincerely hoped it had been put out by the time she got back), to Jimmy, and explanations that were bound to hurt him. To Christmas with her family, with Mabel and Barney. Without Javier.

She dragged her forearm across her eyes and swallowed down the feelings that were trying to break free. She was being pathetic. This was what happened when you didn't live your life properly until you were her age. All she'd had was a holiday romance (or close to a romance) – teenagers survived them so she certainly could. The window had steamed up and she wiped it clear with her sleeve and stared out of the window. And now it was over.

The terminal was busier than she'd expected when she got there and she marched her way resolutely through the happy families that had just arrived, ready for romantic breaks and Christmas shopping. There was a queue at the first airline desk she tried. Ringing Flo again she was surprised when she picked up on the second ring.

'Daisy!'

'Flo, is everything okay? I was out when you called earlier, what on earth has happened? Anna said something about a fire!'

'It's fine, I think. Well, fine, yes. It's just…'

'Is that Hugo I can hear?'

'He, er, he's talking to the fire brigade.'

'God, there is a fire? Is everybody okay? Are you? What about Mabel and Barney?' There was a crackling sound that was a bit alarming. 'Sorry, Flo, this is a really bad line, shall I ring off and try again?'

'No, no I think that noise is Hugo. Don't worry, honestly Daisy,

251

it's all out now. In fact, the fire brigade might have been a bit of an over-reaction. I called them while Hugo was rescuing Mabel. And then I uncalled them. Well, I told them not to bother. But because I'd called them in the first place they said they really had to come out and check the place over.'

'Rescuing Mabel? Oh God, oh she's not hurt is she?'

'She's fine. She flattened Hugo and gave him lots of kisses when he opened the door, which he wasn't exactly thrilled about. I mean he was happy she was okay, but less happy about landing on his arse in the snow.'

Daisy paused for a minute, trying to imagine the aloof Hugo going flying, but it wasn't happening. 'And what about the chickens?'

'No roast chicken, I promise.'

'That's not funny, Flo!'

'Sorry. But there aren't any singed feathers. It wasn't a big fire, just a little one. Tiny. It's all something and nothing really. No real damage.'

'No *real* damage?'

'Only to the cooker really, well the pan. I had a bit of an accident. With bacon and eggs.'

'Bacon and eggs?'

'Cremated.'

'Are you okay, Flo? You're not hurt?'

'Just my pride, and I'm sooty at the edges. But nobody is hurt, and Mabel is fine – Hugo locked her in one of the stables because she was trying to eat the hose and lick one of the firemen to death. I think she fell in love with the black rubber boots. You have one very kinky dog there. Did you know she had a rubber fetish?'

Daisy decided to ignore that comment. 'So it isn't that bad?'

'No, not bad at all. Don't worry, it just looked bad when we saw flames, but that was just the toast, I think. Oh yeah, the toaster looks a bit sooty too. I'm really sorry though, Daisy, I had a hangover and thought a good fry-up would help, then Oli came and I was yelling him out and forgot about them, and then…'

'Oli came? Hang on, Oli is there? What's Oli doing there?'

'Well he isn't here now, he left in a bit of a huff. He turned up out of the blue.'

'Really?' She forgot about the fire for a moment, which obviously wasn't that bad.

'Slime bag. He is so toady, he's not bothered about anybody but himself.'

'But you're okay, Oli has gone? I mean what happened?'

'He brought chocolates and bubbly and wanted me to go back with him.'

'You're kidding!' The man behind Daisy coughed loudly and she realised the queue had moved up.

'He realised that he couldn't live without me apparently, or my PA skills anyway. Sarah just wasn't up to the job, apart from the lying-on-her-back-with-her-legs-open bit.'

'Flo!' Daisy giggled. 'But you're not…?' Daisy held her breath, she'd only swapped a few sentences with Oli and she hadn't particularly warmed to him. And he'd hurt Flo so much, she really deserved better.

'Giving it another go? You must be bloody joking, I've been having far too much fun without him. I never realised what a control freak he was, you know, I mean I quite like a masterful man if you know what I mean.'

'I know exactly what you mean.' It was an unmistakeably male voice interrupting, followed by a 'go away' from Flo.

'What was that?' Daisy frowned, she could swear she recognised that voice.

'Hugo eavesdropping, but he's gone now. What was I saying? Oh yes, Oli was just bossy and a bit of a bully, but I told him I loved being back here,' Daisy caught the wistful note in Flo's voice, 'although I do want to go back to Barcelona, but I'm not doing it just to please him. I've decided to do some freelance stuff and then,' she sounded embarrassed, which was unlike Flo, 'well I've been writing a book, and Hugo thinks…' there seemed to be a lot of mentions of Hugo, 'that I should finish it.' She paused. 'And I think so too.'

'Well that's fab, Flo, I'm really happy for you, and Oli has gone?'

'Well he made the mistake of opening the kitchen door, because he thought I'd got a man hidden in there, but it was Mabel and she kind of bounded out and nearly knocked him flying. He stormed out, then Hugo came in, then he stormed out too.' She sighed. 'It's been one of those days.'

'Hugo? But why would Hugo?'

'It's a bit of a long story.'

'Flo! There isn't something going on between you and Hugo is there? You're not telling me…'

'Well no, I'm not telling you anything.' The sigh travelled over the phone. 'He had a real hissy fit after I told him it was Oli he'd seen drive off. He said I must have invited him, so I went after him to explain. Then when he saw the fire, I mean that was partly his fault because he distracted me. If it hadn't been for him I wouldn't have cremated my brunch.'

'Oh hell, yes, the fire. Blimey, Flo. I'm coming home,' there was a murmur of objection, 'no I am, I'm at the airport,' well, what else did she have to do now? 'Well I'd be coming back soon anyway, I can't leave you.' She'd had her adventure, and she did know now what her heart wanted. And it wasn't Jimmy and his babies. And it probably wasn't another man as she just didn't seem very good at that kind of thing. 'I'm just trying to get a flight. I'll text you when I know what time I'll be back.'

'Daisy, you really don't need to. It's all under control now. I only rang because I thought you should know, but there really is no need for you to come back.'

'I'm here now, look if I can get a flight today I will, and if not… well, I'll ring you. I'm just going to check online now, on my phone, because this queue is hardly moving at all. I'll call you, love you.' Daisy blew a kiss and finished the call.

She'd been a fool over Javier, and she did miss home. Oh, why the hell had she kissed him? And, more to the point, why had he kissed her? Well it had hardly been a kiss, not exactly a full-on snog. She'd just led such a sheltered bloody life that one kiss had been like a promise of more. But it hadn't. Which just showed that, in a way, Jimmy was probably right. Big adventures weren't for people like them, a normal, slightly boring, but totally predictable life with a man like Jimmy – the type of life everybody she knew had – saved a lot of heartache and uncertainty.

She swallowed the disappointment down and ignored the prickle of tears. She was being totally stupid. Her adventure had been amazing – better than amazing. She wanted to be more than a dutiful wife. She deserved to have some of her dreams come true. Even if she needed to have slightly more realistic expectations. Like not expecting the first dishy man that came along to be swept off his feet.

'Daisy.'

Daisy swirled round, her heart hammering. There was only one person with a voice like that. One heartbreakingly gorgeous man, who it would be easier to hate.

'Daisy, thank God I caught you. What are you doing? What's happened?' Javier put a hand on her arm, which made her go all hot and cross. He was looking at her with a concern that made her stomach lurch. She knew she was doing strange contortions, trying to move so he'd let go without actually being too obvious, and without losing her place in the queue. Or dropping her phone. The man behind grunted and shoved his case into her ankle, claiming back the three millimetres of his space she'd strayed onto. 'Where've you been?'

'What do you mean, what am I doing? I'm going home, didn't you get my message? What are *you* doing here, Javier?'

Everybody else in the queue looked round. Great, she had an

audience. And he had a puzzled frown on his face. That, coupled with the fact he was still touching her, and a hot flush was shooting through her body, made her glare.

She shouldn't be cross with him though, she had to be calm; it wasn't his fault that she'd thought the kiss meant anything at all. He was just being nice. Or not nice. I mean, you shouldn't kiss one girl when you were practically married to another one, should you? Not even a peck. Well, not on the lips. And she would never have thought he would be that type of man. Which was why it had made her so cross, and sad, and proved she should stay away. From all of them.

'Is somebody ill?'

'Ill?' She frowned. 'No, nobody's ill. Why've you followed me?'

'I thought something terrible must have happened for you to race off without explaining. What did you mean in your text?'

'I'm going back to England, cutting my holiday short.' It was pretty obvious, wasn't it?

'I don't mean that bit. You said I was relieved of duty.' The frown had deepened and he was ruffling his fingers through the shock of dark hair.

'It was really kind of you to look after—'

'I told you, I wasn't looking after you for Flo. I wasn't being kind, I wanted to show you round, I wanted to be with you.'

Sure. She'd believed that for a time, but now she wasn't sure what to believe. 'Well fine, if you say so, thank you anyway.'

'I do say so. You didn't reply to my text, you did get it, didn't you?'

Well she had seen another text from him when she was on her way to the airport, but she really hadn't wanted to read it. She had to stop thinking about him, move on to whatever came next. Well, she'd been trying until he turned up.

She shrugged. 'I haven't read it.'

'I don't understand, I thought…'

'I was in a hurry.' Why, oh why, had she said that? She didn't need to excuse herself.

'The guy downstairs in the shop told me he'd seen you with a suitcase, so I knew you'd already set off here. Daisy, I don't get it.' He was still running his fingers through his dark hair distractedly and her fingers twitched with the urge to stop him. The woman in front of her turned to look and nudged her husband. 'You never said anything about going home when I saw you. If it was nothing urgent, why didn't you tell me?'

'I only just decided.'

'But if you're not bothered about me, what about your dreams, Daisy? About doing things? Is it so bad here? What happened to the girl who was having a good time, I never thought you were somebody who would just give up, abandon everything.'

I never thought you were the smooth-operator, two-timing type. She could say it, but she wouldn't because he actually hadn't been. It was just her fault for thinking he was being more than just nice and friendly. He *was* being nice. 'I'm not abandoning anything,' she said crossly, wishing she could just push him out of the way, but that would be rude. 'I've got real-life stuff to deal with and I've to go back.'

'To Jimmy?'

'No,' she tried not to glare, but she knew she was, and she was pretty sure she'd just stamped her foot. 'No, not to Jimmy. I need to go back because Flo has set the bloody house on fire. Okay?'

'If you'd let me know, I would have given you a lift here.'

'I thought you were probably busy again. And I was in a rush.'

'Too much of a rush to say goodbye?' His voice was so gentle, with a raw edge to it, that her stomach twisted. But how could he be like this? What did he care?

'I'm sorry. I should have…' She dropped her voice abruptly when she realised she was close to shouting and now had a very interested audience. 'I didn't text you and ask for a lift because… oh it's *complicated*.' She spat the words out, the same ones he'd

257

uttered to her, because it just wasn't fair. People were looking, so she dropped her voice to a hiss. 'I've had a holiday and now I'm going back. And why are you here anyway? You still haven't said.' She probably looked like a mad, spitting alley cat, but she didn't care any longer.

He folded his arms, his voice tight. 'Because I wanted to know the real reason, I thought maybe somebody had died or something had happened to Mabel, I thought you'd have explained otherwise, but it seems I got things wrong.' He shoved his hands in his pockets. 'Looks like I've been a bit of an idiot.'

'What do you mean, got things wrong? Why should I tell you what I'm doing, after all it's you, you…' She stopped herself short, wondering what the hell he meant about being an idiot. 'Look Javier, I am not giving up on anything, so don't make this about me being in the wrong.' She had to say it. 'You're the one that was all for sending me up the coast out of the way for the day.'

'Out of the way?' He looked puzzled. 'Why would I want you out of the way? I told you I had things to…'

'To do, yeah. You're the one that's got the bloody complications, the, the,' what was she, wife? Girlfriend? Ex? 'The family.'

'Family?'

'Family! Like your girlfriend, or partner, or whatever you want to call her, and your child.' Okay she hadn't meant to say it, she'd wanted to just calmly walk away, but he'd cornered her and maybe it was better out than in, as her dad would say.

'Child?' He stared as though he hadn't got a clue what she was talking about, which meant he had to be a very good actor or have a serious memory problem. How could he be like that? That was the really upsetting bit, that he'd seemed so open, so honest. And now this; he wasn't even prepared to be up front and admit what she'd seen with her own eyes. Tears of angry frustration were pricking at the back of her eyes. How could she have been so bloody naïve and stupid?

'Oh, for God's sake. Don't worry about it. There's nothing

to explain.' She did push him out of the way then, because the queue had moved and she wasn't going to risk losing her place. It was easier not to talk about it, to shut down, shut herself off, and make sure she never made the same stupid mistake again.

There wasn't anything to explain – he didn't owe her anything, nothing had happened between them. Even though she did feel let down. Duped. She folded her arms. Oh hell, no, she couldn't just not say anything more. She couldn't just leave it. 'What I don't understand is why you had to lie about it though?'

'Lie? Look Daisy stop being so stubborn and listen to me. I haven't got a clue what you're talking about, but I really wish I had. Especially,' he frowned, 'seeing as I seem to somehow be in the wrong here.'

'You told me you weren't in a relationship – that it was over.'

'I'm not, it is.'

'Not that I care.'

'You don't care?' There was the slightest fan of wrinkles round his eyes, the hint of a lift to his lips.

'No!'

'I'd hate to see you when you do care about something.'

Now he was really annoying her. How could he be so bloody flippant? 'I saw you with your little boy, Javier.'

'I haven't got a child.' The frown deepened. Then something softened in his expression, his voice lost its edge, and he looked almost relieved. 'A toddler?' He did a 'so-high' gesture with his hand and she nodded. 'You saw me with Jaime.' He sighed. 'So this is what this is about. Look, come over here and talk to me,' he stared at the woman behind her, 'in private.'

'I'm buying a plane ticket and I'm going home, and it's none of your business.'

'Maybe it isn't, but I know you shouldn't be going home to marry Jimmy. He's not the right man for you.'

'You're right, he's not.'

'Then stay.' His blue eyes locked with hers in a challenge she didn't understand. 'And apologise.'

'Why? Why should I stay?' She paused. 'And I really don't think I'm the one that has anything to apologise about.' She wasn't the one who'd lied, covered things up. She felt suddenly tired. 'I know you said things were complicated. Well I get it now, you're too busy for me and it's got nothing to do with your sister. It's been really kind of you to look after me, but I'm not actually a baby, I can look after myself.' She looked down at the floor. 'It was just a shock realising that you had a family relying on you; it would have been nice if you'd told me.'

'Okay I made a mistake not explaining properly. I admit it. But that's all, Jaime isn't my son, Daisy. I haven't got any kids, girlfriend, anything. Honestly. Stop for a moment and look at me. I told you it was complicated.' He'd somehow got closer, close enough to touch. He put a finger under her chin and waited for her to look at him, meet his gaze. 'It's very complicated, but I've never lied to you. For God's sake, I thought you trusted me, Daisy? I thought we had something.'

There was a hard edge to his voice that she hadn't heard before, a frustration mingled with something that could have been anger in his eyes. But he was still so beautiful. In fact, like this he was even more striking. An amazing man she'd wanted to believe in. The tears were threatening again and Daisy swallowed hard to get rid of the blockage in her throat.

It had never occurred to her not to trust him. He'd looked after her, spent time with her, kissed her so gently her legs had gone wobbly and she'd felt like she mattered.

'I did.' And that was the trouble; she'd completely, utterly trusted him. Trusted her own instincts. Trusted him. That was why it hurt so much to think she'd made a massive mistake. But now he was telling her she hadn't, that he'd thought they had something, so what was she supposed to think?

'It doesn't look that way from where I'm standing.' He shook his head. 'There isn't anybody else. I really think I should be the one that's angry here, not you.' He held a hand up to stop her interrupting. 'I know I should have explained earlier, but I want to do it now and if you still want to go home after that then I won't try and stop you. I'd really like us to be friends when you go, friends with good memories, even if you don't seem to be bothered.'

He really did seem cross with her. 'I am bothered, actually.' It came out all small and feeble, but she was. She was also confused by this new, determined Javier. She dragged her suitcase over to the row of seats and sat down heavily. 'So tell.'

'This has got *everything* to do with my sister, Daisy. Jaime is my sister's son. It was my little sister, Gabi, that you saw me with.'

Daisy stared as relief flooded through her, and she was pretty sure her mouth was open. 'Your sister? That's your sister, but I—'

'My sister. I thought you knew her? You met her at that get-together, didn't you?'

'We were never introduced, I just assumed...' The reality hit properly. 'Oh God.' She put a hand over her mouth and felt like the biggest, blackest hole ever had opened up in front of her and her stomach dropped into it. How could she have been so stupid and jumped to a conclusion like that? He'd never ever done anything but be honest and open, and she'd let an irrational flood of jealousy swamp all logic. 'I am so sorry.' The words came out on a whisper.

What kind of a person was she to imagine the worst of such an amazing man? Well, of anybody. Infatuated was probably the answer, but it wasn't an acceptable excuse.

'Why didn't you at least ask me?' His mouth was twisted in a look that spelled out pure disappointment. 'I don't get why you didn't stop and say hello, say something, then all this...' He waved a hand.

'I just,' she couldn't look into his eyes, but she knew she had to, 'I took the easy way out.' She took a deep breath. 'I ran away.' At the first hint of something, somebody, really important in her

261

life she'd acted the coward and grasped the first excuse she could to avoid baring her soul, leaving herself open to disappointment, heartache.

She wanted to grab him, kiss him, laugh, cry, but all she could do was stare and hope he'd forgive her.

He was looking at her in that intense way he had, totally serious and all of sudden she was desperate to see the fan of wrinkles at the corners of his eyes, see his mouth curl up. See him happy. Have him forgive her for being such a stupid, stupid fool.

'I'm sorry.'

'Me too.' She wasn't one hundred per cent sure what that meant, and knew she was holding her breath to see what came next. 'Let's go back, talk about this properly?'

He wedged her suitcase between his feet at the front of the scooter, and she was jammed in behind him as they sped back into the city centre, not knowing whether to wrap her arms round him and let that irresistible familiar smell invade her senses, or keep as far away as possible. Which was tricky. Given their close proximity. And the fact he probably thought she was the last person he should ever get into a relationship with.

'I'll carry your case up for you.'

'No, it's okay. You've done enough.'

'Daisy.' The exasperated splutter was so unlike Javier that she forgot about hanging on and let him have the bag. And trudged behind him, counting the eighty-four steps and wondering what was going to happen when they got to the top. It was awkward. Very awkward. And following his trim backside and muscled thighs made it worse. And she couldn't exactly close her eyes.

'I meant it, I wasn't going home to Jimmy.'

'Okay, good, and I meant that there wasn't anybody else, Daisy. But I did think you knew who Gabi was, I thought you knew she was my sister.' He raised an eyebrow. 'With a dog.'

Daisy grimaced and plopped down on the sofa. She was such

262

an idiot, and she'd acted totally out of character. She never normally threw accusations at people or assumed the worse. 'I remember seeing Gabi on that first night. But I just thought...' she put her hands over her face, 'well I got it in my head then she must be your girlfriend. I don't know what came over me, I really don't know why I reacted like that. You've never done anything but be honest and kind.' She'd been jealous, mad jealous in a way she'd never been before.

'Gabi isn't my girlfriend, but she is my complication, Daisy. Like I said to you, she's the reason I came back here, to Barcelona, why I stopped travelling and started this business. She needs me, she's on her own with Jaime and it's not always easy for her. After Mum died...' He shrugged. 'It hit her harder than me, they were really close and then,' he paused, 'well then Jamie's dad went too and it was all too much for her.' His tone had softened. 'She had a baby to look after, a funeral to sort, her whole world had collapsed. So I packed in my job and came here, and promised I'd stay as long as she needs me.'

'Poor Gabi.' She didn't know what else to say.

'I mean, she doesn't really ask for much; she'd kill me if she thought I was saying that. She's pretty self-sufficient, but kids can be hard work. She needs a break sometimes, somebody to chat to. We all need somebody, don't we?' He looked at her and her heart twisted. How could she ever have suspected him of trying to deceive her? 'It's no hardship, I love it here and I love her, but that's why I thought until she's on her feet it was better not to get too involved with anybody. My ex wasn't too impressed when I turned up on a date with a toddler in tow.' He gave a twisted grin, and Daisy couldn't help smiling back. 'I wasn't trying to keep it secret, but when you said you'd probably never come back here it seemed pointless to even try and explain, you obviously didn't feel the same way I did.'

'When you took me for coffee? Asked if I'd come back in the spring?'

He nodded and walked over to the window, so she followed him. Tentatively put a hand on the broad back. 'I didn't mean I didn't want to see you, it was just a surprise, I was trying to work out—'

'How you felt?'

'No.' She paused. 'That kiss was the best thing…' God this was difficult to put into words. 'Javier, nobody has ever made me feel like you do, I've never been kissed like that before,' she held up a hand when it looked like he was about to speak. She needed to get this out, put it into words, for her own sake as well as his. 'Jimmy's the only boyfriend I've ever had and he's just never made me feel like you do. And then, when you asked me if I'd come back.' She stared at him, willing him to understand. 'I was just trying to work out in my head how I could come back, when I could.' She sighed. 'Then you rushed off after, hardly said a word. And I thought it was me being stupid, making something out of nothing.'

'My feelings aren't nothing, Daisy, if only you knew how hard it's been to resist you, I'd been dying to kiss you for a long time. I rushed off,' his voice was oh so gentle, 'because I was upset you'd said no, when I thought I'd got you all wrong, that I didn't mean anything to you.'

'Oh Javier, I didn't mean that. I've wanted you to kiss me for ages.' She swallowed hard. 'I'd decided I'd work it out, make sure I could come back soon, then when I saw you, the three of you, it just all seemed to make sense… I've never been jealous before.' She hadn't; nobody had meant that much to her before. 'And I guess I,' she looked at her feet, embarrassed, 'overreacted a bit. It really hurt.' Hurt was much too small a word, it had been a physical pain.

'I went to chat to Gabi, try and get things straight in my head. I'd thought maybe I should keep my distance anyway, not start something I couldn't finish. But staying away from you was easier said than done, which is why I came back today. Look Daisy, I don't quite know why I came after you to the airport, maybe I shouldn't have, I couldn't help myself, I had to see you, it was just an...'

'Impulse?'

He grinned, the first real smile she'd seen from him, showing his gorgeous white teeth and that cleft in his chin that she wanted to touch. 'More than an impulse, Daisy. I don't know what to say now. I just didn't want you to go back to what you had before. I want you to have your dreams.'

'And that's it?' If that was it, if that was why he'd come to the airport, then she really should go home, because staying here, with him, wouldn't do her any good at all.

He was close enough to kiss, but she couldn't, she shouldn't. 'I don't know. I honestly don't know. Maybe I'm not being fair, being selfish.' His warm hand was on her arm, as though he couldn't help himself. 'When I said at the airport that I wanted us to part as good friends, I didn't mean that,' the grin had slipped, 'I'd like us to be more than friends, Daisy. But I can't follow you back to your home – you do know that? Maybe one day, but not right now. You deserve good things, Daisy, somebody who can be there for you, not a quick fling.'

'Maybe you should let me be the judge of that.' She reached out and touched his chin, she couldn't help herself.

'I don't want you to feel hurt. That's why I've tried not to let anything happen between us, it wouldn't be fair.'

'Life's not always very fair. I want something to happen, Javier. Seeing you is more important than you can imagine, all this does mean something to me.'

'It's selfish,' he traced a finger across her lips; he was so close, close enough to kiss, 'but a few days more, before you leave, is better than nothing.'

'Let's just play it by ear, shall we? Make the most of what we do have, whether it's a fling or not.' Her body closed the gap between them, so that her forehead rested against his. 'Can we start off by kissing and making up, you know after our fall out? I always think it's a good idea.'

He chuckled, and it was so unexpected she stared, and was lost in those deep-blue eyes that were better than any ocean view. 'You do realise you shouldn't have kissed me that first time, Daisy? Until you did that, I was coping.' There was the slightest tremor in his voice. 'I blame you for this.'

And then he kissed her.

It started off like it had the last time. The time when they'd been looking over the city. He'd tasted of coffee that time, the slightest hint was all she'd got, but this time he tasted of something that made her need more. His lips were soft against hers, undemanding, the lightest touch that set off a tremor in her stomach, made the hairs on the back of her neck prickle. His tongue traced a delicate, teasing line along her lip that was almost unbearable, that left her shivery and hot both at the same time.

'Look at me, Daisy.' She opened her eyes, and his gorgeous bright-blue eyes were looking straight at her and she knew she just wanted to savour this moment, even if she never had it again, even if, at the end of this holiday, they went their separate ways.

'Javier.' She breathed his name, and it was swallowed up as his lips met hers again, but this time they were demanding. This time he had the fingers of one hand tangled in her hair, the other holding their bodies pressed tightly together. She clutched at him greedily, drank in the smell of him, the taste of him, felt the stubble on his chin under the tips of her fingers, the silky softness of his hair. Panting, he pulled away.

'We don't have to take this any fur—'

Daisy grinned and wrapped her arms around his neck. 'Oh, I think we do.'

Chapter 22 – Daisy. Sandcastles

'I want you to meet somebody before you go home tomorrow morning.'

Daisy half-turned so that she could look at Javier, who was standing at her side, his arm round her waist. 'I do wish I could stay a bit longer.'

'I wish you could as well.' He smiled, his fingers tightening. 'But we'll make sure there are other times.'

She gazed down from the balcony at the crowds walking below. The time might have whizzed by since she'd arrived, but she felt a different person to the timid but determined Daisy that had arrived here with Anna. It was almost as if a switch had flicked inside her and she realised she could do anything, be anybody, if she wanted to. Or she could just be Daisy, having fun and exploring but knowing she had a home she loved and would always return to.

'In fact,' he leant down and the lightest kiss skimmed her lip, sending a little shiver of need through her body, 'I promise there will be other times. Come on before I forget what we're supposed to be doing.'

'Daisy! I've been dying to meet you properly. God knows why my big brother hasn't introduced us before.'

The petite and very pretty Gabi wrapped Daisy in a bear hug, kissed her on both cheeks then held her at arm's length. She smiled, the same generous, open smile that Javier had, and Daisy felt like an idiot. Again. It was obvious they were related. They had the same gorgeous smile, the same dark hair, and the same amazing blue eyes. Why the hell hadn't she realised when she'd spotted them together? And why hadn't she thought about the fact that the toddler clutching Javier's leg had blond curls?

'I've heard a lot about you, but I gather you've not heard much about me?'

'Well…'

'I really can't believe you did that, Javier. Of all the stupid things.' Gabi looked from Javier to Daisy and shook her head. 'He's never been the type to exactly put his emotions on the line, but to not even explain why he couldn't see you.'

'Will you stop talking about me as though I'm not here? Come on, Jaime, us men should stick together.' The little boy nodded, his shock of curls bobbing.

'Sandcastle.'

'Sandcastle time, you're right. We will do man stuff.' He winked at Daisy. 'Then we will do some grown-up stuff before you have to go.'

'Coffee?' Gabi ordered the drinks and settled down for a chat. 'It's so nice to have a proper chat to somebody in English, I'm sure I'm forgetting how to talk properly. I speak Spanish, of course, but apart from with Javier, the only people I speak English to are foreigners.'

'You've lived here a while then?'

'I moved here before Jaime was born, then fell in love with the place.' She grinned. 'Must be in the genes, Mum was mad about Spain.'

'I didn't realise until the other day, but my parents came years ago and loved it. It is beautiful, I really don't know why it took me so long to come.' Daisy sighed and watched the waves breaking, the surf rippling in over the sand and then retreating. She didn't want to retreat. She wanted to stay. She glanced back at Gabi, who was watching her, thoughtfully, like Javier did. 'Thanks for letting us borrow Poppy, she's gorgeous.'

'You're welcome. Javier said you were really missing your own dog. She's not so gorgeous when she's being bloody minded, you've no idea how naughty and stubborn teckels can be.'

'Teckel?'

'That's what most people out here call them, you say dachshund, don't you?'

Daisy laughed. 'Yes, oh I've got a good idea what they can be like. I groom dogs at home and I've come across one or two of them, but she's still adorable.'

'She has that look to make you forgive her. Like my son does.' She nodded at Jaime. 'And my brother – he has that look when he wants to.'

They both watched the pair playing on the sand.

'I'm so glad you didn't go back early.'

Daisy was surprised at Gabi's comment.

'My silly dollop of a brother is very fond of you.'

'He's nice.'

Gabi grinned. 'He thinks you are too. Oh, come on, don't look like that. He's actually never stopped mentioning you since you first met, not that he realised at first. It was Daisy this, Daisy that.'

'Oh I'm sorr—'

'Don't be sorry, it's fab. He's never wanted to share stuff with somebody like that. I mean, don't think he's a saint, he's had lots of girlfriends.'

That explained the earth-shattering kisses then.

'But he's never wanted to be with somebody all the time, to show them all the bits of Barcelona he loves.' She laughed. 'And he never stole my dog before! It's been like living with a whirlwind; he's dashed in to us, then dashed off again as though he was a man on a mission, but I suppose he was, wasn't he? The clock was ticking away until time was up and you went. Then you went early.'

Daisy wriggled in her seat, feeling embarrassed, hoping against hope that Gabi didn't know the full story. 'Well there was a bit of an emergency at home – at least I thought there was. But there wasn't, and I, well, there was a bit,' major understatement here, 'of a misunderstanding. I saw the three of you and—'

'I know.' Gabi frowned. 'Javier told me, he was so stupid not explaining properly.'

'Oh really, no, it wasn't his fault. I mean I shouldn't have just assumed… I should have stopped, said hello.' She felt so bad, Gabi must think she was pathetic, 'I should have trusted him, I mean I did, do, but I didn't stop to think. I just thought the worst, which is so…' So not her. She still hadn't quite got to grips with why she'd been so stupid, was that what they meant by the green-eyed monster? Something had certainly taken over her brain and left her devoid of her normal common-sense that day. But that was the point, she supposed. This wasn't the old her, this wasn't normal. The old, comfortable her had known what to expect, had never known what it felt like to be head over heels in love. Because she knew now, that's what she was.

The old Daisy accepted Jimmy's flirting with other people because it didn't matter that much to her, he didn't matter. He was just a good friend, not the man who'd stole her heart. But she really shouldn't have let insecurities take over.

'Well I am so glad you did see us though, and you forced him into a corner.' She leaned forward and put a hand over Daisy's. 'You will give him a chance, won't you? You both look so happy.'

'Well I don't really… I mean he's here and I'm going back to the UK.' She was going to say it was complicated and stopped herself just in time. 'And I think it's more a case of whether he'll give me another chance to be honest, I was such an idiot.' Although it did look like he'd forgiven her, but they hadn't discussed the future. Where they went from here.

'Oh he will, he is *so* keen on you, Daisy. Really. He wanted to be with you, get to know you better. When he has been with us he's not really been here, you know. He's had other things on his mind.' She grinned. 'You! He's a brill big brother, he's made a lot of sacrifices for us, but all this isn't good. I don't want you to be one of those things he loses out on.'

'I do like him, a lot, it's just we hardly know each other.' And she liked him even more since they'd got back from the airport and he'd literally swept her off her feet. She could feel the heat rushing to her face.

'I know. I'm sorry. I'm going over the top, aren't I? It's just, I mean, if you wanted to it would be so nice to see you back here. I guess,' she paused for breath, 'what I'm trying to say is what I keep trying to make Javier see. You've got to grab what you can, Daisy. When Javier told me what had happened, and I saw the look on his face, it made me really think. I don't want him to go through what I did. I know I didn't realise what I had until it was too late. Just before Jaime was born, his dad died. One day he was there and the next...' she shrugged, 'life's short, there were so many things that we were going to do together and then it was too late. It just all fell apart, drifted away like that sandcastle of Jaime's.'

Daisy stared at the sandcastle, at the look of consternation on little Jaime's face, and the lump in her throat made it difficult to speak. Not that she really knew what to say. 'Oh no, I'm so sorry, Gabi.' It sounded so lame.

'Oh, don't be sorry, I'm doing okay now. It's taken time, but we are getting there. I'm just trying to explain why Javier is so protective.' A note of frustration had crept into her voice. 'I love him to bits, and he's been so good to us, but I'm just trying to say time is too precious to be using it up on the wrong things.'

Daisy knew exactly what she meant. She'd spent most of her life thinking she had to do what was expected, taking the easy way out instead of chasing her dreams. Following her heart.

'Javier thinks you are brave, he admires you, but he doesn't realise that the same applies to him, that he has to put himself first sometimes. He's always tried to look after people, that's why he does the type of jobs he does I suppose, but he spends too much time with me. He won't listen to me, and he's not good at saying what he wants – but I know he wants some time with you. Trust me.' She grinned. 'He's smitten.'

'I'm going home soon though.' It was a sobering thought, and right now she wasn't sure she wanted to. She was torn between home and her obligations, and the man she'd fallen head over heels for. And she knew now she had, which was why she'd been so devastated when she'd thought he hadn't felt the same way. That they hadn't had a future. 'I promised my parents I'd be home for Christmas' and she had that one last conversation to have with Jimmy, as well, before she would feel that she really could move on.

'I like your brother a lot, Gabi, and it would be fab if he could come home with me.' She grinned. 'But I know he can't, really. I understand.' She looked at the other girl, who was as kind and lovely as her brother. 'This Christmas his place is here with you, and mine is back home sorting my mess out.' Not going back wasn't an option.

'But you might come back next year?'

'I'd love to, I will, but I do love my home, and I know this isn't exactly going to be an easy thing to work out.' But nor was leaving Javier and getting onto that plane. Leaving him was going to be like ripping part of herself out and leaving it behind.

'I know, just leave a door open and you never know who will walk through, eh? Now I'm being too serious, it's a nice day. Tell me about where you live and this massive dog of yours.'

Chapter 23 – Flo. Fanning the flames

'You'd better come to mine for some supper, and bring the bloody dog as well.' Hugo had his arms crossed and his legs at hip-width, but there was a hint of light in his eye that meant he was closer to making fun of her than falling out with her.

'Only if you're going to behave.'

'Behave?' He raised an eyebrow, which made him look wicked. 'And in what way do you mean behave?' Oh God, that drawl set off a chain reaction in her body that could only lead to one place – bed.

'As in listen to me for once and not go off on your high horse.' She wasn't sure how long she could keep up this being-cross business.

'I can't promise that, I quite like my high horse, and you don't seem to have much option, given the state of your cooking facilities.'

Flo stared at the cottage. How could she have done this? Why on earth did she seem so intent on screwing up her life, especially when it had actually seemed on the up at last? 'I'm going to have to paint the kitchen before Daisy comes home. Oh hell, can you buy new cookers this close to Christmas?'

'You can buy anything, darling, but it will be fine, Agas are made to last. Unlike the pan you were using. I'm sure we can get another one though.'

We can get he'd said. He was doing it again; acting the he-man and looking after her. Which was getting to be a bad habit. In fact, he'd been doing it since she'd arrived, dangerous territory. If he'd stop acting like a flaming knight in shining armour, rescuing her from her predicaments (which was so clichéd), then it would be easier to resist him. Although she had already fallen into bed with him once, which was probably one too many times, because she really didn't need another bossy man in her life, even if he had shown a vulnerable side she'd never suspected existed. And he'd just called her *darling*. Although he called everyone that. So it didn't mean a thing. And he supported her writing, and the person she wanted to be, which Oli had never done.

'Oh shit, my writing.'

'Writing?'

'Don't you remember? I was writing when you came round. I'd been inspired by—' oh no, she couldn't say Oli, 'events.' Move on quickly. 'Then you disturbed me, and marched off, and I had to go after you, and that's why I forgot…'

'Your bacon? Wait here, I'll go in and look.'

'But, Hugo…'

'I'm sure it's all fine in there, it was something and nothing, the fire brigade said, only in the kitchen, but you stay here, better to be safe…' He marched off before she could stop him, so she ran after him, slipping and sliding on the icy path.

No way was she 'staying there' like some obedient dog. Even if the place was a bit stinky and the fire brigade had agreed that there had never been any danger. And Hugo had very effectively put the flames out. She supposed they must be bored; not very many fires to be heroic over.

'Your handwriting is atrocious.' He had her notepad in his hand, a surprisingly smoke-free notepad.

'Give it back.' Oh Gawd, it would be so embarrassing if he could decipher it.

'In a minute.' He was grinning, his eyes lit up with amusement, which probably meant he had made out the odd word.

'I'm not used to writing, I normally type. Can I have it, please?' As in now. 'Hugo!'

He held it up higher, just out of reach, looking at the book, not her. Reading. 'What does this say? Oh. Hmm.' He'd got his head down and glanced up through his eyelashes at her, then put a hand on his chin. 'This aristocratic twit in here is totally fictional?'

'Totally. It's fiction. But he's not a twit. And there are elements of truth in all stories.'

'And this bit where he's cooking pheasant and only wearing an apron?'

'I've got a vivid imagination.'

A wicked grin lit up his features, and for a moment she thought he was going to totally embarrass her by starting to read out loud. But instead he lowered the pad. 'It's actually really good.'

'It's only a rough draft, of just a bit…'

'But it is good.'

'Please.' She was used to writing articles for people to read, but this was different, this was fiction. But this had a piece of her, her feelings, emotions, her heart, embedded in each sentence. 'Can I have it?'

'Why?' His tone had softened and he was giving her that toe-curling, intense look of his. 'I was thinking it might be quite good to act out this scene where she—'

'Stop it. It's personal, it's, well it's just draft, not finished, I—' It was words that had poured out of her in response to the way she'd felt, fragments of a story that wasn't yet clear in her mind.

His features softened, as did his voice, back to that level where her legs went wobbly. 'It's beautiful. Really.' He closed the note-book and gently handed it over. 'Sorry, I shouldn't tease. Don't ever let anybody tell you not to write, Flo.' Then he kissed her on the forehead and walked out, pausing in the doorway but not even turning round. 'Oh I've rung somebody to come and board up the cracked kitchen window. He'll be round in the next half an hour, so supper at seven.'

***

Supper was fish and chips, which he'd driven out to pick up from the village chip shop. Served with a nice chilled Chablis.

'You're crazy.'

'I think you'll find 'resourceful' is the word. One doesn't have unexpected guests every day of the week, in fact one very rarely has them at all, which is what I like about living so far from a main road. Now budge up on the sofa so I can join you. Vinegar?'

Flo took the plate he had held out and budged up. They sat in companionable silence. She gazed at the flickering flames in the fireplace as she munched her way through an enormous pile of chips. She'd always loved watching the fire when she was little; the way it constantly changed, shifting into new patterns and shapes, throwing a shimmering shadow on to the walls. She used to challenge herself to sit close to the fire as long as she could, until her face and feet glowed and she couldn't stand it any longer.

'You like playing with fire, don't you?' His voice was mild and when she glanced his way he was steadily eating, one eyebrow quirked into an amused arch.

'I like watching.'

'Fanning the flames.' He put his plate down. 'You fan my flames, gorgeous Flo.'

'Stop it, I'm trying to eat chips.' Her appetite seemed to have died a sudden death though, even if his flames hadn't.

He leaned back on the sofa, stretching his long, long legs in front of him so that she couldn't avoid looking at his lean, muscled

276

thighs. Well she could have gone back to flame- watching. But his body had a magnetic attraction of its own. Rippling muscles were more fascinating than flickering flames any day.

'Thanks for rescuing me today.' Again. 'Even if it was your fault.'

'My fault? So what weird logic is behind the reasoning that your breakfast got cremated?'

'You distracted me.'

He laughed. Did she detect a trace of bitterness there? 'I don't think that was me.'

'Well it was actually.' Flo sighed. 'Oli had gone when I decided to have a fry-up.'

'So he has actually gone?'

'I told him there was no chance of me going back, Hugo.' He relaxed a notch. 'He said he'd wait, but I told him not to bother.'

'So why did he come in the first place?'

'Because I didn't reply to his emails, and,' deep breath, 'he realised I was a better bet than shaggable Sarah.'

'And the bubbly?'

'He forgot it, but I'm sure he'll be back. He doesn't like squandering his money.'

'Ahh.'

'That's why he'd rather I write for the magazine than waste time *scribbling stories* as he puts it.'

'I meant what I said before, you shouldn't give up.' He grinned. 'You never know, one day your kids might benefit from a best-seller.'

'I won't. Thanks.'

'Flo.' He was suddenly serious. Which was also sexy – very. 'You need to change your flight.'

'Sorry?' She was totally confused now. What was it about him that was so good at knocking her off balance? 'What do you mean I need to change my flight?'

'For a wordsmith you really do have trouble with simple words sometimes, don't you?'

'You know what I mean. Stop trying to be clever.' Okay, she was going to have to admit defeat with the chips. She put the plate to one side, hoping Mabel didn't polish off what was left. She was pretty sure she'd read something that said potatoes and canine stomachs didn't mix.

'You can't possibly fly home tomorrow. Nobody flies on Christmas Eve, you'll miss out on the fun.'

'But I've got to go.' Flo looked down at her feet. 'I need to go back, sort out my life, and work out how to pay the rent.'

'You don't have to do that until the New Year, and you need to get some more of your book done. Come on, give me one good reason why you can't delay a bit.'

There wasn't really one. Nothing waiting for her at home quite as tempting as gorgeous Hugo. 'Daisy is coming back, that was the agreement. She'll want her slightly singed cottage back, and there's not really room…'

He twirled a strand of her hair lazily around his finger, her scalp tingled. Expectant. 'You can stay here. I've plenty of room – and an e-nor-mous bed.'

Okay, she was blushing. She knew all about his enormous bed. She leaned in a little bit closer to the heat of his body and tried to speak normally, and not squeak. 'I won't get a refund on my flight, it's too late.' His fingers had reached her tingling scalp, and he'd bent over so that his warm breath was feathering her hair.

'I'll pay for it, and I can give you a better reason to stay.' The low and husky version of his voice should have a health warning. He rested his chin on the top of her head, so that each time he took a breath it reverberated through her. Building up the tension. Making her want him that little bit more.

He stopped playing with her hair and moved slightly away. She looked at him. The spell broken.

'Me. If you don't stay with me, then Christmas will be just

like any other day – you'll be depriving me of something more entertaining.' His eyes were hooded, the self-protective drawl back in place, just in case he needed a rapid retreat.

'Oh, you're good.' She grinned and shook her head. 'You could go to your parents?'

'Too late to kiss-and-make-up, my little Miss Nightingale.'

'It's never too late and,' she paused, whatever he said about his father it was obvious that he missed his mother and she suspected the feeling would be mutual, 'Christmas is a family time, can't you just try? For me?' She added the last bit hopefully and he laughed.

'My parents don't feature in my Christmas fantasies at all, you do.' His eyes glinted and Flo couldn't help smiling. She wasn't going to let him off the hook, if there was one thing she was going to do for Hugo before she went home it was to at least get him to promise to try and make up with his parents. 'The Christmas Eve party won't be the same without you, I'll be lonely.'

'What Christmas Eve party?'

'The one here with you and me.'

'You really are funny.' And adorable.

He reached out then and dragged her onto his lap, and she stilled as he wrapped his strong arms round her and looked straight into her eyes.

There was the slightest of lifts to the corner of his beautiful mouth, but his gaze was serious. Piercing. Strands of his blond hair flopped forward over his brow, and her fingers twitched to brush them back. His dimples were deep, but not with laughter. 'Please?'

He traced the tip of his finger over her own lips, brushed back the hair from her face, and she held her breath. It was turning her on more than ripping off clothes ever had. The emptiness inside her stomach was spreading and she wanted, more than anything, to reach out, but she daren't move. She didn't want to spoil the moment, stop him.

'I'd just like you to stay as long as you can. This is as close as I get to begging, Flo. Please?'

Oh shit. How could she say no? No way.

She looked straight into those dark grey eyes that were studying her so intently and there was a new flutter of anticipation inside her that was nothing to do with sex.

Hugo James wanted her to stay. He was offering her more than a roll between the sheets; it was a glimpse of a different future. If she stayed he could probably take her heart and turn it to mush before he moved on, but she was daring to hope that he wouldn't.

The thought scared her, but it was also far more exciting than anything she'd ever been asked to do before. With a man who had the type of hidden depths she really wanted to explore at least a little bit more.

She swallowed down the feelings that were bubbling up inside her, but couldn't stop the grin escaping. Flo put her hand up, tangled her fingers in his hair, then pulled his face down. 'Show me how much you want me to.'

Chapter 24 – Flo. Christmas Eve

Flo lay back on the bed and looked at the message from Daisy, confirming her flight back and asking what she should do with the keys to the apartment.

Okay, so the best solution was to keep this simple. '*Bring them with you.*'

'*With me?*'

Awkward, but this way she sidled in and got it over with. '*I'll still be here. Decided to stay over for Christmas Day.*'

There was a pause. A long delay. She was just wondering if she needed to add something when a reply came. '*Great! It might be a bit cramped in the cottage though, but I can borrow a camp bed. Mum and Dad will be really pleased to see you.*'

Mum and Dad? Oh. '*I'm not inviting myself to dinner at your parents!*' this was going to raise a few questions. Oh well, in for a penny. '*It's okay about the bed, I've found somewhere else to stay…*'

Her phone rang within seconds of her sending the message. Daisy. A slightly suspicious Daisy.

'Flo, what do you mean? Where are you going?' Then Daisy started to laugh, 'Oh my God,' there was a spluttering sound, 'I get it, it's bloody Hugo isn't it? Oh Flo,' she was obviously cracking up at the other end of the phone.

'It isn't that funny!'

'Oh God, does Anna know? Oh this is absolutely amazing, Flo.' More giggles. 'I always said he needed somebody to put him in his place – and you're just the girl. Oh Flo, how on earth did that hap… No, don't tell me. Just don't tell me.'

'I wasn't going to, don't worry. So, I'll see you later tonight, will I?'

'You will,' there was another giggle, 'as long as you're not too busy.' There was a pause. 'I might be a bit late, I decided I'd go and call in at Jimmy's on the way. I need to talk to him and get it out of the way, I don't just want to bump into him.'

'Oh Daisy, I'm sorry.' She'd almost forgotten the reason Daisy had wanted a break, just as the reason she'd needed to get away had kind of faded into the background. And been replaced with something that made her much happier.

'It's fine. I knew all along it wasn't right, he's not answering his phone or my messages, but I want to see him face to face anyway.'

'He's not been here, and, to be honest, I've not been into the village much anyway so I haven't had chance to bump into him, but you know you're doing the right thing. He'll be fine, Daisy.'

'I know, it's just a bit weird coming back and having to talk about it. It seems ages ago when he asked, like a different lifetime.'

Oh she knew that feeling well. Much as it had hurt at the time, the Paris experience had faded at the edges now, was a fuzzy memory that would probably never go away completely. But it didn't matter.

'I'd better go, I want one last look round Barcelona before I have to go to the airport.'

'Okay, take care and have a good flight. I'll feed the animals and probably take Mabel with me to Hugo's.'

'Won't he mind?' Daisy sounded shocked.

'Mind? Er, no, his dog is in love with her.'

'Just how much time have you been spending round there?'

'I'm not going to answer that. See you tomorrow, Dais, and don't worry about Jimmy, will you? Catch you later, bye.'

The first night after the fire, she'd just ended up staying there because the extent to which he'd demonstrated how much he wanted her to stay had meant there wasn't much night left. And then he'd cooked her breakfast, like you do, because the kitchen was still a bit smelly, and the pan well past the rescue stage. So she'd helped him with the horses, just because it seemed the right thing to do – to show how grateful she was.

And he'd cleared the desk in the study, because he wanted her to have somewhere nice to write (although she spent more time looking through his books, and staring at the many photographs of horses, and him on horses, and him standing next to horses clutching trophies, and the occasional shot of a much younger him with a stern-looking man who just had to be his father, and a very beautiful and aristocratic lady, who just had to be his mother).

So she'd attempted to tidy up his house a bit, which was strewn with horse-related stuff and magazines.

And now, before she knew it, it was Christmas Eve and she needed to clear her stuff out of Daisy's, which was why she was back in her side of the house. Answering awkward questions.

Flo started to pack her few belongings into her suitcase, and Mabel watched her with a worried frown, her chin on her paws and her dark eyes following Flo's every move.

'Don't look at me like that, I'm only going next door, and Daisy will be back later.' She waggled her eyebrows, as though she understood. 'But you can come to Hugo's for our party, you're guest of honour. He said you could, and Rags will be very happy to see you.' The dog wagged her tail slowly and sat back on her haunches. 'Although it might be a bit X-rated, best knickers on just in case.' She waved them in the air, a bit of a mistake when Mabel made a lunge for the scrap of lace. 'Don't you dare!' She hastily stuffed them into her suitcase, out of harms' way, and did a quick check of the drawers and wardrobe, and a glance round the bathroom.

She dragged her suitcase down the narrow staircase, which was a damned sight easier than dragging it up had been when she'd arrived. Although now she just had to be so much fitter, after spending so much time out in the fields and stables, it was hard to believe that so much had happened in such a short time. When she'd first arrived it had been like a little step back in time, back to her childhood. It had been a way to avoid her present, avoid Oli and the job she wasn't sure she liked any more. But it had soon become something far different. More like a glimpse of a better future, a new life that took the best bits of the present and the past and made something shiny and new. Except she wasn't quite sure how it was all going to look when she got back to Barcelona. One thing she did know was she'd be broke.

'Less tapas and wine for one thing, Mabel – that has to be a healthy bonus, doesn't it?'

Leaving a note pinned up by the door, telling Daisy that she had Mabel with her, she pulled the front door shut. 'Come on then, Mabel. Christmas starts here.'

***

'You'll make quite a good groom once I've got you trained up.'

'I'm going to have to teach you how to keep it simple and just say thank you.' Flo laughed and flicked a fork full of straw at Hugo, and before she had chance to retaliate he'd dived forward, hooked her feet from under her, and she'd landed in the bedding. With him looming over her.

'You do realise this was my first proper view of you? From underneath after Mabel had flattened me. If you hadn't been suitably impressive I would have been off by now, you know.' She grinned.

'You're a cheeky mare, asking for a good spanking.'

'Such a stud.' She propped herself up on one elbow. 'All mouth and no trousers?'

'I think you know exactly what I am, dear Florence.' He straddled her, a knee either side, and pinned her arms back in the straw. 'And I know exactly what *you* are right now, far too big a distraction.' He leaned down, intent on his face, then Flo got the weirdest sensation of a vibration right through her pelvis. Even Hugo wasn't capable of doing that to her.

He froze, and peered down. 'Saved by the bell.' And prodded her hip, where her mobile phone was lodged into her pocket, sandwiched between them. 'Which is probably a good thing, seeing as we've got to bring all the horses in and feed them.'

Flo leaned back and fished the phone from her pocket, which had stopped ringing. 'It was Javier. I wonder what's up with him?'

'I don't know. Come on, ring him after we've finished up.'

'Bossy man.' She followed him up to the fields, Mabel loping along at her side. They'd somehow slipped into a routine since the fire – they worked together, side by side, enjoying each other's company – and she loved to watch him handling the horses, a time when it was guaranteed that he'd be himself. Show her the true Hugo: no artifice, no barriers – he couldn't hide when he was with his animals. That was when the mockery was replaced by gentle teasing, and a cheeky humour she loved, when the drawl was replaced by a coaxing but firm tone that made something inside her go all gooey.

Then they'd share a glass of wine, end up cooking together, laughing, listening to music… but soon it would be over. She had to make the most of her last few days, of Christmas.

The ground was crispy under her feet as she and Mabel left a new trace next to the ones that marked where Hugo had strode.

It looked as though they were going to get a white Christmas, and she was so pleased she'd be here to see it. And whatever Hugo thought, the first thing she was going to do in the morning was build a snowman. A massive one. 'Shall we build a snow dog as well, Mabel? And a snow horse for Hugo?'

The light was already fading, the clear sky and crisp white covering on the ground drawing the day out so that they could make the most of every second. She banged her hands together, trying to get the circulation going, knowing that her fingertips would tingle when she went back inside the warm house.

She blew out, watching the warm air dance against the cold, a ghostly whisper of heat fighting the icy stillness.

The horses appeared over the brow, following Hugo, snorting their own halos of warmth like small dragons, the frost already teasing its way into their long lashes and forelocks. They danced on their tiptoes, avoiding the sharp, hard frozen ruts of earth, ever mindful of the tall figure that walked in front. If she'd ever hoped to capture a moment, it was this one.

She closed her eyes, hoping to imprint it on her memory, the freezing air biting at her nostrils as she breathed in, catching at her throat and making her eyes water.

A low whistle made her open her eyes, and through the dampness she realised Hugo was watching her. 'Penny for them?'

'I was just thinking how much I love it here,' she shrugged, 'what more could anybody want?' She looked at him. 'I'll be sad to go.' It was that happy-sad thing again. She liked it here, she felt chilled, comfortable. But her home was in Barcelona. And Hugo was here, in Cheshire. With his horses.

'Well, I don't know if I should admit this or not, but it'll be damned strange without you.'

'You don't fancy coming to Barcelona for New Year's Eve, do you?'

'I can't just leave the horses.'

'Daisy can do them. Just for a couple of days, she'll be back home. I'd like you to know where I am.'

'I think I'd rather like to know as well.' The corner of his mouth quirked up. 'See if I can work out what could possibly appeal to you more than being here with me can.'

Flo laughed, not sure how serious he was being, and then slipped her hand into the one he offered. 'Impossible to imagine, isn't it?'

'It is.' He squeezed her hand. 'Thank you for asking,' his voice had a softer edge than normal, 'I can't think of anybody I'd rather see in the New Year with.'

Which made her insides all squishy and warm.

Chapter 25 – Daisy. Turkey and sprouts

'So this is it then?'

'This is it.'

Daisy looked at the queue that was snaking its way through airport security, and then back at Javier. 'I wish you could come. I'm sorry, I shouldn't say that, it isn't fair.'

Christmas was all turkey and sprouts. A part she loved, and then a not-so-nice bit that you had to put up with. And now she was actually all fluttery-excited inside at the thought of going home to Mabel and Barney, but she had a hard lump in her chest that wouldn't budge. What if she never saw Javier again? What if she never felt this lovely warmth inside that seemed to make the whole world look brighter – as though really, honestly, anything could happen if she wanted it to? She didn't want that light extinguished. She didn't want to go without this man who made everything look better.

'I'm glad you said it.' He kissed the end of her nose. He got her. He got *it*. Which kind of made it worse. 'We'll sort something out, and you know I'm not going to let you give up on your dreams. We're going to work our way through them together.'

'Together' sounded nice, except all those lists and dreams had faded into the background a bit since she'd got to know him. But she had to be sensible about this. 'I might have a new set of dreams though.' He raised an eyebrow. 'Well, that's a pretty ancient list that I thought up years ago, I think it needs updating a bit.' Tweaking to make sure that the really important things, people, took priority.

'Like?'

'Like watching the sun rise here on the beach.' He could say no now if he wanted, be honest, give her some indication of whether the future she could glimpse was anything like the one he had in mind. 'I'm probably not as big as an adventurer as I thought I'd be, and I do want to go home, but,' here was his opening, 'I would like to see some of those things you've told me about.'

'So you will come back?'

'I suppose I should really, shouldn't I?'

'Definitely.' His smile seemed a bit broader, the dimples a bit deeper as he slipped his hand under her hair, rubbed his thumb along her jaw in a way guaranteed to make her lose her concentration and all ability to speak. 'And I presume you'll need a guide?'

'Oh yes.'

'I think I need to come and meet Mabel too, don't I?'

Daisy nodded, gulped, tried not to rub against the pressure and purr. 'I'd like that, she'd like it too.'

'Does New Year's Eve work for you?'

'What!' She forgot about being mesmerised. 'You're kidding? Really? You're going to come over?'

'I thought maybe we should start next year on the right note, you know, as we mean to go on.'

'But...'

'I've chatted to Gabi and she was all for it. But there are conditions.'

'Conditions?'

'Well, I expect you to give me the full works, show me round. I think you owe me a few tours.'

Daisy giggled. 'One tour would just about cover the whole village. It is quiet, you know, no need for a bus, just some wellies.'

'Quiet suits me.' He slipped his arm round her waist, pulled her in tighter against his body. 'As long as you're there.'

'I'll definitely be there, and you can do my stuff – we'll swap the scooter for a horse. You really are coming, you're not joking?'

'No joke.'

'We don't have a big thing for New Year like you do here – it's just few fireworks.'

'We can make our own fireworks I reckon, don't you?'

Oh God, he was just so gorgeous, her stomach was churning just at the thought of being with him again.

'Go on, you'd better go, you'll miss your plane.'

She kissed him. 'Thank you.'

'You're welcome – go.' He took her by the shoulders and spun her round. 'Go before I change my mind and don't let you.'

Was it too early to say it? Was she being daft again? Oh hell, she had to, she couldn't not. The worst he could do was change his mind. She'd save it, no she couldn't.

'Javier, I, well—'

But before she could say what she was trying to, he caught hold of her again and had his arms wrapped around her, his forehead pressed to hers and those blue eyes looking at her as if he'd never looked properly before. Her stomach lurched, it was just such an intent, serious, searching look. 'I think I love you, Daisy Fischer.' His voice was so soft she would have thought there was a chance she'd misheard, except he was so close she couldn't.

Tears sprung into her eyes and the lump that had been lodged in her chest was suddenly in her throat. 'I don't think I love you, Javier.' She swallowed, tightened her grip round him. 'I know it.'

His lips met hers and it was the gentlest, sweetest caress as she leaned into him, closing her eyes so that she could let the smell of coffee, mints, of him, wrap itself around her; properly feel the way his fingers threaded their way through her hair, the sensation of his skin against hers, so that she could hold it. Capture it. Remember it.

'You'd better go.' There was the slightest tremor in his voice. 'Before we get locked up.'

She went. Followed the queue, glancing back all the time. She had a stupid smile on her face, she was waving for far too long as she showed her boarding pass. Holding up the queue as she put her belongings in the trays to be checked. Walking backwards through the arch. The security guys thought she was crackers. She didn't care.

***

'You just always have to win, don't you? Have to be right.'

Daisy looked at Jimmy and the bubble she'd been in since getting on the plane well and truly popped. Reality. She'd known this was never going to be easy, known Jimmy didn't want to hear the truth. To give up on his plan. Because it was just a plan. He wasn't madly in love with her, he'd just decided now was the time to get married and she was the girl he'd known for years.

'This isn't about winning, or being right or wrong, is it Jimmy?' He seemed almost like a stranger now as he glared at her over the table. She'd wanted to part friends, thought maybe they could – seeing as they'd never actually been that involved, committed, until he'd popped the question.

There was no way he couldn't have been expecting this. Which was why he'd been refusing to answer her calls or texts. He'd been avoiding the issue, waiting for it to go away. For her to come home and things to magically revert to how they'd been.

'And what is my dad going to think?'

She tried to repress the sigh. It suddenly seemed easier though, Jimmy wasn't that bothered about her; maybe he never had been.

He was bothered about keeping up appearances, doing what his family expected.

'I'm sorry, Jimmy, I really am, but it just wouldn't be right for either of us. This isn't about your dad is it? It's about us.'

'Well we were fine before.'

'Maybe we've changed? I know I'm going to want to travel, maybe go back to Barcelona, and you hate doing that. And I wouldn't expect you to just sit here waiting for me.'

'If you'd stayed at home with me, where you belong, you wouldn't have got any of these daft ideas. You'll regret it.'

'Oh, Jimmy, I know you don't get it,' she went to touch his hand, but he pulled away, 'but I needed to go, and I wanted to stay out there.'

Jimmy shook his head, looking baffled. 'Are you having one of those midlife-crisis things?'

'Jimmy!'

'Right, if you've got it all off your chest I'll be getting off to the pub. It'll be packed tonight with it being Christmas Eve. You don't get that in old Espagne, do you?' She shook her head.

So that was it. Her head felt lighter as he slammed the door shut behind him. In fact, her whole body seemed lighter.

***

'Happy Christmas, Daisy.'

Daisy smiled to herself, happy but sad, as his familiar, warm voice wrapped its way round her senses. She walked out of her mother's kitchen – where she'd been helping to prepare vegetables – so that she could have some privacy.

'Happy Christmas to you too, Javier.'

'Everything okay? What are you up to?'

'Right now? I'm wearing a very attractive apron and I'm busy with some parsnips.'

He chuckled.

'I miss you.' It had seemed strange waking up on her own on Christmas morning, back in her cottage – with Javier and Spain seeming like a world away. And now, hearing his voice, it was maddeningly better and worse at the same time. She'd been dying to hear him, but now she just wanted him to be there. With her.

'I miss you too, but I'll soon be there with you.'

True, but New Year's Eve and his promised visit seemed a lifetime away. 'I know. I wish I could have stayed with you though.'

'Here, I've got somebody else who wants to talk to you…' She could hear background noises and then a chorus of 'Happy Christmas' from Gabi and Jaime. The laughter caught Daisy in the stomach and a lump rose to her throat, bringing the sting of tears to her eyes. She really missed him. It had caught her unawares, this sudden longing to be with somebody – a feeling she'd never ever felt like this before.

'Are you sure Gabi doesn't mind you coming here for New Year? Will she and Jaime be okay without you?' If she did mind, then Daisy had a feeling she'd be heading back on a flight to Spain some time very soon.

'I heard that! I don't mind at all.' Gabi shouted. 'In fact I'll be glad to see the back of him for a while. You've no idea how much a big brother cramps your style.'

Javier laughed 'Some people are never happy. But, yeah, she doesn't want me. I'm all yours.'

'All?'

'Totally. Mind, body and soul.'

'How do you feel about mucking out horses?'

'Well that wasn't quite what I meant, but you know me, game for anything. Why? I thought you only had one.'

'I have, but Hugo has lots, and Flo's persuaded him to see the New Year in in Barcelona, so I kind of offered to do it.'

'Kind of offered? That sounds just like you! Sounds good to me though, we'll have the place to ourselves, nobody to spoil the fun.' He was chuckling again and the sound fizzed straight down the airwaves and into her bloodstream. 'Look I'm sorry, but I'm going to have to go, Daisy, but it'll seem like no time before I'm with you. Have a lovely day, won't you? I'll call again later if I can.'

'I will, you too, give my love to Gabi and Jaime. I'll call you tomorrow.'

Daisy's mum smiled when she went back in the kitchen. 'Sprouts.'

'Sorry?'

'Sprouts will keep your mind off him.'

'Him?' Acting the innocent didn't exactly work for her; she was grinning and blushing.

'I think you found more to look at than the sea in Barcelona, young Daisy, now come on get those veg prepared. You know I need to have dinner served before the Queen's speech is on.'

***

'I can't believe I've eaten so much.' Daisy groaned as she helped her mother and sister clear the plates. The seconds of Christmas pudding had been a bad idea. All she wanted to do now was collapse on the sofa for an hour, then take Mabel for a very long walk.

'Oh go and answer the door will you, darling?' Her mother frowned, 'did you say young Florence was popping round?'

'I didn't think it would be this early, but she can help us wash the pots.' Daisy peeled herself off the comfortable seat and headed for the door. It was weird thinking of Flo and Hugo as a couple: very weird – not that he couldn't be nice.

He could be unbearable, pompous, and arrogant, but she'd always sneakily watched him handle his horses, wishing she could have such a bond with an animal. He was patient and kind, and amazingly persistent. It was just a shame that the moment he hung up the tack he reverted to the same old idiot. She grinned, but maybe Flo had found the secret to keeping the 'nice' Hugo.

'Flo!' She flung the door open. But it wasn't Flo.

'You can't have forgotten me already!' Javier, with the broadest grin she'd ever seen on his face, was standing in front of her clutching a bunch of red roses.

Flo popped her head round the side of him and giggled. 'You have no idea how difficult it was to deliver this present.'

'But... Flo, Javier.' Daisy looked from one to the other of them, then over Javier's shoulder at a sheepish-looking Hugo.

'Oh my God.' She stared again, just to make sure it was him, then squealed and jumped into his open arms, nearly sending him flying off the doorstep. Squashing the flowers, but she didn't care.

'I thought you only saved hugs like that for your terrible animals.' Hugo's drawl didn't bother her in the slightest, she looked over at him, not letting go of Javier.

'You're a fine one to talk, you're only nice to your horses, or...?'

Daisy looked over at Flo, who was grinning mischievously, then back at Hugo, who didn't look bashful at all now – he looked quite pleased with himself.

'Well are you letting us in for a drink, woman? It's freezing out here.'

'In, in,' she gestured them past her, accepting a hug and kiss from Flo, then eased her body a couple of inches away from Javier. 'But, how did you get here?'

'Plane, automobile, you know, the usual.' Oh those dimples were heaven, she'd missed them so much.

'But I just spoke to you – you were with Gabi.'

'We flew over yesterday evening – she came too.' He grinned.

'She what?' Daisy peered over his shoulder.

'She's not here.' He laughed, and kissed her. 'She fancied a change, so she's spending Christmas with some relatives down south; that's where we were when I rang.'

'But you said you were in Barcelona.'

He grinned. 'You assumed I was in Barcelona; I never said where I was. Then I drove up and, thanks to Flo's directions, managed to find my way to your house so that we could all come here. Well, I did nearly put the car in a ditch at one point I'm not used to icy roads, but…' He pointed down at his feet. 'Hugo lent me some boots to walk over in.'

'But, doesn't Gabi mind? Didn't she want you to be with her?'

'She asked me how the hell she was going to meet anybody new if I was always chaperoning her. She's probably got a point.'

It was just so strange seeing him standing on the doorstep. 'We'll go back to mine later, and you can meet Mabel, and Barney, but you'd better come in and meet my family first.' She watched as he shrugged off his coat. In fact, she couldn't take her eyes off him. He was here. For Christmas. But… 'So you won't be here for New Year?'

'Think you can put up with me until the second of January?'

She squealed again. She couldn't help it. Then she grabbed hold of his hand. 'Mum, Mum you'll never believe…'

Her mother arrived in the doorway of the kitchen, wiping her hands dry on a tea towel, and smiled at Javier. 'Oh I won't, won't I?'

'You knew?'

'Of course I did, darling. We all did, that's why I've just warmed up some mince pies. Come along in, Javier, and tell me all about what's changed in Barcelona. I'm sure the Sagrada Familia is twice the height it was when we were last there.'

Chapter 26 – Flo. Promises to keep

It had, Flo decided, been the strangest Christmas Day she'd ever had – but undeniably nice. She'd headed back to England for snow and mince pies, but instead ended up with the big family Christmas she'd always dreamed about. The one with a crowd, with laughter and giggles over the worst Christmas-cracker jokes ever. One where everybody wore their party hats (even Hugo) and sat in front of a roaring fire feeling too hot, but too stuffed to move.

Listening to the Queen's speech, with Daisy's mum concentrating on her every word, her father snoring and Hugo making funny comments had brought a lump to her throat. She'd glanced over at her friends Daisy and Javier more than once, and wondered why it had never occurred to her before that they'd make such a wonderful couple – comfortable in each other's company, and she'd sneaked as many looks as she could at Hugo's proud profile, with the slightly big, slightly crooked, nose that she'd got so used to seeing.

'Have you had a good day?' Hugo squeezed her hand and she glanced up at him.

'The best.' It had to be said that was partly down to being with the most attractive man she'd ever met, but she wasn't going to give him a swollen head by mentioning it. Even now, tramping across a field of snow, in the kind of silent air of expectancy you only get on a winter's evening, it felt special. 'As long as you don't make me climb over any more stiles.'

'None this way.' He grinned, looking slightly naughty, which could have been down to the way the light was dancing in his eyes or just that disreputable air he carried effortlessly.

In a past life he must have been some kind of scoundrel or lord with a scandalous background. Or she was just light-headed with all the fresh air, and the copious amounts of alcohol that Daisy's parents had plied them with.

'Thank heavens for that.' Hugo and Javier had thought it hilarious when she'd got stuck astride one on the way over. Well, nobody had said a skirt wasn't a good idea, had they? In fact, they'd been laughing so much that when they took an arm each to try and help her down, they ended up trying to head in different directions and threatened to split her as well as her skirt. In the end, once Hugo had stopped staggering about in stitches, he'd thrown her over his shoulder and hiked her off, saying she weighed more than a bale of hay. Hilarious.

Then he'd promptly tripped up over his own foot and landed in a heap with her on top. Which had actually been quite funny as it was about time he was the one with the damp bum, not her. She had, of course, offered to help him strip his trousers off so he could dry – it had seemed the helpful thing to do. Now, though, they were heading home in a slightly different direction.

'It's beautiful, isn't it?'

'Not so nice in the morning when I'm breaking ice on water buckets.'

'Oh stop being boring.' She thumped him playfully, her hand against hard muscle. 'Philistine.'

He chuckled. "*He gives his harness bells a shake, To ask if there is some mistake. The only other sound's the sweep, Of easy wind and downy flake."*

She grinned, hanging on to each word, loving the flow of his deep voice. 'Frost, how appropriate.'

"*The woods are lovely, dark and deep, But I have promises to keep, And miles to go before I sleep."* He paused then, and looked at her. 'So you've covered some of those miles, kept some of those promises?'

'I have.' Some. 'What about you, Hugo?' His dark-lashed eyes were close to hers.

'Oh I've still got a way to go, but I'm planning on covering a few more before the morning.'

She looped her hand through his arm and decided not to comment on that, although her stomach had already started to twist and tumble in anticipation. Talking would take her mind off it.

'Even when we lived here, Christmas was never like this. We had an artificial Christmas tree, so all it smelled of was weird-scented spray, which was nothing like pine needles, and it went up the weekend before Christmas. Then Dad had it packed away in the loft well before the end of the week because he hated the place looking untidy. I always told myself that when I grew up it would be different.'

'And what about when you went to Spain?'

'Well Mum was more fun, she did love to party, but it was mainly just the two of us.' She shrugged. 'Then it was just me and Oli.' She glanced up sideways under her lashes, sorry that she'd mentioned his name. 'I always had a full agenda but an empty heart.' She was even sorrier that thought had slipped out, but it had just tumbled into her consciousness as she spoke. It had never been about passion, just about doing things.

'That's an incredibly sad thing to say.'

'Sorry, I didn't mean it to come out like that.'

'I can't imagine you like that.' His gaze was so intent she blushed. 'Empty-hearted.'

'It's an exaggeration, it was fine, but not like today's been. All huggy and warm.'

He laughed and wrapped an arm around her. 'Huggy.'

'You know what I mean.'

'Well my home wasn't exactly huggy, but I guess I do.'

'Maybe you should do something about that?'

'Don't spoil things, Flo.'

'I can't help it, I just,' she leaned in against the warmth of his body and glanced up, 'I know what it's like to have regrets, Hugo, to get things wrong.' She paused, letting the thoughts straighten out in her head. 'I was too proud to admit I'd made a massive mistake with Oli, that things weren't right. It's just, well, if this is more about pride than ideals...' She shrugged, not sure how much she should say. 'Put it this way, if something happened to them, your parents, would you regret not at least trying?'

'Oh Flo.' He shook his head. 'This isn't just about me.'

'But it is about somebody making the first move.'

'Holding out the olive branch? I wish it was that easy.' His voice was so soft, but so edgy, she wished she'd never said the words. Hugo was all bravado, hiding behind a front that she was actually quite fond of, but she loved the real, warm-hearted Hugo that occasionally emerged from behind the barrier of self-protection far more. She opened her mouth, about to say that maybe it was, but he gave her a warning look and she knew now was not the time.

'Come on, I'll race you back. I recognise where I am now.' Wriggling free of his grasp, Flo started to run. Her wellington boots slipping and sliding in the snow. As the ground dipped down she squealed as she started to slither through the deeper drifts of snow.

'Oh my God.' She lost her footing altogether and, waving her arms like a windmill, ended up on her bottom, sliding a few yards, then rolling. She could hear Hugo's laughter behind her, and then he came whizzing by, rolling over and over until he reached the bottom of the slope and she careered into him. Out of breath.

'Oh my God, we used to do that down the slope at school, on the grass.' Staggering to her feet, she looked down at Hugo, whose eyes were glinting. She really did feel like a kid again: exhilarated, free.

He wrapped an arm round the back of her knees and brought her down onto his lap. 'You're all snowy.'

'So are you.'

Her face was cold, but the moment his lips touched hers she forgot all about it, all about her soggy gloves and damp clothes.

'Have I ever told you how adorable you look when you've been rolling in the snow?'

'Never.'

'Have I ever told you how attractive I find your shiny red nose?'

She shook her head.

'Or the little drip on the end of it.'

'My nose is not dripping.'

'Or how I love your wonderfully warm body?'

She realised too late that he had an ulterior motive, should have known that it was the grin not the smooth talking that was the thing to look out for. Before she could stop him he'd slipped his freezing cold hands up the inside of her jacket, under her jumper. She screamed and went to hit out, but he was too fast. He'd swung her to one side, rolled them both over, and was poised above her. 'I know it's not saying much, but you do know you're the sexiest woman in Tippermere, don't you?'

'And you are the biggest...' She was going to say 'jerk', but he kissed her. Then, while she was still catching her breath, he started to tickle her, and roll them both over and over until they were soaking wet and worn out.

'Oh Flo, what am I going to do with you?' He pulled her to her feet and took her hand in his. Looked at her as though he

301

wanted to say something, then just as abruptly dismissed it. 'Come on, you'll freeze to death. Let's get home.'

Flo looked at the crooked nose she'd grown so fond of, the perfect dimples, the still-grey eyes that she'd at first thought were judging and distant, and now thought were kind. She wanted to ask him why his upbringing hadn't been huggy, why he loved his horses more than life itself, why he insisted on keep saving her. She wanted to hear the promises he wanted to keep. She wanted to know if he was coming to Barcelona for New Year's Eve, and she wanted to know, more than anything, if one more week was all they had together.

She bit her lip and reached out to brush his floppy fringe away. She couldn't ask, not right now and risk spoiling things, because she really didn't know what the answer would be. And she had a feeling that nor did Hugo.

***

By the time Flo had stripped her sodden clothes off, had a shower to warm up, then put pyjamas on, Hugo had got a fire going and was opening a bottle of wine.

'How did you do it that quickly?'

'Corkscrew?' He raised an eyebrow. 'It's a modern invention, even reached Tippermere.'

'The fire, you idiot. It takes me ages.'

'It would if you use damp timber.'

'You're not going to let me forget that, are you?'

'Never. I have to have the upper hand occasionally. It's my male ego. True caveman stuff.'

She settled cross-legged on the sofa, and rested her chin on her hands. 'You're a real hunter-gatherer, aren't you, Hugo?'

'I am. Now budge up and let me pour you a glass of wine, which I, incidentally, hunted down and gathered especially for you.'

'From Majestic?'

'The very same. I had to risk life and limb.'

'I bet you had it delivered.'

'Okay, you're right. Don't I get any small victories? Can't you pretend?'

'I'm sure you very carefully selected it online.' She looked at him over the rim of her glass. 'You are quite the provider, though, aren't you?' She wasn't kidding; he'd done nothing but look after her since she'd arrived. Once he'd stopped laughing at her that was.

'I was brought up to be a gentleman.'

The drawl had strengthened; it was strange how that happened, almost like a defence mechanism when he thought they were straying into territory he'd rather not explore. It could be sexy, beguiling, or it could verge towards arrogant and pompous. God, the man was complicated. The version she liked best was the coaxing, teasing Hugo, the one with a gentle sense of humour who loved his animals and encouraged her to follow her heart.

'But you weren't brought up to do cuddles and hugs?'

'Are you saying I'm lacking in that department?' He raised an eyebrow in a very upper-class way.

'No.' The way he put his hands on her was nothing to complain about, but she wasn't about to let him wriggle away that easily. 'Your mother must have cuddled you, hugged you?'

'Not that you'd notice.'

'But she spent a lot of time reading to you? My mum did, at bedtime, and it was a special, well huggy, time.'

He laughed. 'My mother preferred books to hugs. She gave me them, not read them to me. They were a challenge, a solution.' Flo frowned. 'My mother was an intellectual, darling, and she had my father to contend with.'

'Meaning?'

'He wouldn't have approved of affection, he said it made boys soppy.'

'But she was your mum.'

'And he was a barrister.' He said it as though it explained everything.

'Yeah, so you said.'

'I was enough of a disappointment without my being a mummy's boy.'

'Shagging his boss's wife?'

'Chasing women and messing with horses instead of fighting immoral intellectual battles in dusty courtrooms.' He shrugged. 'That woman was probably the straw that broke the camel's back though. There was no turning back after that. I'm sure he had his eye on her and she'd spurned him.' His eyes had narrowed. 'It was a battle of testosterone as well as wills.'

'And that's why you developed a reputation as a womaniser?' She was, she realised, only half-teasing.

'No, that was because I like women. Although, it must be said, his disapproval probably spurred me on at the start.' The short laugh was humorous rather than bitter, and his eyes were shining in a very naughty way, which she was trying to ignore. 'He did me quite a favour.'

'You prefer horses to people, don't you?'

'A lot of the time. Although right now, I'm rather keen on getting closer to a certain person, if she'd only stop asking so many bloody questions.' He pinged the waistband of her pyjamas, and the drawl, so close to her ear, warmed up a part of her that the wine and fire hadn't yet reached. She nestled in closer and his hand settled on her waist, leaving her smiling stupidly to herself.

How had she ever, ever imagined that life with Oli was as good as it got? She'd been living a half-life of handbags and high heels.

They fell into a companionable silence, both thinking their own thoughts as they stared at the flickering flames.

Mabel was stretched out in front of the fire, with Hugo's terrier curled up between her legs. Her paws kept twitching, and her lips fluttered as she wuffled in her sleep – no doubt chasing imaginary rabbits.

'They're sweet together, aren't they?'

'They are. I never thought Rags would be a fan of a great dollop like Mabel, but you never know where you're going to find the perfect place to settle, do you?'

'You don't.'

'I'd quite like to be curled up between your legs.'

'God, you are so rude. You're doing it again. Don't you ever stop?'

'Not with you around.'

'Can I ask you one more question?'

'I don't suppose it will stop you for one moment if I say no.'

'You miss your mum, don't you?'

'I do.'

'Why don't you get in touch, go and see her?'

'That's two questions.' The drawl deepened, but she had to battle on.

'They're all part of the same one.'

'Very strange logic. Well, dear Flo, I do talk to her occasionally, but it's rather awkward.'

'Wouldn't it be easier for both of you if you tried to, you know, make up a bit with your father?'

He sighed. 'You're like a bloody terrier. You just don't give up, do you?'

'He might miss you too, you know.' And she was damned sure his mother did – they had obviously been close.

'Who said I miss him? I couldn't give a toss.'

'You wouldn't be so angry if you didn't care, Hugo. Maybe he thought you were messing about with horses just to annoy him. Has he ever seen this place, seen what you've achieved?'

He shrugged, which she took as a no.

'You could ask? Just a gesture? It would be, erm, chivalrous. Look. I'm not exactly saying you should kiss and make up – he doesn't sound the type,' she glanced up to judge how he was taking this, but he still looked pretty laid back. In fact he looked amused rather than angry. And as if he was listening. 'But you could invite them to the owner's tent next time you're competing, or something like that. You know, a public thing, so it's just polite handshakes and he could see you doing what you love.' He raised an eyebrow, but he didn't say no. Knowing what Hugo was like, she could well imagine his father wasn't exactly big on being demonstrative. He was a barrister, for heaven's sake, reserved and no doubt pretty stern and scary when he wanted. Stuffed to the gills with British reserve. But this would let them both hang on to their pride, at least be on nodding terms.

'I'll think about it,' he paused, 'if it stops you asking questions.'

'Promise?'

He rolled his eyes. 'Promise.'

'Can I ask another? Just one?' He raised his eyebrow. 'Have you ever really wanted to be with somebody?' It was a daft question; one she wouldn't have dared asked if she hadn't feel so relaxed, so at home.

'I wouldn't have asked you to stay if I hadn't.'

Chapter 27 – Daisy. New Year's Eve in Cheshire

'I've put a list up in the tack room. Don't put that chesnut gelding out if it's icy – he tends to go a bit loopy. Monty needs lunging every day unless the surface of the school is rock hard or he'll seize up, the—'

Daisy rolled her eyes and shook her head. 'Okay, Hugo, we get it, and there's a list.'

He carried on as though she hadn't spoken. 'You need to keep an eye on the old lad. If he shows any signs of colic at all call the vet, and make sure you get Matt, not just anybody.'

'It'll be fine, honest, you're only going for a few days. Honestly, you're like an old woman.'

'They like routine.'

'So do I. Now push off or you'll miss your plane.'

He gave her a piercing look. 'I'm sure you weren't this bossy before you went away, Daisy.'

'Assertive is the word, Hugo, and I was the same, you just never listened to me – you were too busy laughing and telling me off.'

'Was I?' Hugo looked down his nose at her and frowned. 'Nonsense, and make sure you lock the tack room.'

Daisy was trying her hardest not to laugh. 'It'll be so peaceful without you around, Hugo. Mabel and Barney will have a great time.' Hugo looked at her in consternation.

'Does he laugh at you as well?' Flo grinned and looped her arm through Daisy's. 'I thought it was just me.'

'I only laugh when you're being funny. Come on, stop ganging up on me, the taxi's waiting. Although maybe this is a mistake.'

'No way, bugger off and leave us in peace.' Daisy gave him a shove in the direction of the taxi. 'You have no idea how grateful I am to you, Flo, I've been trying to get him out of my hair for years. You couldn't keep him out there permanently, could you?'

'Oh hell, I'm going to miss all this.' Flo threw her arms around Daisy. 'Mabel is brill, and I loved Barney until he dumped me in a ditch, and I even quite liked the chickens.'

'Well I'm quite happy for you to take Hugo, but I'm keeping the rest. That way maybe you'll come back some time?'

'Oh I will, promise.' Flo hugged her tight, then pulled back and wiped the threatening tears from her smiling face. 'Give my love to Anna, won't you? I wouldn't be here if it wasn't for her.'

'I will. Love you, Flo.' Daisy hugged her friend to her again, and then surprised herself by giving Hugo (who seemed so much nicer since she'd got back) a hug as well. She went up on tiptoe to whisper. 'Look after my friend properly, or your horses are in trouble.'

He grinned. 'Look after my horses properly and keep your hound out of my feed room or you're not getting your friend back.'

'Is that new aftershave, Hugo?'

Hugo laughed; a rich, deep laugh that she'd rarely heard before. 'Oh God, you used to be so down-trodden. I like the new Daisy, and the new haircut – suits you.'

Daisy ran her fingers self-consciously through her hair as Hugo gathered the cases and loaded them into the taxi. Flo had done the impossible; made him more human. Although maybe he always had been. Maybe she just hadn't looked hard enough for his nice side, the same as he'd never realised that she was more than the other half of Jimmy.

Javier slipped his arm round Daisy's waist as they waved Flo and Hugo off.

'They'll have a great time. Barcelona on New Year's Eve is awesome. I'm going to show you next year.'

'Promises, promises. I might hold you to that.' She nestled in closer to his firm body. It was hard to believe that he'd been there nearly a week already. That tomorrow would be the start of yet another year. And that so much had changed in her life over the past month. 'Tippermere is pretty awesome too. Come on, I'm going to show you how we make proper mulled wine.'

The cottage was soon flooded with the spicy, fruity aroma that she loved. It was pure festive Christmas holiday: cinnamon, cloves and nutmeg and because Javier hadn't been there to sample it on Christmas Eve she was determined he was going to taste some now.

'I can see why you love being here.' They were sitting together on her old leather sofa, Javier's long legs stretched out in front of him, watching the flames flicker in the fireplace.

'Do you think you'll still be saying that after I send you out at 6 a.m. to break the ice on the trough?' She was only half-teasing. All this was so different to the life Javier was used to, and it wasn't just the cold weather. It was the small village, the fact that there was no wonderful beach, no happy buzz of constant activity.

'Hey.' He put an arm round her. 'How can I not enjoy breaking ice if you're next to me?'

'Do you think we'll be here next year?'

'No.' He traced a finger down her forehead, her nose, stopping when he got to her lips. 'We'll be in Barcelona.'

'You know what I mean.'

'I think we can be together, if it's what you want.' His tone

309

was soft. 'I'm not saying I don't like a bit of sunshine, a walk on the beach, but I'm not rooted anywhere, Daisy.'

'Hippy cat.'

'Less of the cat, if you don't mind. Honest, though, we can find a way to make this work. You want to do more, go to new places – well, we can do it together.'

Daisy smiled. Her mother could have been right about knowing when she'd found the right person. She still wasn't quite sure what the next twelve months would look like, but that was good. Next year was about the new Daisy, the one who didn't feel she had her whole life planned out. 'Mum said that she and Dad can look after Barney and Mabel if I want to go away.'

'I like your parents – they're great.'

'They are pretty good, aren't they?' She grinned. 'Do you want to see my new list?'

'List?' Javier rolled his eyes.

'Well you didn't think I could stop writing them just like that, did you?' She giggled at the look on his face. 'And if you're going to come with me on my trips, you do need to know what I've got in mind.'

'I do?'

'You do. For packing purposes. It's not all flip-flops where I'm going, you know.' There was a loud bang and Daisy jumped up, pulling him over to the window, where they could get a wonderful view of the dramatic firework display.

'Where on earth?'

'It's over at Tipping House. They have a massive display every year and I reckon we've got the best view from here.'

'I certainly have.' He pulled her in closer to him. 'One I'd like to explore in more detail.'

'You're being rude, aren't you?' She glanced up at him.

'I certainly am.'

'There is one minor problem. Well, quite a major one, actually.'

'Which is?'

'Mabel. She's terrified of fireworks. At a guess, right no... be under the duvet.'

He laughed. 'I guess if I take you on, then it's the animals as well?'

'It certainly is. Come on, let's see how masterful you are with an Irish Wolfhound.'

Chapter 28 – Flo. New Year, new start?

Hugo did debonair very well. His long, lightly muscled legs looked perfect in close-fitting chinos and boots, his scarf wrapped ever-so-casually around his neck, his jacket open. He was dangling a bottle of champagne from one hand, the other holding hers.

'You'd almost pass as a Barcelonian, the vintage champagne's a bit of a giveaway, though.'

'One should never lower one's standards, Miss Nightingale. So how much further is it?'

'Not far, follow the crowds.'

They strolled along the front, gazed at the boats in Port Vell harbour, then waited to cross the road, watching the scooters weaving in and out of the traffic. 'We turn right just after Christopher Columbus and head all the way up Paral-lel.'

As they walked up the wide Avinguda del Paral-lel, it started to get busier, everybody heading in the same direction, some already tipsy, some sober, some old, some young and Flo felt the same sense of anticipation she always did as they approached midnight: a new year, new promises, and hope. Except this time the feeling was heightened; this time she wasn't quite sure what she should be wishing for. She just knew it had to be better. More real.

This time last year she'd been hoping that Oli would propose, that she'd be getting married. And it had been for all the wrong reasons. It had all been about appearances, not real love. It had taken a trip back to Tippermere to find that.

She glanced sideways at Hugo as the truth of what she'd been thinking hit her.

She'd fallen in love; it had crept up on her, *he'd* crept up on her, sneaked under her defences. Made her happier and more confident than she'd ever been.

He caught her watching him, raised an eyebrow, and winked. They strolled on in silence, watching the people around them, swinging their joined hands, until at last Placa Espanya was in sight.

It was already busy as they weaved their way through the crowds, heading for the centre, where they could get a good view of the firework display.

The volume of the music increased, the ever-growing crowd pushed them closer together, and Hugo put a protective arm around her.

'I wonder where we'll be next year?' She voiced the thought that had been on her mind, but didn't expect an answer.

'London. I'm doing Olympia at Christmas, then staying over for New Year.'

'Really?' Did that mean him, or them?

'You need to see this whole firework thing done properly – we have a history of decent displays.'

'For dodgy reasons.'

'There is nothing wrong with dodgy, apart from this music.'

'Shush.' She giggled. 'Pour the bubbly.'

'It isn't quite midnight.'

'Maybe not, but who says we shouldn't start celebrating early?

313

And anyway it's well into the new year UK time.' She needed a drink, needed to make the most of their time together.

'Such a rebel.' He fished the glasses out of his bag and passed them to her. 'So how do we do this?'

'Well, you open and pour. I'll hold the glasses.'

'No, I mean *this*.'

She looked at him, his fingers twisting the wire that held the cork in place, his gaze not meeting hers and he looked so boyishly attractive it brought a lump to her throat. She was scared of 'this', she didn't want to lose him – say goodbye – but she didn't want to lose the new her either.

'I don't really do half-measures Flo.' The cork popped and people turned. Smiling faces, but all she could see was his serious one as he poured the champagne. So did this mean that they either did things his way or not at all? 'I'm a fill-it-to-the-brim type of person.' He looked up then, his piercing gaze freezing her in place. Her heart was pounding in her ears, the thump, thump of her pulse blocking out everything but him. 'Until now. I don't expect you to come home with me, Florence, but I'm trying to work out how to play this.'

The crowd pressed closer as midnight neared. The countdown started. People jostled her elbows as she held the two glasses. Studied him. A pulse throbbed in his temple, there was the slightest tremor in the hand that held the bottle, and it suddenly dawned on her that he was nervous. Hugo was as scared about this as she was.

She swallowed hard, cleared her throat.

When she'd first met Hugo she'd done all she could to avoid falling under his spell, and then she'd got to know him. Caught a glimpse of the real Hugo and fallen in love with it. With him. Walking away without a second glance was something she couldn't do, but he'd given her something. He'd given her a bit of herself back, the Flo that had confidence, that had dreams, and she didn't want to let go of that. She couldn't, or she'd be heading right back to where she'd been with Oli. The perfect life that was actually just a façade. 'I can't just leave Barcelona.'

'I know. I'm not asking you to.' They were jostled, pressed even closer, the champagne bottle clinking against the glasses. 'I don't want you to, Flo. I want you the way you are, and you're not just some yes girl.'

But she oh-so nearly had been; the girl that had wanted to say yes to a proposal from Oli, the girl who'd gone along with everything he'd wanted.

Hugo was saying he understood her, and he seemed to, but... 'You've got the horses.' She couldn't just be somebody's groom, slotting neatly into his life. No way was she making that mistake again, even though it would be oh-so easy.

'I have, but I compete all over the world. There'll be times...'

'I've got a book to finish.'

'I know, and I want to be there on launch day, holding back the crowds.'

A shiver ran through her body. He was saying the words as though he meant them. Believed in every one. As though they could make it possible. Make it work. As a team.

'You'll hate my tiny apartment.'

'We can get a bigger one.' He grinned, as though sensing that she didn't want him to offer all the solutions, to run her life. 'Once you're a bestselling author, that is, and have some dosh, and we can balance it with time in my big house.'

'I might get jealous of your horses and your groupies.'

'Then you'll have to come and groom for me now and again, give them your special glare. The girls, not the horses – don't you ever dare try and scare my horses.'

She laughed then. It was hard to imagine what kind of life they could have together, but it was getting hard to imagine one without Hugo in it too. Unconventional was the word that jumped out right now.

'So, Miss Nightingale, I'm still not sure if you're ready.' He looked the full-on cocky and arrogant Hugo again now, the Hugo she'd fallen for.

'Ready?' She held one glass out to him. 'Well, I don't know what I'm supposed to be ready for, but I'd like to find a way to do stuff together, see if we can make it work. Except…'

'Except?'

'If you call me Miss Nightingale again I will hog your favourite horse.'

He stood still for what seemed an eternity. The crowd chanted – the countdown got lower. She was half expecting him to say he'd changed his mind. Then he took the glass.

He took a deep breath, his eyes searching over every inch of her face as though he was trying to memorise it, draw a picture of this moment in his head. 'Florence, I bought this bottle of decent champagne for a reason and I hate to not ask now it's opened.'

She looked at him, slightly confused.

'I tend to agree that Nightingale doesn't really suit you. I thought James might be better.'

'James?' Now she was confused.

'I was wondering if now was a good time to ask you to marry me, but I'm really not sure whether you realise it's what you want yet, or whether I need to wait until you've finished that book of yours.' He paused. 'And you get a chance to realise that I really am as perfect as it gets.' The corner of his mouth twitched, but he looked surprisingly earnest.

'And as pompous and arrogant?'

'And as pompous and arrogant.' He grinned.

'You're being serious?' Flo stared, letting the words sink in, the words she'd been dying to hear just a few months ago. From a different man. Then she shook her head and smiled. Only Hugo would dare ask for the answer before he asked the question. 'And you think that's all that would stop me saying yes,' she really was trying not to laugh, 'just finishing my book? Nothing to do with whether I want to marry you or not?'

'Well, what else would stop you?' He was looking as devilish as he ever had, but did she detect just the faintest hint of doubt in that arrogant tone?

'Oh, Hugo.' She shook her head again. 'You really are amazing.'

'I am being serious, Flo.' His tone had sobered. 'As well as a pompous, arrogant, and amazing man; you'll get somebody who really loves you.'

She stared, feeling light-headed, dazed. He'd said it. He'd said he loved her and he'd proposed.

'We'll drink to that then, shall we?' He linked his arm around hers, not waiting for a response. 'But no promises on the Nightingale front. I'm still going to call you that for now.' The bubbles fizzed in the back of her throat as they drank, so close they were almost touching, and the moment she moved the glass away his mouth was there. Dropping the sweetest, gentlest of kisses on her lips. 'Until you come to your senses and know that you really don't want to say anything but yes. Happy New Year, Flo.'

As people started to move they went with the flow, being carried out of the square. 'I'm glad I've seen you on your own territory – it suits you.' Hugo waved the arm that wasn't draped round her shoulders. 'All this. Barcelona.'

'It does.' She smiled, it really did. She loved the countryside, but she loved her adopted home as well. She liked the buzz, the people, the fiestas, the energy. 'Do you think it would suit you?' It was fingers-crossed, breath-holding time. He knew she wanted to say yes, knew she wanted to marry him, but he also seemed to realise that she needed to test the waters. Be sure she was doing the right thing.

'I'm pretty adaptable.' He shrugged, but his dimples had deepened. 'I'll try anything if it's an attractive enough proposition.'

He paused and spun her round. 'And from where I'm looking this one looks more than attractive.'

'I will come back to Cheshire soon, maybe in a month when I've sorted the apartment?'

'You better had.' He grinned. 'Besides,' he smiled, 'you don't think I'm going to miss you typing *The End* on your novel, do you? I really need to know what happens to that naked chef, and I rather think you'll have to head back soon for more inspiration.'

Flo went on tiptoes and kissed his full mouth. 'I rather think you could be right, Mr James.' She dropped down onto her heels, then traced a fingertip over his generous lips, knowing she could say it now. 'Oh Hugo, I love you too.'

THE END

Acknowledgements

A story is conceived by the author, but there are many influences and helping hands along the way that nurture and transform it into the wonderful end product.

As always I want to say thank you to the wonderful HarperImpulse team: Kimberley Young for her inspiration, Charlotte Ledger for her never-ending support, encouragement and instinct for what will work, and Emily Ruston who has managed to ensure that the thoughts in my head were translated perfectly into words on the page. Thank you also to the fabulous cover designers at HarperCollins – Alexandra Allden who never ceases to amaze me, and Holly McDonald. I do love working with all of you so much!

Alongside the publishing team I've also formed many great friendships as a writer - people who have helped with wine, coffee, words and wisdom. Thank you Mandy Baggot and Jane Linfoot for keeping me sane, The Knutsford Literary Society for their inspiring reaction to the exclusive (un-edited) extract of this story, and to Joanne Robertson who makes me smile and introduced me to Tracy Fenton and the fabulous THE Book Club (TBC) who are guaranteed to give me a giggle when the going gets tough!

Thanks also to Nuria and the team at Hotel Casa Fuster in Barcelona, and to my wonderful friend Georgina, who have all helped me fall in love with this incredible city.

And lastly to all my friends and family, whose friendship and support is priceless.

I came across this recently when I was in Barcelona and love the words;

Cuando descubres la verdadera Amistad ... tienes un gran Tesoro
When you discover true friendship ... you have a great treasure

The Holiday Swap is about friendship as well as romance, about mutual support and understanding, about working together, but most of all about living your dreams. I hope you enjoy it.

Enjoy a Winter Break in Barcelona...

I love Barcelona, and being able to spend so much time out here is a dream come true for me. I'm a bit of a country girl (like Daisy) so I need a place where I can escape the crowds, as well as soak up some culture. Barcelona is the perfect city – it has large stores, chic boutiques, incredible architecture, and a beautiful beach. It's sophisticated and glamorous, and yet also wonderfully laid back. In the winter it's still warm enough to stroll in a light jacket (although the Spanish will be wrapped up in scarves and thick jackets!). So where better for country girl Daisy to start her adventure?

Here are just a few of my suggestions for enjoying a winter stay in Barcelona. I'll be posting lots more on my website – so please do join me there as well at www.ZaraStoneley.com

Sample the cava at **El Xampanyet** (on Carrer de Montcada). It's a really cool tapas bar that is popular with locals as well as tourists. In 'The Holiday Swap' this is where Daisy and Anna spend their first evening with Flo. I love the colourful tiles on the walls and can spend ages studying all the artefacts hung around the walls – I spot something new every time I go. And you really should sample the house cava!

If you fancy buying a nice bottle of cava to savour on your own then check out **La Licorera** (on Calle Taulat, el Poblenou). The bodega opened in 1932 and has been run by three generations of the same family. Look out for the parrot behind the counter – apparently he was given to the shop owners in 1957, and used to confuse the tram drivers as he imitated the whistle signal. He died in 1992 (aged 46) and was preserved by his owner.

Blend in with the locals and hire a scooter from **Via Vespa**. If you're feeling brave you can just set off on your own, or you can book a guided tour. Travelling around by scooter is very popular in the city and it's a great alternative to the tour bus!

Explore the **Christmas market** at the front of the cathedral, admire the fantastic lights around the main streets of the city (including the water and music show at Montjuic's Magic Fountain) and check out the historic Circ Raluy travelling circus that is down by Port Vell – I love the old circus caravans.

Hotel Casa Fuster- for a special occasion this really is my go-to place. It was a gift from Senor Fuster to his wife (how's that for a romantic gesture?) and is the most incredible building inside and out. The hotel is at the top of Passeig de Gracia – one of the main shopping streets - and it's well worth walking the few extra yards to have a look. Woody Allen is just one of the artists who've played on their 'Jazz Club' nights, and the view from the roof terrace is amazing (so are the cocktails)!

Three things to try:

Pintxos – these are 'tapas on bread', a round of baguette with some sort of topping (hot or cold), held together by a small skewer (toothpick). Sample an assortment and then count up the skewers at the end to calculate your bill. These really are delicious, but be warned – they're addictive!

Botifarra – a type of sausage that you'll find on most menus in Barcelona. Very meaty and quite different to our own British bangers!

Patatas Bravas – cubes of fried potato served with a spicy tomato sauce and/or aioli. You'll find this dish on most tapas menus, along with pan con tomate. Try both!

Or capture a warm and fuzzy feeling in Cheshire!

Tippermere might be a fictional village, but Cheshire is very much a real county and has been my home for many years. I've walked my dogs, ridden my horses, visited country shows and listened to the local gossip in many village shops and pubs. There is something special about the UK countryside at Christmas time – which is why I used it as the setting for 'The Holiday Swap'. Florence is drawn back there because it's like nowhere else in the world! Here are a few of my suggestions for wonderful things to do in the winter.

Tatton Park has always been one of my favourite places to walk the dog. In the winter it's quite magical, with a lovely parkland that sweeps down to the water, and a mansion that takes you back in time (I like to imagine I live there – okay maybe a dream too far!). You can stroll through the park where deer roam freely then visit the mansion and listen to Christmas carols. I always used to take my son to visit Father Christmas at the Farm (he's now a bit too old for that kind of thing) and then afterwards treat myself to a mince pie in 'The Stables', followed by a browse through the 'Housekeeper's Store' which stocks delicious food!

Build a **snowman** – if the snowfall has been light, the one place within an easy drive where there is nearly always enough snow to build a snowman is on The Cat and Fiddle Road (A537 between Macclesfield and Buxton) in the Peak District National Park. It's the perfect place for a bracing walk, and if the Cat and Fiddle pub (the second-highest inn in England) is open you can have a warm up by the fire!

Visit a **Christmas market** – these are more often than not at the end of November, or early December but really put me in the festive mood! I love the smell of roasting chestnuts, the cinnamon and spice from the mulled wine, and the scent of pine – not to mention the lovely golds, reds, greens and sparkles everywhere. I love the friendly small village fairs, and the much bigger town and city ones. And I always end up buying presents and decorations.

Visit **The Bull's Head**, Mobberley – there is nothing quite like a cosy, country pub in the winter and this is one of my favourites. Sit by the blazing fire, admire the hops hanging from the beams and enjoy a glass of mulled wine or beer as you sample some of the home-cooked food. If you've been out walking, this is one place where dogs are welcome.

Stock up on some delicious goodies from **The Hollies Farm Shop** at Little Budworth, then for the perfect Christmas find a cottage (like Daisy's) to rent with a fireplace. Make your own mulled wine, stack the logs on the fire, and roast chestnuts or marshmallows.

Three things to try:

Toasted marshmallows – toasted over an open fire (or grilled if you need to!), these gooey treats always cheer me up. Just make sure you don't char them, or set them alight!

Mulled wine – what could be nicer than wrapping your hands round a warm glass of mulled wine after you've been out in the cold? Nothing says Christmas quite like that smell of cinnamon, fruit, cloves and nutmeg.

Chestnut stuffing – my favourite stuffing on Christmas Day is a Delia Smith recipe, www.deliaonline.com/recipes/international/european/british/eighteenth-century-chestnut-stuffing, Christmas wouldn't be the same without it!

Why not visit my website at www.zarastoneley.com where you'll find out more about the secret corners of Barcelona and Cheshire I love so much, plus news, competitions and giveaways. I look forward to seeing you there!

Zara x